DISSENSION

DISSENSION

An Echo Hunter 367 Novel

STACEY BERG

HARPER
VOYAGER
IMPULSE

An Imprint of HarperCollinsPublishers

This is a work of fiction. Names, characters, places, and incidents are products of the author's imagination or are used fictitiously and are not to be construed as real. Any resemblance to actual events, locales, organizations, or persons, living or dead, is entirely coincidental.

EPub Edition MARCH 2016 ISBN: 9780062466129
Print Edition ISBN: 9780062466136

10 9 8 7 6 5 4 3 2

For the Tank Girls, who set a good example

CHAPTER 1

The girl Hunter murdered in the desert was only thirteen.

Hunter eased the aircar closer to the cliff's edge, hovering just above the bleached white stone stained bloody by the setting sol. Emptiness spread in every direction, silent and watchful. Hunter felt it pressing down as she studied the cautious tracks she had followed for the last few miles. The girl had tried to obscure them, as she had been taught, but Hunter knew the desert far too well to be deceived. The tracks ended in a patch of scuffed sand. A broken thornbush trailed over the edge where a desperate hand had ripped through it in a last failed grab at salvation. It was obvious now what had happened.

She settled the aircar in the dry creek bed a hundred feet below. Already the cliff cast a long shadow across the canyon. The day's heat still radiated from the stone, but Hunter could feel the chill in the breeze probing for gaps in her clothing, a mild warning of the harsh night to come. She had to hurry; the scavengers would gather quickly once true night fell. Even she did not want to be caught in the open then.

Her boots squeaked a little in the fine layer of dust, though she could have moved silently had it mattered. Glancing up to the torn spot at the edge of the cliff, she estimated the fall line and began to search the bottom in a systematic grid. It was only a few minutes before she spotted the still form crumpled facedown among the rocks.

The ground warmed her as she knelt. She could see why the girl hadn't called out for help: her shoulders rose and fell with desperate effort, no breath to spare. Hunter rolled her gently on her back.

The girl's eyes were open, pupils dilated wide with shock. Her chalk-white face was bathed in sweat despite the chill. Even so, when the girl spoke, her voice, weak as it was, came out calm, controlled. "You came for me. I knew you would."

"We don't waste anyone."

The eyes, dark as Hunter's own, closed briefly, dragged open again with an enormous effort. "The others?"

"Everyone else returned as scheduled." Eight out of nine, a good outcome for this exercise. Ten sols alone in the desert culled the weak quickly, but none of the rest had called for rescue, and the girl had not had time. The 378s were a strong batch; there had only been fourteen to begin with, thirteen annuals ago. When Hunter had been this age only eight were left. The priests always made more, but it was never quite the same as your own batch.

"That's good," the girl whispered breathlessly. Her eyes wandered up the cliff.

"Tell me how it happened," Hunter said, though she already knew. It didn't matter; there was still a little time, and the girl deserved a chance to make her report.

"I was following some canids." She had to stop and gather air. "I thought they'd lead me to water."

"That was a reasonable plan."

"It almost worked. I smelled the spring, but I let myself get too close to the edge, even though you taught us that the rocks there often crumble." Hunter had never taught this batch. The girl's mind was wandering, or maybe it was only the failing light. Snatching what breath she could, the girl continued, "I was so thirsty, and I thought . . . And then I fell. I broke my leg," she added, glancing at the pink and white splinters thrusting out of the torn flesh. Her eyes came back to Hunter's. "It doesn't hurt. I don't feel anything."

"I know." Hunter edged around a little. "Here, let me help you sit up." The girl was a boneless weight against her, arms dangling, a handful of sand trickling between limp fingers as Hunter knelt behind her, holding her close. "It's all right, Ela. You did well." The lie wouldn't hurt anything now.

The girl's head lolled back against Hunter's shoulder, eyes searching her face as if trying to focus across a great distance. Her whisper was barely audible. "Which one are you?"

"Echo."

"Number five, like me."

"Yes, Ela." She eased one palm around to cup the back of the girl's head, the other gently cradling her chin. "Ready?"

The girl's nod was only the barest motion between her hands. Hunter let her lips rest against the girl's dusty hair for a short moment. She felt the girl's mouth move in a smile against her fingers.

Then, with a swift and practiced motion, Hunter snapped her neck.

In a trick of the sunset the spire of the Church glowed, a wire filament burning in a lamp to guide her home. The crossed antennas rose above like a man with arms outstretched to embrace the city. Beneath, the rose window was an eye gazing out at the horizon.

The sky was dark by the time she stood before the massive doors, staring up and up as she always did when she first returned from the desert. The doors faced away from the compound, setting the line between Church and city with an edge not entirely physical; whoever had built them, long before the Fall, had meant the scale to show a greatness far beyond the mere human. Even before the newer defenses had been added, anyone seeking to enter, friend or otherwise, would have to pause here to consider the indifferent power he faced. The great planks were wider than her torso, bolted top and bottom to make the vertical run three times human height, and the worked-metal bindings looked as strong today as the day they were forged. In the center of the doors, just along the seam at chest height, the bindings flattened into a pair of panels. A hand there, and the door knew who sought to enter. Many fates had been decided with a simple touch.

She raised a grimy palm to the panel. Normally there was no wait. Tonight the doors seemed to hesitate, weighing her worth, before the mechanism clicked and they dragged open, permitting her to enter.

Behind its thick walls the cathedral was cool and dim, conditions that changed little day or night. This was the oldest part of the Church, the hewn stone ancient even before the Fall. Stone walls flanked either side of the cathedral for a few hundred paces. Where they left off, the forcewall, invisible but in some ways stronger than the stone, curved to encompass the whole compound. In the other direction, the Saint's thoughts carried the forcewall in a vast circle separating city from desert, and the canids and other dangers that flourished in the absence of men.

Hunter crossed the nave into the sanctuary. Above her head, the vaulted ceilings arched high, a space calculated to awe the men who used to come here in search of something greater than themselves. Now the echoing silence only mirrored the emptiness of the world. Still, it was a miracle of engineering, this huge enclosure constructed from nothing more than small blocks of stone cemented expertly together. The forebears must have glimpsed long into the future to choose this place as their last refuge against the Fall. It was no allegory, the Patri always said, that the ancient cathedral stood intact so long after the metal and glass of newer buildings had fallen into ruins. The Church simply had the capacity to repair the stone.

The altar rose in the center of the sanctuary, surrounded by the panels and stations the priests tended. Lights played across the screens in patterns unreadable to a hunter, the priests' fingers tapping responses with swift precision. Upon the altar lay the Saint. A glittering crown of copper connected her to the machines that preserved the remains of the city, maintaining the forcewall that blocked the wilderness out, the generators that gave the cityens a bit of light in the darkness and heat to keep them from freezing to death in the winter, and more important, powered the crypts where the priests did their work to keep the Church itself alive; for only the Church could preserve what was left of the world. That was the central truth of all life in the four hundred annuals since the Fall: without the Saint, the Church would die; without the Church, the city.

Hunter bowed her head. She envied the priests, who could know the Saint's thoughts, or what passed for thoughts in a mind that was so much greater now than human. The Saint spoke to them through the boards, but no one knew where her awareness began or ended, or if anything about it could be considered awareness, the way men conceived of it.

Once the crown was on, there was no asking.

The Saint had been a girl once, before she ascended to that altar. Hunter hoped for her sake that it was like a deep sleep, undisturbed by any dream.

Hunter had spoken to the girl, before she became the Saint, had received her words and judged her. Wrongly, foolishly. She wished devoutly that she could speak with her now, confess, ask forgiveness. If she listened hard enough she could imagine that she still heard the girl's voice. But that was all it was, imagining, the way a mind would always try to fill a void. To know the Saint's thoughts was not her place, nor any hunter's. That she even wished it made her unworthy.

Yet she lingered, listening, until she knew for certain she would hear no voice answering her from the silence.

The Patri waited for her at the inner gate, sure enough sign of his concern. He must have been standing there for some time; the motion-activated lights glowed softly where he stood, but the path back to the domiciles was lost in darkness. Another man might have wished for less illumination: Hunter hadn't had time to go back to the spring before night fell, and a quick roll in the sand had done little to scrub the blood and gore from her clothes. The Patri only nodded as she came down the steps from the mundane inner doors. "You found her in time, I see."

Hunter nodded, drawing the little vial from her pocket with a sticky hand. "Her ovaries were perfectly intact. I left the rest for the scavengers; there was nothing of value."

The Patri accepted the bottle without hesitation, secreting it in a fold of his loose-flowing robe. "What delayed you? The aircar landed some while ago."

Dust clung to a wet stain across the toe of her boot. "I'm sorry, Patri. I came in through the sanctuary."

She heard the long breath he let out. "Very well. Go bathe. I will have a meal sent to you if you wish."

Hunter's stomach twisted. "Not now, thank you, Patri."

His wise gaze was nearly unbearable. "Rest, then. There will be much to do in the morning."

Hunter let her normally silent footfalls beat a warning down the stone steps to the baths. Two young priests, interrupted in their dalliance, fled flushed and dripping as she came into the chamber. Steam rose gently from pools heated by the same source deep below that also powered systems throughout the Church, even the altar where the Saint lay. But Hunter did not want to think of the Saint, not now.

She stripped quickly, dropping her clothes in a pile for the young nun who tiptoed in silently to collect them. The fabric was another miracle bequeathed by the forebears; by morning it would be washed clean as if never worn, blank and unstained. She caught sight of herself reflected on the calm surface of the pool, a body lean and muscled as all hunters were, marred here and there by blood and grime; the face a dusty mask with two narrow channels washed clean beneath the eyes. Ela stared back at her without accusation.

She closed her eyes and slipped into the water, floating still as death long after the last ripple died away against the stone.

CHAPTER 2

She went down to the laboratory in the morning. Winter or summer, the temperature stayed the same here in the subterranean bowels of the Church, cool and dank. In the two annuals she had spent tending the listening arrays in the desert, she had grown unused to such confining spaces. She felt the rock ribs pressing close just behind the ancient plastered walls, a bone poking through here and there where repairs had been neglected. Long tubes crossed the ceiling like veins on the back of an old man's hand, a bare few still glowing dimly, providing just enough light to let the priests pick their way along the corridor. For a hunter, it was more than enough.

Doors were set at regular intervals along the hall. Most opened, if they opened at all, only onto the mortuary debris of the Fall. Sometimes the juvenile hunters explored inside those dead rooms, against instructions but well in line with expectations. Hunter herself had done so once. She had found the desiccated remains of two bodies intermingled in a corner, still wrapped in a few scraps of cloth that might have been white once. Far more important, beneath the dead she had spied a rectangular sheaf of prints, fixed together at one end, with a stiff cover protecting the bound edge and sides. Nothing in the Church was worth more than these, save the Saint herself, and she carried it to the priests with an appreciation bordering on awe. That had brought more priests running to search the room for further treasures. There were other items still intact and useful to be collected from the rubble, but it was the papers, burnt and crumbling but still closely covered with the mechanical writings of the forebears, that brought them up in reverent silence. They gathered them up tenderly as children and carried them off to safety, but whether the brown leaves deigned to give up any of their secrets, Hunter never heard, and though she had tried other doors after that, she never found anything else of such value.

She didn't care what any of those rooms might hold right now. Instead she strode towards the meticulously rebuilt laboratory at the end of the hall.

Not a single priest looked up when she entered, though rows of them sat evenly spaced along the pristine tables, bent unmoving over their magnifiers, giving the illusion that the lenses grew out from their eye sockets. The overhead light was dim as the hallway, but each magnifier was lit from beneath, as if the priests huddled over a dozen tiny fires. Their hands worked tiny, delicate instruments, the ends too fine for even Hunter to see unaided. She knew, though, what they prodded and teased beneath the lenses, and how eagerly the next group of nuns waited for them to finish their work and give it over to be incubated through the long winter. The children would look much like Ela, like Hunter herself.

She stood there for a long time, watching what they wrought with the bloody treasure she had brought them last night. Even when she heard the footsteps coming down the hall, she could not take her eyes off the priests and their work. The Patri stood quietly behind her, waiting patiently, breath even as a metronome. Without a hunter's enhanced senses he could not, she knew, detect the minute irregularity of hers, the tiny increase in heart rate she could not prevent when in his presence, ever since she had something to hide.

Since the Saint.

The Patri let her wait some time before he finally said, "When they told me you missed teachings, I thought I would find you here. Would you like to see?"

"Yes, please."

At the Patri's nod, the priest at the nearest magnifier bowed and stepped aside. Hunter glanced at his face. He was thin and sharp-featured, like all his kind, and his eyes were pale, the better to gather the light in this underground lair. His skin was so white she could see the vessels coursing through it, a map to show where to strike, the unprotected soft parts delivered like an offering. She clasped her hands behind her back. He would never be exposed to danger. He had probably not set foot outside the Church since early childhood, instead spending all his waking moments absorbing the teachings, searching for new truths that might be the difference in the Church's survival. One day he, or one of his brothers, would become the Patri. Hunter could not imagine it.

He did not meet her eyes.

The Patri took the stool first, adjusting the dials with an echo of the priests' skilled delicacy. His hands and face were tinted darker now from the sol he walked in above, but where his loose sleeves fell back the skin showed as white as the priest's. "It's been a long time," he said with a wry smile. The young priest nodded nervous encouragement. The Patri stared down for a long time. When he was satisfied at last, he stood up, holding the stool for Hunter.

She took the seat tentatively and set her eyes to the magnifier. "If it isn't in focus, turn the small ring to adjust. Your eyes are sharper than mine." The lumpy pinkish blob in the viewer gained shape as she dialed the knob. "Do you see those little circles?" She nodded minimally, taking care not to lose her view. "Those are the eggs."

"How many will there be?" Her successors, one day, though most of them would never know her.

"Enough for a few batches, maybe less. Many are lost in the enhancement process. We are not as skilled as our grandfathers, and they were not as skilled as theirs. In the first days after the Fall, the eggs might be taken and the hunter survive. Now we dare not try that. So much easier with priests—pair a priest with a nun, and every child is another priest. But hunters can't bear, so it has to be done this way. And of course we only have so many nuns to carry them." His breath rose and fell in a sigh. She felt acutely how his burdens weighed on him.

The priest cleared his throat. "Speaking of difficulty, Patri," he began, then broke off with a nervous glance at Hunter.

"You may speak in front of Echo, Jozef."

"Yes, Patri. I am sorry to have to tell you, but another magnifier broke today."

"Can you repair it?" There was a sharpness in the Patri's question, quickly smoothed. "If there's a way I'm sure you'll find it."

The priest ran a hand through his thin white hair. "We will try, of course, but I'm afraid not. The lens itself cracked. As you know we've been trying to make more, but there is something missing from our technique. We've been searching the prints, but so far . . ."

Hunter had often seen the priests, dozens of them, pale-eyed and soft as Jozef, hunched over the tables in the nave, where the walls were lined with thousands of volumes, lovingly preserved, like the one Hunter had found. Besides the Saint, those prints were the greatest treasure of the world.

"I understand, Jozef. I thank the forebears who

thought to put all those words on paper before the last machine died, of course, but we can wish they had printed us an index, yes?" He laughed ruefully.

Jozef's thin lips curved, without, Hunter thought, much humor. "Yes, Patri. Meanwhile we will try our best with the repairs, of course."

"I know you will, Jozef. We should let you return to your work." He gestured, and Hunter, with a last look through the lenses, surrendered the seat back to the priest.

The Patri laid a hand on her shoulder as they left the laboratory. "You did well to bring her back."

Hunter thought of the broken girl lying in the dust. *It isn't her.*

It is the part of her that mattered, she told herself fiercely. *She knew it too. Do not shame her with your weakness.* "I did what the Church required, no more."

"The Church requires a great deal sometimes."

She stared at the priests manipulating the tiny plates. "We are made to serve, Patri." It was the earliest truth a hunter learned.

The Patri studied her face. Her heart quickened. He would see, surely he would see. "Do you never wish it could be otherwise, Echo?"

"No, Patri," she said, too quickly. "Of course not. The Church is all the world has left. The Saint. Those are the only things that matter. Without them . . ."

"Even with them, I sometimes think."

She stood still, dismayed by heaviness of his tone. In all the annuals she could remember, nothing had shaken him, nothing challenged the calm and clear-eyed judgment that sometimes made him seem as much hunter as priest. He read her expression and smiled. "But not very often. I was sorry to lose Ela, that's all. You are all so precious to me. All those resources that go into your making, and so much we need you for . . . At least you found her in time. It wasn't a total waste; we can make more." He stared into the laboratory for a moment, then shook himself. "Go attend to your duties, Echo. You have a difficult task today, and you are late."

CHAPTER 3

Eight pairs of brown eyes met hers unblinkingly across the blank surfaces of the classroom desks. At this stage the hunters were finally recognizing their strengths: everything was a test, in a way the playful scuffling and half-realized challenges of the younger children were not. The sudden maturation of their bodies sometimes produced erratic moods; it was a dangerous time, for them and everyone around them.

When Hunter had been this age, one of her batchmates had taken a game too far, and drowned a young priest in the baths. Accidents happened, of course, but this wasn't one; and the Patri had had that hunter put down. It was more than just a lesson for the remaining 367s. "I'm worried about the line," Hunter, passing by a cracked door when no one was supposed to be about, had heard the Patri say. "The type is starting to blur. I'm afraid there will be more to cull."

"We will do what we must," the Materna had answered, voice heavy with sorrow. "The Church must be preserved. It is the only hope of the world."

"Yes, I know, and yet the world is changing around us. . . ."

There was more, but Hunter had kept dutifully on her way, not lingering to overhear the rest, no matter how much she wanted to. The words were not meant for her. She had put them resolutely out of her mind and not considered them again until now, when she faced Ela's batchmates with the memory of the laboratory and the Patri's strange mood still roiling her thoughts.

She made sure she showed no uncertainty as she met each girl's eyes in turn. The atmosphere in the room was disturbed, and most of them looked as if they hadn't slept, though they were surely exhausted from the long desert exercise. This batch had not lost one of its own in over an annual. It was always a difficult lesson, both to learn and to teach. Often it played itself out in anger.

One by one she let the girls study her, measure their strength against hers, and one by one they looked away. The seventh, the next to last one left, took longest. Hunter felt the faintest tightening in her belly. When the girl finally blinked it was almost arrogant, a concession but not a defeat. Gem, this number seven was called. An apt name for her, hard and cold. Not at all like Ela. Strange, that those two were the only ones of the batch whose names came easily to Hunter. But then, she spent most of her time away in the desert now, doing the Patri's bidding.

When all the girls were staring down at their desks Hunter finally spoke. "You have questions about yesterday's events. You may ask."

They hesitated, exchanging worried glances. She waited with hunter patience. They were shaken; she could not fault them for caution, though in this case it was unnecessary. At last, when no one else volunteered, the fourth raised an uncertain hand. "In the after-session Priest Dalto said that Ela had to be put down."

"Yes. She had fallen off a cliff and was too badly hurt to survive." There it was, the cold fact. They stared at it as if it were Ela's body laid before them.

The sixth asked, "Are you the one who found her?"

"Yes." Anger flickered across some of the faces, fear across others as they processed her answer. If she had found Ela, she had put Ela down. Hunter faced them calmly, letting them picture the scene, imagine themselves in Ela's place. See Hunter leaning over them, strong, hard hands reaching out, not to save them but to finish everything . . . They had seen death before, of course, but not a killing. One looked away, out the open shutters towards the desert, though the high Church wall blocked the view from here.

"What was her error?" the first asked, managing to sound calm despite whatever emotion widened her dark eyes. Hunter nodded approval.

"That is a good question, but it assumes she made

an error." She paused to let the young hunters chew on that. They didn't like the taste. It was one thing when someone made a mistake, no matter how dire the outcome; the rest always assumed they would perform better themselves. But if Ela had died through no fault of her own, perhaps the same could happen to any of them. Not all of them had thought of that possibility before. Now they would never forget. When Hunter was sure, she said, "In this case you are correct. Ela let discomfort override caution; she slipped seeking water. It was unnecessary." The threat of her own anger caught her by surprise; she dispelled it with a deliberate breath. "What else would you like to know?"

"Did—did she say anything?" It was the sixth again, voice trembling. Hunter hid a frown. Tears, like temper, were not uncommon among hunters of this age, but this was not the place. Perhaps the girl had paired with Ela. The attachments among hunters at this age burned hot, but the girl should have developed better self-control by now.

"She made her report. That was all the time there was."

"Was . . ." The girl broke off. Fay, Hunter finally remembered.

"If you have a question, Fay, ask. This is a time to learn."

Fay swallowed. "Was she frightened?"

Ah. This was an important part of the lesson. She had not expected to be able to address it so directly. "What do you think?"

A little ripple of unease stirred the girls. "I would be," Fay said in a low voice. Hunter raised her estimate of the girl; it was a difficult admission for a juvenile to make, especially in front of the rest of her batch.

Gem barely tried to hide her disdain. "If she was, she deserved to be put down."

"That is an ignorant answer," Hunter retorted. "We are all afraid from time to time."

"I'm not."

"Then you deprive yourself of a weapon, which is also ignorant. Properly managed, fear is useful; it sharpens the reflexes. It increases strength for a short time. It can save your life."

"*Was* Ela afraid?" Fay asked, still too wide-eyed.

The calm white face rose in Hunter's memory, as it would in her dreams when she could sleep again. "No."

"Did she fight you?" That from Gem, of course.

"No."

"I would have. And I wouldn't have been afraid." Not a boast, but a statement of fact. Hunter believed her.

"Then one of us would die, Gem Hunter 378." Gem held her hard stare for a long moment before she finally blinked. The girl leaned back in her chair, unchastened, merely looking thoughtful. She might have been reconsidering her judgment, or thinking about the noon meal. When she next met Hunter's eyes, her face showed nothing beyond a satisfied half smile. And Hunter felt a chill, that had nothing to do with the desert breeze drifting through the window.

CHAPTER 4

The fugitive Saint was afraid.

The girl sat on the bare sand next to the pitiful remnants of a fire, grubby robe pooled around her, skinny arms wrapped protectively around her knees. She looked like a lost child. "How did you find me?"

Hunter drew the scanner from her belt. It must have looked like a weapon; the Saint flinched. Hunter shook her head. "It doesn't hurt." She ran the bluish ray over her own palm to prove it. She gestured, and the Saint reluctantly held out her hand. The green glow of her skin was startling in the gathering dark. "The priests tagged you with it when they made you." Hunter looked at the thin, dirty girl in front of her, swallowing dismay. "We have to hurry. The old Saint is dying. City systems are already beginning to fail. Cityens will die, if you don't ascend soon."

"Yet look at me, hiding in the desert like a rabbit. You must be very disappointed."

Hunter could only stare back at her without answering.

"See? You don't believe I can do it either. Pretend you never found me. No one will know."

For an instant, looking at the frightened child, Hunter wavered. Then: "We are all made to serve. I have to take you back."

The Saint hugged herself tighter. "I don't want to go."

The refectory was warm already, although the enormous fans, broader than a hunter was tall, pulled fresh air through the walls on either end. The nuns took up three long tables in the middle of the massive room, laughing and chattering away like the cityen girls they were, while the weanling 388s stalked each other around their legs. Perhaps twenty of the nuns had babies at breast—the 390s, those would be—and another dozen or more were gravid, by the looks of them ready to deliver in weeks, another batch of hunters for the Church. There would be no Saint among these births. The priests made those singly, far from the hunters and nuns. And none would be needed for a long time yet.

The nuns sat spread legged in their loose robes, patting their ponderous bellies while a pair of the newer girls, tithed late last year, took their turns bringing the steaming bowls from the kitchen and passing heavily laden platters. Hunter paused, smelling greens, a luxury she had missed in the desert. The oblivious nuns carried on their conversation, apparently gathering information from one of the new girls who had sat down with them.

"He did that?"

"Yes. My cousin told me. And didn't ask for anything in return." The women's eyes were round with admiration.

"I heard something like that too," another one put in. "When Yeral was sick, that Bender who runs the melter, he sent some men to help until Yeral got well again."

"A Bender?" the first woman asked dubiously. "Why'd he help them? It's not even his same clave."

"Don't know. Got to take care of each other, I've heard some say, but I don't see why, when we've got the Church already taking care of us. If the Benders'd asked, a medical priest would've got Yeral better before they needed the Warder's help. Don't know why they didn't send for one. Maybe—Saints, Luida, watch that child!"

It was too late: a 388, reflexes not as advanced as her ambition, misjudged a pounce and fell with an unhunterlike cry, startling a nursing baby whose flailing limb knocked over a glass. There was a tinkling crash, and another peal of laughter as the serving girls scurried to clean up before the weanlings could make it worse.

Hunter kicked a bit of glass off her boot. She would not be sorry when the Patri sent her back to the peace of the desert. Dodging the worst of the mess, she made her way towards the farthest table, where a group of hunters were consuming their meal in a somewhat more orderly fashion. They noticed her coming, of course, and their conversation stilled, then resumed, a pause just brief enough for her to wonder if she had imagined it. She took a seat with a nod she hoped passed for companionable, and focused on the plate the breathless young nun put in front of her.

"Echo Hunter 367!"

Even in a crowd of like-sounding hunters she would never mistake that voice. She rose to face the woman just arriving. "Criya."

"It's good to see you." Criya reached out to clasp her shoulders briefly—more demonstrative than hunters usually were, but in this case it was permissible. The 367s had had bad luck, six lost at once when their aircar crashed in the chaos while the old Saint was dying, and now there were none left except herself and Criya. Even now Hunter still half expected to see Delia or Freyn, who had lined up for so long on either side of her that they seemed to have grown from her shoulders like extra arms. Sometimes, when they were first gone, she'd wondered what it would feel like to stand with other batches, the 370s, for instance, between Dava and Fallon. But they had their own fifth, Evlin, and that would never be Hunter's place.

Criya was right, it was good to see a surviving batchmate.

And annuals ago they had been close. Hunter reached back in memory, trying to recall the attachment they had shared; found instead Fay's face, and

Ela's. What would it have been like if Criya had died when they were that age?

But Criya was here, speaking to her now. "Well done with Ela. You were always good at finding things." She grinned, pulling up a stool; the poor serving girl brought yet another plate. "I hope if I'm ever lost they send you to look for me."

Before Hunter could answer, a dry voice said, "Not much chance of getting lost in the city, is there, Criya?" It took Hunter a moment to place the speaker: Indine, a 362; Hunter had spent little time with that batch. Another of them, Nyree, looked on with a cold smile.

"More than staying here watching over nuns and weanlings, Indine. There are new habited areas all the time. I don't know why cityens can't stay put where it'd be easier to watch over them. They've spread out so far we can hardly keep order everywhere at once. Although," Criya added, laughing at the commotion yet another 388 was causing, "you still might have the more difficult task."

Hunter let the banter sail over her head. Hunters used it for practice, the quick exchanges, probes and thrusts no different from any other kind of sparring. There were rarely serious injuries, and even if there were, one learned. It had never been Hunter's strongest skill, and today she had no heart for it. She concentrated on her greens and was reaching for a second portion when the fans stopped turning.

She was half out of her chair, hand on her belt where a static wand would be if they carried them inside the compound, when the power came back. It hadn't been more than a second or two, but that should have been plenty of time for the others to react as well, readying themselves to face the threat.

Instead they sat in their chairs, eyeing her as they would a small piece of equipment that had malfunctioned unexpectedly, more curious than alarmed. The nuns and tiny hunters seemed not to have noticed anything at all. "It's a bad circuit," Indine said around a mouthful. "They reported it at teachings."

Hunter sat back down, chagrined, and the others resumed their conversation where she had interrupted it, ignoring her, but she knew they could sense the heat in her skin, mark the effects of the fighting hormones coursing wastefully through her blood. "Is something wrong?" Criya whispered, leaning close.

"I didn't know about the circuit, that is all."

"Things break from time to time, Echo. There is no reason to be so alarmed; this isn't the desert. The priests will fix it."

The fans hitched once more, then caught, turning steadily through the rest of the meal. Hunter hoped no one noticed that she had lost her appetite. But Criya, each time Hunter looked, was watching her.

Hunter watched Ela's batchmates practice with projtrodes under the careful tutelage of Tana Hunter 337. She wanted to confer with Tana, but she had no excuse to interrupt the exercise. The juveniles were working in the modeled ruins of a city building that had been assembled in the farthest corner of the compound. It was a good day for a lesson, the hot sun recharging the trodes nearly as soon as they were empty and giving the targets plenty of power to pop up lifelike from within the rubble. Tana had been training batches since Hunter was younger than these juveniles were now.

It had been Tana, inadvertently, who had given her her first glimpse of the city the Church preserved. Eight-year-old Hunter had hesitated at the wall for just a moment, balancing the injunction never to leave the compound without permission against the assignment another teacher had given to follow Tana without letting her know. True, Tana had announced that all the day's training was complete; but Hunter reasoned that if Tana didn't know about the surveillance exercise, she couldn't properly cancel it. Far worse to fail in a mission than to break a housekeeping rule, she had decided that night; and so she skittered over the wall and set off after Tana through the twilight.

The Church sat in what had once been the center of the city, before the Fall. It was hard to imagine how many people had lived here then; millions, the priests estimated from the salvaged records and the span of the empty ruins. Now everything to the north and west was hundreds of annuals abandoned, leaving the Church at the far western edge of the forcewall that circumscribed the city's remains. Though the force-wall recognized the denas that all humans, made or born, had in common, and let their bearers pass back and forth with no more sensation than a faint tingling of the skin, cityens still regarded that boundary with an almost superstitious awe, as if a few steps one way or the other made any compelling difference. Even now few lived anywhere close to it. Past the forcewall was the desert, where habitation had given way to ruins, and beyond that, the true wilderness, where it had never spread even before the Fall. The great Church doors stared down a wide expanse of ancient stone steps at the straight main road that led to the city. Abandoned buildings that once lined that road had long ago fallen to ruin, leaving open space on either side. The contracted population occupied only three small claves, scattered among the ruins to the north, east along the river bend, and more recently further south.

Hunter had slipped along that road from shadow to gradually deepening shadow between the infrequent light posts, which twinkled on one by one as Tana approached and darkened when she passed. Hunter followed as close as she dared—too close and Tana would hear her; too big a gap, and her separate passage would trigger the lights again. Besides that, nighttime was unsafe even inside the forcewall. It was not canids who made the danger here, but the human predators that the Church had never managed to stamp out despite its best efforts. Refusing to shiver, Hunter had pressed forward, concentrating on her quarry.

Tana visited three small shops that evening, doing

nothing more than inquiring with the keepers about the state of their inventories, before she knocked on the partition of a grain grower's space. Hunter slipped around to the side, where standing on tiptoe she was just able to put an ear to the cracked window. ". . . Kept some back from the store," she heard Tana finish a sentence.

"Please, I've done everything I was supposed to." The grower's voice cracked as he spoke. "I only took a little extra . . . with the children growing so, and we have another baby coming . . . I was afraid there just wouldn't be enough. The harvest this year . . ." His words trailed off miserably.

"Everyone gets a fair share," Tana reminded him mildly.

Hunter could practically hear the man hanging his head. "I know. It's just that—our first baby died, the way they do, and even though the next two are with us, my wife, she's still afraid. She asked me please, just set aside a little, in case there's another sickness, and this being a bad year, who knows what would happen, if we couldn't feed them, maybe the Church would take them both for nuns, and who would we have left?"

"Why would she think such a thing? The Church never took more than one daughter from a family, even in the old days. And now there are so many, most families aren't asked to tithe at all."

"That's what I said. But my wife—they told her things would change, the Church had a new plan. . . ."

"Who told her that?" Tana asked sharply.

Fear entered the man's voice. "I—I don't know."

"Is your wife here?"

"No, she isn't. She—" His voice changed. He must have turned his head, the kind of involuntary glance that gave away a nervous liar every time. "She isn't here," he finished weakly.

"Well then." Tana's voice was uncharacteristically gentle. "I know you're a good man. You don't want to get in any trouble with the Church, do you?"

"N-n-no."

"Here's what you can do, then. When your wife comes home, remind her that the Church is here to help. In fact, I'll stop back again next week to check on you. I'm sure by then the matter of the grain will be forgotten, especially if your wife remembers where she heard those rumors."

The man had practically babbled with relief. After a few more minutes of meaningless pleasantries, Tana came out into the narrow alley leading back to the street. The light globes were small and far apart here, but there was enough illumination for Hunter to see the disgusted crook of her mouth. Curiosity must have made Hunter careless; Tana disappeared in the next slip of shadow and didn't reemerge. Hunter stood there, perplexed, until iron fingers closed over her shoulder and dragged her into a pool of light. "Echo Hunter 367?"

"Yes, Tana." Hunter forced herself to stand straight and still.

"What are you doing here?"

"Tracking you, Tana."

"Tracking me? What are you talking about?"

"That was our exercise today, but you weren't supposed to know. I've failed."

There was a strained silence, during which Hunter was sure Tana was sorting through appropriate punishments. Then, unexpectedly, the older hunter broke into a laugh. "Failed? Not to worry, Echo. You've done well. Very well. But it's getting late; let's get you back to the Church. Tracking me," she said again to herself, still laughing.

Hunter fell in beside her, working to keep up with the long strides. "Tana, I think that man's wife was really there. His voice sounded strange."

Tana sobered. "I know she was. My words were really for her."

They walked in silence for a time. Then Hunter said, "Why was he afraid of you? Hunters don't hurt cityens, we protect them."

"Sometimes the things we do to help seem harsh to them. That makes them frightened, or angry. The nun tithe, for instance: they love their daughters. They hate to give them up, even though they know it's the right thing."

Hunter thought about things she had seen in her lessons. "Are you sure? Sometimes in the desert we find dead ones."

Tana sighed. "I know. We think those are children who ran away, or whose parents died or couldn't take care of them anymore."

"That seems awfully wasteful. Why wouldn't someone else help them?"

"The city isn't orderly like the Church, Echo. Many things aren't the exact way we'd want them to be, but we have to focus on the big things. If we find children like that in time, we give them to someone who can take care of them. If not . . ." Tana shrugged. "Some losses we have to accept."

"I still don't understand why the man got so upset," Hunter pressed. "The tithe is like a lesson, isn't it? Sometimes *our* lessons are hard, but they make us better, so we can fulfill our function."

"What's simple for us, Echo, can be very confusing for the cityens."

Then, Hunter had been satisfied with that.

Now, many annuals later, a pause in the steady firing of stunners drew her attention back to the 378s. Tana had called the girls over to her. She pointed at something in a crate, then at the model house. Two of the girls carried the heavy container behind a bit of imitation wall, where they were lost to view for a moment. Then they came running back to wait breathlessly with the others. Hunter felt the echo of their excitement in her own quickened heartbeat.

A shadow moved beyond the mock wall. The young hunters surveyed the ruins, projtrodes ready. Another movement, and a *pop* followed by twin metallic *pings* as the projtrodes struck uselessly against brick. All was still. The girls waited, rewinding the trodes. Tana lobbed a stone over the wall, stirring whatever hid there. A dark form streaked over the wall, not towards the girls but away, where instinct must have told it freedom lay. There was another quick series of *pings*, a pause, then one more *pop* and an agonized howl. The canid fell down where it was struck, limbs jerking in the dust. The girls stalked carefully over to it, stunners ready. It was a juvenile, nothing compared to the huge beasts of the desert, but still dangerous. Tana, her own weapon put aside, calmly pointed out the effects on the animal, which continued to twitch disjointedly, odd high-pitched noises coming from its foaming muzzle. The breeze carried off most of the discussion, but Hunter still caught snatches.

" . . . Conscious but . . . interfere . . . nerve pathways . . . Careful, sometimes heart . . . Pain."

The girls stood still, the yard soundless except for the animal's squeals. Then a girl's voice, higher pitched but calm. " . . . Try it on each other?"

Even from here, Hunter saw the change in Tana's posture as the old woman shook her head emphatically. "Over," Hunter heard her pronounce. The girl who had asked clearly wanted to argue. Gem, Hunter realized with a chill. Tana shook her head again and turned to walk away. The girl lifted her trodes. The other juveniles stood frozen. Tana kept walking, though Hunter was certain that she felt the weapon leveled at her back. Hunter held her breath, bracing for the shot. When it came, she flinched despite herself. Tana kept walking, ignoring the sharp *pop-pop-pop* as Gem wheeled away, firing her projtrodes close range at the canid, the other girls joining in until the last charge ran out and there was nothing left but a pile of mangled bloody fur at their feet. Tana never turned.

Hunter took a step in Tana's direction. Then: "Am I interrupting?" The voice came from nearby, though she had not registered the footfalls coming up behind her.

"No, Materna. I was just watching the exercise. It's finished anyway."

"Would you walk with me?"

"Yes, Materna." Hunter stifled a sigh. The Materna's company was always vaguely pleasant and just the slightest bit trying, as if she were still the cityen girl she had been so long ago. And now Hunter would miss her chance to talk to Tana.

The old woman linked an arm through Hunter's. All this time and she had never lost that odd cityen habit. "I've scarcely seen you these two annuals, Echo, since you brought the Saint back to us."

Heat rolled up from the baking sand. There was one last *pop* from someone's trodes. The sanctuary where the Saint lay would be cool and quiet. "My duties have kept me in the desert," Hunter said stiffly.

"I don't mean to chide you, child." The Materna peered across at the 378s. "Have you seen enough to say how they're coming along?"

"Their skills are appropriate for their stage. The loss rate has been acceptable, all things considered."

"It was so sad about Ela."

Hunter kept her face impassive. "Better on an exercise than somewhere her failure could hurt the Church."

A pause. "She was a nice child." The Materna's plump face was lined, tired, devoid for once of her usual jovial smile. Hunter suddenly wondered if she had borne Ela. Hunters were lost often, true enough; but the nuns who had incubated them in their own bellies and nursed them until they weaned always mourned, perhaps not as women in the city mourned their born-children, but still there was a kind of attachment there. And the Materna, having carried hunters from who knew how many batches until her body aged past that usefulness, still sometimes seemed to see the children they had briefly been, long past the time they had grown into what they were made to be. Hunter wished she had spoken less harshly. "But I suppose you're right." Another pause, as the old woman's gaze drifted over the 378s. "This is a difficult time. The Church must be certain of us all. Are you worried about any of the others?"

Hunter's mind was full of worries. What she had told the Materna was true; this batch was doing better than many. How would one know if the line were failing? One juvenile lost to the desert was hardly a mark of decline. It was also true that the training was harsh not merely to provide the girls with necessary skills, but also to expose weaknesses before they wasted more than just the one. But what of the other signs Hunter had seen in her brief exposure to the batch? The softness of the sixth, unable to hide her grief over a lost friend; or Gem, whose cold self-confidence was even more disturbing. She worried about all of them.

She opened her mouth to say so. But then, before she could suppress it, an image floated into her mind, the watery reflection of a dusty, tear-scarred face. Hunter's chest squeezed tight. *It is not their fault I doubt them.*

Misinterpreting her silence, the Materna said, "You needn't protect me, Echo. Even if it were one I carried, if there were weakness, I would want to know."

"No, Materna."

The old woman searched her face. After a moment, defeated by the blank hunter mask, she gave up. "If you say so. Help me back to my quarters, Echo, if you don't mind. And then you can go see the Patri. He's been asking for you."

The Patri's chambers nestled in a wing of the cathedral, where he could work in peace away from the distraction of the domicile buildings, close to the Saint. Hunter hesitated at his door. *There is no reason to be anxious.* He had summoned her here often, to give her instruction before a mission or hear a report afterwards, or simply to have her assessment of some matter or other, as he might gather useful information from any hunter. And he taught, as well, with the insight of an intellect designed to be superior, to see events with a longer view. Such lessons were challenging, but Hunter had always looked forward to them eagerly, and returned to them over and over in her thoughts long after. But it was more than the teachings he imparted that made her treasure their sessions. In the

Patri's presence she had understood most directly the service for which she was made.

Nothing has changed, she insisted to herself. Yet waiting here before the Patri's chambers she felt her heart speed up, her breathing quicken as if she faced danger. She stood a moment, schooling herself to calm.

Her diffident knock seemed to boom in the deep silence.

"Enter." She made herself walk in slowly, then turned to face the Patri, hands laced calmly in front of her, as if merely preparing herself for another lesson. If she thought about it that way it was not so difficult. It helped that his chambers looked the same as always, the desk littered with prints, stacks of them piled on the side table, the floor. Her nose twitched at the familiar smell, musty paper overlaid with the mineral scent of ink. The Patri's joke with Jozef had had more than a core of truth. The priests marked for him everything they found that could bear on whatever issue he faced. She waited while he finished the page he was studying. "Come in, Echo. Please sit down."

"Thank you, Patri."

It was hard to sit quietly while he contemplated her with the same sharp scrutiny he brought to every problem. Only since apprehending the fugitive Saint had she imagined any cause to fear his regard. "Are you well?" he asked.

Perhaps Criya had told him about the incident in the refectory. "Yes, Patri."

"That is good." He assessed her over steepled fingers. "My assignments have kept you far from us these past few years."

He had sent Hunter as far out in the desert as the aircar could take her, to the limit of the transmission towers' reach, and three days past on foot. Hunters could go no further; those who passed that mark never returned. There she tended the arrays of dishes that could relay the faintest signal of any surviving city to the Church, if any existed. It seemed doubtful. Hunter had stumbled across ruins, here and there, bony outlines of the places men had once flourished; but the wilderness had long since taken over, and only the canids and the smaller predators stalked the remnants of the streets and nested in the caves of rubble. Sometimes, since the Saint, Hunter stood there at the edge of the world, poised on the brink of stepping off; but duty always brought her back.

"Yes, Patri." She added, to ease his burden when he sent her away again, "It is not a hardship." Too late, she realized how *that* sounded.

He let it pass. "I envy you a little, you know. I haven't left the walls for"—his lips moved, counting silently—"almost sixty annuals now. Sometimes I wish I could go outside again."

Hunter could not remember ever hearing the Patri express a wish for himself. "We could take you," she told him. "Tana, I, a few others; enough to keep you safe. Not in an aircar, they aren't reliable enough to carry you, but we could go slowly. This would be a good time for you to see the desert. There hasn't been any rain, but the worst of the windstorms are past—"

He stopped her with a wave of his hand, amused. "No, no. Thank you, Echo, but the desert never appealed to me. The priestly denas, I suppose. Now, the city, that's a different matter. I've been there once or twice, a long time ago. Not since I was Patri, of course. But even then, to see it starting to thrive, under the Church's eye, to understand what it is we strive so diligently to preserve—"

He tapped the print he'd been reading; upside down to her, it appeared to be a capture of the sanctuary in some vastly earlier time, when the equipment was still being assembled. "I try to imagine what it must have been like for the forebears, knowing that the Fall was coming, that everything they knew was coming to an end, and still directing all their efforts to preserve some seed of humanity that the Church might use to regrow the world again. This is an original print, from the time just before the Fall. The horror they faced was unimaginable, and still they served. Every Patri since has measured himself against those men."

To test oneself, not against the task at hand, a batchmate, or the physical challenges of the desert, but the dust of time—a hunter could not comprehend such a thing.

"Patri, anything I can do, the least service—"

"You retrieved the Saint, Echo. That was far from the least service."

Her belly tightened. There was much that had happened with the Saint that she had never told. Not what had happened; she had described that all, in precise detail, without variance, as often as required. But no one knew what she had thought in that dark night. How she had nearly failed. Had wanted to, for that one instant, when instead of the city's salvation she saw only a frightened, desperate child.

That she must never confess to anyone, not even the Patri.

"Any hunter would have done it, Patri. I only happened to be the one."

The corner of his mouth drew up. "As I happen to be Patri now. We have no luxury to pick our circumstances. The city thrives, Echo, but this is a dangerous time, perhaps as dangerous as any since the Fall. There are still not enough cityens to guarantee our survival, and yet there are so many, we scarcely have enough food, enough power. It is a difficult balance. The smallest wobble either way could tip it. If we could find other cities, other Saints to help—" He broke off; she saw again the weight of his burdens.

"Surely the Church will provide, Patri. The Saint is young and strong."

"Yes." His eyes fell to the print; he sat lost in thought for a moment before he looked up at her again. "What I spoke of is a problem for the priests. You need not concern yourself. But I do have another duty for you, now that the matter with Ela is resolved."

Hunter spoke quickly, so that she didn't have time

to think of Ela. "I can pack tonight, Patri, and be back at the farthest arrays within four days at the most."

"Criya will tend the arrays."

She blinked back surprise, laced with dismay. "Patri, I am most familiar with the desert. I assumed—" She broke off under the weight of his mild gaze. "Forgive my error, Patri."

"It is forgiven." He studied her, lips pursed. At last he said, "I have sent you away too often, Echo. I want you close for now."

"I am honored, Patri," she said, but her stomach knotted again. Her mouth felt dry; she should have drunk more this morning. "May I know my assignment?"

"I have decided that you will work with the juveniles for a time. It is good for them to gain from the experience of many different hunters. It is also good to assess them from many vantage points. As I said, this is a difficult time. We must identify any weaknesses, and act to correct them however necessary."

The type is starting to blur, she heard in memory. *There might be more to cull.* She forced herself to meet his eyes. "My service to the Church in all things, Patri."

"As it should be." The ritual words hung in the air.

Then the Patri said, "Report to Criya any new information she should have about the arrays before she leaves. Then see Kam Hunter 364; she has the details of your assignment." As she rose he added, "I am glad you'll be watching over the young hunters, Echo, as I watch over all of you."

She finally caught up with Tana that evening. By the time Hunter arrived at the training ground, the 378s were already passing around stringy meat, the remnants of the canid they had killed. That was part of the lesson too: nothing went wasted.

Tana, perched on a piece of broken wall where her presence would not distract them, nodded greeting as Hunter approached. Her gnarled hands cupped a bowl of grains she must have brought from the refectory. "My jaws are too stiff for canid," she said. "Not that I ever cared for it." She smiled crookedly. "It's a good thing we have the Church. I would never make it outside now."

Hunter did not want to picture the old woman outside. Struggling, fighting. Lying in the dust, perhaps, at the bottom of a cliff whose edge she had misjudged . . .

"You'd find a way," she said.

Tana raised an eyebrow. "I'm not so old you need to lie to me, Echo." Her gaze flicked back to the 378s. Hunter could not help noticing the way she had to squint a little to bring them into focus, the dark irises clouded with too many years in the sun, the whites shot through with red.

"I'm sorry, Tana. I meant no disrespect."

"I know. You meant to be kind. That's even worse. No, don't worry. I'm not going to fuss like the Materna. Though I'm as old as her, you know. I remember the year she was tithed in to the Church. Those days, the girls wanted to be nuns. It was an honor, and their life here was so much better than anything they could expect in the city."

"It still is." Hunter thought of the conversation she'd eavesdropped on so long ago. "And I still don't understand why the cityens have such difficulty accepting the need. Without the nuns, the Church couldn't survive. Without the Church, *they* wouldn't survive."

"Yes, I know the catechism. The cityens know it too, that's not the problem. They're like the juveniles; we have to help them put their knowledge into practice. Sometimes it's easier than others. But you haven't been in the city lately, have you?"

"I'm taking a training patrol there tomorrow."

Tana grunted, amused. "I'm sure you'd rather the desert."

"I serve wherever the Patri sends me."

"I'm not criticizing you, Echo. It's not against the catechism to enjoy our duty. And you're good out there, the best we've made in a long time, I think." The praise only added to Hunter's unease. Why would the Patri *not* send her where she was best suited to serve? Hunters occasionally rotated duties, it was true, for freshness or cross-training. But she feared a darker reason. *He wants to keep me here. To watch me.* Tana asked, "What batch are you taking?"

Hunter flicked her eyes in the direction of the 378s.

Tana laughed outright. "That will make it even more interesting. This batch is a challenge, Saint knows."

The 378s passing the plate were quiet, almost somber, though even from the back Hunter could tell

Gem's studied casualness from the other girls' ever so slight reluctance to taste the butchered animal. They'd be thinking how it had been alive one moment, meat the next, their doing. Remembering things that hadn't mattered in the hot excitement of the chase, harder to face now as they stared at their dinner, the way it had trembled, trapped and frightened, the sounds it had made as it died.

"Be careful of Gem," Hunter warned.

"My eyes still see, Echo. Just not as far as they did." The corner of Tana's mouth turned up in something that wasn't quite a smile. The plate went round again; Gem took another portion. "We were bloodthirsty like that once too. It's in the denas. She'll make good use of it. We all do."

Hunter had known Tana all her life. That did not make what she was about to ask safe. The juveniles, beyond earshot, had finished their meal and begun practicing the weaponless combat techniques that every hunter learned from earliest childhood. Hunter watched them for a moment, then said, "Do you think . . . You've seen more hunter batches made than anyone besides the Patri and Materna."

"Dozens," Tana agreed.

"Do you think something's happening to the whole hunter line?" There, it was out. She waited for the reprimand that such a question deserved.

Tana only cocked her head. "Like what?"

Hunter let out a breath. "I don't know. Maybe that . . . that it doesn't replicate the template the way it used to. That there's more drift away than there should be."

"You really think something's wrong with Gem?"

Not only with Gem. "I don't know. She's strong. Quick to make decisions, even where she should be more cautious. Very certain of herself."

Tana's mouth quirked up. "That sounds familiar."

"But there's more, Tana. An arrogance. A lack of respect. Saints, she aimed her stunner at you today. She might have fired."

"She didn't." Tana shrugged without particular concern. "Besides, what if she had? I'm almost past my usefulness. If she learned something, it wouldn't have been a total waste."

"Tana . . ."

"Kindness again, Echo? Now, that *is* peculiar in a hunter. Much more worrisome than arrogance." She shook her head at Hunter's expression. "I'm teasing you. Yet another strange behavior. Maybe you're right after all."

"I don't understand you."

Tana smiled again, distantly. "I don't especially understand myself either. This last annual or two . . . One day, Echo, I looked around and realized I was the last of my batch. Not long after that I was the oldest hunter left. Up until that moment, I felt like I could sit down with a training cohort and start it all again. Then I knew there was only forward, and that it was always going to be shorter than backward. Of course, that was before you were weaned. So I was wrong, by the numbers. But in here," she said, tapping a finger against her graying temple, "it was true all the same. And now I've begun to think odd things, to wonder. . . . Perhaps it's not an accident that we don't usually survive so long. We aren't made to question. Yet here I am."

Hunter's heart sped up. "Tana, what kind of things do you wonder?"

For a moment Tana seemed about to answer. Then Hunter heard the distinct *whoosh* of breath from lungs as one girl missed a breakfall and landed flat on her back in the sand. Tana rose, setting her bowl aside and dusting herself off. "I'd better stop them before bones are broken. It would be a terrible waste if anyone had to miss a training patrol with *you*."

CHAPTER 5

Hunter led the 378s into the western edge of the north-
most clave, one of the earliest areas reclaimed as the
population had rebounded from its nadir. Here, the
buildings had substance, some of them reclaimed and
rebuilt ruins, others constructed entirely new, albeit
from reused metal and stone salvaged elsewhere in
the city. Between them, sometimes running alongside
the road itself, small plots of crops grew in haphazard
rows, not the grains that were grown in mass in the
stads, but vegetables, edible plants, even small fruiting
trees. It reminded Hunter of the priests' garden behind
the domiciles. Water would always be a problem, but
cityens had placed cisterns everywhere to catch the
precious run-off from the rare rains.

This area was often used for teaching. The city was
a confined space compared to the desert, but there

weren't nearly enough hunters to patrol every alley in every clave. Instead they concentrated on maintaining order in the most important parts: the north end where cityens had begun to accumulate goods, the stads where the grain was grown, the west road that led to the Church. This particular zone was safe, and the cityens living here were used to hunters and unlikely to be alarmed by their exercises. Other places, where men found themselves farther from the Church's watchful eye, would be different.

"How," Hunter asked the juveniles as they studied the street, "would you take control of this block if you had to? Fay?"

The girl hesitated, dark-circled eyes closing in thought. It should not be so difficult for her to concentrate. "I—I would order the cityens out."

"That is a child's answer, Fay. Suppose they disobeyed. What then?"

"I would remove the cisterns," Delen said.

"Not unreasonable. But do you know where they all are?"

"No," Delen admitted. She thought a moment. "But I could survey in advance. Then when the time came, I'd be ready."

"Good," Hunter said. "Hunter patrols routinely gather such information. You must always be aware of the resources at your disposal. You have a question, Ava?"

"Might the cityens not keep additional supplies

within their living areas? It would be more convenient for them, and they might have enough to last them several days."

Hunter nodded. "That is a disadvantage of Delen's plan. Lack of food or water will eventually force prey to emerge, but it can require some time."

A few cityens had gathered to watch them curiously, from a respectful distance. Hunter regretted her choice of words, though probably they hadn't heard.

Gem, inattentive, frowned down the axis of the road. "Gem Hunter 378, what is your thought?"

The girl brought her gaze back to Hunter without haste. "I would station hunters with projtrodes at each end of the street. Then I would start a fire in the central building. When the cityens emerged I would stun them all. If any resisted I would force them back inside."

Hunter regulated her breathing. "That would be unnecessarily destructive."

"I would have control of the block."

The juveniles eyed Hunter, waiting for her answer. At last she nodded. "Your plan lacks subtlety, but it is technically correct. That is adequate for now. Let us consider another scenario." She led them on, deeper into the clave, until they came to a metalsmithing shop. The report she'd received had said the man here was friendly to the Church; he was certainly happy to have juveniles to show off to, even if they were juvenile hunters. He probably didn't mind the gold grain chit Hunter gave him either. He took his time showing

the 378s around his work area while his usual customers waited in the front room. "So there you have it. I
used to have to hammer every piece separate. Now,"
he boasted, "we can melt it, like as you see, and pour
it into molds. Not so long since we figured it out, but it
already makes a big difference."

"You didn't invent that, it's Church tech," Gem said.
"I've seen it in the prints."

"Be as it might," the smith said, his tone a bit less
friendly, "it's us that figured it and us that's using it
now, so seems just as like it's ours. Anyway, it meets
the need, and that's what matters."

Hunter watched closely while the juveniles debated
that. "It seems a fair assessment," Delen said. "We
sometimes come up with the same solutions indepen-
dently on an exercise, and everyone is credited."

Gem hesitated, then nodded, apparently accepting
the soundness of Delen's judgment. The man, humor
restored, showed them where he kept the fuel and how
he fed the forge. Gem, Hunter thought darkly, was
probably marking that among her resources. At last
the lesson ended, and the 378s gathered in the street
outside the shop. "A word," the smith said quietly from
the doorway. Hunter hung back to listen. "North is
quiet, everyone knows that, but sometimes we hear
talk. Nonsense, mostly, people being how they are,
but there's a bit of it I think the Church might want to
hear."

"Go on," she said.

He glanced back into the shop. "There's lots of cityens know how to pour metal now, and other things too. What I said to that young one—I don't want you thinking I've mistook my place. Everything we've got is given by the Saint, one way or the next. I know that. But I hear there's some in other claves as may be forgetting the Church's help in that and this. Saying we can find our way ourselves, the like."

"Do you know who these 'some' would be?"

His burly shoulders lifted in a shrug. "Benders, Wardmen, I don't know. Don't know for sure it's true, even. Just a thing I heard, that I thought the Church would want to know."

She would have questioned him further, but just then an irritated customer came out to find the cause of the delay. "I need to get that wheel fixed, Tren, I have a load to take to market day. Are you—oh, begging pardon, respected hunter, I didn't know you were still here. I can wait, Tren." He scuttled back inside.

"Best be going," the smith said. "Commend us to the Church."

"The Church is grateful," Hunter answered, dropping another chit into his palm.

The young hunters walked back towards the Church in silence, absorbing the day's lessons. The spire rose before them in the distance, and atop it the metal mast whose light-charging panels, flashing as they slowly rotated in the setting sun, drew the eye from every point in the city, and beyond. At the very apex of the mast a dish rotated ceaselessly, listening for signals from the desert arrays. Even at night, lit only by the power coursing through it, the cross glowed, pulsing almost imperceptibly in a slow, steady rhythm, like breathing, or a heartbeat. The Saint's, perhaps, for she regulated the flow of power to the spire as she did all the other functions of the Church. Hunters could see that light from a long way away, like a star set low against the dark shadow of the earth, unblinking and immovable. It had accompanied Hunter through many long night watches, a fixed point to settle on while the rest of the sky circled through the hours.

Fay said, "When they first dropped us in the desert I looked for it. That was how I knew which direction I should go."

"That was proper, Fay. A hunter can use any stationary mark to take a bearing, even without wayfinding equipment."

"Why—" The girl swallowed. "Why didn't Ela think of it?"

Because she was weak. But she hadn't been. She had simply made a mistake. A single misplaced foot. "I don't know, Fay. Perhaps she tried. Perhaps she made a series of small errors that compounded."

"Would the Saint know, if we could talk to her?" Delen asked.

"We can't." The words came out harsh. "Only the priests know the Saint's thoughts."

Gem looked at her. "You knew her before she was the Saint. The ascended one, I mean. I heard the Materna talking about you with the Patri."

Talking about me. Saints. She had to gather her wits

to make a sensible reply. "Hunters chanced to meet her from time to time. You were too young."

"What was it like to see her grow?" Ava's eyes were huge with curiosity. The 378s would not likely see another new Saint in their lifetime.

"Like seeing any of us grow, I suppose, only by herself, instead of in a batch." Lonely, she had thought the girl, surrounded by priests and older nuns all the time, but no one like her around her, ever. "She wasn't trained the way we were, of course. She wasn't ever going to have to live in the desert, or even in the city."

"Soft," Gem judged.

Hunter shook her head impatiently. "The Saint's brain needs many complex connections for the interface. The energy goes into that instead of physical development. And she must be exactly like the original." It was impossible to imagine the courage of that first woman, putting on the crown when no one could have known whether she would succeed or her mind would be burned to cinders, and all the hopes of the city with it. "If not the Church will reject her, as it does intruders who try the doors. She would die the instant she ascended the altar."

"Is that why she ran away? Because she was afraid she would die?"

"She was braver than you or I could ever be. And remember, Gem Hunter 378: it is blasphemy to doubt the Saint."

CHAPTER 6

When the power failed it had brought down more than just the homing beacon guiding Hunter and the fugitive Saint. Junctions had exploded in the surge, collapsing buildings, hard to know how many amidst the chaos. A crowd milled in aimless panic. Someone had gotten a light working, its faded beam sweeping in an unsteady arc. Others were climbing precariously through the unstable wreckage, desperately pulling at the debris. This was only a minor spasm compared with the calamity of the Fall, yet the damage shook Hunter deeply. She heard the cries and moans of those trapped beneath the wreckage. The crowd itself seemed shocked into an eerie silence.

The Saint looked on in horror, face twisted with the pain of the city tearing itself apart before her. Hunter grabbed the girl by the shoulder. "Come on, we've got to go."

"I can't!" The girl tugged away. "I have to help them."

"Help them by fulfilling your purpose."

But the girl tore away before Hunter could stop her, walking into the open. In the bluish sweep of the searchlight, her uncovered face and hands glowed green. Someone shouted, "It's the waiting Saint!" At first fractured among a hundred voices, the call coalesced into a reverent chant that raised the hairs on Hunter's neck. "Saint," the crowd called, and the Saint went towards them.

"Saint!" A single voice rose above the others, whose murmur abruptly dropped into expectant silence. A figure separated from the others. A man, carrying a small, still bundle. "Use your power! Heal my son."

The Saint's hand dipped slowly towards the broken child. The man drew back in fear, but a gentle murmur from the Saint and he steadied, holding his small burden out like a sacrificial offering. She laid a hand on the boy's still chest.

For a long moment they stood just like that. Hunter forgot to breathe.

Nothing happened.

The charge ran out of the air. The saint staggered back. The father hunched over his dead child, weeping.

The crowd howled its despair. Hunter turned and grabbed the Saint, and then they were running, fleeing the desperate mob through the failing city. After a while the cries and pleas behind them faded beneath the sound of their own harsh breathing. Around another corner, and Hunter ducked into a deep shadow, dragging the Saint after her. She could hear the distant noises of destruction, but no close pursuit. She eased cautiously back into the street, trying to catch her bearings after their headlong flight.

She whirled at the sound behind her, thinking they had

been caught, but it was only the Saint, fallen to her knees, weeping, nothing more now than a frightened girl with no-where to turn. The girl who had been supposed to save them.

She couldn't even save one child.

"It's not your fault," *Hunter told her wearily.* "There's nothing you can do. I'll take you somewhere safe."

The girl stood up then, her tear-stained face hard and angry. "Take me to the Church," *the Saint commanded.*

Hunter sat on a hard wooden bench, the silence echoing in her head. She had delivered the smith's information, such as it was, to the Patri, but it was the memories that troubled her. She strove to match her thoughts to the silence, empty, waiting. Even the occasional murmuring of the priests as they tended to the Saint barely rose past a whisper so as not to disturb the mind that spun all along the great net to the city, and upon which they all depended. The body itself withered, consumed by the strain despite the tubes that brought nourishment to it and carried waste away, the priests who hovered, studying panels and adjusting minute dials, tending her with the same dedication as their forebears had done for Saints every day since the Fall. This shriveled thing had been that girl who stepped bravely to her fate only a few annuals ago. Since her return from the desert, Hunter had come day by day to honor that sacrifice.

She knew she would never be worthy.

In an alcove off to one side, a priest sat at an ancient

box, its front covered with dials that were no longer lit from within. Wires snaked from the back of the box to the wall, where they ran like a vine up the tower, until they tied into the metal dish at the top of the spire. The dish sent out its signal faithfully as a beating heart, to the arrays Hunter tended in the desert and beyond, and it listened. It had been listening since the Fall. A priest sat always at the receiver, like the one Hunter watched today, praying for a sign that the city was not alone in the desolate world. He wore small speakers over his ears, but Hunter's sharp hearing picked up the static of the carrier, empty and gray as a winter sky.

After a time she rose to leave. The priest at the receiver ignored her, intent on his listening, but she knew that no voice spoke to him. If other cities still lived they did not call out.

Her hand was on the door latch when the priest cried out. She froze, transfixed, for the space of a quick-drawn breath before she saw that he was tearing the speakers off his ears in pain, not astonishment. The other priests jumped to help but she got there first, wincing as a high-pitched squeal screamed through the speakers. "Are you injured?" she shouted, trying hold his head still. He pushed her away, grimacing, at the same moment she smelled the first smoke.

She whirled in a full circle, scanning the sanctuary for fire, seeing none. Priests babbled at each other, in-audible over the obscene noise. The smell grew more intense. It was sharp and bitter, not like wood smoke. She clamped her hands over her ears as the speakers kept on shrieking, and finally saw it, a black tendril rising from the back of the dialed box, with a lick of orange at its center.

She leapt unthinking between it and the altar, as if her body could block the flames. Then she tore her shirt off, beating at the fire while the smoke steadily thickened. A priest, braver than the others or quicker witted, dove behind the box, tearing at wires until he had it disconnected from the other panels. Her ears rang as the speakers went dead all at once. She gestured violently and he rolled out of the way so she could kick the box on its side. It burst open, spilling charred wire intestines onto the floor. She beat at them until she was sure there was nothing left to spark anew.

The priests were already back at their panels, even the one with blood running down from both his ears. Fingers flew over dials and switches. Intent on their work, the priests ignored Hunter as she pulled her sooty shirt back on, watching the Saint fearfully. She had no way to know what harm might have been done.

The Patri burst in through the vestibule door, breathing hard, a sanctuary priest right behind him. The Patri ran to the largest panel, studying its lights and symbols, then began barking orders in a tight voice. Hunter heard the words *circuit, amperage, flux*, but the sense of what he said eluded her. It seemed to be working, though: his shoulders, rigid at first, began to relax as the blinking grew steadier, less frantic. Finally he sighed, satisfied with the patterns. Then he saw Hunter.

"What are you doing here?"

"Patri, the Saint. Is she—"

"Get out of here. *Get out!*" He strode towards her as if he would push her through the door.

She backed away. "But, Patri, is she—"

"The Saint is my concern, not yours. A wire failed. Tell *no one* you saw more than that. No one! Now *go!*"

She fled through the vestibule, down the steps into the gated yard. The lights must have flickered, or there'd been some other sign of trouble; a small crowd of nuns and hunters had gathered there. They seemed more curious than alarmed, though a murmur rose at the sight of her, disheveled as she was. Indine approached her, nose wrinkling at the clinging smoky smell. "Echo Hunter 367, what is amiss?"

Hunter rubbed a hand across her stinging eyes. "Bad circuit," she said.

She tried to see the Patri the next day, and the next, to make amends for whatever offense she had given. But each time she approached his chambers she was told he was unavailable, communing with the Saint and unlikely to emerge that day. Finally, with a sinking in her gut she decided that there was no choice but to wait for him to send for her. She could not risk angering him further with her impatience.

Tana had been in the city with a training cohort during the incident. The priests made barest mention of it in teachings, and the lights and all the other systems seemed to be functioning normally. The dish still circled steadily on the mast. But a bad circuit in the refectory was one thing. A failure in the sanctuary, where harm might come to the Saint . . . And the Patri's alarm had been so great. His demand for secrecy worried her, almost as much as his anger. She wished she could discuss it with Tana. That was impossible, given the Patri's prohibition. But on the fourth day after the fire, while Hunter helped her inspect the static wands that the juveniles had been learning to rewire, Tana said, "Indine told me she saw you coming from the sanctuary again."

The battery case in Hunter's hands came apart with a sharp *snap*. The weapons area was in the lower level, at the opposite end of the hall from the priests' laboratory. Despite the subterranean cool, the room felt airless. "Why did Indine feel it necessary to report to you on my activities?"

"She didn't, particularly. I asked her to report everything that took place while I was away. Don't look so surprised, Echo. I'm the oldest hunter in the compound. People tolerate my eccentricities, even that I've become curious as a new nun. Besides, you go to the sanctuary as often as a priest. Indine hardly needed to tell me that."

The trigger wire had come loose. It was a frequent finding in beginners' work, as the flexion when the case snapped closed stressed the connection. Hunter set the wand aside as an example. It wouldn't fire in this condition. If a life depended on it, someone would die. "Your information is old, Tana. I have not been to the sanctuary in days."

Tana inspected another wand. Her bony fingers were still deft as a priest's, though the thickened knuckles made her slower than she had been when she'd taught Hunter this skill all those annuals ago. Tana squinted at wiring, adjusted something, then said, "For a long time I went every day too. The priests got so used to me I could study the boards without their noticing. But I don't imagine that's why you go. Or why you've stopped."

Hunter searched for a permissible response. "Did Indine say anything else about the sanctuary? Or report any other—concerns?"

"A few. A 385 broke her arm attempting to scale the wall. She is expected to make a quick recovery. One of the gravid nuns has developed an insatiable taste for redberry. The priests have caught her three times in the garden. Fortunately, the crop is expected to be generous this year. I'm glad, because I like redberry. Do you have a pry bar there? This case is jammed." Hunter took the wand from her and twisted the sections apart. Tana grunted in disgust. "Thank you. As you can tell, Indine's reports are very thorough. She didn't say anything about the sanctuary other than that an unimportant piece of equipment failed and was easily replaced."

There was nothing unimportant about the listening devices. But even if the dial box couldn't be replaced,

Hunter could think of no reason for the Patri to withhold such information.

Tana frowned at a tangle of wiring. "Things fail more often these days than they used to, or at least I think so."

Hunter felt a prickle of alarm. "Surely the Patri would say if something were amiss."

"There are things even I do not ask the Patri, Echo."

"If you did . . . do you think he would tell you?"

"If it served." Tana huffed a breath out through her nose. "A hunter would say that that would be the only reason for her to know."

"What do you say, Tana?"

The old woman's face was as inscrutable as the Patri's. "I say you are still a hunter, Echo."

They returned the repaired static wands to the storage cabinet, next to the projtrodes. Those were all the weapons the Church had to protect the city, besides the hunters. It seemed a thin margin for survival.

Tana locked the workroom door behind them. "One other thing Indine told me," she said, glancing down the hall. "The priests finished with Ela. The recovery was adequate. There will be a few more batches of us to make." Her lips quirked in that peculiar, crooked fashion that was not quite a smile. "Another way I'm not of any use."

CHAPTER 7

Hunter cycled through a teaching round, working in a different area each day to refamiliarize herself with the way the various skills were taught. The irregular schedule disturbed her sleep, already troubled enough. The dreams would fade eventually, she hoped; meanwhile she lay in her cell in the domicile each night and counted breaths. That was what they taught the juveniles to do, when difficult parts of their training kept them up at night. It didn't work. Behind the numbing drone of numbers, her mind still churned. Tomorrow she would be in a classroom, leading the 388s through their first real day of training. There were fourteen of them, a good-sized batch.

She hoped none of them would have to be culled.

There had been fourteen 378s as well, Hunter recalled. Her thoughts turned darkly to Gem.

The girl performed flawlessly in every exercise. She

attended teaching and duties without fail, absorbing information, working efficiently with batchmates or other hunters. If she asked a question, it was a good one, and given an order, she complied quickly, without complaint. If there was any challenge in her demeanor, it was only that her excellence demanded the same of everyone around her. Only Hunter, when she met her eyes, saw the cold arrogance there, patient, measuring, waiting for Hunter to fail.

And not just Gem. Hunter knew the others watched her, as Criya had, and Indine. Oh, they still included her, still made room at the table or in their training exercises, but she felt the distance that had come between them, as if she had been marked somehow and they too waited to see what it meant.

She skipped the morning meal, leaving the refectory directly after teachings to walk the circumference of the compound. It was hot already, the height of summer approaching fast. In the desert, she would be considering the day's shelter, ensuring that she had sufficient water and shade to wait out the stifling noon. Sometimes as the slow hours passed she would indulge herself by picturing the daily routine of the Church, what she'd be doing if she were there. The best parts of those reveries involved her lessons with the Patri, the anchors that held her to a hunter's purpose.

She had been closer to him there than here.

After an hour she was back to the arc of wall winged from the cathedral. It was tall enough to shade the path; a few nuns and priests were strolling here, enjoying the relative cool. She left the path then, intending to cut through the gated yard to the domiciles, where the 388s awaited.

And there, as she came around the corner, stood the Patri. He was standing on the steps to the vestibule, speaking with the Materna, frowning over something she'd said. They noticed her only a fraction after she saw them.

The abrupt stilling of their faces made her stomach drop. Even so, she lengthened her stride, determined at least to try to speak with him. The Materna limped up to the vestibule, leaning heavily on the rail. But the Patri, standing on the step, waited, his face unreadable.

"Patri." Now that she stood before him, everything she had rehearsed dropped into the dust. "My service to the Church in all things."

"As it should be."

"Please, Patri, I must speak to you."

"I am here, Echo."

A pair of nuns waddled past, nattering about the heat. *Hurry*, she urged them, *before he changes his mind.* She burst out, "Patri, whatever happened in the sanctuary, if I was at fault in any way—"

"We agreed not to speak of that matter, Echo."

She stood mute, more baffled by his cool politeness than by his earlier anger. She couldn't let him go with only this. She asked stupidly, "Are you well, Patri?"

"Yes, Echo, thank you."

"And the Materna?"

"She is finding the heat more difficult to bear these days."

"I'm sorry," Hunter said.

He inclined his head. "It is the natural order of things." Then he said, "Is there something else you wished to speak of?"

Facing that placid stranger, she almost told him no. But then she asked: "Is all well with the Saint, Patri?"

She braced herself for anger or dismay. But she didn't see even the least change in his expression. He only said, "There is nothing you need concern yourself with. I must go, however. The priests are waiting for me. You have duties as well."

"Yes, Patri," An emptiness took root inside her chest. She said again, "My service to the Church in all things."

He looked at her. "Remember that obedience is the foundation of service, Echo."

After that her sleep was worse than before.

A few restless nights later, she was called to aid the infirmary priest with a gravid nun who had grown ill. "The child was malformed and died inside," the priest said. "There's contamination in her abdomen." He stabbed tubes into blood vessels while the woman lay staring at the ceiling, cheeks streaked with tears that seemed as much from grief as from the spasms that rocked her heavy body.

Hunter looked at her flushed, drawn face. Illness was less familiar to her than injury; hunters were almost always lost to violence.

Like Ela.

"Will she survive?"

"With the Saint's help," the priest said, deftly connecting the tubes to a complex pump of some kind, itself attached to wires that ran into the wall. "She's young and has more bearing years ahead; it's worth the effort to try. This will filter the blood until her own body can do it. The Saint manages the process." He adjusted a dial, pale eyes narrowed in concentration. "I need more blood to prime the pump. Let me see your arm."

Later, lightheaded and barely conscious, Hunter lay on the cot next to the nun, listening to the rhythm of the woman's breath slowing, smoothing into sleep while their blood flowed together through the machine. She imagined the particular fine thread of the Saint's enormous attention devoted to just this task, the preservation of one cityen's life, a tiny thing of no importance in itself, yet worth saving if it might yet be of service to the Church. So the Saint kept the balance, a constant calculation of resources, unending myriad judgments that had kept the city alive since the Fall.

Hunter could not go to the sanctuary, but she could, in the small hours of the morning, slip into the gated yard and watch.

She sat with her back against the fence, hands laced around a knee, as she had sat around a hundred campfires. Up so close, the glow of the spire washed half the familiar stars away. If she were in the desert, she would see a long tail spiraling off that constellation there, and the dim red eye that blinked over the horizon at this time of year just there, but from here even her sensitive vision could make out almost none of those familiar patterns. It was enough, even so, to bring those desert camps to her in detail, from the taste of the smoke in her throat, pungent and resiny, to the small hissing creaks the rocks made as they cooled in the night, to the way, trapped once by a pack of canids, she had lain with a pebble pressed painfully into her thigh for long hours when she dared not move.

She wondered if the Saint had a thread of thought for her.

After a while she let her forehead drop on her drawn-up knees and closed her eyes.

Her attention snapped back to the yard when the lights abruptly came on.

It wasn't unusual for young hunters to be out at this hour; they might have had an exercise or some practice they had come up with on their own, or maybe tonight they just couldn't sleep either and had decided to get an early start on their day. What *was* unusual was to see a motionless figure on the ground, another kneeling beside it, and two more girls standing very, very still above them. Hunter uncoiled to her feet and took a silent step towards them, then stopped, easing back into the shadows: Tana, emerging from her own night watch, had gotten there first. The old hunter squatted by the body on the ground, a hand on its neck for more than a minute, unspeaking. Then she rose, the lines of her body hard, angry. "What happened?" Her voice conveyed no emotion at all.

The kneeling girl stood slowly, wiping her palms against her thighs. "We were practicing choke-downs." That voice was cool, striving for nonchalance. Gem.

"Why did you disable the motion sensors?"

"To practice in the dark, Tana."

The old hunter blew out a breath. "Were you using safety precautions?"

"Of course. Standard tap-outs. She never gave one."

One of the other girls shifted slightly. Delen, it looked like. Tana turned to her. "Is that correct?"

"I—I thought I heard her tap out."

"And you?"

The third girl looked from Tana to Gem to the shape at her feet. "I thought so. I'm not sure."

Tana said to Gem, "Are you certain of your report?"

"If she tried to tap out I didn't realize," Gem said.

Tana nodded thoughtfully, arms crossed, a finger pressed to her lips. "Four hunters beyond their first decade, in a practice setting, a controlled situation. One is dead and three are uncertain what happened. That is not an adequate performance, not in the least. Obviously you need remedial training. We will begin now. You first." She crooked her finger at Gem, who didn't move.

"Respectfully, Tana, I disagree with your assessment. Our training has been adequate. We're uncertain because Fay failed to tap out correctly. It was her fault."

Fay. The girl who had cried for Ela. Hunter's fists clenched, nails digging into her palms. She forced them to open again.

Tana appeared unimpressed by Gem's explanation. "If that is the case, then others could also be confused. Therefore I want to be sure—absolutely sure—that each of you demonstrates adequate understanding of the proper tap-out technique. Step over here."

Gem wiped her palms again over her thighs, the first hint of nervousness she had betrayed, but still did not move. Tana merely asked, "Which choke were you practicing?" The girls shifted again, no one answering. "Which one?"

"The sentry hold, behind."

Tana raised an eyebrow. "A dangerous maneuver. Quite difficult to control, as we have discussed. That is why we don't practice it in class. But since you felt the need, I will demonstrate. Over here, Gem. Now."

Gem obeyed this time, turning to stand stolidly facing the other girls while Tana stepped behind her. Tana snaked one arm around Gem's neck, palm facing inward, the other pressing between the girl's shoulder blades. Gem came up on her toes but made no attempt to counter. Hunter could hear the air whistle in her throat. "This is the common sentry hold," Tana said in a calm classroom tone, "but as you see, it's inefficient. She still can breathe. This way is better." She turned her front hand so the palm pointed down and locked her other hand around it, pinching the girl's throat between the sharp bone of her forearm and her lanky bicep. It was only a second before Gem's hand slapped against her own thigh.

Tana kept squeezing. Gem slapped again, hard enough for Hunter to hear clearly across the yard. Tana ignored the tap-out, squeezing, until Gem began flailing, grabbing with both hands at the forearm barred across her throat, increasingly desperate until suddenly she gave a jerk and her body went abruptly limp. Tana let go and stepped back, letting the body fall unceremoniously to the ground beside the dead girl.

Tana turned to the others, unconcerned. "Tell me what you observed."

Delen said shakily, "She tapped out, but you didn't stop."

"Which arm did I use to apply the hold?"

The girl took a deep breath. "Right, Tana."

"Are you certain?"

"Yes."

"You saw her tap out?"

"Yes, Tana."

"Which hand did she use? You?"

The other girl swallowed. "Left hand. Palm against her left thigh, twice. The second was clearly audible."

Tana nodded. "That is correct. Did I release the hold immediately?" The girls exchanged a look. "You should not need to consult with each other. Did I release the hold immediately?"

"No," Delen said, and the other shook her head, *no*.

"Then you clearly observed me breaking a standard practice safety procedure, yet you said nothing?"

"That is correct, Tana."

"Is that what happened when Gem practiced the hold on your sixth?"

"I—" Delen straightened. "Yes, Tana. That is what happened."

"And you are both now certain?"

"Yes, Tana," they replied in unison.

"Then you've learned enough for now." Her booted toe probed Gem's body; it was met with a strangled moan. "Get her up. Apply the field-healing techniques you've been taught, assuming that you recall *those* adequately and do not need additional training. If she is not fully recuperated in an hour, take her to the priests. Be sure," she added acidly, "to describe clearly what happened to her."

"What about—" Delen barely glanced at the dead girl next to Gem, then looked away quickly.

"What about her?" Tana asked, very softly.

"We should call the priests, to harvest the ovaries," Delen said.

"Take her to them yourself," Tana said. She looked down a moment at the two bodies, one beginning to stir, the other eternally still. "What a waste."

Tana stalked away from the juveniles. Hunter rose, thinking to follow her to the domicile, but the other woman turned abruptly, striding towards the sanctuary. "Tana," Hunter called softly, not wanting to draw the 378s' attention. *"Tana!"* She was sure the old hunter could hear her. But Tana kept going, straight past Hunter, through the door and into the sanctuary, where Hunter dared not follow.

Tana didn't come for morning teachings. Hunter collected two bowls of grain from the refectory and took them to Tana's cell. The old woman lay on her bunk, hands behind her head, staring at the ceiling. Hunter offered her a bowl. Sighing, she swung her feet to the ground, taking the food without enthusiasm. "I saw what happened last night," Hunter said.

"I know. I saw you watching there by the gate. What were you doing up at that hour?"

"Your eyes are still sharp."

Tana made a disgusted little sound. The skin beneath her eyes was dark. "If Gem had remembered the counter for that choke-down, she could have executed it easily. I remember being young and strong like that. It was very long ago. I was surprised that she panicked."

"She thought you were going to kill her."

"That's exactly when she should *not* have panicked. I wouldn't have. Neither would you."

"No." Hunter forced down a bite of grain that tasted like dust. "We have to go to the Patri. She's already wasted Fay. She must be prevented from doing more damage."

"I've been to see the Patri," Tana said, staring at the pattern in her grains as if the Patri looked back from there.

Hunter caught at her spoon as it nearly slipped from her fingers. "What did he say?"

Tana's mouth quirked, in that way that was not at all hunter. "There is a plan, Saint knows."

"Is he going to put her down?"

"I don't know what he's going to do."

"But, Tana, she's so"—Hunter cast about for the word—"unsound. He must see that."

"I'm not sure I know what sound is anymore."

The food in Hunter's belly turned to ice. "What are you talking about?"

"Gem, Fay . . ." Tana ran a gnarled hand across her eyes. "Myself. These last few annuals, the changes . . . I don't know what to think. Sometimes I sit in the sanctuary like you, and ask the Saint. I think I've learned to read the patterns, Echo. But I don't like her answers."

This was too like the crumbling rock at the edge of the cliff. Hunter heard her own voice thin, tinny, protesting like a child. "It's blasphemy to question the Saint." But this was *Tana*. Hunter said, "Whatever you think, you've always been a good hunter. A good teacher. You still are, Tana."

"Sometimes the lessons seem awfully hard." Tana rose with a creaky effort, collecting her bowl and spoon. Then she smiled, a real smile, not the crooked grin. "I've always liked you, Echo, from that time you were a fierce little hunter tracking me through the city." She sighed, a long outgoing breath. "Maybe you're right. I hope so. We'll find out."

CHAPTER 8

The Patri sent for Hunter the same day.

It was long past the evening meal; though it was still just light, the yard was devoid of people. Hunter restrained herself from running, but her heart pounded as if she had been; she took an extra moment at the Patri's chamber door to settle her breathing. Then she went in.

He had been waiting for her; the print on his desk was closed, his hands, fingers interlaced, resting atop it. He studied her, expression neutral, for a long moment. Finally he said, "Sit down please, Echo."

She sat with both feet on the floor, hands in her lap. She forced herself not to clench them into fists. He had arrived at some decision, she saw it clearly in his face. She must make herself ready to receive it. She focused on the room, the stacks of prints, the paper-strewn desk. The window framed a view across the yard, small, but centered squarely on the sanctuary. She wondered for the first time whether every Patri had sat here, or this one had chosen it specifically.

"I erred," the Patri said, "in leaving you so long in the desert. I was busy with the new Saint, and your performance with the arrays was more than adequate, so I did not consider the disadvantages of such prolonged separation from the Church. The independent functioning of a hunter is an asset, but it must be balanced with obedience. It is only since you returned that I realized my mistake. I must confess, Echo, I have been surprised by what I see in you."

The walls pressed inward. She breathed slowly, deeply. *He is going to have me culled.*

He smiled faintly. "The Materna has reminded me, however, that all that time alone left you without proper guidance. Your deviations have been minor, considering. And as the Materna has also reminded me, an intelligent man does not waste a valuable resource from temper, or in haste. I have a new mission for you. I know your performance will ease my mind."

The shock was so great that she could not identify what she felt as relief. Numb, she asked in a voice that she struggled to control, "How may I serve, Patri?"

"I have begun to hear things about the city, rumors that disturb me. From the nuns, mostly."

"The nuns?" Her mind struggled with the change of focus. She forced herself to think. "Patri, I know we can never disregard information, but the nuns seem somewhat . . . less than reliable as observers."

"That's true, but they do talk." He smiled wryly. "Most of what they say is gossip, city nonsense. But there is a common thread running through it, more than usual. It seems to circle around a man, a cityen. The girls don't know this man, but they know *about* him. Not facts, but stories, which is even worse. Little pleasantries about things he's done. A kindness here or there, extra food to a family having a hard time, a few men to help in a garden if a cityen falls sick and can't, that sort of thing."

"I heard the nuns in the refectory speak of a man like that," Hunter recalled. "But how could one man, doing so little, disturb the Church?"

"He hasn't, yet. But he could someday. There is something on the boards I don't understand, a pattern the Saint is trying to show me. . . ." He pursed his lips in exasperation. "Her thoughts are not like ours. I read the boards, of course, but sometimes I despair of ever truly understanding. But I *can* foresee a time when cityens begin to turn to such a man as I've described, instead of to the Church. At first innocently enough, only for those little things, but gradually more and more. A clever man, a patient one, could cultivate loyalty among the cityens." His eyes narrowed, and his voice grew harder than Hunter had ever heard it. "The tithe is coming, and I'm concerned that it will provide a focus for the misguided."

"You think cityens will refuse to tithe?" She couldn't keep the consternation out of her voice. "Even they couldn't be so shortsighted."

"They are undisciplined by nature, Echo. I don't expect them to like or even understand all the things the Church must do. That is part of my burden, and I accept it willingly. But I fear that a time may be coming when they think they know better than we do. They talk of change, and I will *not* tolerate anything, anyone, that threatens the plan the forebears put in place, that saved us all. We've come too far, and it is all still too fragile. I won't let it go to waste. That is why these stories worry me."

This was a tactical problem, something Hunter could understand. "Do you want this man put down?" she asked.

The Patri's eyes opened a little wider, then he shook his head, amused despite himself. "Thank you, Echo, no. That might bring its own complications. I don't want to make a martyr of this Warder, as they call him. No, this is a time for subtlety. I need to know what's happening. How to control the situation, or even better, to arrange for this man to discredit himself. It may not be difficult, no matter how the cityens view him now. For all their intensity, men's passions are short-lived."

Hunter turned possibilities over in her mind. "It should be straightforward to find such a man and observe his behavior. His activities would only serve their strategic purpose if everyone knew about them."

Fingers steepled. "I agree. However, the hunters who routinely patrol haven't discovered anything. There may be nothing to find, but I'm concerned that their familiarity with the city may obscure their vision. You bring a different perspective."

Different brought a small shiver of unease. She thrust it away. She would perform adequately; he would be pleased. "When shall I begin, Patri?"

"Three days from now. The cityens have taken to marking the solstice with a fest. It will provide an opportunity to observe many of them at once, and a focal point, perhaps, for plans this Warder or another such might make. You will be a hunter sent by me to show the Church's support for the celebration."

Camouflage. Something else she understood. "I'll prepare at once." The sense of anticipation was familiar; the darker thing behind it, less so. She wondered if it was fear. Gem would mock her, if she knew.

Gem. In the stress and its relief, Hunter had forgotten. "Patri, I must report on another matter."

He had already reached for a print; now he returned his attention to her. "What is that?"

"Gem Hunter 378, Patri. Last night she killed another of her batch."

"I am aware of this, Echo. Tana and I discussed it."

"Yes, Patri, Tana told me. But as you directed me to watch the juveniles, I wanted to report it to you myself."

"Thank you, but I am not unduly concerned. It was a training accident; they happen."

"I don't believe this was an accident, Patri. There has been a pattern in her behavior. Surely you see."

He closed the print with a thump. "What I see, Echo, is your difficulty remembering your place."

The safe ground Hunter thought she had found vanished beneath her feet. Her heart raced anew while he stared narrow-eyed at the pattern she had shown him. Then he sighed, relenting. "I accept my fault in this, and my responsibility to correct it. I know you are willing; you only need a little help. And after all, I am fond of you, Echo; you showed your true nature in bringing back the Saint."

And she realized: *he doesn't know.*

He must never know.

He was smiling at her kindly now. "We will be as we were, Echo. Only trust me as I do you. That is all I ask."

Voiceless, she could only nod, forcing herself to sit still and bear that gaze that searched out her every flaw. At any moment, he would realize his mistake. But after a long time he nodded, seeming satisfied. "Attend to your preparations. You must be ready."

"My service in all things, Patri."

"As it has always been." The Patri reached for another print. When she was almost at the door, he said, "Echo. I'm sorry I spoke so harshly. I don't like to lose my hunters, you know this. But if the girl couldn't defend herself in a practice exercise—well, better to know now. This is not a time for weakness. Thank you, again, Echo. That is all."

CHAPTER 9

She began to shake as she crossed the yard. A normal reaction, she told herself. She had perceived danger; her body had responded accordingly. The fighting hormones, unused, needed to burn themselves off.

A group of hunters practiced in a corner. She walked the other way, where they could not observe her distress.

It was the greatest danger she had ever faced. If he had seen—but he had not. She drew a breath, willing herself to calm. He had given his instructions. Now she must simply focus on one task at a time, the small things that pieced together into larger wholes, until the mission was complete and she had regained his trust.

Perhaps, in doing so, she would regain her own.

The steeple glowed softly ahead. The girl had given her life for the Church; surely she would approve.

You must not think of her now. Only the Patri, and his will.

Hunter turned away from the sanctuary. Then, in the soft darkness between the failing of the sun and the automatic lighting of the lamps, instinct spun her back towards the practicing hunters before she even registered what had caught her eye.

The sounds arrived at the same time, the *zzzzzphttt* of a static wand discharging and the soft *huh* of the last breath leaving a body. Then someone screamed, a sound more shocking in the Churchyard than either of the first two.

She disarmed the girl holding the static wand without bothering to order her to drop it. The girl's wrist broke with a sharp crack but she made no sound other than a surprised grunt. Hunter did not have to see her face to know it was Gem. She hooked her foot around the girl's ankle and used the hand at her neck to slam her facedown into the dirt, then knelt with a knee in the small of her back while she reached over to check Tana's throat for the pulse she knew she would not find. After a moment she rose, hauling Gem up with a fist in her collar. She was dimly aware that there were others gathering around, but they were nothing to her. "Make your report, Gem Hunter 378," she hissed.

The girl gave a choking gasp, unable to drag air past Hunter's grip in her collar. Her face began to go dusky. "Nothing? What good is that?" Gem tried to say something, lips moving soundlessly. Hunter refused to read whatever the plea was, twisting the cloth in her hand tighter even as Gem's good arm beat frantically in a reflexive tap-out. At the last second Hunter gave a final shake, then let go, thrusting the girl away in disgust. Gem staggered, but did not fall. Ignoring her, Hunter bent to scoop up the static wand, checked that the pack had fully recharged, then set the safety mechanism back in place. She turned back towards Gem, who was still whooping for air. "Make your report."

Gem's hand clutched at her battered throat. "She—she was holding the weapon, discussing the safing device, when it discharged suddenly."

"Don't lie to me. Tana has been handling weapons far too long to make such a careless mistake."

"The wand must be faulty," Gem said hoarsely.

"Do *not* lie to me."

"I'm not. Ask them." Gem jerked her head at her stunned batchmates, the six who were left, who had been watching in a motionless semicircle all along.

"Well?"

The girls nodded, rendered speechless by the impossible sight of Tana on the ground. Hunter could not believe that they had willingly conspired with Gem to kill her; she must have coerced them somehow into verifying her story. Were they that afraid of her? And one of them had actually *screamed*. By the Saint, the whole batch was faulty.

"Return to the domiciles, all of you but Gem. Go *now*." Obeying without hesitation, the girls fled. Good. She returned her focus to the girl in front of her. "If you didn't kill her, then why was the wand in your hand?"

"She dropped it as she fell. I caught it. It was a reflex."

"Am I to believe you are that fast?"

The girl's voice came arrogantly calm. "Yes."

"Well, I don't. You'll have to prove it." Hunter reversed the weapon in her hand and tossed it to Gem.

She made no effort to catch it. The wand fell at her feet.

"Pick it up. I said, *pick it up.*"

Gem bent slowly, then rose with the wand steady in one hand, injured wrist cradled against her chest. Her face was dark with suspicion. Hunter said, "You were fast enough to kill an old woman. Now you have one chance to stop me. If you miss it will be your last lesson. Arm the wand."

Gem started to say something, then stopped, face settling into expressionlessness. Awkward with one hand, she finally disengaged the safing device and raised the wand.

Balanced on the balls of her feet, Hunter waited. Let her opponent get nervous. She was young and fast, strong enough to be dangerous, but not experienced. All Hunter had to do was distract her, trick her into discharging the wand before she had the one clean shot that would save her. In the recharge gap Hunter would find all the time she needed.

But Gem's eyes kept flicking past her, over Hunter's shoulder. Give the girl credit; despite her pain and shock she was still thinking. It was a good trick; Tana had probably taught it to them. Saints. *Tana.* That empty shell on the ground—Hunter's nails stabbed into her palms. She forced her fists to open, one finger at a time. Blood pulsed through them, heavy, aching.

Now Gem's eyes widened, as if she really saw something coming across the yard. She was good, very good. Hunter didn't take the bait, instead watching the girl's face with the intensity she shared with the other predators of the desert. Then Gem made her mistake, raising her wand hand in a quick motion as if to catch someone's attention. Before she could bring the weapon back to bear, Hunter was on her.

The girl was on her back with Hunter's fingers clamped around her throat in an instant. The wand flew somewhere into the dark; Hunter heard it hiss as it discharged harmlessly into the ground. She shifted her hand a little, fingers seeking the most effective grip to crush the girl's trachea, clean and simple. This time she wasn't letting go.

The lamps all around came on full with a blinding flash. "Echo Hunter 367, cease!" Hunter froze, an automatic response to the Patri's command. It was barely enough to save Gem's life. Breath rattled back into the girl's lungs with a painful wheeze. Hunter's fingers eased reluctantly, but her hand stayed at Gem's throat, ready. "Let her up."

Hunter twisted to look at the Patri over her shoulder as he hurried across the yard, 378s trailing behind. The little fools had gone to him, not to their quarters as she had ordered. They too needed a lesson. She would teach them later, when she had more time. "Echo," the Patri repeated firmly, "let her up."

Hunter rocked back on her heels. Water streamed

from her eyes as she squinted into the harsh light. "She killed Tana."

"I didn't," Gem croaked from where she lay. Wisely, she did not attempt to rise.

"Ava and Delen told me what happened," the Patri said. "Tana was holding the weapon when it discharged. It was a terrible accident."

"You can't believe that, Patri. There's no way Tana—"

"The weapon must have been faulty."

She heard her voice rising as she strained to make him listen. "Tana would have checked. It's standard procedure, she would have—"

The Patri interrupted gently. "I'm not blaming Tana, Echo. Of course it wasn't her fault. The weapon malfunctioned."

Her heart pounded. How could he not understand? Gem had hated Tana, that was so obvious; she had only waited for the right opportunity, finding it here tonight in the last training exercise the old woman would ever lead. . . . Hunter thrust to her feet, a last shove warning Gem to stay down. *Find it,* she ordered harshly. The other 378s scattered. In a moment Ava was back, carrying the wand gingerly, live end carefully averted. Hunter studied it without touching. In a moment she had found what she was looking for: the faintest scratching at the edge of the wiring panel, as if someone had used the point of a knife or some other sharp tool to pry the access open. In the twilight, with her aging eyes, Tana wouldn't have been able to see it. By the Saint, Gem was clever. Hunter pointed. "Look, Patri, right here. This weapon has been tampered with."

"It was an accident, Echo." The Patri's voice hardened into an unmistakable warning, but she overrode it as she would a malfunctioning alarm in the aircar, her mind parsing the data more accurately than any sensor relay.

"Patri, the marks on the panel are plain. Please, look for yourself." Around them a small crowd had begun to form, priests and nuns and no few hunters alerted by the commotion.

"Remove the power pack, Ava, and give me the wand." The girl obeyed the Patri instantly, slipping the solar cell from the firing mechanism with an expert twist and laying the two parts in his waiting palm. He studied the device, face unreadable, before he slipped the harmless pieces separately into the deep pockets of his robe. He stood for a moment, bent at the waist as if the slight weights dragged him down. Then he straightened, turning at last to address those who had gathered in a loose circle. "Someone please take Tana's body to be prepared for disposal. Gem, see the medical priest immediately. The rest of you may return to your duties; no other assistance is required. Thank you."

"Patri—"

"Silence, Echo Hunter 367."

Static hissed from some malfunctioning receiver nearby. Hunter stood paralyzed as if the stunwand had been turned on her. Gem got to her feet shakily,

broken wrist held tight against her chest. She looked
at Tana's body and bowed her head briefly. Then she
looked at Hunter. Something she seemed about to say
died on her lips at whatever she saw in Hunter's face.
She turned on her heel, pale face blank, and disappeared into the dark.

"It wasn't an accident," Hunter said, too softly for
even the nearby hunters to hear. "Please, Patri. You
must listen to me. First Fay, now Tana . . ." Her voice
trailed off. He had blamed them both.

"You are mistaken. Go to your cell, before a worse
thing happens."

"I must make you see—"

"Do not trade on my fondness for you, Echo." There
was no sign of that fondness in the Patri's eyes, only a
chill colder than a hunter's stare.

It seemed to freeze her heart. She took a step back
from him. "Tana talked about difficult lessons. . . . She
knew this was going to happen. *You* knew."

She could see his pupils dilate despite the spotlights'
glare. Could he feign such shock? Real or not, it was
followed quickly by anger. "Go to your cell. *Now*. Stay
there until I send for you."

Priests and nuns were staring. A defective circuit
between her brain and her feet left her rooted to the
spot, motionless as Tana. The old hunter's eyes stared
up at them, empty, indifferent. It didn't matter to
her why she had died. "Someone tampered with that
device," Hunter said, projecting her voice to be heard
across the yard.

Everything went so still that she could hear the words bounce uselessly off the cathedral wall. Then the crowed stirred, parting to let someone through. The Materna limped forward, leaning heavily on her cane. "We know you cared for Tana, Echo." She laid a gentle hand on Hunter's shoulder.

Hunter struck the Materna's hand off, drawing a murmur of consternation from those gathered and a quick step forward from the closest hunter. Brit, one of the few remaining 364s, a particularly stolid woman, but more than ready to protect the Materna. Fools; they thought *Hunter* was the danger here. Could they not see?

The Patri and Materna exchanged a glance.

And all at once she understood. They had maneuvered her into this position. All this time, letting her think she still served, while they conspired. . . . Gem had heard them talking about her, she had said so in the city. The girl must be in it with them. And their faces that day on the sanctuary steps—the Patri knew. He had always known.

He had only needed an excuse.

Hunter looked into the Materna's kind brown eyes. "You are trying to make me look unsound."

"You are not thinking clearly." The Patri forced a reasonable tone between lips drawn thin with anger. "I will look into this incident. You need not concern yourself."

"Not concern myself?" Hunter's voice spiraled upwards. "Tana was *murdered*." The word caught in her throat. Her lips against dusty hair. A neck snapping, quick as a last breath. "The line is failing," she whispered, so none but he could hear. "The whole Church is in danger—"

"*Be silent*," the Patri hissed. "Before your words become the danger."

And in that instant, she saw the entire edifice of the Church, the foundation of the world, crumbling to nothing as if it had no more substance than a handful of sand slipping through nerveless fingers.

"No!" she cried. "How does it serve to be silent? Tana is dead. Who is next, Patri? The line is failing. The *Church* is in danger. From *us*. From *you*. What must happen to make you see? The fire—" She drew a strangled breath. "The Saint herself is in danger, yet you will not admit the truth!"

In her peripheral vision she saw the startled faces of the hunters and priests who had gathered, their eyes widening in shock, their lips moving although some barrier prevented the sound from reaching her ears. She could only hear her own words, crashing in waves against the inside of her skull with a violence that rocked her on her feet. Balance failed as the ground gave way beneath her. She reached out for a support that wasn't there, slipped to one knee.

The Patri stared down at her, pale features glowing bone white under the hot lights. His eyes were lost in pits of shadow. "Echo Hunter 367." The Patri's voice thundered across the Churchyard. She knew what he was going to say before the words split the air. Pain ripped through her chest as if someone had turned the stunner on her. "Prepare yourself. Contemplate the Saint, and your own failures. As of the dawn of the new day, for the unforgiveable crime of blasphemy against the Church, you are excommunicated from the sanctuary of this body."

He turned on his heel and strode away. The lights dimmed behind him, or maybe something had gone wrong with her eyes. It did not matter. Nothing mattered; nothing ever would again. When the hunters stepped forward to haul her off into the darkness, she did not even resist.

The Patri granted her grace to gather a few supplies before the hunters led her through the sanctuary to the outer doors. The whole Church seemed to follow behind her on that last walk, the hunters and priests and nuns gathered in a cold, silent mass that absorbed all the light, all the air from the sanctuary. Her head swam dizzily, and objects swam in and out of focus until she stumbled as she walked. Brit seized her by the arm to hold her upright, normally bland features a mask of contempt.

They let her pause one last time before the Saint. The silent, wizened body, tireless in its sacrifice, rebuked her for her weakness. When the massive doors slammed shut behind her, cutting her off from the Church with a boom that echoed down the dusty stone road, the relief was almost as great as the pain.

Almost.

She stood for a long time alone, a hundred paces off the road, staring back at the steeple as it began to shine in the first rays of the sun. She didn't look away, even when the glare burned her eyes, until finally she could see nothing but a light so bright it turned to blackness in her brain.

Then she dragged herself to the forcewall, and out, into the desert.

CHAPTER 10

Hunter paused only briefly, pretending to wipe sweat
from her eyes. Whoever was watching had been there
for quite some time but offered no threat; let him think
she didn't see him. It wasn't the first time either: for
days now she had been aware that she was being observed.

She looked around at her handiwork. The watcher
must be very patient or very bored, or both. In two
weeks she had done nothing more than secure her shelter, using materials scavenged from the ruins to rein-
force the walls and roof of a hollow space created by a
stone-white tumble of debris. She had chosen to camp
a little way past the northern limit of the forcewall, a
half-day walk from the city proper, though no cityen
with sense would want to come here. The proximity
offered some protection from the larger predators that
lived farther out, and a trickle of water ran through the

remnants of an underground conduit she could reach by climbing through a hole and down a twisted metal ladder that she guessed predated the Fall. She wasn't the first to have found this spot. The remains of other shelters, and some of those who had been sheltered, were scattered here and there among the ruins.

She lifted another stone, judging its size and shape carefully as she brushed sand and grit from its pocked surface. By now she had a space, not much more than a burrow in the rocks, to sleep under cover from sun and protected from any predator bold enough to hunt this close, and a smaller vestibule where she could light a fire if she wished without filling her shelter with smoke. She had been careful to clear the area around of any flammable materials; the ruins were marked everywhere by fire, and she had no wish to die that way. She had not troubled to store edible plant material as she would in the desert proper, for scrubby vegetation, roots reaching deep for the buried water, had established itself here and there among the crumbled rock. Instead she methodically gathered and stacked ancient bricks, bits of pipe, even twisted metal bars and other parts that had once been structural. The desert was filled with such riches. Her predecessors had not managed to strip everything of value even in four hundred annuals, and there would still be resources for the clever four hundred annuals from now, if they could manage to make it that far. She could not envision what the city must have been like at its height, when these vast wastes had been densely inhabited, the great empty spaces filled with buildings, people, life. What the Church guarded now was nothing but a fragmentary remnant.

She could survive indefinitely in the desert with much less effort than this; it seemed foolish to invest so much energy in a structure she had no intention of inhabiting. Yet she kept working ceaselessly. If she paused, if she let her guard down for so much as one moment, she was there again: standing in the Churchyard that night, in that moment when words against the Patri burst their way through her lips, when she had actually accused him before the body of the Church, had named him capable of—of what?

It wasn't only what she had said that tormented her now, though the words had been deserving of his wrath. She had spoken recklessly, in anger and dismay, but words alone were insubstantial. They could be reexamined later, if later came. Far worse was what she had felt, in that awful moment.

He had done nothing but pocket the stunner. Yet she had accused him, as if he had triggered it himself. Tana was dead; a weapon's case was scratched. She had no other facts, no evidence of wrongdoing. Yet something had happened in her brain, some defect uncovered by the shock, perhaps, and in that moment she had *doubted*—not only the Patri, who after all was just a man, but *everything*. She would not have thought that a hunter could even be capable of such a transgression. She could scarcely believe it of herself. She tried not to think about the Saint at all; even in memory, the girl and what she had become deserved better than to be sullied by the touch of Hunter's thoughts.

Sometimes in the night when she had just managed to fall into a restless sleep, she awoke with a start, imagining it all the nightmare of some toxin, some incapacitating wound, until her outflung hand struck rock, and she remembered where she was, and why. Then she knew, deeply and beyond any doubt, that she had earned this exile. She did not know whether it was mercy or the worst punishment of all that the Patri had not simply had her put down, culling her as she deserved. Either way she determined to do her penance, as long as she was able, and when she finished she would walk farther out into the desert and find an end.

Yet sometimes she doubted whether she could hold even to that simple plan. She found herself, in her weakest moments, making contemptible excuses for herself. Could the Patri, she wondered then, have planned this all? In one way it could serve his purpose: an exiled hunter, one publicly humiliated, might seek shelter among the cityens, make common cause with the disaffected. Might find her way, eventually, to the very man the Patri sought: the Warder. *Be ready*, the Patri had told her; had he meant for this?

No, surely not; it was impossible. For then his plan would have had to include Tana's death—her murder. And he would have had to count on Hunter's reaction, expected her to go against all her training, the very purpose for which she was made, and do what no one could have guessed she would—he would have had to

know, to *use*, how very unsound she was, how fatally
deep her doubts—

No.

These were only her excuses. She only wanted it
to be the Patri's plan so she did not have to face the
enormity of her failure. She kept recalling her meeting with him, the way he had offered her forgiveness.
The way he had trusted her. She had proven that she
was unworthy, that was certain. Maybe it was his own
weakness. *I am fond of you,* he had said. There might
be hope there: if she could somehow do his bidding,
regain his trust, one day—

She buried the thought away where she could not
betray it too, then emptied her mind and set the next
stone in place.

Some hours later she sat in the cool shadows of the
vestibule, carefully stripping meat from the bones of
three of the tiny animals that scurried among the rocks
throughout the ruins. Hunting here was easier than in
the remoter desert. The canids rarely came close to the
forcewall, and the small game was less wary, though
soon the ones nearby would learn that her approach
meant danger, and then she would have to venture farther for her meals. Or into the city.

But not yet. She gathered the bones in her hand,
and, after deciding that she did not need to extract the
meager marrow for a soup, walked a little way away
from her shelter to bury them.

A shadow followed her, making tiny scuffing
noises. Bare feet, she judged, and small. She bent to

move a rock, making a show of setting down her pack, that her observer would know still contained meat, then shifted far enough away that he or she might underestimate her range. When the shadow moved, she was ready, striking with hunter speed to grab the wrist attached to the hand that closed around her bag.

A male child, hardly bigger than a toddler, dangled in her grip, face screwed up in pain. The arm she held was alarmingly thin, the bones her fist enclosed scarcely more substantial than those she had just buried. She set him down on his feet with a hard thump, not letting go, though her grip eased. "You need to be more careful when you scavenge from predators larger than you."

"Are you gonna kill me?" He spoke with the slurred drawl of the cityens, so familiar from the tithed girls who only gradually acquired the precisely measured syllables of the Church over their years as nuns.

"I will if you try to steal my food again." She let him ponder that for a minute, then released his wrist. He stood rubbing it silently, still eyeing her bag with cold calculation. She revised her estimate of his age upward to eight or nine annuals. She wondered with mild interest what he was doing out here, and how long ago he had come. It must have been some time: he was filthy, with long matted hair that had been hacked short enough in front to stay mostly out of his eyes. The shirt that hung around him had enough intact seams, barely, to keep it from falling off. Either he wasn't its original owner or he had once been much heavier. She doubted the latter. Bones stuck out of him everywhere, not the sinewy lean build that a hunter girl his age would have, but the desperate thinness of starvation. "As it happens, I have extra. Here." She tossed him the last two little animals from her bag. Beneath the faint squeak of her shoes on dust as she walked away, she heard him scrabbling in the dirt.

She almost turned back, to warn him that he should take shelter before some larger scavenger came to steal his meal in turn. Then she stopped herself. He was not a hunter child having a lesson. However he had gotten here, he had survived until now. How long that lasted was not her concern.

Close to morning she became aware of sounds around her in the ruins that she had not heard before. She was not without defenses: the static wand was one of the things her hands, still competent even with her mind whirling in turmoil, had thrust into her pack that night. She had checked it carefully, as soon as she was alone, for signs of sabotage; there were none. Now, lying in the shelter, she refrained from reaching to assure herself that it was nearby; she had laid it close to hand before settling to sleep, and she knew it was still there. The faint urge troubled her, nonetheless.

With the languid movements of a sleeper, she rolled onto one side, looking through barely slitted eyes towards the opening of her vestibule. The watchers were unlikely to notice the way the apparently haphazard post propping the roof could be pulled out in a second, trapping any invader under a fall of stone and brick while she escaped through a bolt-hole from the shelter.

She heard the noise again, saw transient darkness as someone passed the crack in the curtain. Someone small, followed by another, and another. Just children, but enough of them could be a threat. She feigned sleep for a long time, waiting to see what they would do. Nothing happened. A small breeze kicked up as the dawn drew near. It brought her the scents of the desert—silica, dust, a hint of vegetation. Nothing of predators tonight. Closer, the mild but distinct taint of prepubertal humans, unwashed. She frowned in the dark. Hunters that age would already know to stay downwind if they wished to remain undetected. One of her watchers carried with him the smell of her last meal. Maybe he and his friends hoped to steal whatever else she might have to eat. If so, they were surprisingly patient. Maybe they were smarter than that. Either way, she could likely handle untrained children. She rolled onto her back, settling in for a wakeful night.

But just in case, she pulled the static wand closer.

When she rose at sunrise, her watchers had disappeared. Probably, like the little animals she ate, they found refuge in the cracks and crevices and caved-in structures that spread for miles out from the force-wall. She studied the scuff marks outside the vestibule. Three or four of them, none bigger than the boy she had captured yesterday, one considerably smaller. Still big enough, perhaps, if it had a blade, or a large rock, and she grew careless.

She checked the traps she had set the night before, carefully disguised so that other animals would not steal her prey. Normally she would skin and clean what she caught far from her camp, scattering the offal in a way that would not draw scavengers. Today she brought everything back, settling on her heels outside the shelter, making certain that what she was doing would be easily visible to anyone peeking out from nearby gaps in the rock. "I seem to have extra again today," she said aloud. "I would welcome company." There was no answer. She shrugged, cooked all the meat over a tiny fire she lit with the static wand, and ate a small portion with more gusto than she felt. The rest she left cooling while she went off noisily to collect more water. When she came back, it was gone.

She followed that routine for three more days. On the fourth morning, instead of leaving the camp, she settled back on her heels out of arms' reach of the food, but in plain sight. She heard little rustling noises, small bodies rocking back and forth in indecision. Finally a stone chinked nearby as someone, hunger winning over fear, crept out of his hiding place. The same small male child she had first seen. He looked from her to the food and back, plainly judging whether he could dash off with it before she could grab him. "If I wanted to catch you I would have already."

He frowned, cracking dirt in unaccustomed lines. She lay back on her elbows, a position that looked relaxed, though she could rise from it fast enough if she chose. "Go ahead, I've been leaving it out for you and your friends."

At *friends*, his eyes darted telltale to a crevice that must widen out into a hiding place big enough for all of them. She carefully did not follow his gaze. "You can take it. I won't chase you."

Finally hunger prevailed. He darted forward, scooped the treasure into a bag he had slung over his shoulder, and went running off without a word. She smiled to herself; he had the good sense to head away from his hidey-hole. She went inside her shelter. A few minutes later she heard the barest of scuffling as he slipped into the opening in the rocks she had marked.

The next day she waited again. When he appeared she said, "You don't have to run away."

Immediately the scowl, a show of anger to hide fear, common tactic for a small creature that could not afford to look weak. "What d'you want?"

"Nothing."

"Ever'one wants something."

She shrugged. "I don't." Which wasn't true, Saint knew. But what she wanted she was not ready to name, even to herself.

He squatted nearer than he should, still underestimating her. Not his fault; wary as he was, it was cityens he had experience with. She admired his discipline; he couldn't keep his eyes off the meat, but he made no move towards it. "You can have it."

He looked at her with frank disbelief. His eyes were

muddy brown, the color human irises tended towards when nothing special was selected, and it looked like his hair would be brown too if it were ever clean. His skin was tan and already weathered beneath the filth. "How long have you been living outside the wall?" she asked.

"Long time." He shrugged. "Me and—" That was almost a slip, admitting that he had companions. He covered it quickly. "Me and myself."

"Well, you and yourself look hungry. Take the food, there's plenty."

He reached out, finally, and put the pieces in the bag. All of them. "Don't you want to eat any now?"

He licked his lips, then swallowed. Another tiny glance towards his hidey. "Not hungry now." Going to share it fairly with the others, then. That was impressive; they wouldn't have been able to blame him if he said he had to eat some so she wouldn't get suspicious.

She nodded, and he stood, settling the bag on his hip. The slight burden seemed to weigh on him more than the mass of the food accounted for, the drag of responsibility. He seemed awfully young for it. "I'll have more tomorrow."

Again the look of puzzlement. He seemed for a moment about to ask her something, then thought better of it. He still had the presence of mind to take a different route away.

She had been awakened by a nightmare long before she opened her eyes. When she finally did the three small forms gathered round jumped back as if she had shouted. "S'all right," the boy said, boldly settling back in his place. "She won't hurt us."

"You crazy," a smaller voice said fiercely, but they did not run.

"He's right," Hunter said mildly. She sat up, very slowly, locking her hands around her knees where they could see them. There was her boy, a female who was even smaller than he was, though she might have the same annuals, and a tiny figure of indeterminate gender, barely old enough to walk, sucking noisily on its fingers. They rearranged themselves around her, small dangerous animals shifting into position. Hunter looked at the boy. "This is who you've been taking the food to?"

"Uh-huh."

"You've done well to provide for them."

He scowled and kicked at the dust. "There was more babies in the spring, but they wouldn't eat the meat."

"Didn't have no teeth," the fierce girl said, scowling as if it had been a character defect. "Never do."

"Are there many babies out here?" The edge in Hunter's voice surprised her; it made the children pull back warily, poised to run if she did anything unpredictable.

The boy looked around as if checking whether any infants had suddenly appeared. Then he shrugged. "In the winter, mostly. When'ts cold they was all stiff when we found 'em."

"Dead," the girl pronounced with satisfaction.

Sometimes in the desert we find dead ones. That was what she had told Tana, long ago. She felt her hands clench across her knees and made a physical effort to relax them. It was a chance to gain information closer to its source. "Where do they come from?"

The boy's face screwed up in puzzlement. "Mating, I guess."

She wiped a palm across her eyes. "Yes. I meant, how do they get outside the wall? How did you?"

He shrugged. "Once day our matr' didn't wake up. Then our patr'. After a while there was nothing to eat."

The girl was his sister, then. Maybe the smaller one as well. "Didn't you have anyone to take you in?" A clever child like this, he could work, that was clear. Some cityen should have found him useful enough to keep. And the girl would have been worth it too.

He bit his lip. "Din't like them. S'better out here." His glance at the girl told Hunter more than enough about why.

"They leaves the babies," the girl put in fiercely. "Heard 'em talk. Can't feed 'em no more, that's what they say. Leave 'em to the Saint to feed. But I don't see how's they can eat much anyway, when they got no teeth."

Hunter thrust to her feet, scattering the children like the tiny animals she preyed on. Winter was a bad time to bear young; even the cityens knew that. Everything was scarce then. The arid ground froze hard, and what couldn't hunt and hadn't set aside a store had scanty chance to see the thaw. But once they made the young, even if they did it at the worst possible time, to leave them out to die—the waste was unacceptable.

She turned to the frightened children. "If you come back tomorrow, I'll have more meat. Enough for all of you."

The next day they were there again, squatting in a half circle around her when she awoke, dirty faces serious and unblinking as hunters. This time they didn't jump back so far when she sat up. She smiled to herself. Hours later, when she returned, they were still waiting. She cooked it for them, and they ate like the canids, tearing into the meat while it was still too hot to hold, tossing the pieces from hand to hand until they cooled and gnawing down to the bones. The girl sucked the marrow noisily from a long thin bone then held it up critically to the light to be sure she hadn't left anything. Then she tucked the sharp bit away somewhere in her rags, in case she needed an awl, perhaps, or a dagger. The other two were no less thorough; there would hardly be anything left to bury by the time they were done eating. Seeing the way they picked over the bits, Hunter tossed them the rest of her share too. The boy hesitated, a faint quizzical look on his face, but at Hunter's encouraging nod he set into it as if he hadn't eaten anything before. Even after so few meals, they all seemed the slightest bit less gaunt now, though perhaps that was her imagination.

The next evening as she got her gear together she said as casually as she could, "Hunting's good right now. I can show you, if you want to come."

The boy and girl looked at each other, while the toddler made sucking noises on its hand, then back to her. Suspicion darkened the little faces. "What d'you want?" the boy asked, as he had the first time she captured him.

"Nothing. I told you before."

"People says things th' don't mean."

"I don't."

He shrugged with weary disdain. "Why's you any different?"

Because I'm made to be, she almost answered, the calm certainty as much a part of her as blood and bone and sinew, before she remembered who she was and why she was here, and that nothing was certain anymore. Instead she said, "I mean this: I don't need anything from you. The hunting is good. I can show you. Teach you to hunt for yourself." She threw her pack over her shoulder abruptly. "Come or not. It doesn't matter to me."

She took a random heading out, all her attention directed back. There was a brief whispered argument, then silence; they were not coming. The sharp twist of disappointment caught her by surprise. Then she heard tiny sighs, and the scuff of feet—a hesitant, worried sound, but they followed nonetheless.

They turned out to be quick students, not surprisingly; after all, they had survived this long. There were limits to what she could teach them; they simply didn't have a hunter's enhanced senses to track prey or follow the scent of moisture. But their eyes were sharp, even if they couldn't see in the dark; she could teach them the telltales of animals following the same path to water night after night, and how to lie still and wait, and how to fashion a few strips of cloth from the rags that barely covered them anyway into deadly nooses. The girl had a particular aptitude for the stealthy wait followed by the quick snatch and shake that severed vertebrae. Even the toddler seemed to understand the importance of keeping still and quiet during the hunt, and made sure to suck his fingers silently, as if he knew already that liabilities got left behind. They studied the marks her boots made, and each other's bare footprints, and learned to tell them apart, and how to hide themselves invisibly among the rocks. The only thing they would not learn was to scavenge along the edge of the forcewall for the bodies of small creatures that had not learned to avoid the charge. They simply refused to go so close to the city, no matter what resources they might find there. Otherwise, considering what they were, she could not criticize their progress.

Days passed, turning into tens. One evening as they prepared to go out she said, "I'll stay here. You check the traps."

Instantly those suspicious looks again, that she hadn't seen in recent days. "We can't go alone in the dark," the boy objected. "S'dangerous."

"You know what to do. The past few nights I haven't done a thing except watch."

"You was there."

"I won't be here forever."

Even as she said it she was sorry. Not for the words, which were most likely true, but that she had taught them to depend on her, even for this short time; to trust her. The glances they exchanged, weary and unsurprised, told her they had known all along that she would abandon them, and been foolish to hope otherwise. The boy's face twisted up into a little scarlet ball, though he made no sound. The toddler, hand crushed in the girl's suddenly too-tight grip, uncharacteristically spat out his fingers and began to wail before the girl cuffed him into silence with an accusing glare at Hunter. "I don't need to eat tonight," Hunter said harshly. "If you want something, go get it."

They went without her, in the end, desolate. She stared all night at the roof of her shelter, unable to rest. She shouldn't have sent them. The boy was right; it was dangerous. They had been doing well enough before she got there, staying to their hideys and taking only what came to them, sufficient to survive, marginal as it was. Now she had taught them to ignore those traits that had kept them safe, encouraged them to try to become something they were not. They would fail, and it would be her fault. Her ears kept straining for the smallest sound to tell her they were coming back. None came. Towards dawn she sat up irritably, drawing on her boots, preparing for a rescue mission, or worse.

The laughter came ahead of them. The boy tossed the bag proudly on the ground at her feet. It made a heavy thumping sound. She let go a huge exhalation, then nodded. "Good. Now I'll teach you how to dry the extra, so you have something saved for when times are bad."

They spoke no more of her leaving, though the fact of it sat in their shelter like the fallen stone Hunter fingered in an idle moment. On close inspection she could see that it wasn't a natural rock; in fact, it wasn't stone at all, but some kind of heavy cast resin, too irregular to have been structural, unbroken and shiny as new beneath the thick layer of dust. It was pretty enough, though what its use had been she couldn't imagine; its purpose had died along with the men who had made this dead place live before the Fall. The ruins were full of such artifacts.

She kept on teaching the children, stubbornly rejecting any consideration of how it was justified, that effort spent on three abandoned juveniles of no particular value to the Church. She told herself that it was sufficient for now to protect them, give them what chance of survival, however vanishingly small, she could. And it helped keep her mind from the stray images that tried, stubbornly as a stalking predator, to hunt her down in those careless moments when her attention wandered.

Ela, broken at the bottom of the cliff. Tana, face up in the dirt. She had not protected *them*.

The delay, she told herself, was for a purpose. An excommunicated hunter would not immediately seek shelter in the city. No one would believe that. Much more in character that she should linger in the desert, pitifully trying to find meaning in teaching cityen children as if they were young hunters being prepared to take their place in the Church. As if she struggled to find her own place in a world that had changed and left her behind. Yes, this was the behavior anyone would expect of her in this situation. That was always the best disguise. Only with cover well established could she make her way into the city, find the man, the Warder, who so troubled the Patri, and eliminate the threat. Then the Patri would welcome her back, praising her for a mission so well performed, for understanding what had been his plan all along, and being true.

It could be so.

She told herself, in the nights when she attributed her sleeplessness to the need to guard the young, that she would make it so.

Meanwhile she could not manufacture an excuse to leave her exile and go inside. The devastated hunter of her story would not seek the company of cityens. A different opportunity would have to present itself, one arising on its own. If it took a very long time, that was not her fault.

And when it finally did, she refused to name the sinking in her gut as anything close to regret.

"Som'un brought another baby," the fierce girl said between bites, picking a stringy bit of tendon out of her teeth. The hunting had been good.

"Where?" Hunter tried to keep the sharpness out of her voice. It was not the girl's fault.

"By th' rockslide." That was what the children called the tumbled-down pile that had once been a span of the ancient road, just outside the forcewall. "Saw 'em lurking at the edge when we was out. Waiting for dark. They don't like no one to see."

Hunter stared up into the deep violet of the sky. If the girl had waited a few more minutes to speak, it would have been too late. In the dark the canids would already have gotten to the defenseless infant, making short work of it as they hissed and snapped and fought each other over the rare bounty of such high-yield prey. She would have shaken her head at how near the chance to move forward had come, and been disappointed to miss it.

She would have stayed.

But the girl hadn't waited, and Hunter would do none of those things. "You stay here," she ordered no one in particular. She changed out of her hunter shirt and trousers into the scavenged city garb that had waited at the bottom of her pack for this moment, then gathered her few belongings quickly, the static wand, the sun charger. The hunter clothes she left rolled in a corner of the shelter; the children might be able to use them, and she couldn't risk having them found on her in the city. She hesitated over the weapons, then handed her knife to the boy. The composite blade was still as sharp as the day it had been cast. Of all her belongings it was the most valuable out here. "Keep this for me."

He looked from it to her, not taking it. "You going after th' baby?"

"Yes."

"Coming back any time soon?"

A deep breath that hurt. "I don't know." He deserved better. They all did. "Probably not."

He nodded, looking away, and took the knife, tucking it carefully inside his rags. "'Kay."

The words flew out of her mouth before she could stop them. "You could come." She was appalled by her weakness. The city had already rejected them once; she wouldn't be able to protect them if they followed. She had no right to interfere. But: "Come with me," she urged, against all common sense.

"Not goin' back there," the girl spat. She threw down the last bit of her meat and stomped into the shelter, dragging the toddler after her. The boy stayed where he was, rocking a little, arms around his knees. He didn't follow when Hunter turned away at last.

She didn't look back, walking away casually the way she would on any brief excursion, ignoring the thing inside her throat that was trying to strangle her breath as mercilessly as she had tried to strangle Gem that awful night. At first she headed into the desert, not towards the rockslide where the baby would be left. No sense drawing attention to her departure; the children might be protected for a while yet by the predators' wariness of her, though that would wear off eventually as the impression of her presence faded from the place. The desert had a short memory for the unimportant. The children would be gone one day too, either grown enough to move on, or more likely, taken by a canid or an illness or a fall over the edge of a cliff. . . . At least, being gone herself, she wouldn't have to know.

Enough. She wrestled her thoughts around to her current task. A few hundred paces into the desert and she ducked behind a pile of debris, waiting. She had been half hoping the children would follow her, but there was no sound of pursuit; even the small animals, sensing a hunter in their midst, had frozen in their hiding places among the ruins. Still, she waited a long time. When she was finally convinced that she was really alone, she slipped out from her hiding place and doubled back towards the city. This time she used every hunter skill to hide her progress. Just before full dark, she settled into a lookout by the rockslide.

She was lucky, today; the breeze blew away from the city. Most of time the forcewall kept the city inside as much as it kept the desert outside. Today the wind must have been skipping up and over the wall, for she could smell and hear the foreign world inside. There were the plain animal scents of people, of course, especially the ones who didn't wash often. Other odors were distinctly human-made: cooking fires, smoke, the sharper smell of metal, machine oil. Above the hum of the forcewall, which cityens could not hear, she caught sounds alien to the desert quiet: wheels rumbling along stone, the occasional slam of a door, voices, all far away.

Longing for the Church exploded in her chest with a physical pain that she had not experienced in weeks. If she were there now, she would be sitting down to the evening meal in the refectory, watching the weanlings fuss, listening to the juveniles describe their day to each other, what skills they had learned; or maybe she'd be walking, half annoyed and half amused, with the Materna as the old woman took her arm and said—

Enough. Hunter concentrated on breathing, in, out, in, out, in, until her thoughts were quiet and her senses were available to scan the area. If the fierce girl were right, and if Hunter's need for subterfuge hadn't delayed her too long, she should find some sign soon. She sniffed the breeze; nothing. She should be able to hear something, but maybe the city noise was obscuring it. She half turned her head, one ear tuning back into the desert frequencies. Still nothing. She refused to hope that the girl had been wrong, or that the baby was already dead.

In a moment when the breeze stilled between inhale and exhale, she heard it, a thin, dry wail. That was all she needed. Two minutes later she had the baby in her arms. It was a boy, fat and dirty, and too hungry and exhausted to do more than squeak a faint protest as she lifted it from the cradle of debris it had been left in. Its umbilical cord was still attached, knotted to stop the blood, and it was carefully swaddled in a scrap of now-soiled blanket as if whoever had left it out had not wanted it to be cold while it waited to starve to death.

She wrinkled her nose. Baby smell would draw canids and anything else circling for easy prey. She spent a moment and some of her water to clean the excrement from the baby's buttocks and discard the old blanket, exchanging it for a soft cloth from her pack. Reinvigorated, the baby began to cry. She gave up on stealth and dipped a finger in the water. The baby sucked eagerly. It was strong, and like all young animals it wanted to survive.

She would not let it go to waste.

CHAPTER 11

Hunter stood so close to the forcewall that the hairs on her arm lifted gently towards the current. Even to her, the forcewall was nearly invisible, marked only by an occasional scintillation that cityens wouldn't be able to see at all. There was nothing else to show a transition, the same sun-bleached white gravel gleaming on either side of the border. Then again, no other demarcation was necessary: the goal, after all, was not to trap cityens inside, but only to keep the outside out, and there was nothing outside that could heed a sign had there been one. The forebears must have felt a dizzying pain, amputating the limbs of their city at the farthest inhabited edge they thought they could defend. It must have been hard too to condemn those left on the wrong side to be consumed by the chaos of the Fall. A hunter-cold decision, that, to sacrifice so many to ensure the survival of the rest. Not coincidentally, the first hunters had been made around that time, an implacably superior weapon against the desperate abandoned men whose bones a shift of wind or rain still occasionally unearthed at the foot of the forcewall.

Hunter felt a foolish reluctance to test that boundary. She chided herself for her weakness. The forcewall carried no danger for her; since those desperate early days, it had been modified again to let men cross when the need arose. The wall wouldn't care that she had changed from her hunter garb to a cityen's woven shirt and trousers and loosened her hair, grown ragged in her time in the desert, to fall forward over her face. Anyone who looked closely would still know her for a hunter, but in her experience cityens did not often look closely. And even if they did, they were no threat to her. No, her hesitation had nothing to do with physical danger. She stood still another wasted moment, as if that could change anything.

The baby stirred restlessly; it had remembered that it was hungry and the water hadn't satisfied it. Lips rooted against her shirt. "That won't help you," she told it. "But we'll find something."

She set her shoulders and strode through the barrier unimpeded.

The path that ended here had once been a wide road, but after centuries of neglect was now no more than an impression of direction through the rubble. She followed it nonetheless, the sounds and smells of men gradually coming closer. After a short while by the standards of the desert, she came around a turn to

the edge of the inhabited part of the city. She did not
bother to stop. Contracted as it was, the city still had a
fringe, the ragged margin of existence. The lights here,
wired to a distant transmission tower, were far apart
and dim, giving scarcely more illumination than a full
moon on a clear night. The few people she saw were
almost as thin and dirty as the children she had left outside, and probably less likely to survive. Their shelters
were certainly less sturdy than the one she had left in
the desert, most of them little more than a roof of salvaged polymer laid across rough walls of hand-stacked
stone, and scarcely differentiated from the untouched
piles of rubble surrounding them. Around one corner
she crossed paths with a man arguing with no one, ges-
ticulating wildly at the air. Bones showed through his
skin as if he had forgotten to eat for many days. She
slowed, wondering if she could spare the time to do
something. By the Church's calculation enough grain
was harvested every year to sustain the whole population of the city *and* still make the tithe; but the Church
could not set the food in front of every individual anymore. Every population had a proportion that failed,
no matter what.

She thought of Tana, Ela. The Saint.

The baby squalled, and she moved on.

The hovels gradually gave way to sturdier shelters.
This was the far edge of North, well beyond the part she
had showed the 378s on their training exercise in some
other life. Thin sheets of polymer covered a surprising
number of the windows, and most of the individual

dwellings even had lights, for behind the translucent panes she saw figures moving, scowling out, she imagined, at the stranger pausing to scrutinize their possessions. She wondered what the cityens living here had traded or stolen to earn such luxury, and whether they were fitter than the unfortunates she had seen earlier, or merely luckier. In the desert it would have been some of both. The roads had been rebuilt too, smooth enough to accommodate the wheeled carts pulled by the last few people scurrying to safety as true night grew close.

"Excuse me." She stopped politely but inescapably in the path of a man whose clothes were notably intact and whose cart was weighted with a large sack of grain. He frowned, seeing nothing but a ragged woman and her child. Interesting that he seemed more annoyed than frightened; order must prevail in this part of the city. Or perhaps he was just stupid.

"Yes?"

"I found this baby unattended. I wondered if you could tell me where I might take it that its matri would check for it?"

"I wouldn't know." He yanked his cart around her and went on. She suppressed a brief surge of irritation and made no effort to stop him. A little further on she found someone more helpful, a man who eyed her uneasily, stepping back to what he incorrectly estimated was a safe distance before suggesting that perhaps she could obtain more information at a certain trade not far away, and also some milk for the child, which by now had begun to wail again in earnest.

His directions sent her south, towards where the city had reached its greatest heights just before the Fall. The shells of the buildings still reached for the sky, thirty or forty levels stacked one above the other, though the tops had long ago sagged and crumbled in on themselves. Hunter knew from her own experience that it was possible to climb at least partway up inside some of the buildings using old stairwells and the shafts of mechanical lifts that could be climbed like vertical tunnels. It was hard to imagine the number of people who must have lived here before the Fall, to fill all that space; millions, the priests said. And once there had been city upon city like this, now silent, as far as the ears in the desert could hear. The cityens who were left were like the scavengers in the desert, crawling among the ruins with no thought of what had been lost and no goal greater than the day's necessities. Only the Church remembered, and dreamed to make men more than what they were.

The empty sockets of the buildings frowned down at such dreams. She turned back to the road. Fittingly, the trade she sought occupied the front corner of one structure that had not been very tall to begin with, and had therefore been easier to restore. From the street, it looked like most of the ground level was still filled in by debris, but the heavy door was marked with a sheaf of grain, the symbol for supplies, and light seeped out under the sill. She tried the door gently; it was locked. That couldn't stop her long, of course, but forcing her way in might lead to confrontation, and that would not serve her purpose just yet. Instead she knocked, at first politely, then pounding hard with her fist, the way a desperate woman with a hungry child might do late at night with no other hope.

"All right, that's enough! I hear you." The door opened a crack, just enough to let the occupant blind her with a bright light aimed at her eyes. Her pupils damped it down immediately, but she blinked hard anyway, giving an impression of helplessness that apparently satisfied the torch holder, for she heard a clank of chain and the door swung wider to admit her.

The room she entered was smaller than she would have thought, and crowded with shelving on which were stacked all manner of goods, some in bundles, others in bins, still more just laid out in the open. It looked innocuous enough—foodstuffs, cloth, a few mechanical tools, all perfectly legitimate to trade. Someone had known enough to rig a proper power drop into the room; the light was steady and clean, not the flicker of candles or lamps. The beam in her face was handheld, a Church device that had somehow found its way here.

She blinked in earnest when the trader switched it off. "What do you want?" he asked, keeping the heavy stick he held in his other hand ready for a quick swing. His frown took in her unkempt hair, dirty clothes, and finally, the exhausted baby. Good; she wanted him to mistake her for no more than a distraught cityen. He might not be used to such people, by his appearance: like the man with the cart, his clothes looked newly sewn, scarcely a stitch undone. And if she wasn't mistaken, the reinforcing patches at elbow and knee were the same woven polymer thread the Church used in the hunters' clothing. The last time she had been in the city she had not seen that; she would have to tell the Patri.

Then with a lurch in her gut she remembered that she would not be reporting to the Patri.

"I need milk for this baby," she grated, shifting the wailing boy in the crook of her arm. "Human, if you have any."

The trader continued to study her closely, stick still raised. Maybe he could see better than she thought. "Nothing else?"

Laughter almost caught her by surprise. Nothing he had could possibly be sufficient for her needs. She choked back a dangerous despair along with the laugh. "Yes," she said recklessly. "Information."

The tip of his stick tapped a thoughtful rhythm against the flooring. The sound echoed hollowly. There must be space under the floor for goods he didn't want to display. Interesting. "I assume you have chits, or something else to trade?"

She smiled briefly and set the object she was holding on the table, watching with satisfaction as his eyes widened. "This should be enough for some milk. And some information."

He reached eagerly for the device. Her free hand clamped over his wrist. He thought about swinging the stick, but stopped when she smiled at him again. She nodded and let go. "Milk first."

He was back in less than a minute, and the milk smelled sweet. The baby lipped impatiently at the cloth nipple, its cries quickly replaced by enthusiastic sucking noises. "Nice baby," the trader said, all friendly now.

"It's not mine. No, I didn't steal it," she added as she saw him computing how a woman would end up with a baby that new that wasn't hers. "I'd give it back to its matri, if I could find her."

"I haven't heard of any missing babies," he said. His eyes were locked on the object sitting on the counter between them. It was simple, mechanical, but very old. She might have come by it any number of ways.

"Where do you get human milk?" she asked casually.

He shrugged. "People bring it in, not my problem where they get it. Baby dies, milk keeps coming, who knows."

"*I've* heard sometimes people leave babies outside the forcewall. If they did that they'd have extra milk."

He looked up sharply, genuine distress crossing his fleshy face. "I wouldn't trade with the kind did that."

"Hmmm. With a place like this you must have people come to trade from all over the city. Maybe some of them would talk about that kind."

"People talk, that's not my interest. I just trade. Goods or chits or grain, whatever you want, makes no difference to me."

"Well." She reached for the wayfinder she had set out to entice him. "This is too much to trade just for milk. If you don't have any information—"

"Wait," he interjected swiftly. "What do you want? Ask, maybe I'll know."

For just a moment she debated simply asking about the Warder. If he existed, the trader was exactly the kind of man who would know about him, and she was sure he would talk; he wanted that device. But he'd also be eager to trade back to the Warder the story that a stranger had come in asking for him personally. That would be too suspicious to explain away if her plan worked. A less direct approach would be better. And the trader's reaction had given her a clue. "Where can I take this baby that someone would take care of it if I can't find its matri?"

Relief crossed the trader's face; he'd been worried that he wouldn't earn the wayfinder. "Easy enough. Keep going south, through Riverbend, to the old clave by the stads where they grow the grain. Follow the numbers down, you'll find what you're looking for."

She didn't have to feign surprise. "Riverbend? I know that place. Nothing but crazies and gangs, even the hunters never got it cleaned up. You're sending me into a trap." She made to pocket the device.

"No, no, it's not like it used to be." He shook his head earnestly. "Still rough around the edges, sure, but plenty of people live there now, regular cityens. Anyway, you're just passing through, no one will touch you. You'll see. The baby will protect you."

"The Church protects the people," she said automatically. The tone caught his attention. Questions started in his eyes, where she came from, why she knew so little of the city. Hastily she slackened her features, let her hair fall forward. "At least that's what those hunters say."

The trader grunted. "Hunters? Don't see them around here very much, do we? Leave us to sort out our own troubles, except when they come to take the tithe."

She looked at the suckling in her arms. "Maybe they'd have taken this baby to the Church, if its matri took it to them instead of leaving it outside." But they wouldn't have, and she knew it. If the fierce girl had heard her she would have spat her disgust right on the trader's clean floor. The thought hurt, a sharp pain under her ribs.

The trader shrugged, uninterested in conjecture. "Maybe."

She paused, as if considering whether to trust him. "You know, maybe it's not so bad the hunters don't come around. I've heard people saying we don't need the Church like we used to. We'd do fine on our own."

He'd heard that too, and still thought it dangerous, by the way his face closed up. "Like I said. People talk, it doesn't mean I listen." He set another container of milk on the table. "Here's my part. That, and you take the baby to the Ward. You go there, ask for help. It will find you."

She fingered the wayfinder in her hand. She felt a curious reluctance to leave it. In truth, it had little value; there were plenty more in the priests' store. No harm would be done by letting the cityens have it. But she had carried this one for a long time, and it had always led her back to the Church, no matter how far the Patri's orders had sent her. *You don't need a wayfinder to get back from the city*, she told herself sternly, and stood up, settling the baby's solid weight against her chest.

She tossed him the wayfinder. "Fair enough. Here's mine."

CHAPTER 12

The city took a long time to cross on foot, and night made it seem longer. Between the claves where the cityens clustered against the dark, the wind probed deserted alleys, and every footfall echoed with a deathly emptiness that Hunter never felt in the clean distances of the desert. Even the lightstrings hung as a guide to the safest route from North to Riverbend only made the surrounding darkness more impenetrable. The way she followed was as desolate as if no one had survived the Fall. As if even the Saint couldn't hold back the dark. She smelled stone cooling, flinty-sharp, but no other animals except herself and the baby, and the only sound was the distant hum of the transmission lines, almost below even her hearing. *All you do is wasted*, a serpentine voice hissed in her thoughts. *The Church is nothing against the end of the world.*

She closed her mind to it and kept going.

She might have been walking an endless dusty loop, passing the same ruined buildings over and over, the same burned-out lamp sputtering dead warnings into the night. It was illusion, she told herself, born of night and distance and fatigue; she knew her steps carried her steadily south. She paused for a moment to wipe a smudge from her vision, then shook her head and resumed her dogged trudge, ignoring the temptation to tear off a bit of cloth to mark her passage, in case she circled this way again. As her path curved near the river, the breeze picked up an oily tang that burned in the back of her throat. She wondered if cityens could taste it. Fortunately the baby, having guzzled most of the trader's milk as she carried it along, slept soundly. Despite the trader's reassurance, anyone about in the Riverbend now would not be someone whose attention she wanted to attract. She kept to the edge of the clave as best she could, working her way past it towards the Ward.

Finally the air began to clear and light leaked back into the streets. At last she crossed the no man's land between the claves and arrived at the edge of the Ward. Like the Church, this part of the city had been ancient before the Fall, and when the population had shriveled to its tiniest remnant, it had holed up here, where the city had begun as a fortress an eon ago. The small scale of this clave was comforting for a walker, especially compared with the vast empty paths striping the desert. The buildings stood close together, blunted towers that had never overreached like the blind giants farther north, the stone alleyways they'd grown up around so narrow and twisting that aircars couldn't follow them. Even the ground vehicles city-ens had used before the Fall would have had a hard time navigating this area, and there was no evidence that they had tried. In other parts of the city and along the desert roads hunters ran across rubber wheels and other preserved parts that showed where vehicles had died, but if any had been left here, they had long since been salvaged for scrap or dissolved into rust.

The buildings themselves were in decent repair here, many of them built of the same stolid brick and stone as the Church. It would have been a simple matter to clear rubble, shore up walls and roofs, and wire the lightstrings that ran every which way off the clave's main transmission hub. Though the street she walked was narrow, it was well maintained, and showed the marks of many recent passersby. At some of the inter-sections the buildings bore painted numbers, counting down towards a center of some kind. In this early part of morning the streets were still empty, but it was the emptiness of sleep, not death. Though it was still quiet, Hunter could hear the sounds of a day slowly waken-ing, a wheel or two rumbling over stone, the creak of hinges arguing not to open. Someone would notice her soon.

When she came to an open square where four streets met, she paused, pretending to study her choices un-easily. She walked a few paces to the left, then turned back in the other direction, scanning the upper floors of the nearest buildings for anything lurking there, occasionally glancing back over her shoulder. A few hundred paces past the square and a turn, followed by another, and another, and she ended up back where she had started, as someone truly lost might do. By now a sullen dawn was beginning to stain the cobble. She let her steps flag, paced a bit more, then flopped down on a bit of curb, head hanging. The baby, which had been sleeping contentedly in the crook of her arm all the while, chose this opportune time to let out a shriek of protest.

"Do you need some help?"

She looked up through a curtain of dirty hair. A young man stood near, but not too near, as anyone with sense would faced with someone as wild as she no doubt looked. Though he appeared more than adequately fed, he balanced lightly enough on his feet, ready to respond if she made a sudden move. She doubted that he was some innocent who just happened to be passing by. Worth trying, then. "I'm looking for the Warder."

A little laugh, not especially unkind. "Really? Why?"

She had worked out her story in the long night's walk. She would give them one mystery to solve; pleased with their own cleverness, they would not probe her deeper secrets. "I have something to tell him."

"You look hungry. Whyn't you tell me whatever it is? I'll take you somewhere you can get something to eat, and then I'll go tell'm."

At the mention of food, her stomach rumbled helpfully. "No. Only him. You won't believe me, so he won't believe you."

"Whyn't you let him decide?"

She pushed herself to her feet, shoulders setting stubbornly. "No. The children are too important. If you won't help me I'll find someone else." She started away across the square.

"Wait, wait." The man hurried up beside her. "What about children? I see you have th' one. You want help with it, I'll get you some. Just tell me what you need. I'll speak with'm myself, I promise."

"Take me to the Warder. Then you can hear."

He spoke to her gently, reasonably, the way one did with someone who might react unpredictably. "Something special about your baby? More'n just having it, I mean?"

She let a hint of defiance trickle into her voice. "Yes. Very special."

He hesitated a moment longer. "All right, then. Come with me, I'll take you to'm. He's busy, but he won't mind." She studied him as they walked. He wore the kind of baggy outer shirt cityens made from salvaged polymer they melted and spun into fiber, then wove into decent cloth, neither as new as the trader's nor as worn as her disguise. A blue stripe ran down one side, brightening the otherwise drab color. He had a round, pleasant face framed by a tangle of curly brown hair that made him look like a little boy, though the breadth of his shoulders belonged more to a man.

The street was beginning to stir, cityens emerging

to face their daily struggles, and though she drew an occasional puzzled glance, he seemed familiar to many of those they passed. People liked him, she thought; they waved and nodded, and he smiled back, a warm, open grin that made her think of how rarely hunters smiled. As they walked he whistled, not the imitation of animal sounds that hunters practiced, but a pretty tune, the way a happy man might as he ambled on his way. After a while it brought someone else.

"Hallo, Justan," the newcomer said. He was younger than his friend, and considerably leaner, with the wiry build of a youth just coming into full manhood. His overshirt was nearly identical to the first man's, fitted closer to his frame but still loose enough to conceal a weapon, if he carried one. *Some kind of uniform?* Hunter wondered. The stripe was the same on both. It didn't indicate a rank: the new man clearly thought he was in charge. "What'd you find there?"

"I was checking th' edge and met this woman wandering down from th' Bend. Says she wants to see th' Warder."

"Really?" The man looked Hunter up and down, wrinkling his nose. "You think he wants to see her?"

"I do. She won't explain, but she seems to know something about some special children." He turned to Hunter. "Go on," he encouraged her. "Tell Loro." She shook her head dully, as if she were too worn out to try to explain. Justan shrugged at Loro. "He'd want t' know."

"If it's true. Could be she's making it up, just to get

close. Everyone wants to see him these days. Trying
to get something, all of them. Probably this one too."

"Could be. He'll like the baby, though, they always
cheer him up. Gives 'im hope, he says, doesn't he?
Might as well take her. Worst thing that can happen is
it'll just be a story."

Loro puffed out his cheeks. "Right. Best be sure.
You go back to the edge, keep an eye out for any trouble come down from the Bend. There was a fight at the
edge last night."

"Heard about that from Teller. Just too much ferm,
he said."

"Yeah, well, if ours didn't go drinking ferm with
theirs to begin with, we'd have a lot less chance for
trouble. You don't worry about that, just go watch. I'll
take this one in."

Justan nodded amiably. "*You* don't worry," he told
Hunter, dropping a friendly hand on her shoulder.
"Whatever it is, the Warder'll take care of it." She felt a
tiny twinge of regret as he walked back down the way
they had come, leaving her with the frowning Loro.
She must be more tired than she thought.

"Let's go," Loro said gruffly, pointing in the opposite direction. As she made to follow, he stopped her
with a hand on her arm. It was gentle enough, but she
felt the strength of his fingers underneath, despite his
lean build; he probably worked at it. His hands were
decently clean, nails pared short. His dark hair was
clean too, almost as long as hers and tied back neatly
out of the way. A man who took some care in how he

looked. She noted the detail as a matter of course, in case it came useful later. "Better not try any nonsense with the Warder. I'll be watching."

She gave him the blankest look she had. "I don't know what you mean."

"Good." He led her to a building not far down the street and knocked a signal rhythm on the door. It cracked open. A whispered conversation followed, and the door opened onto a brightly lit hall, occupied by someone who did not smell quite as good as Loro. While Loro watched closely, the new guard searched her clothes, finding only the utility edge she had tucked into her waistband to give any searchers the false confidence of having disarmed her. "Wait here," Loro ordered, and disappeared down the hall, leaving her with the guard, who studied her and the baby with frank curiosity, but asked no questions. She leaned back against the wall, closing her eyes, feigning exhaustion until Loro returned. He wrapped a cloth around her eyes and led her up the stairs and deeper into the building. She counted the turns automatically, memorizing the layout as they walked. What sounded like two more men stood outside the fourth door on the left. Loro knocked respectfully, then they ushered her in and pulled off the blindfold.

Treasure filled the room.

Paper covered the desk, stacks of it, sorted carefully by size, edges aligned with concentrated care. The walls were lined with shelves holding piles and stacks of prints that must have been salvaged from all over the city. Most of the covers were stained and torn, of course, but a few looked as though they'd been protected, wherever they'd been hidden, almost as whole as the day they'd been made. Hunter's fingers twitched with the urge to feel those delicate sheaves in her hands, turn the yellowed, brittle pages to parse out the words that had been printed before the Fall. It would be a lifetime's study, the volumes in this room, worthy of every priest the Church could spare. The Patri would be ecstatic, when she told him—

"Loro says you wanted to see me?"

She came back to the present with a painful jolt. The voice was not the Patri's, and the man behind the desk could hardly be less like him. For one thing, he was older, with thinning hair that must once have been some shade of brown, now worn of color, the flesh of his face drooping softly past his jawline. His brown eyes had more than the beginning of a gray film around the edges, and beneath his shirt his shoulders were hunched in a way that suggested more bone than muscle. Despite the morning warmth he wore a vest over the shirt, woven from thicker fibers that had frayed badly at the hem. The clasped hands emerging from his shirtsleeves were wrinkled and spotted with too many annuals in the sun, and the thin lips trying to curve a smile had a faint bluish tinge beneath the surface color. He looked a bit like a priest who had spent too long at a magnifier, only without the sharp edge. "Are you the Warder?" she asked with what she hoped seemed like anxious respect.

He chuckled gently. "These good people call me that at times, it's true. There's really no such thing, you know. Fetch that chair, would you please, Loro? Now, what do you need, child?" *That* was so ridiculous that she felt her eyebrows rise. "It's just an expression," he said with a sheepish little shrug. "To an old man like me everyone looks so young, you see. But never mind, never mind that. How can I help you?"

She lifted her elbow, showing him the bundle in the crook of her arm. "It's this baby."

The two men who had been guarding the door had come in with her and Loro. That was poor planning; it left no one to stop her if she meant to escape. Unaware, one of them laughed. The Warder's smile turned apologetic. "You flatter me, child, but I'm certain that it isn't mine."

"It isn't mine either, sir," she countered with the mildest edge.

Pale eyebrows lifted towards his thinning hairline. "Do you need milk? Food for yourself? That's easily arranged. You didn't have to come all the way to me for that, you know. Loro there would have helped, or anyone in the Ward. We take care of each other here you know."

There was much interesting information in that brief statement; she set it aside to process later. "I do need milk, sir, but that isn't why I wanted to see you."

"Help finding the father, then?" The man behind her sniggered again. "Now, now, Teller. Don't be like that. We don't know this poor young woman's story yet, do we? She's not from the Ward, that's clear enough. Other claves might not have fine young men like you to help our friends stay out of trouble, you know." Teller subsided, and the Warder's smile came back to Hunter. "I'm sorry, child; truly sorry. Personal disputes are always so uncomfortable. We'll help you with the baby, of course we will. If I could give you some advice, though, I'd say to try to forget about whoever he is. If he won't help you, he isn't good enough for you anyway."

"Yes, sir, thank you, but it isn't a personal dispute. I don't know where the father is, but I don't know where the mother is either. You see, sir, this baby really isn't mine. I found it."

No one laughed at that. The Warder leaned forward, elbows on his desk, eyes suddenly narrowed, and his voice grew sharp although the kindly mask didn't falter. "Found it where, child?"

This part of the story had taken longest to work out. She could not reveal where she came from, not yet; that would be much too suspiciously direct. And she would not expose the little camp and the children she had left behind. It had been their choice to stay. Yet she had to give the Warder a loose thread to tug. That was why she had left the wayfinder with the trader: he would show it off eventually. No sense in having a treasure like that if he kept it to himself. If the Warder's people were clever enough, they would connect it to her, and begin to guess what she was. And who. A hunter in their midst could be a spy. But the excommunicated hunter, rejected and alone—managed properly, she could be an asset. They only had to think they had figured it out themselves, discovering a secret she had hoped to hide. It might take time, but that was the one thing she had more than enough of. "Near the forcewall. Way past the northern clave."

There was a long silence. The Warder pursed his thin lips. "How do you think it might have gotten there?" he asked at last.

"Someone left it. They do that sometimes, didn't you know?" She didn't need to feign the anger that tightened her voice. The children would be waking about now, if they had slept, to the first morning without her. . . . She jerked her attention back to the Warder.

"No one I know would do that," he said.

"I've seen it, more than this once."

"That is hard to believe, child. There are still so few babies, even now, you know. Every one is precious." He meant it; she saw the distress in his eyes, not quite strong enough to be anger. She wondered if he had that in him, reminded herself that the Patri thought him dangerous, though he didn't seem so sitting here.

She shrugged, not quite respectfully. "You don't have to believe *me*. This baby is proof, if you're interested in that." The man who had brought her, Loro, didn't like her attitude; he frowned, taking a half step towards her from his position behind the Warder's shoulder. She pretended not to notice, focusing on the Warder.

The Warder shook his head; Loro stopped, scowling. "Tell me exactly how you found him."

"Simple enough. I was walking up there, just inside the forcewall. I heard a baby cry, I went to look."

"Interesting, interesting. I hadn't thought that was such a common part of the city for people just to be walking." He might send men to search; it wouldn't be her fault if they found nothing.

Hunter permitted herself her own apologetic little smile, as if he were too clever for her. "Well, maybe I wasn't just walking." He waited, fingers fiddling idly with a stray fiber on the hem of his vest. She made a show of hesitation. "I thought it might be a convenient place to, well, let's say leave a few things I didn't want anyone else to find."

"What kind of things, child?"

She shrugged again. "This and that. I thought I might be able to trade some of it later. But now you've found me out." She let the smile show again, a little more anxiously. "Maybe you'd like to trade? Or," she added hastily as his eyebrows climbed again, "I can just give it to you. In appreciation for your help with the baby."

"Pardon me for saying so, child, but if that's how you see things I'm a bit surprised you would care so much about a child."

She sat up straight, putting on an offended scowl. "It's one thing to try to get a little extra to carry me through hard times. It's another to leave a baby out to die."

"Or steal one, and make up a story to try to gain the Warder's favor," Loro said with a barely suppressed snort of derision. It disturbed the baby, which started, gave a disconsolate wail, then lapsed into a defeated whimper, its little face pinched and miserable. The shopkeeper's milk hadn't been enough to make up for the feedings it had missed since it had been abandoned.

"Now, now," the Warder began, hands fluttering, but Hunter decided the appearance of maneuvering had gone on long enough.

"Look," she said, standing so abruptly that hands reached for weapons in panic. She glanced back over her shoulder at the knives and rods. "You don't need those. Whatever else you think, this baby needs food and someone to care for him. If you don't want him I'll find someone else."

The Warder studied her face intently. She let him see it nearly undisguised for just a moment, then slipped the mask back on. That should be enough; if he could not follow the trail of clues she had left, he was not worthy of the Patri's concern. This would all have been a waste. What she would do then she did not even try to consider.

The Warder tugged the thread free from his hem, flicked it away, then nodded slowly. "I believe you."

He turned to the puzzled guards, who had understood nothing. "Take her to the clinic." He frowned still, but it was thoughtful. "Lia will look after her."

CHAPTER 13

Loro led her out a different way from the one she had
been brought in, accompanied by a few of the men
they had picked up inside. It would have been a reasonable precaution, had she been a cityen. As it was, she
knew from the twists and turns exactly where down
the block the bolt-hole would lead. It would be no difficulty to find it again if she wanted to come at them
that way. Even so she gave them credit for their desire
to protect their leader; they were cityens, not hunters,
neither bred nor trained for this. It would be impru-
dent to underestimate them, just as the small predators in the desert had to be respected even when they
posed no immediate threat.

It was well into morning when they emerged into
the street. In the desert the children would be settling
down to wait out the day's stifling heat. The boy by
now should be pulling the blacking curtain across the

entrance to the nest, as she had taught him. The fierce girl would be hunkered on her heels by the burned-down fire, chewing a piece of dried meat and garnering her courage to face the terrors waiting in her dreams. Would the boy remember to set the tripwire so that if a canid sniffed too close around the tunnel entrance they would have warning? The net above the entrance had been secure, Hunter had rechecked before she left; but how long would that last? If it frayed and broke, the rocks might fall on one of the children if they bumped the pillar as they left. She should have reviewed it with them again. She should—

"This way," Loro said. He took her arm to direct her, not roughly, but it was enough to jostle the baby, which began to howl yet again. Hunter babies were quieter, despite the nuns' influence.

"I hope it's not far to wherever we're going."

"It's not." The baby gave one more loud protest and began to root around against her chest. One of the guards tittered, leering at Hunter. "Not much *she* can do about that," the man said. "Good thing we have Lia."

"Who's Lia?" Hunter asked.

"Our med," Loro said briefly. "Now be quiet."

The guards were not nervous, exactly, but alert. She wondered if they had enemies, or simply an abundance of caution. The city was much like the desert. There would be predators here, too, sniffing about, ready to take what was better than they had, if there were no hunters present to stop them. There mostly wouldn't be. Order and safety flowed from the Church down, but in a place like this, it had to be enforced primarily by the cityens themselves.

The guards took her down a few blocks, then up to another doorway. Like the Warder's, this building was made of old brick, but it was only one room high, and probably not much more than three or four rooms inside. A garden had been dug along the walls, a few vegetables but mostly green plants—herbs, it looked like. Hunter thought she recognized some of them from the priests' gardens in the Churchyard. The guards did not bother her with blindfolds or false passages this time. Apparently this was a public place. Nonetheless, she noted the way piles of old brick and stone stacked here and there in the street let individual walkers approach, but would deny any large group a straight run at the door. Another sensible precaution, one that suggested something of value to protect.

The front door opened onto an anteroom, empty except for a scattering of unmatched chairs, obviously created from scrap, but large and soft, with cushioned backs and bottoms. Sheets of thin-rolled resin, translucent enough to give the room a cheerful brightness, had been placed into shutters that closed over the many windows, bisected so they could be opened to let in the breeze. People who came to this room would be comfortable while they waited.

Loro crossed the room to the far door, gesturing for her to follow. The others trailed at her back; it could still be a trap. Her shoulder blades prickled. She had distracted them with the knife she'd let them find; the thin plastic slice sewn into her shirtsleeve would be more useful here anyway. Pretending to shift the baby to a more secure grip, she slipped the fingers of her right hand into the gap in the seam. One quick tear and a whirl at neck level, and she would have three fewer guards to deal with. The baby sniffled as if it knew and disapproved of her plan.

Loro disappeared through the door. The man behind her gave a small push. Her fingers twitched in the seam; then she went inside.

The room reminded her of nothing so much as the priests' laboratory in the Church, though this one looked simultaneously as if it had been cobbled together yesterday and had been there since before the Fall. There were six beds lined up against the long wall, narrow but comfortable looking, with clean sheets turned down at one end. The blankets were the haphazard color of salvaged polymer shredded to fine fibers and twisted together, then rewoven into a soft, light fuzz. There were windows here too, and these were open, admitting the smell of the city, not too unpleasant this warm morning. The wall across from the beds was lined with shelves full of boxes and bottles, neatly arranged for easy access to their contents. At the far end of the room was a small desk, with another door propped half open behind it. Remarkably, yet another sheaf of prints bound along one end lay open on the desktop.

The young woman studying the prints looked up as they entered. "Hello, Loro," she began, then stopped at the sight of Hunter coming behind him, carrying the baby. She stood in a quick, graceful movement, smoothing her long skirt down. "How can I help you?" Her voice was warm and light.

"Are you the med?"

"Yes, I am. Is your baby ill?"

"It isn't my baby," Hunter said yet again. Her voice sounded harsh, abrupt, compared with the woman's soft tone. "I found it. In the desert," she added.

The woman drew a quick breath, glancing at Loro. He nodded. "He told us to bring her to you."

"Please, lay him down here. The rest of you can go." Loro nodded agreement, and his men filed out of the room. He stayed, lounging against the wall with a casualness that did not fool Hunter. She ignored him.

The med patted a hand on the examining bed. Hunter found herself oddly reluctant to relinquish the child, although it was obvious at once that the woman knew her work. She unswaddled the baby, inspecting him all over in a rapid glance. He chose that exact moment to demonstrate his excretory functions. The woman cupped a hand to deflect the stream, not before the first drops splashed onto her skirt. Her eyes crinkled around the edges. They were almost the exact shade of the canids' eyes, golden brown with a dark rim, and occasional flecks of green mixed in. And they were sad, Hunter saw, not a transient mood but a deep, abiding sorrow that lingered even as she laughed over the baby. "Well, at least we can tell that he's had enough fluid." Outraged at being wet, the infant howled. "And his lungs are strong." She toweled him off, pressing on his belly, peering into his mouth before she let him suck on a fingertip. "That won't fool him long. What have you been feeding him?"

"Human milk." Hunter waved the empty container. "That's all I had. I got it from the trader who sent me to you. I only found him last night." She frowned at the disjointedness of her report.

The woman didn't seem to notice. "That would be enough. He's just a few days old; babies are born with extra fluid. It helps them survive."

He wouldn't have survived in the desert.

"Milse, could you come in here please?" A man popped his head in through the door behind the desk. He wore a loose robe like the Warder's, not the shirt and trousers of Loro's men. Probably some kind of helper or apprentice then, rather than a guard, but it was hard to be sure. There were just a few meds scattered through the city, Hunter knew. They were valuable enough to warrant protection, but usually it came from the Church. Sometimes the hunters even brought them in to share information with the medical priests who went from time to time to tend the sickest cityens. She wondered if the hunters knew about this med, who said to the man, "Bring me some of that milk we have in back, would you please? Thank you." Milse was back in a moment, sack in hand, then stayed, hovering off to the side.

"Could you do me one other favor, Milse? I still need that magnifying lens Exey was working on. He said it would be ready today. Would you mind checking? I can handle the beginning of visits without you."

"Of course, Lia. Happy to."

"As if he needed an excuse to run around the city," Loro said, with the half scowl that Hunter was beginning to recognize as his habitual expression.

Milse smiled tartly in response and went out through the door behind the desk. That meant another exit that way, Hunter noted almost without thinking. Two doors, all the windows; easy enough to get out any time she needed to, though this was exactly where she wanted to be for now.

"You said you found him abandoned?" The med looked perfectly comfortable with the baby sucking away contentedly in her arms.

"Yes." Hunter's voice hardened. "Someone left him to die."

"Poor woman," the med murmured. "It must have seemed less cruel than letting his struggle drag on if she couldn't provide for him." She shook her head, eyes briefly closing. "The Warder tries to help them when he hears."

"I met a man who I was told was the Warder. He said there's no such thing."

"It's our nickname for him. He doesn't like to take so much credit."

"He also told me the children are too precious to be abandoned in the desert."

The remarkable eyes dimmed. "He remembers the way it was when he was young. But even the children are having children now, or so it seems. Faster, I'm afraid, than we've learned to feed them all. It's a great change from the days when hardly anyone could bear, but it brings its own problems."

"People can just ask the Church. They help whenever they're asked, don't they?"

"Not everyone can even manage that. Sometimes we have to help ourselves." The woman studied her face openly. "Someone from the Ward might know that."

Hunter shrugged. "I'm not from the Ward."

"No, I can see that," the med said thoughtfully. Hunter waited, but the med did not ask. She only said, "It was a long winter. Until the new grain comes in, some of us will struggle." The baby stopped sucking, beginning to fuss. She shifted him over her shoulder, patting him expertly until he spat with satisfaction and settled back, snuggling his cheek against her shoulder. She smiled suddenly. The way it lit her eyes put an infinitesimal catch in Hunter's even breathing. "But I think I know what we can do for this little man. I delivered a dead baby of a young woman a few days ago. It would have been her second child. She'll still have milk. If we can help her with the food, she would welcome a baby to raise. Loro, do you remember? It was that woman down the alley towards the river. Send someone, if you would, and tell her the Warder asks. She'll understand. Don't worry," she added, sitting down to settle the baby more comfortably. "We'll be fine until you get back."

Loro pushed away from the wall he was slouching on. "I'm not leaving you alone with her," he objected.

"It's fine. She won't make problems here, not when she went to all this trouble to bring the baby." Hunter covered a breath of astonishment. No one could be *that* much of a fool. Loro looked more unhappy than surprised, but he didn't argue. That was interesting too. He fixed Hunter with a warning glare until she nodded her understanding, then disappeared the way they had come, pulling the door closed behind him.

"So now," the med said when they seemed to be alone, though Hunter could hear Milse, or someone, lingering beyond the not-quite-closed back door, and more than one set of footsteps in the anteroom. Loro wasn't as trusting as the med. "What about you?"

"Me? What do you mean?"

The med's smile, gentle as it was, didn't belong to a fool at all. "We've agreed that you're not from the Ward. I don't know anything else about you, other than that you care something for abandoned children."

"I just try to get by, like everyone else," Hunter said, wondering if the Warder had sent word ahead, and whether this was an interrogation. She stood up, just to see what would happen. The med seemed unperturbed. "Well, now that the baby is taken care of, I can leave you to your work." The guards met her on the threshold as she opened the anteroom door, and she stopped, pretending to be surprised. She recognized one, the first man she had met in the Ward. "Am

I some kind of prisoner, then?" She hadn't expected it to be quite this easy.

"What is this, Justan?" the med asked with a frown. Either she hadn't known, or she could feign surprise tolerably well.

Justan ducked his head, clearly embarrassed. "Loro said. Sorry, I told'm you wouldn't like it, but he says she has to stay until th' Warder's ready." Hadn't known, then.

"Ready for what?" Hunter pushed.

Now he was avoiding Hunter's eyes as well as the med's. It was almost amusing. "To decide what to do with you."

"Now listen, Justan—" the med began.

"I'm sorry," he repeated, and he looked it, ducking his head again so that his curly hair fell over his eyes. "Best not t' argue with you, Lia, I know." He slipped back out of the room, door closing behind him with a firm click.

The med stared at it in exasperation, then let out a sigh. "These days they think everyone is going to make some kind of trouble. I suppose I can't blame them. All these babies, the Bend and the Ward are getting full enough to bump right up against each other. . . . Another problem we should welcome, but it's such a strange time." She frowned absently, contemplating the strangeness, then remembered Hunter with a reassuring smile. "Don't worry. The Warder is kind to everyone. He's probably just humoring Loro. We don't take prisoners here; he'll let you go if that's what you want."

That was the last thing Hunter wanted, but it wouldn't do to seem too eager to stay. "I hope it doesn't take too long. I'm not used to sitting and waiting. I'm a—let's just say, I trade. I make my own way."

"Well then, let's make a trade. When Loro gets back, we'll give the baby to the woman. Meanwhile, I could use some help, nothing too difficult, but it will give you something to do until the Warder sends for you."

Hunter made a show of pretending to consider it was a choice. "All right, then."

The med smiled again, and dropped a hand lightly on Hunter's forearm. The soft touch brought a reflex shiver. "Good," the med said. "They'll be here in a few minutes."

CHAPTER 14

Hunter didn't know yet where the back door led, but apparently everyone in the clave knew where to find the public entrance. As the med finished feeding the baby and swaddled it comfortably on one of the cots, she said, "Would you ask Justan to send in the first visit?"

Cautiously, Hunter cracked open the front door. Justan, who must have been standing right there, thrust himself into the gap, then relaxed with a sheepish grin once he realized she wasn't trying to escape. She glared at him for show, but it was hard not to smile back at his boyish, open face. Then she looked over his shoulder. She'd been aware of the growing hubbub outside, but until now she hadn't realized quite how big a crowd had gathered. The anteroom had filled with people, who now overflowed the chairs and sat on the floor or leaned up against the walls wherever they could find a place. Some of them wore bandages or clutched sturdy sticks for support; others had the unmistakable pinched look of sickness and pain. "She says she's ready," Hunter said doubtfully.

The med did not seem daunted. At her nod the first person limped in, a woman with a leg wound that needed cleaning and rebandaging. Hunter helped her up on the table, then undid the old dressing. The med did the rest of the job with quick efficiency and a light touch that made the woman smile gratefully even when it hurt. The next visit was a man no older than Justan, with a hand wrapped from fingertips to elbow. Lia readjusted the splint. "That will do fine if you leave it another seven or so. No more punching people in the skull with it, right?"

The man colored bright pink. "Yes'm," he mumbled. She patted him on his good arm and sent him along with a smile that turned him even redder. So it went, one after another, some who knew the med and greeted her with respectful friendliness, others deferential strangers. The way they just walked in with their bags and carryalls and Saint knew what concealed under baggy cityen's clothing made Hunter's palms itch. To be sure, Justan was in the anteroom, and a pair of guards lounged in the corners outside the curtained area where Lia did her examining, but they wouldn't do the med much good if someone really meant her harm. Relegated to holding basins and bandages while the med worked, Hunter imagined half a dozen ways she could defeat their security if she wanted to. It would be simple, especially if it wouldn't matter that some died.

The med caught her eye as she was studying the guards. She smiled, sadly, and shook her head, as if she knew exactly what Hunter was thinking. Hunter's face grew hot, unaccustomed shame at the direction her thoughts had carried her.

These cityens were not here to threaten Lia.

"Hand me that, would you please?" The med's voice was gentle, forgiving. Hunter passed her the tool, a simple unpowered amplifier with an earpiece and a diaphragm that she placed over the sick man's chest to listen to his breathing. The priests in the lab had something similar. Hunter wondered whether they had passed the tech on or the cityens had thought of it themselves. She knew so little about the city. Why had the Patri sent her so unprepared? *He didn't send you*, the darkest part of her mocked.

The med frowned as the man coughed painfully. She listened a little longer, then leaned back. "Good, you can button up again. May I see your feet?"

The man shifted uncomfortably. "I . . . um, I haven't washed them yet today." He probably hadn't washed them in a month, judging by the rest of him.

The med dropped a kind hand on his shoulder. "That's all right. I won't mind."

Scarlet, the man removed the scraps of plastic sheeting and straps that passed for his shoes. Hunter's nose twitched at the smell. The med touched a blackened toe, moving it back and forth gently. "Does this hurt?"

"No, mam. Really I don't feel't much."

The med nodded. She pressed her thumb into the shiny skin above one swollen ankle, leaving a depression that stayed. "Are they always big like this?"

"Worse, most times." His eyes crept anxiously to her face, meeting her gaze for the first time. "Is't bad?"

It was the same sad smile she had given Hunter. "You've been a hard worker, haven't you?" The man nodded dumbly. "Your heart is a little tired now, that's all. Go ahead, put your shoes back on. I have something for you."

While the man reassembled his rags, the med perused the row of jars neatly arranged on her shelves. Someone knew how to write, maybe the med herself; each jar was carefully labeled, the letters tiny to save the precious paper. After a moment the med reached for a small jar, which she handed to the man. "I want you to take a pinch of this, just what you can catch between these two fingers, morning and night, dissolved in some water. Every day, don't miss any. Come back in a seven to see me."

The man coughed again, then nodded, clutching the jar close. "Yes, mam. Thank you. Thank you."

The med watched the door shut behind him, a welcome break in the endless flow of cityens. She passed a hand over her eyes. "They say that once the Saint could work healing. I'd like to have seen that."

A thin girl, standing over a man with a child in his arms. Hope rising like electric current from the gathered crowd, rising in Hunter's heart, wild and dangerous as a predator at night. And shattered, just like that, the child dead, the father keening his grief to the dark. "It isn't true." Hunter caught her ragged voice back before the med could make anything more of the words, then said with the measured interest of a stranger, "That man's heart was failing?"

"Yes." With a little sigh, the med sat down for the first time that morning, absently rubbing her neck. "Probably his kidneys too; they usually go together in someone with feet like that."

Hunter nodded, thinking of some of the old priests she had seen. "And the dry rot."

The med studied her face. "You have some experience with these things."

"A little." Careful; she did not want to go too far down that line of questioning yet. It was too soon. "What was that you gave him?"

"Foxglove. It might help him for a little while."

"It won't make a difference in the end, will it?" The med shook her head. "Then why waste it? You gave him all you had."

"I can make more, as soon as the plants flower. I grow them out front. It shouldn't be too long."

"What if someone comes before then who it really would have helped?"

The med shrugged tiredly. "We'll just have to hope that doesn't happen."

A hunter who thought like that would never survive. No wonder the forebears had seen the need for the Church to keep the city alive. "Hope won't make it happen or not happen."

The med's gaze was sharp, troubled. "He was standing here in front of us. Would you have sent him away with nothing?"

"I wouldn't waste something that could go to better use." Almost before the words were out of her mouth Hunter regretted them. She wasn't here to teach the med.

The woman frowned towards the shelf of jars. Most of them were closer to empty than not. Her shoulders rose and fell. "I can see why you would say that. But people need hope. That's what the Warder always tells us: we have to have hope, if we're ever going be more than animals, scrambling for something to eat, killing each other if there isn't enough." She glanced at the quietly sleeping bundle on the bed. "Leaving babies to die."

The Church had never taught that the old world was some kind of paradise. "We were like that even before the Fall."

"I know." The med's hands were open in her lap. She turned them over, studying first the backs, then the palms. If she learned anything, it brought her no comfort. "But we don't have to be like that forever. The city's changing, growing. Why can't we?"

They talk of change, the Patri had told her. It was an unexpected opening. Some part of Hunter drew back, inexplicably reluctant to use the med this way; she shut it out, knowing no chance could be wasted. "Why not send some of the people to the Church, those priests that come around, like other claves?" Hunter asked. "It's their problem, protecting the cityens, isn't it?"

"The Warder says we can't ask the Church to do it all. We have to take care of each other too. You must think so too; you got yourself into some trouble helping that baby."

"That's not the same thing," Hunter said.

"No?" The med's eyes crinkled with gentle amusement, and Hunter felt a stab of guilt at the deception that had stolen that smile. It was something that should be earned. She wanted to, suddenly, and reminded herself angrily that she could not afford such distractions.

"No," Hunter insisted. "Anyway, as I see it, cityens mostly get by. The Church keeps order, and what do they ask us for? A little grain, a few girls from time to time to make their nuns, it doesn't seem so much. . . ." She let the words trail off, inviting the med to fill the gap.

"I wouldn't say that to—" Whoever the med had been about to name, she changed her mind. "Well, never mind. Let's just say that the price for order can seem high. Though sometimes I wish we had a little more of it, especially when people have had too much ferm and I spend all night sewing them up and setting bones." Her attempt at a laugh fell a little short.

Before Hunter could answer, a knock sounded on the door and Justan looked in. "Ready, Lia? There's more."

Lia stood, stretching, hands on the small of her back. "There are always more. Too many."

"What d'you expect, only med in the Ward." Justan's round face creased in concern. "Want me to send them away until tomorrow? Nobody's bleeding so hard as you can hear it."

"And *that*," Lia said, "is why you're not the med. Send the next one in, please."

The next one was, in fact, bleeding, though not very hard; Lia stitched the wound with a fine thread of polymer soaked in fermentate and left Hunter to bandage it after. The next two the med sent away with more powders from her jars, then one more with stitching. Lia was right, there were too many. Last winter's grain shortage showed itself in the weak and sick who came through the door, privation leaving their bodies without the resources to repair damage that would not otherwise have been so serious.

A gravid woman entered, swollen almost as big as the nuns. She clutched her man's hands throughout the examination, the two of them following Lia's every movement in something that looked to Hunter like terror. The med, eyes closed in concentration, shaped her hands this way and that around the woman's full belly, then reached up inside. At last, she opened her eyes and smiled. "You're doing wonderfully now that the sickness is past, Tralene. Just a few more weeks."

The woman's eyes brimmed. "Do you think . . . do you think this one will be all right?"

Lia washed her hands in the basin Hunter held. "This baby's the right size, and he's right way up."

"He!" the man exclaimed. "Is it a boy? I'll have a son?"

Lia laughed. "I'm sorry, Drayton, I shouldn't have

said. We won't know until the baby's here. You just take care of Tralene, make sure she eats the extra portions the Warder sends, and I think whichever it is, it'll be nice and healthy."

The woman said, "Thank him for us, Lia. And you, thank you, I don't know what I would have done, after the first one, I—I—" She burst into a flood of messy tears.

"Thank you, Lia mam," the man said earnestly. "And tell the Warder—anything, any way we can repay his kindness . . ."

"He doesn't need anything, Drayton, you know that, but I'll tell him that you said."

"The Warder does all this and asks for nothing?" Hunter asked as she helped put a clean cloth over the examining table. "Strange kind of trade. He'd never make it in my place."

"Maybe you haven't found the right place," Lia answered. She smiled, but her golden eyes were serious.

There's no way she can know. The catch in Hunter's breath brought Lia's eyes to her face. Before the med could question her she said with a shrug, "I know the teachings. Saint preserves the Church, and Church preserves the city. That's good enough for me."

"Really? I'm not so sure the Church can teach us everything. Sometimes I think even the Saint doesn't know all of it, or all about us—what's inside us. Don't you ever feel like we have to find that for ourselves?"

Blasphemy, the deepest-rooted part of Hunter wanted to charge, but the med wasn't a hunter, and the word didn't fit the open, unguarded gaze Lia offered her, a look that made Hunter feel as unworthy as she did in the sanctuary. The Saint had looked at her like that once too, in the desert before Hunter had dragged her back to face the altar.

She swallowed the painful swelling in her throat. "People in this clave say some strange things," she said, struggling to keep her tone light, conversational. "Must be what the Warder teaches you."

The med looked at her. "It's what I believe," she answered simply.

Suddenly Hunter did not want to probe any more. Fatigue bore down on her, the sleepless night and the long walk and the strain of all the posing. She told herself she should stop before she made a mistake that cost her the position she had worked to gain. There would be time to press on later. *Weak*, said the voice in the back of her head. "Maybe you're right," she conceded.

The med held Hunter's eyes a moment longer. "Well, one thing the Warder *does* say is that what you do matters more than what you think. Let's see if between the two of us we can find a way to help a few more of those people out there."

They made their way through the line of visits. Hunter observed how the med approached the problems, what questions she asked, the way she poked and prodded and studied. Hunter had seen the priests work like this in the infirmary, the med would fit in well with them—

The room grew suddenly distant. The med's lips

were moving but it was the priests' soft interrogation she heard, the shadowless infirmary light that made her blink in surprise, twitching her nose at the sharp smell of chemicals and disinfectant, all for a moment more vivid, more *real* in her mind than where her body stood, this foreign room where she had no place—

"Are you all right?" the med asked sharply as Hunter grabbed at a chair to stop the dizziness.

"I'm fine," she muttered, clasping the metal hard enough to hurt. "I just—"

All at once there was a commotion at the door, shouts and someone bursting through. Without thinking Hunter leapt in front of the med, shoving her down behind the marginal safety of the chair. She reached automatically for her static wand before she remembered it was hidden with her other gear in the desert camp. Instead her hand closed over a tall medicine bottle; a quick flick of her wrist and she held a jagged glass dagger, cold and comforting. Guards who had been half dozing in the corners so long Hunter had almost forgotten them sprang alert, too late to prevent the entrance of two men, faces taut with panic, supporting a third man between them who was screaming every breath and spraying blood everywhere. "Help me! Oh, Saint, help me, please!"

"Get him down!" Hunter dropped the shard of bottle and pushed all three of them towards a bed. They wrestled him across; he was white with blood loss but thrashing so in his panic that they could barely hold him. "Keep him still. I said, still!" She couldn't even see where he was bleeding from, only that he was soaked with it and every time he moved another stream spurted from wherever it was. "Stop it," she told him urgently. "I'm trying to help you, hold still." But he was too far gone to listen. She reached for his throat. The sleep hold might kill him, weak as he was, but he would die for certain if he kept thrashing. The guards stared uselessly, weapons dangling.

But the med was already kneeling at the top of the bed. "Look at me," she said, taking the man's blood-spattered face between her hands. "Just look at me. You'll be all right. *Look.*" Somehow her calm demand cut through the chaos. His eyes, barely focused, searched hers out, and all at once he went limp, unresisting. Hunter thought for a breath he was dead, but the blood was still pumping.

From the mangled remains of a hand, she saw now. He must have caught it under something heavy and moving. Gobbets of flesh hung stripped from bone; glistening pinkish fragments spiked out in no relation to where fingers should have been. Someone made a retching noise. Hunter swallowed a wave of her own nausea and ripped the remains of his sleeve up to the shoulder. She wrapped the rag quickly around his upper arm, pulling it tight as she could. She scanned the room, searching. "Give me your knife." The guard stared at her stupidly. "*Give* it to me. And the sheath. Hurry." Fumbling, he handed it over, staring as if he expected her to cut the man's throat. Instead she tied the sheathed blade quickly in the rag, then twisted, using it as a lever until it pulled the cloth tight enough to staunch the spraying blood to a slow ooze.

Hunter drew a breath, but before she could speak the med said, "Get his clothes off. What happened to him?" She inspected the rest of his body quickly while the man who answered averted his eyes.

"He's a grower down at the stads. Crop powder exploded in his spreader. Must've been a spark."

"Did anything else happen, or just the hand?"

"Just the hand."

Hunter didn't see any other injuries either. The hand might be enough. The man's breathing was heavy, irregular, his face slack. Hunter looked at the med. "The hand has to come off if he's going to have a chance."

"I know." The med stood, wiping her bloody palms calmly on her skirt. "I have what we need."

By the time they were done, the man's friends had retreated to the outer room and one of the guards had fainted in a heap in the corner. The man had come awake once, screaming hoarsely for mercy; Hunter had no choice but to apply the sleep hold then. But he kept breathing, and now the clean cloth wrapped tightly around the stump of his wrist had only a little stain on it, and they had gotten dry sheets under him and tied him loosely to the bed, in case he woke again.

Hunter wiped a gory hand on her pants. "He should live, unless he lost too much blood."

"Yes." The med had a streak of red across her chin, another splotch on her forehead. Her face had never lost its calm. She was thoughtful now, evaluating Hunter as she had the patient. "You've done this before."

"There are accidents everywhere. Sometimes I was in a position to help. So I learned."

The med did not press her. "There's a water tap through there. You can wash; I'll clean up in here. Teller"—this to the guard who had propped his fainting comrade against the wall and was slapping his face none too gently to revive him from his stupor—"please find some clean clothes for—come to think of it, I never heard your name?"

Hunter took a deep breath. "Echo."

"Echo." The med smiled, and it turned her eyes to honey. "It's good to know you. Teller, please bring some clean clothes for Echo."

The med looked like a child with her wet hair tied back in a string and a too-big shirt with rolled-up sleeves hanging loosely over her long skirt. They were her own clothes, from a small chest in the back room; she had lost weight recently, or never cared to adjust them properly. The clothes the man Teller had found Hunter fit her better; worn and patched as they were, they would be perfectly serviceable. She looked, she knew, like a guard, or a hunter; she would find no trace of a child if she searched her own image in a glass.

The baby she'd brought to the Ward, which had miraculously slept through the screaming and all the other noise, woke with a start and began wailing at the top of its evidently healthy lungs when Lia shut the door with a gentle *click*. Laughing, the med scooped it up. "I think there's enough milk still in that bag. Pass it here, will you? Loro should be back any time now with the girl." And indeed it wasn't long before the baby had been sent off with a wide-eyed young woman, still walking gingerly, and the med's promise that the Warder would make sure the nursing mother got enough to eat to keep the milk coming. Before they left, Loro had demanded a summary of the morning's activities. His face clouded forebodingly over Justan's explanation of Hunter's role, but Lia forestalled him with a pat on the arm. "I think the Warder would want to know," she said, and though his nod was curt, he chose not to argue, and his hand was gentle enough as he took the limping girl's arm to help her out the door. Hunter watched them go, the girl already smiling and cooing at the baby as if it were her own. Just like the young nuns with their first-born in the Church, the priest-made babies that would be the new hunters, already fiercely demanding to be fed, to be cleaned—

Her chest tightened, crushing inward on her heart. She tried to take a deep breath—*it will pass, it will pass*—Saint, it was worse here than in the desert— and with another dislocating jolt, it was the children she saw, waiting forlornly for her in the camp where she had abandoned them, the fierce girl squatting on her heels banging rocks together with a scowl while the boy plucked at his rags and worried— *Stop it*, she told herself savagely. *Don't let them see*. Nothing but breath, one in, one out, past the constriction, in, out, until finally the constriction began to give way. She wiped sweat surreptitiously from her face, hoping that Lia wouldn't notice, hoping that if she did she would blame a belated reaction to all the blood. . . .

She jerked fully back to the present, still primed for action, at a knock on the door. But it was only a visitor, a stranger with a little pack for the med. It held bread, and a bit of cheese. "There's enough for two," Lia said, offering her a generous half. Hunter shook her head, though her stomach rumbled loud enough for the med to hear. "When was the last time you ate?"

In the camp, this morning, no, yesterday . . . "It doesn't matter. I don't want to take your share."

"Don't worry, the Warder will send more." She pressed the bread into Hunter's rough, sunburned hand. "I told you: we take care of each other here."

Hunter slipped into the daily routine without resistance. It was easy enough: she simply didn't ask again about leaving, and if the Warder had any further plans for her, or even remembered that she was there, no one brought it up. If she didn't think of the Church, the Saint; if she didn't think of Tana, or the children in the desert, what they would be doing, whether they had found food—*no, don't think about it*—this duty was no more difficult than any other, and more comfortable than most. She had shelter in the form of her own pallet in a corner of the main room, and there was enough food, brought to the med by some or other emissary from the Warder. There was always a guard or two, but they appeared to be there as much to manage the crowded anteroom as to watch over Hunter. Loro, clearly their leader, came every day, sometimes more than once, bringing Lia news or supplies, or occasionally sharing a meal; those times he could almost seem pleasant, at least with the med. Towards Hunter he maintained a cold hostility by which she understood that he viewed her as a threat, though she didn't think he knew exactly why. He manifested it mainly by ignoring her as thoroughly as possible, which only made it easier for her to fade into the background and observe.

Once, after he walked out the door in just such a way that Hunter had to step inconveniently aside or take a shoulder as he passed, Lia laid a light hand on her arm. The incessant physical contact among the cityens was hard for Hunter to adjust to. Hunters never touched but for a purpose, but the cityens did it all the time, casually, just as they laughed and chatted. The med's touch was soft and gentle, like everything about her; Hunter didn't object. "He doesn't mean anything by it," Lia said. "He's just protective of me. We've known each other since we were small; he thinks of me as a sister."

Probably not a sister, Hunter thought, a tiny spark of wry annoyance catching her by surprise, but she didn't argue.

The days might have dragged, but she had useful

work to pass the time, assisting the med when she saw the ill or injured people who made their way to the clinic. Milse, whom Hunter had taken for Lia's assistant, seemed happy enough to pass off those duties, pronouncing that Hunter could do them better anyway. There was another advantage as well: the people talked. Not quite as much as the nuns, but enough for her to begin to put together a picture that she could take back to the Patri. It would be much like all the other times she had reported to him: he would listen intently, fitting her observations into the larger picture he had, his expression of concentration so like the priests as they looked through their magnifiers— then the shock of remembering that she could not expect to sit with him again, would never— *No, don't think about that. Focus, here, now.*

It was like any other wound, she reasoned wearily. The pain and fear were normal, to be used when possible, tolerated when not. There was no sense dwelling on them. Shaking herself, she listened closely, rarely speaking, only occasionally asking just the right question, casually, not to draw suspicion, the way a stranger might wonder, mildly curious, how they did things here.

Much of the talk circled back, one way or another, to the Warder. It seemed that everyone had a personal tie, a time that he had extended extra grain chits before they had been earned, sent food when someone was too sick to work, dragged a boy back from the lawless gangs of the neighboring Riverbend and set him to honest work trading labor for chits down in the stads. Hunter hadn't realized how critical the flow of chits had become, at least in the Ward. From what she gathered, many people didn't even hand them in directly for grain rations anymore, as the Church intended; they simply passed them among themselves as tokens, trading for one thing or another until the chits had somehow obtained a value of their own. The Warder must have gathered a considerable store to himself, to be able to pass them out in exchange for nothing more tangible than the cityens' goodwill. It was, she thought uneasily, another thing the Patri needed to know, when—if—she reported back to him.

Meanwhile, she told herself that she was still doing a hunter's duty protecting the cityens, if not in any way she had before. She maintained the guise of the suspect trader, skilled more from practice than from training, but it didn't take long for Lia to see that Hunter could attend to the less seriously injured herself, freeing the med to see the worse hurt and the ill. For them there often seemed to be no answer; yet most of them left somehow comforted, like the old man Hunter had seen the first day.

Lia smiled at all of them, but in the evenings, sometimes, Hunter saw the smile fade, and the med's golden eyes grew sad and weary. "I don't know where I'd be without your help," Lia said one night as they shared yet another meal of bread and cheese. "Milse tries, but he doesn't really like blood and mess. He's much happier flitting around the clave trading for supplies and gathering gossip for the Warder. And anyway, it isn't usually this bad. The sickness last year . . . Most of these people never really recovered." She shook her head. "We need a good harvest. If we go into next winter without enough for them to eat—well, I don't have to tell you."

"No." Hunter studied the med's shadowed face. "You should take on apprentices. There's too much work for one."

"Apprentices?" The med laughed ruefully. "I'm not much more than one myself."

"That's not true."

"It is, you know. Jonesen was the real med here, he'd worked with the Warder for I don't know how long. Before I was born, probably. We lost him near the end of the sickness. Most of the rest of the city meds too." Hunter wondered briefly if the Church had known about that, or cared. Lia went on, "He took me on when I was just a girl. He used to watch me with the other orphans in the Warder's shelter. He said he saw something in me, I can't imagine what." Her mouth curved at the memory, eyes misting. "I had the sickness myself, and Jonesen never left my side, even after he started getting ill. I would have died without him, but by the time I was well enough to do anything, it was too late for him." She smiled again, with an effort. "Who was it who taught you?"

But Hunter's mind had snagged on something else. "The Warder shelters orphans?"

"Yes." The med pursed her lips in surprise. "Didn't

you know? He takes them in, all that make their way to him, if there isn't anywhere else for them to go. I thought that's why you brought that baby. . . ."

The children would be safe here.

She refused to call the thing beating wings against her ribcage hope. It was simply good sense, she told herself, another duty she could fulfill. Three lives that didn't have to be wasted after all.

She only needed to go back to the desert to retrieve them. They wouldn't want to come, at first, especially not the fierce girl, but they'd be sensible enough once they understood that there would be food and a safe place to sleep. It would take some time for them to get used to being around so many strangers; the boy probably wouldn't speak to anyone for weeks and the girl might never give up hiding food and weapons, but at least there wouldn't be canids sniffing around their camp every night, and the toddler would adapt quickest of all. She felt a strange lifting in her chest as her lungs tried to take too deep a breath. It would work. It must. All she had to do was—

"Are you all right?" Lia was staring at her, eyes wide with concern.

"I need to see the Warder." She looked straight at Lia, no disguises now. "Please."

CHAPTER 15

"**C**hildren!" The Warder's voice thinned with anger as the pointless questions tumbled out. "How could you just leave them there? Children alone in the desert? Why didn't you bring them with you?"

"I asked them," she said sensibly, "but they were afraid. They didn't want to come."

"*Asked* them? For Saint's sake, what were you thinking? You should have *made* them. There are times you don't ask children what they want, don't you realize? You make them do what's best for them, because you know and they don't. I can't imagine leaving them to face all the dangers beyond the wall. It's been sevens now! Why haven't you said something before? So little food, and the canids, and the hunters have warned us that in some places there are holes in the ground, and terrible falls if you aren't careful. . . ." He shook his head, looking at her, anger running out of him all at once. "I see I'm not telling you anything you haven't already told yourself. I just wish you had made them come."

"I didn't know you would take them in."

His voice rose again, bafflement rather than anger this time. "Saints, child, what do you think we are?"

She couldn't think of anything to say.

The Warder puffed a frustrated breath, twizzling a stray bit of thread between his fingers. "When you first came to us, I asked Loro to look around where you found the baby you brought here. Where you told us, and," he added, apologetically, "a little bit farther. Just in case you might have, well, been confused about where you'd run across him. Abandoned children . . . I wasn't sure whether to believe you, but if by chance there were more nearby, I wanted to find them right away. Of course I didn't think to ask you, I just assumed that anyone who knew such a thing would have said . . ." He shook his head, frustration directed at himself now. "I should have thought more carefully. If Loro had known exactly where to look, he would have found them, you know." Behind him, Loro nodded, frowning at Hunter as if he blamed her for thwarting his efforts. It would have been a triumph for him to bring more children to the Warder. For a perverse moment, she was glad she had set a false trail. Then sense kicked in with a profound ache.

"He wouldn't have. They wouldn't want to be found, not by strangers. But they're out there. They know me; they wouldn't hide if I went back."

The Warder did not answer directly. "Lia tells me that you know your way around a difficult situation. She likes you, and she's very grateful for your help. That makes me grateful as well."

"The Ward is lucky to have her," Hunter said. *The children*, she urged him inwardly. She could only focus a small part of her attention on anything else. *I want to go look for the children*.

"Yes," the Warder agreed. It took her a fraction of a second to realize that he was still referring to Lia. "She's our only med since last winter, you know."

"She told me."

He nodded. "A dark time for us all, a very dark time. Lia thinks you could be a great help to us, if you would be willing to stay." Behind him, Loro twitched. The Warder must not have shared his plan with him, or maybe the offer had been spontaneous.

She gave a small shrug, as if it didn't overly matter to her whether she stayed or not. It was nearly true in this moment. "I'd like to go look for the children myself," she said again.

The Warder leaned back in his chair, fingers steepling. "Loro, please don't feel that you need to stay. Echo and I will be fine. I'm sure you have other things you have to see to."

Loro straightened. "Nothing that can't wait."

"I appreciate it, you know I do, but truly, it isn't necessary for you to inconvenience yourself. Please, I would just feel guilty for wasting your time."

"No, sir, really. I don't mind staying."

"Yes, I know," the Warder said gently. "But you may go."

Loro came around the side of the desk so Hunter could see his face. He did not speak what he was thinking, not in front of the Warder, but his glare made it perfectly clear. She was beginning to find him tedious. "All right, then, if you're sure you don't need me." The Warder nodded again, leaving him no choice.

After the door closed, the Warder said apologetically, "He's a bit on edge right now. There was a little incident with the Benders last week. We don't really have any problems with them, you know, just every now and then the young men's tempers run a little hot. Especially with the tithe not so very far away. He's just always been protective of me."

It was the same excuse Lia had made for Loro. Maybe it was even true. "I can't fault him for being cautious," she said, which was also true; but it only made it more surprising that he would leave her alone with the Warder, unless it was a test. Or maybe the Warder was really enough of a fool to trust her. Either way, she wanted to be done with it and out searching. There wasn't much time to spare. If the children realized they were being hunted, they would disappear.

"Especially in these times, perhaps." The Warder paused, eyes wandering to the prints on the shelves behind her. "I've had word that the Church excommunicated a hunter some weeks ago."

All Hunter's attention snapped to the man in front of her. She had planted the trail carefully to lead to this moment, but that made it no less dangerous. If they suspected her of treachery—well, there had been guards outside the door when she arrived, and test or not, Loro no doubt needed only the slightest excuse. If it came to that, she could almost certainly escape with her life, but that was worth nothing if she lost her foothold in the Ward. "I heard that too," she agreed noncommittally.

The Warder looked directly at her. "Was it you?"

"Yes." She sat calmly, letting him study her, a scrutiny almost as thorough as the Patri's, despite the filmy eyes.

"Why did they do it, child?"

"I asked too many questions." He would have heard that much at least, and there was no reason to lie. Still, the words pricked at the back of her throat like tiny splintered bones that stuck going down.

He nodded slowly. "Then you went to the desert. That's how you found those children."

"Yes." She hesitated, weighing how far she could go. If she pushed too hard, he might cut her loose altogether, leaving her back where she had started the day she entered the city, or worse. She could not risk that. But the soft lines of his face sagged, reminding her that there might be another way with him. And she wanted that other way, or everything she had worked for would have been wasted. "I'd like to go look for them, please."

The Warder rose, walking to his window. Another test, perhaps, his back turned to her and nothing between him and the drop but a thin pane of glass. But this was not the Church: a hunter might be bold enough to tempt her that way; she doubted that a cityen would. And besides, whatever rumors of discontent had reached the Patri, the cityens had four hundred annuals of the hunters' protection behind them. The Warder would surely not think one capable of such a thing. Even one who had been excommunicated.

The Warder looked down across the city, hands clasped behind him. "How many do the Church estimate lived here before the Fall?"

"Four million," she answered, startled by the heaviness in his voice.

"And perhaps forty thousand of us now. Barely enough to inhabit the edges of these ruins. You would think, after four hundred years, that we would have started to recover." He tapped the glass with a fingernail. It rang like a crystal bell. "Oh, some ways, we have, we have. We've unearthed some of the old skills, rebuilt some of the simple machines. We have fabricators now, you know, more than a handful, who can make wonderful things like this window. We even understand some of the machines we've found buried in the ruins, though we can't begin to repair or remake them. Primitive, our ancestors from Before would have called us, but we are making progress. Sometimes we even figure out how to do a thing ourselves, before the Church shows us." *A time may come that they think they know more than we do.* But the Warder's voice held sorrow, not triumph. "Last winter, more of us died in the sickness than had been born in the spring. That hadn't happened in a long time, at least since I was a boy. Many of the children, our most precious resource, were left without parents."

"I know that part," she said, an edge creeping into her voice.

"Yes, of course you do." He paused, pressing the pads of his hand lightly against the pane, like Lia examining the gravid woman's belly. "A few more years like that, and there won't be anything left of us but a handful of savages, fighting with each other for scraps." His sigh was not for whatever he saw out the window. "Sometimes I think we're just postponing the long slide down into the dark."

"The Church will preserve us." Her reply was automatic, like the signal sent from the sanctuary out into the desert. What did it mean, if there was no one to hear? Her reflection hung mute beside the Warder's, ghostly in the glass.

The Warder spoke to the ghost. "Sometimes I wonder. Priests who huddle over instruments, never venturing outside the Church walls, a few hunters copying yourselves over and over—what for? I know the teachings, of course I do, but sometimes I have to wonder. Why do you keep doing it? Why do we?"

How dare he question? She stifled the flash of anger. He was a cityen; he could say what he wanted, even if he trod close to the edge of blasphemy. It was not his responsibility to share the Church's burden. Besides, he probably didn't even understand what his words meant. She said, "The Church, the Saint—they *will* preserve the city. It has always been that way, since the Fall. It always will be."

He turned to face her, and she saw that he understood completely. "You believe that, do you?"

"Yes." It was not the Warder's gaze she felt, but Tana's, sightless eyes staring at her, seeing the lie. The betrayal.

"Yet they threw you away," the Warder said, very softly. "Your hunters and priests."

The jagged bones in her throat stabbed in time with her pulse. "They did what they thought best," she whispered.

"Because you asked questions? Wanted answers for the death of a friend? Yes, I know *that* part too."

That morning on the Church steps came back to her, vivid as blood spilled fresh across bleached sand. The Patri's words, the ones that cast her out. *Disobedience. Doubt.* He had proclaimed them for all to hear, Church and city, so they would mark her anywhere she fled. Surely it had all been part of his plan. It must have been. The only way to set her on this path, bring her to this place . . . Yes, it would have been easier if she had been warned, had known what he was going to say; but then her reaction might not have been convincing enough. He had taken the safer course, trusting her to trust him, as she had promised. He had counted on her not to give in to the very things he accused her of in public. He could not have known the things she struggled not to think, still refused to consider now.

No one could.

"The Church has no room for doubt," she told the Warder and herself. "They were right to do what they did."

The Warder smiled at her sadly, as if he heard what ran beneath the words. "Not if they wasted you, Echo."

She could not answer, only stared at him, voiceless as her dead.

"Well." He dropped heavily back into his chair, then forced a smile. "You must think me terribly weak, giving in to these dark thoughts. It's true. I'm not strong, like you, but fortunately, the Church is forgiving. They can put up with an old man's ramblings. And they've lasted this long, you know, so they can't be utter fools. Maybe they'll take you back someday."

"Maybe," she whispered.

His eyes rested on her, judging more kindly than she did. "Think about my offer: until that day comes, work with us here. We would welcome it, and your skills would be put to good use. That would bring you some comfort, I think. And as I said, Lia likes you."

She was so distracted that she nearly missed the victory. The pieces had lined up neatly as a training exercise, ever since the infant had appeared in the desert—earlier even. Since that terrible day in the yard. If she'd been testing the young hunters, she would have made it more difficult than this. It was, she estimated dispassionately, a nearly perfectly executed plan. And now it could not hurt to ask—in fact, would only encourage the Warder to think *he* had won— "I'm

very grateful for the offer. And I'd like to be useful."
Yes, that would be just what she should feel and say.
"But I'd like to look for the children first, please."

He hesitated, torn. "I understand how you feel, believe me. That any child could be lost, through care-
lessness, let alone on purpose—you know how terrible
that makes me feel."

"Yes, sir."

Fingertips worried at a hem. "So you understand
how much I want to let you go. But Lia is stretched
thin—I know that she would deny it, but I see how
hard the work is on her—and there must be things
you know that she doesn't, after all. You can help her,
teach her. . . . The desert is dangerous, isn't it, even for
a hunter? I don't like to have to say this, but it's been
more than three sevens now, hasn't it, and the chances
that those children survive seem, well . . . I'm so sorry,
truly. But it would only compound the waste if something happened to *you* out there."

"One day," she bargained, like a cityen arguing over
chits. "That's all I ask. Then I'm yours."

He should say no. His argument had been sound, a
safe plan to make the best of his resources. He knew
it too, she could see that in his eyes. But he looked at
her as if it mattered how she felt, and he gave in. "Very
well. I suppose a day is not so much to ask. Loro will
go with you—yes, I think it's necessary. I know you
can handle yourself, but two are safer than one, even if
the one is you. I wouldn't like an accident to befall that
a simple action could have prevented."

She didn't argue further; she had her victory, after all. "Thank you," she said, swallowing hard.

"One other thing, Echo."

She waited.

"Most of us don't know what—who you are. Hunters look alike, but with that long hair, and wearing our clothes—or maybe it's just that up close, the resemblance isn't as great as we expect. At any rate, only Lia and myself are certain. Best to keep it that way." He pulled on his hem, nervous for the first time. "We've kept with your story that you're a trader from the north clave, but we, you know, added a bit. We've been saying you had some trouble there, and spent a while living alone on the edges." Like the deranged man she had seen talking to himself when she first came into the city. She raised an eyebrow, amused despite everything else. Tana would have laughed outright. The Warder's thin lips curved into a relieved smile at her reaction. "Well, you know, it will go a ways towards explaining anything—unusual—that you do. But please, be careful, especially with Loro. He has no great love of the Church. They took his sister, you see, when he was a boy. I'm afraid that no matter how well he understands the necessity, he'll never forgive them for that. Better for everyone if you don't remind him of his grievances."

Little changed after that day, except that sometimes the faces of the children added themselves to the rest of the silently watching dead in Hunter's dreams.

Maybe if she had respected them less, regarded them properly as cityens instead of pretending to herself that she could teach them the same skills that helped juvenile hunters survive the desert—*but Ela didn't survive*—maybe they would have been afraid to stay alone, and Lia would be looking after them now, and they would be safe. But there was no point imagining things that had not happened, Hunter told herself, and wishing against what had simply wasted energy that could be put to better use helping Lia now.

Saints knew there was enough work to be done. Sometimes, if the waiting room emptied long enough before dark, the med, attended by Loro or another guard, even went out to see those who couldn't come to her. Hunter would have found these excursions both useful and diverting, but Loro and his men always found an excuse to prevent her. She was not a prisoner, exactly, but they contrived to limit her movement nearly as if she were, and the times she was left alone, there always seemed to be at least one guard about, who would watch over her politely but carefully, with the explanation, when she asked, that there was nothing at all unusual going on, they always watched the clinic like this. She wondered if the Warder had set them to it, or whether it was all Loro's doing. Despite his youth, the men clearly followed him, and she could see why; he was brusque with them, but in a comradely way, and there was no denying the air of competence he brought to everything he did.

That was why, despite the urgency coiling in her

chest, she had taken a long way round to the camp when they went in search of the children, laying down any number of false routes and detours so that Loro would not be able to return to the spot without her. Knowing at once from the empty smell and cold silence that the children were not there, had not been there for days at least, she gave only a cursory glance inside the remains of the shelter. She spent the rest of that dead day peering into other cracks and crevices, never hinting to Loro that the search was long since over. She told herself that the children had learned well from her, had moved on as a precaution once she left them, too clever to leave a sign, were out there somewhere unharmed, maybe even watching, warmed to see that she had returned for them after all. Just in case, she scuffed a squiggle in the dust outside the shelter, the field mark she'd taught them for *safe*. They would recognize that, and her familiar bootprints.

Beyond that there was nothing she could do for them.

Lia was out again this evening, and the clinic felt intolerably airless. Hunter stood, shoving her chair back with a squeal. Justan, dozing on one of the beds like a curly-haired canid on a sunny ledge, leapt up at the noise. She brushed by him, strode through the empty anteroom, and yanked the outside door open to face the two startled clinic guards. "I'm going for a walk," she said politely.

They eyed her, uncertain they had the authority to let her go alone. Any number of options to fix that presented themselves, but most of them would have involved exposing more of her skills than she was ready to do. Instead she stood waiting until Justan caught up, then turned to him with what she hoped was the right amount of contained desperation for the trader she was still playing and said, "I just need to stretch my legs." Which was true; and if one of them went along, he might feel like talking. She could at least put the dull hour before Lia got back to some good use.

"How 'bout I go with you?" Justan asked.

"I'd welcome that," she said, wishing with a twinge that it had been one of the guards she knew less well, who now resumed their stations with the satisfaction of men who had done their jobs. She knew they were trying. Like Lia's patients, the guards talked, enough that she had learned there was a tension running through the city, something making the men worried and ill at ease. It seemed to do with the nun tithe, coming up as the harvest neared. And they weren't lying to her about watching the clinic: even here, inside the Warder's stronghold, they checked before they opened inner doors, and if young men, strangers to the clave, came to the clinic, they sometimes searched them before admitting them to Lia's presence. Their efforts would be insufficient, Hunter thought, fingering the small blade she had purloined from Lia's tools, if there were a serious threat, but they could not know that.

They are not hunters, she reminded herself. And, with a little chill: *they have done all this without any hunter's help.*

The street was empty. She craned her neck, studying the darkening sky. The lightstrings washed it out; she could only see a few of the brightest stars. Justan said, "Best time of year to see them. I could stand out here a long time watching."

They resumed their walk. "Want some of this?" He offered her dried meat from a packet he'd secreted somewhere. She shook her head. He took a generous portion for himself. "Sure?" She shook her head again. The meat had been smoked; the smell tickled high in the back of her throat. He passed her his water holder.

"Noticed you don't talk too much," he said.

She considered. "I do when I have something to say."

"Good way to do it. Most people aren't so sensible, I suppose. Some cityens, they talk all day long, never take a breath."

She thought of the nuns. "What do they talk about?"

"Most everything, I guess. Day's a pretty long time. Figure you can fit pretty much most things in it."

"What do you fit in, Justan? When you're not guarding me, I mean?"

He chewed thoughtfully for a moment. "Well, I'm pretty sure you noticed I try to get my meals." He patted his belly, which in fact protruded a little way over his belt. He must have been miserable through the winter's shortages.

"What about your work?"

"Oh, Loro keeps me busy. This and that. Ward's pretty spread out these days. Always somewhere needs a little help. Sometimes even the Bend. Pretty much only place we don't go's into North."

That was an interesting tidbit. "Not friendly to the Warder?"

"Not friendly to anybody. Got too much they're trying to keep. Don't want to hear too much about sharing."

"They share with the Church, don't they? Pay the tithe?"

"That's different. Nobody's going to argue with the Church. Those hunters see to that. You'd have to be a crazy fool."

Hunter scanned the sky, but the stars were still hidden. "What would happen?"

The frown marred the boyish features. "Can't say for sure. Seems like they'd make examples, though. So no one would try the same thing again."

I'd set fire to the building, Gem had said, *and force them back inside.*

"I don't think they'd do that," Hunter told him.

Justan stopped walking. They were almost all the way around the block. He smiled. "You're nicer than most traders, Echo. I've been thinking. Maybe we could—"

She whirled away.

"Wait, I didn't mean to—" Then Justan heard it too: a shout, and feet pounding hard across the pavestones.

A running figure appeared at the end of the street, moving fast. "Quick, back to the clinic," Justan said, everything else forgotten.

But the runner had already seen them and changed course. Hunter kicked a stone aside, making sure of her footing. Justan put himself between the approaching man and her. *Saints. Protecting me.* She closed her hand around the little knife in her pocket. The runner slowed. "Justan, is that you?"

"Teller? What in the Saint's—" In the lightstring's glow, the arm of Teller's shirt was dark and wet.

"Benders," Teller gasped, clutching the arm. "I need Lia."

Justan nodded, grabbing Teller's other arm. "Anybody following you?" The man shook his head. "All right. Voren"—this to one of the clinic guards who had come running at the noise—"you stay out here. Keep an eye."

They were inside the clinic a minute later. Lia hadn't returned yet; Hunter got out the necessary supplies while Teller told his story, a towel clamped over the jagged cut the length of his forearm. "We were just out making checks. Heard about something happening on the edge of Bend and North, so we swung up to see. There was—"

A signal knock sounded on the door, and Loro flew in. "Teller! I heard. What happened?"

"I was just saying. There was a bunch of Benders, blocked off the end of an alley. Some hunters were headed that way. Don't know what they wanted, but Benders got the idea they'd try to keep them out. We had to take care of that quick."

Hunter's hand froze on the pack she was unrolling. "You got this in a fight with hunters?"

Teller snorted in exasperation. "Course not. Benders. Had to get that barricade down, didn't we? Hunters got there after. They thanked us." He laughed shortly. "Even offered to escort us back, like we'd need it in the Ward."

Hunter busied herself with the instruments so the men couldn't see her face. They could have come here. Hunters could have come here. Her chest ached at the thought. "Did they say their names?" she asked, trying to sound merely curious.

"Think we'd ask? Hardly tell one from the other anyway, they're all the same to look at, aren't they? We just thanked 'em and got the Benders out of there before they could make more trouble. Last thing we need is hunters thinking cityens are getting in their way. Don't want no confrontations."

"Not yet," Loro said.

CHAPTER 16

Occasional reports of hunters trickled in after that, but from what Hunter could glean their activities remained routine. They patrolled the stads south of the Ward, protecting the grain that was nearly ready for harvest; they escorted medical priests to the parts of the city that had no access to a med. Once, to Teller's dour satisfaction, they took away a Bender whom they'd caught stealing crop powder, even though he could have had it free for his crops if he'd just asked. The relative quiet was advantageous; Hunter needed as much time as she could get to understand the situation in the Ward. It seemed more complex than the Patri's information had led him to believe. When Hunter reported back to him—if she ever did—she had to have the details right.

Yet against all sense, a thread of disappointment wove through her relief.

Meanwhile the need to play the cityen role wore at her. Over and over, the guards made mistakes she would not have tolerated in young hunters she was teaching, missed potential threats that even the children—*no, don't think about that*—would have recognized. Saints, they even trusted her now alone with Lia, leaving her to sleep unguarded in the clinic, separated from the med only by a door whose primitive lock would not stop her for a dozen heartbeats if she meant to get past it. . . .

She fretted all the while they let Lia wander the streets, accompanied only by a guard or two, or even just Milse; if the Warder had calculated that Hunter was too valuable to lose, there was no equation at all that justified risking their med. And Hunter suspected that the visits Lia made were to those too ill to be moved, for whom there was nothing she could do anyway; she almost always came back downcast, and said little about where she had been.

After those visits Lia spent much time searching through the prints, studying page after page under the lightstring's harsh glare until she finally retreated to her room, in the back of the clinic, defeated. One such evening when the guards had left and she sat sorting through random sheets while Hunter repaired a broken chair, Lia looked up suddenly, eyes red-rimmed, and asked, "Can you read?"

"Yes," Hunter answered, startled, the hammer dangling from her hand.

"Would you be willing to help me with these prints?

The pages are so random, just bits and pieces gathered from wherever people found them. . . . Jonesen knew them better, but he had just begun to show me. It's so frustrating. Sometimes I see someone sick and I know the thing to do is in here somewhere, if I could only find it. . . ." She broke off, passing a hand across her eyes.

"You can't expect to help them all," Hunter said. "Even the Saint can't do that."

"Can she really heal?" Lia asked wistfully.

There had been the nun whose blood the Saint had cleansed, and others from time to time. But Ela, Tana . . . "Sometimes. If the sickness is temporary, and the body is strong enough. Not someone like that old man with the heart," she added. For some reason it seemed important that Lia not blame herself for him.

The med riffled the corners of the stacked prints. "Maybe not," she said with a sigh. "But there's plenty in here to help others. I thought if I could mark them somehow, make a list of what there is, I would at least have a place to start. It would go faster, if you could help me."

"I can do that," Hunter said, pulling the chair to the desk.

Lia touched a fingertip to the back of Hunter's hand as she reached for the first print. "Thank you, Echo."

Hunter would have expected to find the work dull as she had always imagined the priests' to be. For hours in the evenings after visits, she sat across the worktable from Lia, sorting through sheets trying to match like-sized pages or similar lettering styles. It turned out to be not so different from the times she spent in the desert, studying some prey in minute detail, lying motionless as a stone while she absorbed every facet of her surroundings. Surprisingly, she began to look forward to the task. The pages, yellow with age and brittle as old bones, some of them partially burned or with bits torn away, made a puzzle she could concentrate on, keeping her mind from other, darker thoughts. There were a few captures, images preserved astoundingly lifelike, with some tech that had long been lost. Mostly, though, the prints contained unadorned text, page after dense page, as if someone had tried to cram the most information into the smallest possible space.

Most of the content was meaningless to her, and probably would be to the med as well. It was not that she could not read the words; rather, the world before the Fall was so far removed that prescience alone had been insufficient to preserve their sense across the chasm. She imagined the forefathers in the last spasms of the catastrophe they knew was upon them, scrambling to leave a legacy, trying to prevent their accumulated knowledge from hemorrhaging away into the dark. They must have known the hopelessness of the attempt even as they made it. She admired their doggedness, little good though it had done.

Yet every now and then she came across a fragment of unmistakable value, a bit on the diagnosis of disease or treatment of an injury. Those always won a smile from Lia. It was its own form of pleasure too to watch the med transcribe her notes in a tiny, precise hand from the random scraps they found into orderly columns on the sheets of blank print Milse brought her. "Exey sends his love," Milse said one day, flitting in with a small stack of the material.

"He's amazing," Lia said, holding a sheet up to the light. It was fine textured, not quite white, and thin enough for the light to shine through it. "He takes the old prints that are too damaged to read, finds some way to soak them and roll them out, and dries them back into sheets." She waggled the delicate stylus she used to write. "It's a big improvement. On the old ones the ink bled so much I could hardly fit anything onto a sheet."

"He always brags about being the best fabricator in the city," Milse said. "Course, all the Benders brag, but in Exey's case it's actually true, not that I think anyone should tell him so. The best thing is, he's helping the millers get another windwheel working. Once it's fixed it'll only take a few minutes to get a whole sack of grain ground, fine as you could want. It'll take an hour off my day. And wait until you taste the bread." His eyes widened in exaggerated appreciation, then narrowed dramatically. "We'll have to fight off Justan to let anyone else get a share."

Lia laughed. "That's hard enough already."

"Speaking of, where's Justan been? Used to hang around here all the time. Now I never see him anymore."

"He traded off with Teller, I don't know why. I've lost track of the days, Milse," Lia added ruefully. "When's market again?"

"You work too hard," Milse reproved her. "We're halfway through the seven. You should take better care of yourself."

"I'm fine," Lia protested.

"You're not! Look at you. You see people all day in the clinic, then you sit up half the night like this. Saint's sake, take some time for yourself. Sleep, go to market. Get out of these rooms for a little while, for something other than some awful bloody mess. And you," he added, jabbing an accusatory finger at Hunter. "Just because you never need to rest doesn't mean she doesn't."

"Don't go on at her," Lia murmured, setting the writing tool aside with a sigh. "She just does what I ask."

"Well, I think she looks like someone who knows her own mind," Milse grumbled. "I know the Warder gives out that you're some crazy woman from North, but I don't believe it. I know what you really are."

"Leave her alone, Milse," Lia said with a laugh, but Hunter heard the sudden tension in her voice.

"No, go ahead, I'm curious." She was more than curious: if people knew she was a hunter, she hadn't picked up any sign of it. Nonetheless, she casually uncrossed her legs and let her feet rest lightly on the floor, just in case he reached for anything in the pockets of his overshirt. "You really know?" she asked.

Milse crossed his arms emphatically. "I do. You're

really a perfectly sane woman from North. You've just realized there's something better to do than spend all your time piling up your own chits, like try to make things a little better for everyone else." He broke into a broad smile. "The Warder's message is getting around at long last; take care of each other, don't wait for someone else to do it. One of these days, everyone will listen. I'm glad you did. Our Lia needed the help, more than I could give, for certain. I just wish that *you'd* give *her* a few orders for once. She'd listen to you. Try telling her to eat and sleep, for starters." With that, he bounced triumphantly out the door.

"Well," Lia said, after a bemused pause. "That wasn't quite what I expected him to say."

"Maybe he's right," Hunter told her.

"About what?"

"Listening to me." She felt a strange lightness in her heart. "Go and get some sleep."

It was one of the captured images fished out of a stack of prints that brought Hunter up short, fingers pressing hard to the table to keep her motionless while her vision blurred and her throat tightened around a hard lump. She forced her face to stillness, but Lia noticed anyway, forehead creasing with concern as she reached across the table to slide the page out from under Hunter's nerveless fingers. Her lips pursed in a soundless *ooh* of dismay. "I'm so sorry, Echo. I wish you could have found them."

"It doesn't matter," she said to Lia. They hadn't discussed the children since the day Hunter had failed to bring them back.

"It does matter," Lia chided gently. "You must have cared about them very much."

Hunter stared unseeing at the capture. "I taught them what I could while time permitted, that was all." *The loss rate has been acceptable*, she remembered saying once. Ela stared at her impassively. Tana. They didn't say whether they would still agree. Her shoulders twitched in a spasm she forced into a shrug. "What happened after that wasn't up to me."

"Oh, Echo." Lia's golden eyes brimmed. "Don't you even know when something hurts?"

Very early the next morning they were awakened by a frantic pounding on the clinic door. Sounds of argument brought Hunter to her feet and ready, but it was only Justan who entered with an urgent message for Lia. Quickly gathering supplies into a bag, the med told Hunter, "Come with me. We have to hurry."

Loro stood in the frame of the outer door, blocking the way of a man craning his neck to see in over Loro's shoulder. "Exey," Lia exclaimed. "What's wrong?"

"My brother's wife," the man told her. Exey was the fabricator who made the paper, Hunter remembered. "It's the baby. She's been trying since yesterday, but it won't come. She's gotten awfully weak. No one knows what to do."

"Benders," Loro spat.

"Cityens," the man retorted. "Same as you. Lia's all our med, not just the Ward's."

"I'm not taking her into the Bend, not at night."

"My brother's wife is at my shop," Exey said harshly. "Neutral ground, just like this place."

"Please, Loro," Lia said, getting between them. "There isn't much time."

"It's too dangerous."

"*Please.*"

Loro puffed out his cheeks. "All right then. We'll all go. You first, Justan. Go ahead, take Teller." But to Hunter he said, "Not you."

"I might need her help. Please," Lia repeated. "We have to hurry."

Loro shot a dark look at Hunter as if he suspected that she had devised whatever incident it was specifically to work her way further into Lia's favor. Hunter returned him her blandest stare. "You've never needed help before."

"I haven't had it before," the med said sharply, caught up in the tension, then her tone softened and she smiled. "You'll be with us, Loro. Nothing will happen."

Loro hissed a breath through his teeth, shaking his head, but he held the door open for Lia to pass. As Hunter went to follow, he barred the way with his arm. "Do exactly what I say out there, hear me?"

If she pinned his hand against the jamb it would be a simple matter to snap his elbow with a quick strike. The temptation was so shocking that it froze her in place. Loro saw her hesitate and misunderstood. "Good." He jerked his hand back, letting her pass. They were halfway down the street before she trusted herself to breathe again.

Exey led them in a race through still-dark streets Hunter had not seen before, though she recognized the general direction as Bend-wards. They passed quickly from the broader passages of the Ward to narrow alleys that had barely been cleared, snaking among tumbled-down wrecks that might not have been touched at all since the Fall, and the few lights strung along the road were very far apart. The claves abutted closely here, she recalled from the maps she had studied, but what seemed a short distance on the map made for a nervous trot in the dark. Loro and Exey went first. Justan hurried Hunter and the med close behind, eyes darting from mounds of tumbled debris to the twisting turns of the way ahead, moving nimbly despite his girth. Teller followed last of all, making certain no one could come up behind them.

Once they had to skirt what looked like a flattened mound of purposely burned fiber. Melted polymer had hardened across the dust. There were footprints in it, bare ones. Whoever had made them when that plastic was hot wouldn't have been walking for a long time after. "What happened there?" she whispered to Justan, hoping Lia hadn't seen.

"Benders," he hissed back. "With a grudge. Come on, this isn't a good place t' stop."

Hunter stayed as close to the med as she could, extending her senses in all directions to search out any threat. Her heart pounded out of proportion to the exertion. She had run through streets like this before, hurrying another girl along a dangerous road. That had ended in death. But this time nothing happened, and after a while the alleys began to widen again, rubble clearing into more orderly spaces, until finally Exey stopped them in front of a shop, displayed wares just visible behind translucent panes on each side of the door. A few people had gathered outside, murmuring and pacing anxiously the way cityens did when they had nothing useful to offer. Family, Hunter supposed, or neighbors.

Loro made them wait while he went inside. Even through the door Hunter could hear a long muffled groan, followed by a series of sobbing breaths. Exey bounced on his toes, craning his neck to see in, anxious as if it were his own woman in there. Finally Loro returned, jerking his head at the doorway, and Lia rushed inside, Hunter at her heels.

A brief glance as they passed through showed a room much like the trade Hunter had visited her first night in the city, goods neatly stacked around a clean-swept wooden floor. There was no time to see more; Loro led the way down some stairs into the workshop proper. It reminded Hunter of the priests' laboratories in the vaults of the Church. Workbenches along the walls held various equipment laid out in orderly fashion, tools mounted above with equal precision. A large table that probably belonged in the center had been pushed to one side to give more space on the floor. Lightstrings had been rigged much more carefully than usual, in a pattern that would give excellent illumination to the benches and table. Most of the lights were off; only a single string of shaded bulbs lit a woman who lay on a pallet on the floor, her swollen belly bared by skirts that had worked their way up around her chest as she writhed. She groaned again as Lia knelt by her legs, making a rapid assessment. Hunter moved quickly to take her shoulders, propping her from behind, and making sure no flailing hands could reach the med.

"Shh . . . Shh . . ." the med crooned. "You're fine, fine. . . ." She looked up at the boy wringing his hands by her side. Exey's younger brother, no doubt. "This is her first, isn't it?" He nodded, white faced with fear. "That's why she's having such a hard time. We just need to turn the baby. She'll be all right."

Hunter heard the tension behind Lia's reassuring words. She remembered the woman at the clinic, whose first baby had been wrong way up.

That baby had died.

The young father clutched at the edge of the table. Lia said, "Why don't you wait outside? It won't help if you faint on top of us." The boy fled almost before she finished telling him to go. "Loro, could you send someone for more water? This will be messy."

Hours later, Lia washed as best she could in a corner while the exhausted woman held the baby to a small breast while the young man, nearly as pale, sat beaming by her side. "Th-th-this is all I h-have—" The boy couldn't get the rest out, only pushed a still shaking hand in Lia's direction, something shiny in his palm. Offering payment, Hunter realized, but not the old stamped gold chits the Church issued; rather, these were coppery, irregular, as if someone had melted wire and poured it into home-made molds.

Lia shook her head, smiling. "Don't worry, I—"

"We don't need that," Loro interrupted from the doorway where he'd been rebuffing anxious visitors. "Here's how you pay us back: anyone asks, you just say the Warder sent help when you needed it. Sent it free, even to the Bend. Make sure everyone knows. Hear me?"

"Of c-c-course. I w-will."

"Good." Loro glanced down at the swaddled form. "Boy or girl?"

"Girl," Lia said. She stopped smiling.

Loro's gaze darkened. "By the time she's old enough, it won't matter."

That night, when they sat across Lia's worktable alone as usual, Hunter said, "You didn't need my help this morning."

Lia spread her hands palm up, unabashed. "I wanted you to see."

"I've seen babies born before."

She sounded too like a young hunter trying hard to

act unimpressed, but Lia took no offense. Instead the med asked curiously, "The ones the nuns bear? Is it the same?"

Hunter remembered the young women in the brightly lit infirmary, each tended by a priest and one or two of the older nuns, everything calm and orderly until the strong squalling babies fought their way into the world with hunter fierceness. All while wide-eyed older versions of themselves watched, learning first-hand where they came from. "Some of it is." Considering, she admitted, "I only saw a few."

"I've lost track of how many I've helped bring out by now. It's a good change. Jonesen, the old med I learned from—" Lia's eyes misted, before she went on briskly, "He told me that his teacher's teacher remembered when it first happened that more babies were born alive than dead. Even then most of them didn't survive. Healthy infants, ones formed right, were so rare, people would come from all around to look at them."

Hunter nodded. "If the first generations hadn't listened to the priests and coupled with the mates they were assigned to, it would have been even worse. Without the variability there wouldn't be any cityens at all."

Lia looked at her thoughtfully. "There are still hunters. Are you really all the same?"

Gem, standing over Tana's lifeless body in the Churchyard. *Do you think something's happened to the line?* "The denas are. How they're expressed can vary."

Lia's golden eyes rested on Hunter. "I've seen hunters before, of course, but never anyone like you."

It was hard not to look away, to speak evenly past the constriction in her breath. "I was made the same as every other."

"It must be quite a process. I can't imagine a whole Churchful of you."

"It isn't exactly—" Hunter started to explain further, then stopped at the light in Lia's eyes. She was, she realized, kindly, gently, being *teased*. It was so unlikely that she could only sit there with her mouth open, waiting helplessly for it to shape words.

The med grinned, pleased with herself. "Well, it doesn't matter anyway, I guess; the cityens can only make babies their own way." She chuckled, the habitual gravity falling away unexpectedly, a momentary glimpse of what she'd look like happy and carefree, like the pampered nuns. If only she'd been tithed as a child, Hunter thought with a sudden pang, those lines wouldn't be carved so deep; the little laugh she gave now would come so much easier. "And they seem to like it. Good thing, too: the city's going to need all the children we can make for a long, long time."

"The city's going to need the Church for a long time too."

Hunter regretted the words instantly as the med's face turned sober again. "People don't like the tithe very well."

"I know." Hunter remembered the lesson Tana had tried to teach her so long ago. "But if they thought about it, they should. The Church just takes a few girls, and their life is so much easier than in the city. They're provided for, they're given shelter and plenty to eat even in a bad annual—the people who care for them should be happy to have them chosen."

Lia leaned back in her chair, eyelids starting to droop. Exey had awakened them very early. "If they got to choose, maybe they would be. But the girls are just taken away, want to or not, and even if it's not that many, every family is sure it will be their daughter. *You* wouldn't know, but being so helpless feels awful. It frightens people, and that makes them angry. Afterwards, when they remember why the Church did it, they do feel better, but it isn't easy. It's always been like that, long as I can remember, but this year . . . Somehow it feels different. The tithe is soon, and people are saying things. . . . Almost like they're planning to do something about it this time."

Everything went still inside Hunter, the way it did in the desert when she finally sighted her prey after a long time tracking. *The tithe is coming, and I'm concerned that it will provide a focus for the misguided*, the Patri had said. Lia sat across from her, trusting, innocent. That couldn't be allowed to matter. The Patri's doubts had centered around one particular cityen. If he had plans, and if he had confided them to Lia . . .

"Have you asked the Warder what he thinks?" Hunter asked, mouth dry.

"Yes, of course."

"And?"

"He told me that it was natural, in the circumstances I see people in, to hear the worst of their fears, and that I don't need to be concerned about it. We didn't discuss it again." The corner of her mouth lifted. "He doesn't want me to worry, and I don't want him to worry that I'm worried." The med stifled a yawn. "Sorry. Long day. You must be tired too, even though you never seem to show it."

As if the words made it so, a weariness flooded through Hunter that had nothing to do with the hours awake. "I'm fine."

"Liar," Lia murmured, then sighed and pushed herself to her feet. Hunter rose too, reaching an arm to steady her. The med leaned into the support for a moment. "Goodnight, Echo. Thank you for watching out for me today."

And Hunter stood a long time, staring at the closed door, a hand to the cheek that burned where the med's lips had ever so lightly brushed against it.

CHAPTER 17

"Welcome, my dear." The Warder kissed Lia on the cheek, gesturing for her to enter. A cool, slightly damp palm met Hunter's hand. "Welcome to you too. We're glad to have you join us."

"Thank you." This room was part of his living quarters, in the same structure as his office; she had never been brought here before. This time she wasn't blindfolded. Up one set of stairs on the shady side of the building, the quarters occupied a corner, with windows that opened wide on each side to let in the breeze. The windows had real glass here too, not the repurposed polymer used so many other places in the Ward. It was, she thought, the only real sign of luxury she'd seen around him. Whatever extra resources he had, he didn't waste them on himself.

Even this late in the evening it was still hot outside, but someone had managed to rig a drop that ran a small fan, providing extra ventilation, and that along with the thick walls made the room quite comfortable. Loro, Justan, Teller, and a few other men Hunter recognized but did not know had already sat down at the table in the center. Loro patted the one empty chair between himself and Justan to show Lia she should sit there, favoring the med with a smile and Hunter with a self-satisfied stare as she was left to take a seat further down the table. She suppressed a sigh. Hunters got over these games as children.

"Here we are," Milse announced, backing through the door bearing a platter heaped with greens in one hand and a serving bowl of roasted grains in the other. He set them down with a flourish next to a loaf of the usual bread, so fresh it was still faintly steaming. The smell made Hunter's mouth water. "Last scraps of the week. Eat up, they won't last another day."

"It all looks wonderful, Milse, thank you." The Warder started the platter and passed it along the table.

"I don't know how you do it," Lia marveled, reaching for the greens. "Look, Echo, your favorite. Scraps, Milse? You always come up with something, but this is amazing."

"Well, I've had more time, since Echo's been helping you with visits these last few sevens."

"That's another reason to be glad you're here," the Warder said with a smile and nod at Hunter. "Although when I invited you to stay, I didn't realize it would have such direct benefits as on our mealtimes. It only shows how we can turn chance events to our favor if we just take care of each other. This time it's worked out all for the best."

"Uh-huh," Milse agreed, with an arch look at Lia that unaccountably made the med turn pink.

"Oh, stop," she said, but she was smiling.

The conversation wandered off from there, Justan telling some convoluted story about a friend of his, the friend's cousin, and an introduction he was angling for that had them all chuckling, even Lia. Teller, whom Hunter had rarely heard speak other than to curse the Benders, took it up from there, and the merriment escalated until people could hardly eat for laughing. Looking around the table, Hunter wondered if the Patri's fears were mistaken. It was hard to see any threat in these people. Even Loro, laughing along with the rest of them, was only a boy trying to protect his own, and doing, she had to admit, a creditable job. The Warder himself, unassuming and almost bashful, even here among his inner circle, seemed least likely of anyone she had met to challenge another cityen, let alone the Church. The Patri knew more, she reminded herself, saw broader patterns. But he hadn't been certain; that was why he had sent her to investigate.

If he had sent her. The tired old argument began again in her head, drowning out the cheerful conversation. She closed her eyes, willing her thoughts to silence.

"Okay?" Lia asked softly, touching her hand beneath the table.

Hunter caught herself back to the present, cursing

herself for letting the weakness show. She nodded, and the med sat back, but her face was troubled, Hunter's fault. Ignoring a stab of guilt, Hunter made herself turn her attention again to the others.

"Don't know about th' rest of you," Justan was saying around a mouthful, "but night b'fore market's always my favorite."

"That's because it's the one time you get to stuff yourself as much as you want," Milse snorted. "No saving up for the rest of the week."

"Jus' doing my duty," Justan protested, chewing heroically. "Can't have this good food going t' waste." He waved a crust in Hunter's direction. "Bet you didn't eat like this where you came from."

"No," Hunter said, thinking of the refectory.

"Where was that again?" Loro asked, folding a portion of grains into a broad green leaf with quick, deft movements. Up until now he had ignored her. She sighed.

"North. I thought you already knew."

"I know that's what you say."

"Loro, please don't," Lia murmured.

Ignoring the med, Loro said, "It's just sometimes I wonder."

Hunter asked mildly, "Why would I lie about it?"

"I don't know. Why would you?" Everyone was looking at them now, even Justan, cheek puffed out around a bite he was forgetting to swallow.

"Now, now," the Warder said, hands making vague patting motions in both their directions. "Let's not ruin Milse's good work with an argument. Everyone's welcome in the Ward, isn't that what we always say? Helping each other means helping strangers too."

"Yes," Loro said, "but not every stranger comes straight to your table, especially when we don't know anything about them." It was, for once, a completely sensible point of view. Hunter hoped the Warder didn't listen.

"You just let me worry about that, Loro. Echo's been with us for many sevens now, and she's shown that she's a friend, hasn't she? See, Lia agrees too. Now, let's speak of other things, shall we? Now that I think of it, I've been meaning to ask—do you know if the Benders got the mill fixed?"

After a stiff pause, Loro gave in, nodding. "They did. That print you sent Exey was just what he needed to work it out." Lia rewarded him with a smile, and he continued in a fair attempt at good humor, "The millers said they'll grind all your grain chit-free forever."

The Warder beamed. "I hope you told them that won't be necessary. The print was a gift."

"I did, but I don't think they'll be taking your chits anyway."

The lights flickered, and the fans slowed, just long enough for everyone to stop eating. Then the power caught again, and the moment of apprehension passed. "Exey thought he might be able to rig the mill to help when that happens too," Loro said.

"There's no end to that man's cleverness," Milse said. "But let's not lose sight of what's important." He pointed at the empty platter where the bread had been. "We'll have double loaves this seven. Even Justan will be sick of it."

"I can take the grain to the mill if you'd like," Lia said amidst the laughter. "I was planning to go to market tomorrow anyway." She shot a mock-innocent look at Milse, who *harrumphed* under his breath.

"Tomorrow's no good," Loro said. He glanced at the Warder. "I have plans, I can't take you."

Lia's eyebrows went up. "I've been going to market since I was old enough to carry sacks. I don't need an escort." Her smile took any sting out of the words. Of course, Hunter thought wryly, that smile could take the sting out of almost anything. Only a fool as stubborn as Loro could manage to frown back at it.

"I just don't think you should go tomorrow. There was some trouble in North again."

"Hunters?" Hunter asked, as casually as she could.

He shot a scowl at her. "Not this time, but could've been. They're everywhere these days. Getting ready for the tithe." He tore off a piece of bread. "It's making people tight. They're arguing over every little thing. The fest is coming, there's a lot of ferm around, and it's so Saints-be-praised hot—you never know what's going to happen next."

"Maybe Loro's right," the Warder said.

Unexpected anger flashed through Hunter. She had never heard Lia ask a thing for herself, and for them to deny her such a simple pleasure—

"Echo can take me," Lia said.

"Don't be ridiculous," Loro snapped.

"I'm not being ridiculous! It's only market, for Saint's sake. She may not be one of your guards, but I think if there's an argument in a chit line she can probably find a way to get me out of it. Couldn't you?" Hunter nodded solemnly, trying not to choke on the sip of water she took to hide her expression. "Besides, no one's going to start any trouble at market. Ward, Bend, even North, we all depend on it just the same."

"Trouble doesn't always think so clearly," Loro said. "Neither do the Benders. They're happy enough when you help them with their babies, then they're all friendly. You don't know them like I do, though. Yesterday there was a fight on the edge, a bad one, just because one of ours tried to cut through the gap without an invitation."

"They're just cityens, Loro. Same as us. I know everyone's tight right now, but we'll be dancing together at the fest this year like always."

"Sure we will." He squeezed a crust as if it were a Bender's neck. "What if you're wrong?"

"Then Echo will take care of me."

"I don't think—"

"You know, Loro," the Warder interrupted, smiling in apology, "I think Lia might be right. It's only market, after all. Neutral ground, no matter what else is happening."

Loro gave him a quizzical look. "Do you want me to go with her, then?"

"No, no, your errand is more important. I think Lia

will be safe enough with Echo." Loro stared at him another moment, then nodded slowly. The Warder turned the conversation then to other matters. There had been something behind that exchange, Hunter felt certain, but she had no way to probe further without being obvious, so she reluctantly let it pass. Lia, delighted with the outcome, spent the rest of the evening taking every opportunity to charm Loro back into good temper, and for the most part she seemed to succeed. Whenever his gaze happened to fall on Hunter, he frowned, but it was more thoughtful than angry, as if he were just on the verge of puzzling something out.

Given the circumstances, she would have preferred the anger.

The shortest route to the market took them past the stads. In the distant past the huge open structures had been stages for some kind of public spectacle, gathering places that between the pair of them would have held three times the population of the present city. The upper levels where seating must have been had collapsed onto themselves, the giant ramps dead-ending only a few strides after the first turn, but the outer walls still made a pair of three-quarter enclosures. The open ends faced each other, creating two vast empty areas, pavement long crumbled away, that had been easy enough to dig into fields over time as the city needed more arable land for food. The priests' crop powder made the grain grow plump and dense, and so

far the cityens had not outgrown the space. Beyond the
stads a herd of bovines grazed on weeds and stubble,
tails flicking in the heat.

"We store all the grain in there after harvest," Lia
said, pointing to the sheltered end of the smaller stad.
"It keeps better that way. People pick up their ration
and only get it milled when they're ready to use it. Or
at least they did. Nowadays, lots of times the millers
get it instead and bring it to market already ground."

"Yes, I know."

"I always forget. I keep thinking of you as a stranger,
arrived from someplace else. You probably know the
city better than I do."

Hunter shook her head. "I haven't been to this part
in many annuals. Not since training exercises when I
was juvenile."

"Really? Have you stayed in the Church all this
time?"

"No. Out in the desert mostly."

Lia's eyes widened. "I've never been outside the
forcewall. Most of us haven't. I think some of the
boys go outside to show off, sometimes. The only one
I know who spends any time out there now is Loro;
that's why the Warder sent him with you when you
went to look for the—" She broke off, touching Hunter's shoulder softly in apology. "Anyway. Loro says the
outside's exactly the same as the fringes inside and you
wouldn't even know there was a forcewall if you didn't
feel it tingle as you walked through."

Hunter's gaze wandered north. "Close in it's just

like the city. But when you go farther . . . I've been as far as the aircars can go." She paused, trying to think how to let Lia see it with her eyes. "When you turn around, all you see is nothing. The priests say that even before the Fall, the city didn't extend that far. There were small buildings maybe, but not the size of the ones inside. There's nothing much left of them now, just mounds where they fell and got covered over by dust, and a few pieces of metal sometimes. Everything that was made has burned white from the sun. It even sounds white sometimes, the way the wind can blow across the spaces. The only color is a little bit of brown where brush is rooted deep enough to find water. But I've been there right after the vernal rains, and then all the brown turns green. It's still silent, except for the wind, but if you know where to look you see the small animals scurrying everywhere. It's the one time in the annual that conditions support their reproduction." She smiled grimly to herself. "The predators do well then too."

Lia was silent for a moment, digesting that. Then: "Do all hunters go there?"

"For training." Hunter veered abruptly from that subject. "But most of the time they're assigned to the city. There's enough to be done here."

As she spoke, her eyes sought the opening to the giant U of the stads. From this distance she couldn't make them out, but they had to be there, her hunter cousins, inconspicuous in their nondescript Church garb but unmistakably hunter in their posture, the easy balanced way they would be standing relaxed but alert, watching as cityens wove in and out with baskets and pull carts. Hunter had stood with them as a juvenile, consciously mimicking their stance, small thumbs hooked into her waistband, refusing to fidget for what seemed like interminable shifts on guard duty. There might be a juvenile with them today too, another cohort getting ready to slot into place.

Lia followed her gaze. "Do you miss them very much?" she asked softly.

Dust kicked up from the street; she had to clear her throat to answer. "I can't see them from here."

She knew from Lia's expression that that wasn't the question the med had asked, but that was all the answer she had.

Hunter expected the market to seem smaller, less chaotic, than it had when she was juvenile. Instead it was the opposite: where she remembered a few rows of carts offering little more than a selection of greens and some sacks of flour, now the market overflowed out of a square three long blocks on a side. Most of the carts carried grain products still, Hunter saw, in sacks of varying sizes that might hold a day's supply or a week's, but some offered other wares as well, a bright pile of round red fruits she recognized as pommes, a stack of white bricks that must be some kind of cheese, even rolls of reclaimed polymer fiber already combed into sheets and ready to cut for clothing. Right next to those a particularly enterprising cityen had set up a display of tools, needles, straight cutters, and even some delicate-looking shears that he was currently demonstrating on a scrap of his neighbor's fabric. The metallic *snick* carried clearly above the timbre of voices.

"Let's see if we can find Exey," Lia said, squinting across the square. "You'll like him. He's very clever. Come this way, he usually sets his cart over there."

"Wait," Hunter said, but Lia had already set off through the crowd. Hunter caught up quickly, positioning herself at the med's shoulder. She didn't like the way cityens crammed into the tight walkways between the carts, shouldering past each other to get the attention of the carts' harried managers, who could barely keep up with the pace of the shouted orders. Even though it was early, a few of the carts were empty already, their managers shrugging with upturned palms and weary smiles as those who had stood in line shouted their complaints. It seemed good-humored, mostly; there was enough for everyone, she estimated, even if some of them had to go to the back of a different line. It was easy to imagine, though, what would happen if supplies really ran short. A crowd like this could turn into a riot as fast as thought, smiles turning to snarls, the laughter morphing into something ugly, a growl she had heard before, when she had dragged a terrified girl through darkened streets, the mob snapping at their heels as they fled towards the Church, where the empty altar waited. . . .

"There it is!" Lia turned off the main walkway

into a narrower path that ran behind the largest carts. "Exey!" she called.

The Bender was working inside the bed of a covered cart, one flap pulled back. It was brighter inside than the small opening could account for. Hunter saw the glowlamp burning above a workbench, got a glimpse of a complicated device the man was working on amidst a nest of wire and tools before he hopped lightly down, pulling the flap closed behind him. She looked around, puzzled, seeing no power line attached to the cart. He followed her gaze to the roof of the cart, where a device much like a sun charger lay spread along the covering. "Just something I'm trying out," he said with a little grin. "Why pull all your power from the Church if you don't need to? Hello, Lia my sweetest, you always bring the sun into my day."

Lia ran to meet him with a hug, keeping an arm around his waist as Hunter approached less precipitately, studying the cart with interest. It looked like something she might find in the priests' underground laboratories, the display surface laid out carefully with bits and pieces of gear and wire. There were a few things, like a spark-striker, that Hunter recognized, and many whose purpose she couldn't quite make out.

Lia laughed. "Exey, this is my friend Echo. You met once before."

The man reached out to clasp hands. He was taller than Lia, taller even than Hunter, but wiry, his forearms hard with muscle and his grip strong and sure despite the delicacy of his long fingers. He wore his gleaming dark hair past shoulder length, pulled efficiently back out of the way, but the clasp that held it was a bar of polished copper, surface dimpled with the perfectly spaced marks of a tiny hammer. It must have taken many hours to beat a thick piece of wire so flat, and more to shine it until it glinted, catching the sun as Exey turned his head and smiled. "I remember. You came with Lia when Mari was having her baby."

"Are she and the baby well?" Hunter asked politely.

"Yes, very, thanks to Lia. You should see that girl. Hardly a month out, and already she's mostly got her eyes open, thinking all the time. Except when she's eating, which she's also extremely good at. Or peeing, yet another talent. Not to mention the other, of course. Yes, altogether she's an amazing little thing."

"You're just a proud uncle," Lia said, smiling.

"Oh, no, I'm perfectly unbiased. Just because she's the first baby any of my brothers and sisters have made, that's no reason to doubt my judgment, is it? Besides, how can she help being brilliant, when her uncle is the best fabricator in the city? I tell you, soon I'll be making her one of these." From his tray he lifted one of the objects Hunter hadn't recognized, a thin stick the length of her forearm, topped with a circle of triangles, shiny on one side and dull on the other, slightly curving, like a canid's ear. She was still trying to imagine what it was when Exey touched one triangle with a finger, setting the whole wheel to spinning atop the stick. Perfectly balanced, the blades blurred as they whirled around, the dark and light sides flickering as they spun. Lia laughed with delight. "That's what all the children say when they see it," Exey said. "You can have it if you'd like, but I have better toys for you. Look."

He pulled out a tray full of bright baubles, shining yellow trinkets of no obvious utility, but pleasing to look at all the same, like the decorative carvings barely visible in the high vaults of the sanctuary. "This one, I think?" He lifted a short chain of faceted beads connected by tiny links that let them spin free, glinting in the light like the toy he had shown Lia. The last bead sparked red as fire, a jewel captured in a yellow-threaded basket.

"Oh, Exey, it's beautiful." Lia's smile sparkled like the jewel.

Exey presented the piece with a grand sweeping gesture, offering it to Lia on his palm. "Have it."

Lia clasped her hands behind her back reluctantly. "I don't have any spare chits this week."

"Have it anyway. You don't need chits with me."

"But I can't just take it from you for nothing."

"Why not? It's not worth anything. Completely useless, though decorative. There's so much of this stuff lying around, people bring it to me when they find it. All I do is polish up bits and put them together."

"Everyone tries that, but only you have the eye for it."

He smiled, a little ruefully Hunter thought. "You always know the right thing to say. See, that's payment enough." He dropped the bauble into her hand, closing her fingers over it to forestall any protests, then turned a critical eye on Hunter. "You, on the other hand, look entirely useful. Not at all like my usual customers. But," Exey continued with a sly glance at Lia, "not without your own decorative qualities." He rummaged in the tray. "Here, I think this is just about right."

Between his fingers dangled a miniature of the bar that pulled his hair back, only this one made of the same gold as the filigreed piece he'd given to Lia. A rectangle the length of Hunter's smallest finger and perhaps half as wide, it had no design at all, only myriad planes hammered at impossible yet completely inevitable angles, the surfaces polished so fine that they reflected sun like so many shards of mirror. He held it up by the side of her face, measuring. "Yes, it suits you fine."

"It does," Lia agreed. "Echo, it's perfect."

"I have nothing to exchange for it," Hunter said stiffly.

"You could owe me," Exey suggested, then added hastily as she glared, "No, I agree, that's not such a good idea. Fortunately, a clever cityen like me can always find a solution: I'll give it to Lia. We've already established that she never needs to trade with me. So it'll be hers. Then she can give it to you."

Laughing, Lia took the piece and reached up to clasp it to Hunter's ear, then stood back to admire it. "Here, put your hair back so we can see it. That's better. Yes, it's beautiful. Perfect for you."

Hunter ducked her head, skin tingling where Lia's fingers had traced a soft line before withdrawing. The tiny unaccustomed weight tugged gently at her earlobe. "Thank you," she managed.

"Thank Exey," Lia said.

"Oh, no," the fabricator said. "She wouldn't have taken it from me."

"Well then, thank you for giving me something I could give her," Lia answered, eyes still crinkled with delight. "It's not easy to make our Echo smile like that."

And she was, Hunter realized, all the way back across the square.

CHAPTER 18

This part of the market was even more impossibly crowded, hot as the desert with the late morning sun beating down in earnest. Hunter, sweating in the spun fiber of her cityen's shirt, indulged in a brief wish for the comfort of her old clothing long hidden away at the edge of the forcewall. Lia was red-faced, her dress damp and clinging around the neck, but she didn't seem to mind; her footsteps were light and quick as she wove her way through the aisles between the food traders' stations. "Look," she exclaimed, pointing at a basket in one of the smaller stalls, which was really no more than a two-wheeled cart. "The pommes are finally ripe! Have you ever had one?" Before Hunter could answer Lia picked two, red and shining, and addressed the trader. "Morning, Samin. How much are you asking for these?"

"Three chit," the trader replied. "Oh, morning to you, Lia. Nice to see you here, it's been a long time."

"Three chit?" Lia's eyes went almost round as the pommes. "It hasn't been *that* long, Samin. I haven't forgotten I could get a whole basket of grain for three chit."

The trader shrugged elaborately, feigning uninterest while his eyes began to glint with the thrill of the chase. "Grain's easy, they grow a whole stad full of that. Trees, now those are hard. Risky too, what with having to plant them at the edge of the clave and all. 'Member last year, it was so hot there was no pommes at all? Lucky I'm asking three, on account of you're the med and all, those others I told four."

"Mmmm, I'm sure." Lia favored the fruits, then the trader, with a narrow stare. "This one looks bruised. Say two. You're probably not getting half a chit per hand from anyone else, but I'm feeling generous today." That drew a snort from the trader.

The haggling went on for a little while, both of them obviously enjoying the game. It was, Hunter decided, like sparring, a ritual with particular rules, designed to hone important skills in the safety of a structured environment. She watched closely, following the bout with interest until Lia, finally triumphant, proffered her one of the pommes with a victorious flourish. "Here, for you. Try it."

Hunter took the gift with peculiar reluctance, holding the smooth globe to her lips. Its tangy sweet smell tickled her nostrils. She closed her eyes, remembering a day long ago, hot like this, she and her small batchmates sitting under the leafy branches in the tiny grove next to the priests' medicinal garden. The girls had tended trees and plot alike all summer, learning patience and the vagaries of crops. The pomme had been the most delicious thing she ever tasted. She hadn't had one in annuals.

She touched her tongue to the smooth, warm skin. Before she could bite, a high-pitched whine sounded over the hubbub of the market, a piercing mechanical sound that didn't belong here. Her heart skipped.

The last time she had heard that sound, Tana had died.

"Back," she ordered Lia, thrusting the med into the scant cover of the stall. The trader, thinking her clumsy, glared and grabbed at a tumbling fruit. She ignored him, searching for the source of the disruption.

"What is it?" Lia asked, a tiny streak of juice from the forgotten pomme dribbling down her chin.

"I heard something." She scanned the crowd quickly. No one else looked the least alarmed, the haggling continuing, the cityens hauling their burdens home in the heat, unaware. *Too high for their ears*, she realized. *Where was it?* The sound didn't come again, but she knew she hadn't imagined it.

There, by the alley leading north, a ripple as someone made his way against the flow of the crowd. Hunter heard a curse from that direction, but it sounded merely annoyed, a foot stepped on, not murder. Even so . . .

"Thank the Saint I found you. I knew you'd be looking for pommes," Milse panted, then lowered his voice with a worried glance at the oblivious cityens. "Don't let anyone else hear, or there will be a riot. There's trouble over by the Bend gap, people are hurt."

"Take me," Lia ordered, hand automatically checking for the kit she always carried slung from one shoulder. With her free hand she took Milse's arm, acting as if she were merely sauntering along with him through the market. Hunter followed, jamming the untouched pomme in her pocket, all her senses trained ahead. "What happened?"

"I'm not sure. Some hunters came, and then there was a crowd—"

Lia's sudden stop nearly jerked Milse off his feet. "Hunters," she breathed. "Are they still there?"

"Yes, when I left, I don't know—why does it matter? We're not going there; you have to get back to the clinic where it's safe."

"Don't be ridiculous." Lia turned to Hunter, face etched with worry. "You have to go back. You can't let them see you, not in the middle of trouble."

For the briefest moment Hunter was tempted to listen. Her clothes, her grown-out hair—none of that would matter. Even if they got the barest glimpse of her, they would know her for a hunter immediately. And there was only one hunter she could be, so disguised, so diminished. She would be completely exposed. Everyone would know, hunters and cityens alike. Then the Warder would have to turn her out, for though she might be useful to him while no one was looking, openly sheltering a cast-off from the Church would raise far too many questions about his intent.

She would lose everything she had worked for; she couldn't risk it.

"Why in the Saint's name not?" Milse demanded.

Lia stammered uncharacteristically. "It's just—it's just—"

"I had some trouble with them in North," Hunter put in, taking Lia's bag from her. "Don't worry about it. We'll all go." She did not even try to talk Lia into returning to the Ward; the med would never consent to leaving the injured.

"But—"

"Either I'm coming or you're not going. Milse, show us the place."

They followed him then, walking as calmly as they could until they got free of the crowd, then breaking into a trot.

Hunter felt it blocks away, the silence, not desert quiet, but something ominous, the close tension before an explosion. She ran lightly, held back by Lia and Milse, whose footfalls drummed painfully loud, advertising their approach in a way that made her belly tighten. "How much farther?"

"Up there." Milse pointed, panting. He wasn't used to moving so fast, especially in this heat. "Just past that corner."

Hunter pulled him to a stop, barred Lia's way with an arm. "We don't want to run at trouble. I'll go first. If you don't get a sign from me in five minutes, get Lia straight back to the clinic. Don't stop for anything. *Anything.* Milse, you keep her safe, understand me?"

She didn't even look at Lia, just turned and walked casually towards the corner, making herself small and ordinary, like any cityen headed home from market.

It was like being hit with a stunner. There they were, two hunters and a priest. All her muscles clenched at the sight, and she had to concentrate to make her diaphragm move enough to pull a breath into her lungs. The hunters stood just this side of the small square the street emptied into, backs to the wall, facing a knot of angry cityens, some carrying stones and even makeshift clubs, though they had not yet gathered the courage to charge. Someone had tried something, though: a still body lay in the empty space between the hunters and the crowd.

From this distance Hunter couldn't recognize the hunters' faces, but by the way they stood, one relaxed and ready, the other still slender with youth, bouncing ever so slightly on her toes, she guessed that this must indeed have started as a training exercise for the younger girl, accompanying the older hunter and the priest on whatever business they had in the city. The hunters stood slightly angled to each other with the priest shielded behind them. Their hands were empty still, but Hunter recognized the high whine of holstered stunners charging, beyond the cityens' hearing. Hunter's fingers twitched reflexively, the fighting hormones coursing through her bloodstream just as they must through theirs, heightening every sense, bringing preternatural clarity to every sound, every motion. She felt her own lips curling as theirs would be, and almost ran to stand beside them, shoulder to shoulder, where instinct and training told her she belonged. The pain of separation shot through her body, sharp as it had been on the morning of her exile. She took a deep breath, wiping her palms against her pants, and stayed where she was.

If the hunters had been alone, they would be gone already, slicing through the thinnest part of the crowd and down the alley opposite before the cityens had a chance to stop them. They probably wouldn't even have to do more than stun anyone. The priest made the situation more difficult; to get him out they would have to force the mob back long enough for him to pass. That would mean inflicting more serious damage. They were doing all they could to prevent that: waiting patiently, letting the cityens think about what had happened to their fellow, saying nothing to amplify their anger. The tactic seemed to be working: as Hunter watched, pressed into the shadow of a wall, a few of the clubheads drooped, a sullen muttering beginning to relieve the silence. One or two of the stragglers at the back of the crowd broke off, slinking back down the street to safety, not even noticing her as they passed.

Then Loro stepped forward from the mouth of the alley.

Of course, Loro.

"Don't let them get away with it," he shouted to the cityens. Clubs rose again, but uncertainly. He marched into the middle of the square. "We know you're carrying weapons," Loro shouted at the hunters. "Throw them down."

The older hunter turned to study him. Brit, the 364 who had escorted Hunter to the gate the last time she had walked out of the Churchyard. And the other one was Ava, the 378. Saints, that batch was at the center of everything that went wrong. Ela, Fay. Gem. "Tell your people to withdraw," Brit said. "No one else will get hurt."

"We're not letting you go. You can't fight all of us."

"We can," the hunter advised. "But we don't want to."

Loro took another step forward, pulling the front of the crowd with him. "I don't think so. How many of those paralyzers can you throw before your charges run out? Seven? Eight? There's way more of us than that. And the wands have to touch someone to bring him down, we know that too. You can't get us all."

Brit considered, then dismissed him to speak directly to the crowd. "We don't *want* to fight you, cityens. We're here to serve you." She scanned the faces, probing for hints of who really wanted a confrontation, who looked just as willing to slink away and call it a victory.

"Serve us by stealing our daughters?" someone shouted, but there was a question in it.

"Look around. It's only us and this priest. The priest was checking on a woman in North who had given birth, that's all. We're leaving. We're not taking anyone. Let us pass, and this small trouble is forgotten." Some in the crowd nodded, murmuring agreement.

"Don't listen to her," Loro urged the crowd. "They were spying on us, seeing which girls they want when the tithe comes. We're not stupid, they can't fool us that way. Rad, you know it, you lost a daughter to them. Jolen, you too, it was your sister, same as mine. They were here for the census, that's what they were doing. Well, this time we're not going to let them!"

The angry murmur rose again. The idiot, he was going to get his own people killed. The hunters wouldn't start the rush, but they would end it. Hunter edged deeper into the shadows, feeling the mob's mood teeter back and forth on the edge of disaster as Loro continued to goad them. The last thing it needed was for her to give it a push.

She whirled at the familiar footsteps gliding up behind her. Lia stood on tiptoes to peer over her shoulder. "What's happening? Have they seen you?"

"No. I told you to wait for my signal!"

The med's eyes dropped. "I was afraid for you. I couldn't just wait." Then she raised her head defiantly. "Besides, Milse said people were hurt. Where—never mind, I see. I need to get to him."

"It's too dangerous. Loro has them ready to riot."

"Loro?" Lia surveyed the crowd again. "I was afraid of something like that. I sent Milse for the Warder." She took a deep breath. "Hope he gets here soon."

"Wait—"

But before Hunter could stop her, Lia was heading for the center of the square, making no effort at stealth. The cityens parted for her as she strode forward, shoulders squared and head lifted, and walked straight up to the fallen man. There she knelt, turning him over and running her hands along his body, while the silence of absolute astonishment fell over the square. Finally the med looked up. In a completely matter-of-fact voice she said, "Loro, I need to get this man to the clinic right away. Give me a hand, will you?"

"Lia, get away from there now!" Loro's voice held genuine panic. Whatever mischief he had planned, this was sending it badly awry.

"Don't move!" The young hunter suddenly had projtrodes in her hand, aimed dead at Lia.

"Get away from her!" Loro shouted, lurching towards the hunters.

It was the exact wrong move.

Ava jumped forward and dragged the med to her feet, trodes to her head. A hunter might survive a discharge there, but no cityen would. Hunter's heart squeezed until she could hardly breathe. It was a standard tactic: when outnumbered, use the most valuable available currency to bargain with, and do whatever necessary to make your adversary understand the seriousness of your stance. Gem would have killed someone by now, just to demonstrate how far she was willing to go. There was no doubt that Ava knew what to do. Hunter had taught her. But Saints, that whole batch was so erratic. . . . If the girl panicked now, it could cost Lia her life.

Hunter weighed possibilities furiously. With surprise on her side, she could overpower Ava, that much was certain. She could probably occupy both hunters long enough for Lia to escape, especially if the crowd erupted. It would only take one spark to ignite them, and Loro looked ready to explode. The hunters would then kill Hunter, and maybe some of the cityens. None of that mattered, as long as Lia got away— *No*, she hissed at herself. *You have a duty to the Patri. Save the mission.* What other choice was there? She could do nothing, hoping that between Brit's good sense and Lia's stature, order would prevail. That approach made the most sense. It risked nothing but Lia and maybe the hunters' lives. One cityen against the Patri's mission, two hunters against the crowd of cityens. In the long run, what took place here was insignificant. Her priority was to keep her cover, letting the confrontation play itself out without her interference.

She strode forward into the square, scattering startled cityens like the tiny mammals in the desert, hands spread wide to show she had no weapons. "Stay calm, everyone."

Ava's trodes jerked off Lia to point at her. Brit had her proj out now too, but held it averted while she assessed this new dimension of the problem. "Who—" She broke off, astonishment showing plain in the normally impassive face. "Echo Hunter 367. Is that *you*?"

Hunter took a deep breath. "Brit Hunter 364. I'm glad to see you."

Loro, staring, made an inarticulate sound of rage and took one step towards Hunter, hands balled into fists, before he managed to stop himself. *Later*, his furious gaze promised her. There were other exclamations, some surprised, others more ominous, as the cityens gradually realized that a disguised hunter stood among them, and tried to figure out whether she stood with them or against. Lia's lips shaped a soundless *no* in a face white as dust.

Brit's startled survey took in Hunter's clothes, the hair that had worked its way out of its knot and snarled around her sweaty face. "I doubt that."

"We aren't enemies."

"No," Brit agreed, "we aren't." She studied Hunter the way she might any oddity she found in the desert, coolly interested. The crowd around them might as well not exist. "I assumed you were dead. No other hunter has been excommunicated in my memory; I would have thought there would be no purpose to living." Lia made a sound, and Brit glanced that way, then back at Hunter. "You must have found something, unless—" She gestured slightly with the trodes. "Do you need assistance?"

Hunter's face burned. "I need no help from you. But I can give you some. This confrontation"—she waved a casual hand towards the cityens behind her, trying to convey indifference—"serves no one."

"I agree. You probably heard what I told them. It was true: we only want to leave. What do you propose?"

"Safe passage, for you and the priest, if you leave them their med."

Brit smiled grimly. "I can make our passage safe if I have to."

"I know. But you'll have to kill at least a few of them. It would be a waste."

"That's true." Brit considered. "We'll take the woman with us. As a calming influence on her more precipitate friends, like that one over there. You stay here to help discourage them."

Hunter shook her head. It was absurdly like bartering in the market. "Leave her. I'll come with you. Better numbers."

"But it gives us no cover."

"Three hunters shouldn't need cover, Brit Hunter 364."

A flicker of something crossed her stolid face. Disdain. "Don't try to shame *me*, Echo. I don't want to hurt these cityens. Besides, how can I know which side you'll take? No, my plan has fewer variables. As long as everyone else behaves, the woman is safe with us. We'll let her go at the Church steps."

Hunter weighed her choices. Lia stood perfectly still, both hands clutching at Ava's rock-hard arm around her throat. She would be feeling that strength and reckoning how easily it could squeeze the breath from her, should this negotiation go awry. Hunter met her frightened gaze, tried to reassure her. "As far as the forcewall, then," she said to Brit, "and I come with you too. When we get there you release her to me. Unharmed," she added, with a hard look at Ava. The young hunter's face betrayed nothing, but the knot of her larynx worked up and down.

"That would do." Brit nodded, then raised an eyebrow. "But do you speak for them?" The crowd had edged closer. They had kept quiet enough to hear most of the exchange, but now voices were rising, fingers pointing as they held their own debate. The naked hate in Loro's eyes chilled her. Only fear for Lia held him back. Brit smiled, coldly amused as she read their mood. "I'm not sure you've helped us, Echo."

"They're reasonable people," Hunter answered, loud enough for all the cityens to hear clearly. "They won't do anything foolish."

"No, no, indeed, we won't." Hunter didn't have to turn. She heard the crowd murmur as the Warder stepped past her. Finally she risked a glance behind, where Milse stood bent at the waist, gasping; he must have run both ways to get the Warder here so quickly. By contrast the Warder was barely breathing hard. The chatter died to a tentative hush as he addressed hunters and cityens alike. "I think safe passage is a good idea."

"But, *sir*," Loro objected, coming up to stand beside the Warder. "They were here to take the census. To count our girls, for the *tithe*."

"Perhaps. If so, we owe them that duty." The Warder raised his voice for all to hear. "The Church protects us, and we respect that, and honor it. But," he said, and his voice grew uncharacteristically stern as he turned to the hunters, "you did not protect us today, it seems. Is that man dead?"

"No," Lia choked out. "I just want to—"

"These people attacked us," Ava broke in, tightening her grip on the med. "We had no choice but to defend ourselves."

Hands jammed in his pockets, the Warder regarded her curiously. "May I ask your name?"

"I am Ava Hunter 378."

"Three seven eight? You are still young, then, if I understand the way you name yourselves. You must acquit yourself well, for the Church to send you on such an important mission. Still, young Ava, forgive me, but it seems that this one has not come out so well, has it?"

Ava flushed, but before she could speak Brit interrupted. "It would be best to end this before there is a chance for any accident." She made a show of putting away her trodes. Only Hunter knew how quickly they could be back in her hand and firing. "Release her, Ava."

Ava obeyed instantly, pushing Lia away, no harder than necessary to get her clear. Hand to her throat, the med stumbled up against Loro, who threw an arm around her. Catching her breath, she shrugged it off, kneeling once more by the fallen man. She gestured impatiently, and Hunter brought her bag, careful not to make any sudden movements. It brought her so close to the hunters that she could smell them, the slight sourness that betrayed Ava's fear though her face showed nothing, the flint that was Brit. Her throat closed painfully.

"Thank you, Ava. Thank both of you," the Warder said. "I think you should go now, you and your friend. These people are hot and tired, and no doubt they're also ready to go home."

Brit inclined her head. "The Church will remember

your assistance, sir. When the Patri asks, what name shall I give?"

The Warder plucked at his hems for a moment before answering. "My name's not important, respected hunter, not in the larger vision, though some call me the Warder. Please tell the Patri we cityens stand with him, with him and the Church. And if you will, commend us to the Saint, and tell her we are grateful."

Brit's face was unreadable. Hunter wondered if the Patri had spoken of the Warder to her, before he had discovered Hunter's uselessness, or after. There was no way to tell. "I will," was all Brit said. At the jerk of her head, Ava backed off down the empty alley, shielding the priest who stuck close as her shadow. It was working: the crowd hung back, its surging anger damped. Brit waited, watching the cityens, until Ava and the priest were safely away, then turned to follow them.

"Brit," Hunter hissed at her as she passed. "Tell the Patri I still serve. *Tell him.*" The hunter paused but didn't turn. Hunter knew she could hear. "*I still serve.*"

Brit said nothing at all. Then she was gone.

The cityens milled around with the uncertainty of a mob deciding it was just a crowd. They began to disperse in little groups, still muttering, but anger dissipating. The Warder walked among them, smiling and nodding, helping them unknot themselves. "I need to get this man back to the clinic," Lia said briskly, ignoring all that. "Echo. *Echo.*"

"What?"

"Can you carry him?"

"Yes, of course."

"Good." Lia started to rise, brushing dust off her skirts. Hunter reached down to help her up.

"*Don't touch her.*" Loro shoved Hunter back with a two-fisted punch to her chest. "You *filth.*"

People who had been walking away paused, looking back. Hunter felt their attention focus on her, danger ratcheting up again. The Warder, speaking to someone on the other side of the square, didn't seem to notice.

"Just pick him up, Echo," Lia murmured. She took Loro's hand with a smile, but her eyes were furious.

Hunter hesitated, then obeyed. The man was beginning to stir as she lifted him. "Let's just get away from here," Lia said.

"How can you—" Loro began, but Lia stopped him.

"Not now," she said. "*Not now.*"

Ignoring the crawling between her shoulder blades, Hunter turned her back on the crowd and led the way back from the square. A few sets of footsteps followed for a little way, but then broke off, and finally retreated. She kept going, not slacking her pace until she was convinced that there was no pursuit. The man she carried was heavy, and when a few minutes along he began to struggle in earnest, she set him down on the curb.

"Let me see him." Lia studied his face, felt around his head as he blinked, dazed. "Nothing's broken. What's the last thing you remember?"

"Someone said . . . hunters, a girl needed help. . . . I can't—" He shook his head, stopped with a wince.

"Don't worry. You got a good knock on the head, but you'll be all right. Is there anyone we can send for?"

"Salry," he mumbled. "I promised Salry I'd be back before . . ."

"We'll find her," Lia promised, then chuckled shakily as his eyes drifted closed. "She's not going to believe his story."

"She will when word gets around what happened," Loro said, eyes gleaming. Something was beginning to replace the anger in them, something Hunter didn't like at all. "We had those hunters trapped. We could have taken them, easy. Would have, if *you* hadn't gotten in the way."

"They would have slaughtered you," Hunter said flatly.

"Don't think I won't take care of you next, you filthy, spying—"

"Loro, stop it!" Lia said.

"I'm not stopping it, Lia. She lied to us. She's one of *them*. When I tell the Warder—"

"The Warder knows," Lia said. "She's a friend, Loro. Can't you see that?"

"They're never our friends, Lia. They pretend, so they can take what they want." He spat, then turned on Hunter with a gleam of triumph. "But they don't want you, do they? Not even good enough for them, I guess. Maybe it's lucky for you."

"Loro!" Lia began, but he ignored her.

"Just watch," he taunted. "They won't come back here any time soon. They know what happened. So do you. You just wait. This is only the beginning."

It wasn't worth arguing. Shaking her head, she brushed past him. He called her a filthy name, laughing, thinking he had won, then Lia said something to him, anger plain in her voice, then the two of them were arguing. Hunter shut her ears, ignoring them both, and walked away.

The guard at the clinic entrance smiled pleasantly and let Hunter in, a sure sign that word hadn't traveled this far yet. She retreated to her corner pallet, glad the place was empty. She would deal with the cityens when she had to, but for now all she wanted was a little time to herself. Sitting cross-legged on the bed, she tried to focus on her breathing, let the disturbance of the market settle, drain away until she was calm again, quiet, quiet. . . .

"Echo, I'm so sorry." Lia stood by the foot of her bed, twisting the strap of her kit bag over and over.

Hunter opened her eyes reluctantly. "For what?"

"I heard what she said, that hunter. About not having a reason to live. It was a cruel thing to say. She had no right."

"She thought it was true."

Silence, while Lia thought her way through that. "I'm sorry," she said again at last.

"You don't need to be." Then, because Lia's eyes

began to fill, Hunter added, "I'm sorry too. It wasn't the market day you planned."

The med choked out a weak laugh. "Hunters, a mob—no, that wasn't the kind of day anyone had planned."

Maybe it was, Hunter thought, with a sudden chill. She remembered what the injured man had said, and how Loro had just happened to turn up to stoke the mob. *I have plans*, he had said the night before.

And he had wanted Lia to stay away.

There was no point in burdening the med with her suspicion. Lia still stood uncertainly, liquid gathering in the corners of her eyes, threatening to spill. Hunter shifted on the bed, felt something press into her hip. Reaching into her pocket, she drew out the forgotten pomme, now sadly bruised. Lia bit her lip, a dismay Hunter thought had little to do with the condition of the fruit. "Don't worry, it'll still be good. Sit down, we can share."

Lia sat, finally beginning to smile as she took the proffered pomme. Hunter cut a small piece for herself. The crisp sweet taste, exactly as she remembered it, made her close her eyes, holding the half-chewed bite in her mouth for a moment before she remembered to swallow.

"Do you like it?" the med asked.

"Yes," Hunter answered. "I do."

"Good," Lia said softly. "Then my market day wasn't wasted after all."

CHAPTER 19

Loro was both right and wrong. More and more often, guards or cityens brought word of hunters moving through the city, singly or in twos or threes. Taking the census as Loro had accused, Hunter thought privately, or making some other kind of preparations. She wanted to observe them for herself, but the Warder would have none of it. "I'm sorry, Echo, truly," he said. "But we'd best keep you far away, where it's less likely anyone will be tempted into doing anything foolish." Whatever they were up to, the hunters provoked no further overt dissension in the city. The tension that had led to the confrontation near the market still simmered, but it seemed to have no focus at the moment.

And hunters never came into the Ward.

Yet Hunter was troubled: her living among the cityens was unprecedented, as Brit had so helpfully pointed out. It should provoke some kind of reaction from the

Church. She made her calculations grimly. If the Patri had seen the Warder as a threat before, how much more dangerous would he be with an exiled hunter at his side? The solution to that problem seemed obvious: send a hunter patrol to demand that the Warder hand her over or have her taken from him by force. The Warder might hate to give up such a valuable asset, but even in losing her he would still win something, for by acceding to the Church's requirements, he would make himself seem all the more a model cityen. And if the Warder were *not* what the Patri thought, he would be even more willing to let them take her. If she fought back, well . . . the Patri had feared making a martyr of the Warder, but he would have no such concerns about eliminating her. Besides, if they came for her it could only lead to one end, and it scarcely mattered where they finished it.

No, it was certainly not fear of the cityens that held them back. And yet . . . There could be another explanation. Maybe Brit had carried Hunter's message back. The Patri might be pleased to learn that she was still on his mission, insinuating herself among his enemies as he had planned, carrying out his directive to watch, and learn. He would hold the hunters in hand, waiting, watching in whatever ways he had, to see what value she might still hold. If that were the case, if it were not all her desperate grasp to justify the unforgiveable . . . She schooled herself not to hope, chided herself for being tempted by a wish.

And, buried before it was fully born, the fear that she no longer knew what it was she wished for.

Something else bothered her too, and it was a great deal more concrete. "Milse," she said a day or two after market, when Lia was out of earshot. "I've been wondering. How did you get the Warder to the square so fast?"

"Oh," he said. "Didn't I tell you? I met him halfway. He was already on his way to market." Milse shook his head soberly. "That was lucky, wasn't it? The Saint was watching out for us that day, for sure."

Hunter thought darkly that the Saint most likely had nothing to do with it at all.

Surprisingly, the Warder's people seemed indifferent to Hunter's unmasking. It made her daily life easier, if anything. If Loro were angry with Lia or the Warder for keeping Hunter's secret, it didn't show. Striding triumphantly around the Ward as if he himself had defeated an entire hunter patrol in personal combat, he actually grew less hostile to her and instead adopted an air of tolerant magnanimity that was considerably more annoying. Only once did it give way to something else entirely, when he caught her aside at the clinic where no one else could hear. "Did you know a girl named Luida? Short, with long brown hair, and always laughing?"

The nuns all looked like that to her. "I didn't know most of their names. I'm sorry." For an instant, he was only a disappointed boy. "Loro. Their life is good there."

He cursed and pushed her away.

Justan, good-natured as always, held no grudge.

Sitting across from her at the evening meal, he had just shrugged and reached for more bread. "There's enough for us all," he said. "Better t' share than waste." If outsiders were troubled that the Warder had a tame hunter among his people, or if they even connected that hunter with Lia's helper in the clinic, Hunter saw no sign. With some chagrin she remembered how carefully she had worked to lead them to identify what she was at the proper time. It seemed it didn't matter at all. She wondered, uneasily, what else she might have been wrong about.

Or perhaps the cityens were simply distracted. Something was going on, something unrelated to her. The tithe was coming, of course, and the hunters' stepped-up patrols buzzed in the background like static. But there was something else too. Hunter felt it in the mood of the cityens who still streamed daily into the clinic: a kind of excitement that ran under every interaction, an alert anticipation not unlike that of a hunter before action, only with a lighthearted edge entirely unfamiliar to Hunter. She remarked on it to Lia one day.

The med answered absently, absorbed in the print she was indexing. "It's the harvest fest." At Hunter's puzzled silence, Lia set her stylus down, eyebrows raised. "I thought you knew. The Church always sets the day."

"I forgot all about it," Hunter admitted. No wonder: hunters didn't particularly mark the harvest fest; it was nothing to them, though for the cityens it was a welcome time to set aside trivial disagreements and celebrate another annual of survival.

The med shook her head in mild exasperation. "Somehow I'm not surprised."

That stung peculiarly. Lia saw, and touched her arm. "I'm sorry, I shouldn't tease you about things like that."

"It doesn't matter."

"You always say that, Echo, but it does." The med twirled the stylus in her fingers a moment, thoughtfully regarding its tip, then asked casually, "Can you dance?"

"Dance?" Hunter repeated, bewildered.

"Yes, dance—you know, put one foot after another in patterns, to music, with a partner." A mischievous twinkle lit Lia's eyes. It was a rare thing to see in the usually grave med, and it showed her unexpectedly young. Again Hunter was struck by the absurd wish that the Church had taken Lia for tithe, raised her carefree and lighthearted, with none of the worries she carried here to wear her down. It was too late now; the lines in her face were carved too deep to smooth away, even in a moment like this. And yet—and yet—

"I know what dancing is," Hunter said, perplexed as much by the turn of her own thoughts as by the med's.

"Yes, but can you do it?" Lia was laughing now, like an innocent child.

Hunter remembered it bone deep. The carefully choreographed steps in the yard, blocks and blows, throws and parries, parries and strikes, every beat precisely measured, pattern repeated over and over until repetition set the hunters free of the form— "Yes, I can do it." Better than most, as it happened, though they all were skilled. Not just in practice either, but the applications, in the field, the flowing lithe movements so much a part of her nature that her body had seemed to move on its own, the girl dead at the foot of the cliff almost before she knew what she had done. . . . She forced herself to see the face in front of her: Lia, not Ela. Lia, smiling still, the golden eyes warm, the upsweep of her mouth full and sweet, asking her if she could dance, with no comprehension at all of what it was that stood before her. "I can do it," Hunter repeated, more to herself than the med.

"Good. Then you'll come with me. There's always dancing the night before the fest."

Hunter stared at her.

Whatever Lia saw in that look made her face crumple in on itself. "I'm sorry, Echo, I should've realized." The words tumbled out, faster and faster, as the med averted her eyes. "Of course you wouldn't want to go to something like that. It's just a silly cityen thing, anyway. It's probably just as well, now that I think of it. There might be other hunters. The other day in the market . . . I saw the way you looked at them. I never thought about it before, but there aren't that many hunters compared with cityens, are there? Of course you would all be friends. Even if"—she hesitated for a moment, choosing her words more carefully—"even if you aren't part of the Church anymore, I know you miss it awfully, at least sometimes." She drew a breath, staring at her hands in her lap, recollecting her composure. "There was a while I didn't want to go to the fests either, to be honest. After the sickness, when so many had died, I used to wonder what anyone had to celebrate. Everything was so terrible, and there was nothing anyone could do. . . . How could they dance? How could they possibly be happy? But then I realized, *they lived*. That was why they were celebrating. They lived. Sometimes that seems like enough. Doesn't it?" Her luminous eyes searched Hunter's for the answer.

I don't know. That was the truth. But suddenly she could not say it to Lia, who stood before her looking so forlorn, for this instant closer to the young girl who did not yet realize what lay ahead than the woman who had spent half the winter nursing those dying around her, until she nearly died herself, who was barely recovered even now, face thin in the slanting afternoon light, eyes smudged with weariness that came from far more than this day's work. It seemed not so much to ask, that Lia should take an evening to forget, and be happy.

With an effort, Hunter made herself smile. It felt stiff, strange. Had it been so long? "Maybe so," she said.

Lia's eyes widened in surprise. The corners of her mouth curled up slowly, leaves unfurling at an unexpected touch of sun. Her eyes glittered, catching the light. Hunter felt her own face soften in that reflected warmth, and she meant it when she said, "I'll be happy to go with you."

The cityens had cleared the ground floor of a low building that clung to the riverbank, probably a storehouse of some kind before the Fall, when boats plying the water would have needed a place to unload and resupply. It had been a good choice of locations once, overlooking that narrowing where every boat had to come within weapons' reach. There had likely been some encampment here long before there was a city. The roads leading to the place remained straight and broad, equidistant from Ward, Bend, and North. Good neutral ground for bringing the claves together.

But the Fall had changed more than the cityens. The river didn't run now except after the rare hard rain, and all that remained of what must have been a tremendous bridge were a few broken metal stumps sticking out of the oily dead sludge like shattered bones, jagged ends scarred over with age. On shore, ancient fire had blackened the building's brick and caved in the back part of the roof, but the simplicity of the squat design had saved the place from total destruction. Nothing nearby it had survived, leaving a zone of almost desert-like emptiness all around. At odds with the desolation, the place was gaily lit tonight, though so far from the transmission lines it was done with simple torches instead of lightstrings. The sounds of drums and pipes bounced through the heavy air. Even outside, Hunter could smell the fruity tang of fermented grain. She frowned to herself, seeing the resources wasted on ferm when there were still so many to feed.

Not tonight, she told herself sternly. *You promised.* Besides, the Church didn't disapprove. As Lia had said, it even set the fest time. It wasn't by mistake that the day fell when many cityens would still be occupied with the mechanics of getting the harvest in, and the start of the celebration would create a welcome distraction. That the nun tithe followed almost immediately was even less coincidental. After all, only a few families gave up their daughters, and for the rest, a few days of dancing and drinking fermentate went a long way towards dulling any sympathetic pain.

They had arrived a little bit late, it seemed; voices echoed from inside the building and there was a growing queue outside. It took a second to see what was causing the delay: a little knot of men loitering outside the door, two on one side and three on the other, grouped in just such a casual arrangement that everyone who entered had to pass between them. Hunter recognized one of the three, a man who had come once to the clinic. The others were unfamiliar, but she noted the two groups watching each other almost as much as the door. The pair of strangers must not be the Warder's men. Benders? North seemed less likely; they were too concerned with themselves there to offer to share the task. She watched as the men unobtrusively surveyed everyone who entered, occasionally exchanging little nods that marked the entrant known to one side or the other. Like the market, this place belonged to no one clave, and any manner of cityens could come. The scrutiny suggested that some of them could bring trouble.

Suddenly it was more than Hunter wanted to face. But Lia's features were lit by excitement as much as the torches; she couldn't change her mind now. And it was a good opportunity; ferm loosened tongues, and she might learn something worthwhile with all those cityens gathered in one place. Something to help the Patri. She forced a smile and motioned Lia towards the door.

All five guards straightened up as one.

Lia smiled at the man Hunter had recognized. "Rander, how are you doing? Is your arm better?" She had to raise her voice to be heard over the drums.

The man's dour face split in a grin as he raised a hand, showing a pink scar, neat stitchmarks still faintly visible, lined all along the underside of the arm. His fingers flexed into a tight fist. "Good enough for all I need. Thanks t' you."

"I'm glad I could help." Lia took Hunter's arm, dragged her forward a step. "This is Echo, I don't think you've met her yet. I asked her to come tonight."

So simple: nothing more than the choice of a dance partner. Who could argue with the med over that? Nonetheless the men exchanged wary glances. Rander shifted awkwardly from one foot to the other, wanting to please Lia, worried about letting trouble past the door. "I don't know. . . ."

Lia frowned. "The fest is open to everyone, Rander."

"Yes, mam, I know, but you know how't is. You want it t' be safe. We're not s'pposed to let in, well . . ."

"Who gave you those instructions?"

"I'm not sure I should—"

"Well, whoever it was, you can send them to see me later. *After* you let us inside."

The poor man looked to his fellows, trying to decide what to say, but they offered no help at all. Whatever plan they'd had for this eventuality had failed to account for Lia's determination. In other circumstances Hunter would have laughed out loud. Now she just wanted to get out of the bottleneck. Oblivious cityens pushed up behind her and Lia in the queue, in high humor but impatient at the delay. By the tone of the voices, some of them had clearly found a source of fermentate already. Hunter stifled a sigh. It wasn't worth risking a disturbance. "You go ahead."

"But—"

The line behind them rippled as someone pushed through. Hunter turned, body instinctively shielding Lia from whatever trouble was coming. Loro, striding up to the door with his hands in his pockets and a careful not-smile playing across his face. The timing couldn't be accidental. "Rander, Samno." Loro nodded to the Benders too, who respectfully returned it. "Evening, friends. Lia, glad you finally decided to come. I thought you might not. Everything well?"

"Very well, thank you, Loro." Hunter thought she heard the slightest brittleness in Lia's tone, but the med's smile was bright as always.

"Good." Loro turned from Lia to face Hunter, eyebrows raised in exaggerated query. "You don't seem to be the type that would enjoy a fest."

Maybe a disturbance would be worth it. "I thought I would try," she said mildly.

He had shaved; the light glinted off the smooth line of his jaw. He wasn't that much older than the 378s, she was reminded again. Important to remember, that hormonal volatility, especially in this setting. He might already have had some ferm himself; he stood particularly square shouldered, and closer to Lia than he usually might. She didn't seem to notice. His fists balled in his pockets. "Are you planning to try anything else?"

Hunter cocked her head, considering. "Dancing, maybe."

The smooth jaw tightened. "We have to check *strangers* for weapons."

Rander and the other guards shuffled uneasily, smelling the tension in the air. "Loro," Lia started to protest, but Hunter interrupted her.

"No, it's all right. It's a sensible precaution." She held her arms out to her sides, feet slightly apart, waiting. Loro hesitated almost imperceptibly, making himself angry. Hunter lifted a brow to show that she had noticed. Scowling, he stomped forward, running his hands roughly over every part of her body, patting for the weapons he knew full well she wasn't carrying. Instead of tensing with embarrassment or anger, as he obviously meant her to, she relaxed into his touch, letting him feel her weight, the solidity of her musculature, and judge whether he could move her if he tried. When he stepped back, glaring, she didn't even indulge in the insolence of a smile.

He stared at her for a moment, then snapped around to Lia, taking her arm. Fortunately he wasn't rough with her. "What are you waiting for, then? Let's go in."

The Warder's men hastily stepped aside, and after a second the other men did too, letting Loro and Lia push by, followed by Hunter, unobstructed. The med turned a smile on Loro that would make any amount of trouble worthwhile, but Hunter thought her voice carried the faintest note of annoyance. "Thank you, Loro. For a minute I thought Rander wouldn't let us in."

That restored some of his good humor. "He was just being careful, like he was supposed to. We don't want anyone spoiling the fest. Come this way, the ferm is over here." A bit of copper flashed between his fingers. "My chit. Then you can dance with me." Lia cast a worried look over her shoulder. Hunter shook her head and went the other direction as Loro guided Lia into the crowd.

The fest wore on in a din and crush of bodies that made Hunter wish for the peace of the desert. The drummers had started out tapping on their metal vessels by hand, but had long since transitioned to banging with rods of different lengths and thicknesses that produced a surprising variation in sound, all of it loud, and the pipers were red-faced from trying to keep up. Besides the music, the conversation and laughter and general commotion from hundreds of people packed

into the enclosed space was enough that cityens standing next to each other had nearly to shout to be heard,
ratcheting the sound level ever higher. It hurt her ears.

Across the way she saw Lia, trapped in Loro's encir-
cling arm while dancers swirled around them. Hunter
wondered why the med put up with him. It certainly
wasn't for his diplomatic skills. Hunter sighed and
found herself a place against a wall to wait and watch
the revelers. She frowned to herself. All this disorder
would make good cover for activities other than dancing; cityens who might draw attention speaking to
each other in normal circumstances could easily have
arranged to meet here, where the noise and distraction of the crowd would cover any conversation. She
scanned the room, but saw nothing to concern her,
other than an unsafe density of cityens. People kept arriving, and hardly anyone seemed to be leaving. There
must be a back way out, though, for there was a nondescript opening set off with a curtain, through which
the musicians had emerged. A few other cityens came
in and out as well, mostly carrying food and jugs of
ferm to resupply the table across the room. It was even
more crowded over there.

She found herself wondering what the children
would make of all this easy prey. Enough food was
falling from clumsy fingers to feed them for a seven.
A small, determined body could weave its way at knee
level among the crowd, feeling carefully inside the
pockets of the distracted, perhaps skimming a pouch
or two to search later for treasures from those fool-

ish enough to let their belongings hang loose. A clever child could—no. Hunter shook thoughts of the desert out of her head. Her duty was to watch. Though nothing had happened that was worth seeing, other than Lia's dancing, which drew her eyes again. Not surprisingly, the med was good at it, graceful and light on her feet, weaving easily with Loro through the lines and squares as the lead drummer called the patterns. Loro was reasonably skilled as well, Hunter had to admit; he and Lia made an attractive pair among the many on the floor.

Hunter touched her tongue to the ferm she'd been carrying without drinking. It tasted sour, yeasty, crude compared with the stuff the priests made from time to time as a relaxant. Once past juvenile experimentation, most hunters rarely drank it, disliking the way it dulled the senses. That was obviously not a concern for the cityens here tonight. By now more than a few could barely keep their feet, and the pairings in the shadowy corners were hardly cognizant of onlookers.

Someone leaned up against the wall right next to her, so close his hip touched hers when he turned. Crowded as the place was, she could hardly begrudge him the space; without a glance, she slipped half a step sideways to give them both more room. He laughed softly, closing the gap again. "Don't worry. I'm only saving her place."

She did look then. It was Exey, the clever fabricator from the Bend. His long hair was pulled back to show off another of his filigreed creations glimmering in one ear, and he wore a loose white shirt embroidered with a design to match. He smiled when he saw his gold bauble dangling from her ear. "That looks nice on you. Lia has good taste." When she didn't say anything he asked, "Enjoying the fest?"

"It's interesting enough."

"It's more fun if you dance. But I don't suppose hunters do that. No offense," he added quickly at her glare. "I'm sure someone wants to ask you." He laughed again. He was nervous, she realized. He hadn't been, that day Lia had introduced them in the market. Before he knew what she was. "But I imagine you have other things on your mind."

She shrugged noncommittally, pretending to take another sip of the ferm. He was after something, clearly, and she remembered how he liked to talk. He'd fill the silence if she let him. And indeed, when she failed to respond, he continued, "The nun tithe, for example. That was quite a thing you did in the square. We heard about it over in the Bend. You saved some cityens' lives, no doubt about it." He paused, waiting for some reaction.

He hadn't approached her just to say thanks, she was sure. "Hunters are supposed to protect cityens," she said neutrally.

"Right. That's why we—my friends, I mean, I'm just the messenger—we thought we should give you something in return."

Ah. "I'm listening."

He looked around to be sure no one else was, lowering his voice though even a hunter wouldn't have been able to eavesdrop with all the noise. "We have some news we thought you'd want to hear." For a moment she thought his nerve would fail him and he wouldn't say whatever he had planned to tell her. He took a big sip of ferm for courage, leaving his cup at his lips so no one could see them move. "Everyone knows Loro hates the Church, right? Well, he's been talking, all about how he sent those hunters running himself."

Losing interest, she leaned back against the wall. "That's hardly news."

"Oh, I agree. Saint knows, I never met a man so impressed with his own skills. Well, I suppose I mention from time to time that I can fabricate a thing or two, but that's another story."

Maybe Lia would come back soon. "If that's all you have to tell me?" she asked pointedly.

"No, wait. Yes, Loro's always talked himself up, and he's always hated the Church, and everyone knows both of those things. What everyone doesn't know is that now he's planning to do something about it."

This was more interesting, but Exey didn't need to know she thought so. "I think the Church can handle Loro."

"We thought so too," he said with an anxious little smile. "But things have changed. A lot of cityens are listening to him these days. That means a lot of them could get hurt. You were there; you saw what almost happened in the square. What probably would have happened, without your help."

"The Warder handled that."

"Maybe so, maybe not." His eyes crinkled. "I'm sure that it didn't hurt his cause any to have you there looking all scary and intimidating while he made one of his noble speeches about unity and love." She glanced at him quickly, but couldn't tell where the joking stopped.

She shrugged. "None of this has anything to do with me, Exey. Loro is the Warder's man. If you have a problem with him, why not go to the Warder?"

Something flickered across Exey's face, too quickly for her to read before he covered it behind another long pull on his ferm. Wiping foam from his lip, he nodded. "We thought about that. In fact, if not for you, I'm sure that's what we—my friends—would do. It isn't entirely clear, though, that he would listen to us. In fact, it might make things worse. Look at it like this: Loro's been the Warder's right hand for a long time now. The Ward and the Bend, they get along just fine. Oh, sure, a little skirmish now and then along the edges, but nothing more serious than that. That's the beauty of balance, after all, both sides nice and even, and Saint knows North is too busy with its own self to—no, never mind, North's not the point. The point is this: if now the Bend comes along, says Loro's a problem, the Warder needs to rein him in—well, somehow we just can't see the Warder taking us at our word."

She was sure there was more to the story, maybe much more. If the Bend was that worried about Loro, they could eventually find a way to deal with him. "What else aren't you telling me, Exey?"

His eyes flicked away and back. "Nothing, of course." He was a good talker, but not a great liar.

She let it go for now. "Fine. But I don't understand why you think the Warder would listen to me and not to you."

"Yes, well, that's the thing, you see. We don't want you to tell the Warder. We want you to tell the Church."

Her mouth was suddenly parched. She took a deep drink of her own ferm, ignoring the sourness, until her throat loosened up enough for her to be sure of her voice. "What in the Saint's name makes you think I'd go back to them?"

He tried to smile. "That's a reasonable question. We debated even suggesting it, believe me. Me especially, since I was the lucky one who got to tell you." When she just kept staring at him he took a deep breath, plunging ahead. "We tried to figure how we'd feel in your position. Thrown out of the Church, I mean—no offense. We'd be angry, sure. I'm not saying you are, mind, just that we would be. But we'd also figure the Church had only done what they thought was right, even if they were wrong. And we'd still want to do the right thing ourselves, even if we *were* angry. Once we had a chance to think about it." Now it was his turn to leave a silence to be filled.

She drank again. "What would this right thing be?"

Now he looked straight at her, and he wasn't smiling. "What Loro's planning changes everything. He has to be stopped. This isn't some little dust-up between the claves he's talking about. What he's planning—it threatens everything. *Everything*. Only the Church can save us."

"Save you from what?" When he didn't answer, she said, "Don't be a fool, Exey. Listen to what you just said. *What* is Loro planning?"

"I don't know specifics. Only that it's something big."

She said roughly, "Even if what you say is true, you haven't given me anything to go to the Church with. Saints, Exey. Are you telling me cityens are planning to rebel? That hasn't happened in four hundred annuals. You think the Warder wouldn't believe you. You can't imagine what the Patri would say if I went back to him with nothing more than this." Her voice had risen; she lowered it with an effort. "I need proof."

"It's coming." It was something he didn't like, something dangerous. His long, skilled fingers shook, spilling a little of the ferm onto his fancy shirt.

"What is?"

"I don't know."

"Tell me *now*!"

"*I don't know*. No, don't do that, people will notice. We're just two friends talking at the fest; you can't strangle me here." She let go of his shirt and he sighed gratefully. "I like you, Echo. You make Lia smile. But as I said, I'm just a messenger. My friends thought it would be safer if I couldn't tell, no matter how, ah, tempting an offer you made." His dark eyes shone liquid in the torchlight. "They told me if you asked, to just say this: be ready. The time will come, and you'll know."

The music droned on. *Be ready.* An echo of the Patri's last charge to her. Hunter scanned the crowd, searching for Loro, but didn't see him. The warehouse seemed an unlikely place for him to start trouble; despite Lia's concerns, no hunters had appeared, and the drunken revelers would not make much of a militia, if that was what he had in mind. She didn't want to confront him in the midst of all these cityens, either; better to deal with him later, someplace the damage would be easier to contain.

On the far side of the room she spotted the Warder, seated comfortably at one of the few tables, smiling and nodding amiably as cityens came by to pay their respects. There was no sign that he planned to do anything more than that. It was a night for dancing, not for speeches.

She wanted to do much more than be ready. Part of her wanted to do exactly as Exey's friends suggested, run straight to the Patri with their story, beg his forgiveness and lead the hunters back to crush Loro's rebellion herself.

The more rational part judged that urge with a disapproval very near to contempt. What she had told Exey was true: this wasn't intelligence worth bringing. Perhaps the Patri didn't know Loro by name, but he was already worried about restive cityens. So what if he had suspected the Warder instead; that was more than close enough. Besides, Brit and Ava would have reported on Loro's actions in the square by now. There was nothing for Hunter to add. She had to have more, if there was more. She wondered uneasily what proof Exey meant. He might be lying about not knowing, but his fear had been genuine.

She wished she knew where Lia had gotten to; the floor had grown too crowded to see every dancer, and Hunter felt peculiarly uncomfortable letting the med out of sight. On the raised dais, the musicians, having taken a short break, settled back into their places with a metallic clatter. A new sound joined them, the twanging whine of metal wires stretched to various lengths across the top of a box. It reminded Hunter of the wind singing across the guy lines that steadied the transmission towers.

At that moment Lia reappeared, carrying a ferm. It might not be her first one; she was steady enough on her feet, but her face was flushed. Maybe it was just the dancing. "Whew," she said, taking a sip. "I wasn't sure Loro would ever let me go. Good thing the Warder got here. It distracted him just long enough." She took another long swallow, and that mischievous look was back. "I looked for you out there. I thought you said you could dance."

People trickled back to the center of the floor, making a disorderly line of pairs that had to double back on itself to fit the space as the music picked up. "I can."

"Well, why haven't you?"

What had Exey said? "No one asked me."

Lia stared at her, expressions flitting across her face too fast for Hunter to track. Her laughter, when it came, was a little choked. "But of course. I should have known. All right then, I can fix that. Echo: will you dance with me?"

Hunter looked down at her, feeling an unfamiliar tightness low in her belly. "Yes. I will."

Lia's golden eyes glowed in the torchlight. She took Hunter's ferm from her and set both glasses aside. Then she took Hunter by the elbow and guided her lightly to the floor, where they found their places in the twin rows of dancers, facing each other across an arm's length of empty space.

The musicians struck their tune, drums counting out a smart rhythm while the pipers pitched in merrily. Wires jangled, and the drummer began to call instructions. Lia reached out, waiting. Hunter raised her palms to match, and Lia took them, fingers intertwining. Her grip was strong and gentle, like the med herself. Their eyes met, and this expression Hunter recognized. Hunter let her hands slide to rest gently on Lia's waist, acutely aware of the flesh and bone beneath the soft spun fiber. Then they were skipping sideways down the line, under the raised arms of the other couples, until they got to the start, where they broke apart to clap the beat for the next pair coming. Simple, this cityens' dance, compared with the endless patterns she had counted out so often in the Churchyard, and of no utility at all. Yet Hunter found herself in no hurry for the music to end, and she was glad when the line began to repeat itself, and Lia reached for her again.

They were halfway back to the Ward when it happened. "Let's go home," Lia had asked, though the dancing seemed likely to go on all night, and if anyone else had left, it had made no diminution of the crowd and noise inside. Hunter was oddly hesitant, but the med insisted, pleading fatigue, and together they slipped out a side door. "Careful," Lia said. "If Loro sees us he'll be angry."

"Does that matter?" Hunter couldn't hide the sharpness in her tone.

"Don't *you* be angry, Echo, please."

"All right, I won't." And she wasn't, when Lia smiled. A strange contentment filled her as the med took her arm, leaning into her against the night air's chill, and she was warm where their bodies touched, and wished the walk were longer.

Then she heard the footsteps.

She knew immediately it wasn't just other festgoers heading home. It wasn't friends of Exey's come to meet her privately either: those were no honest footfalls, echoing off the stone; they had the peculiar muffled quality of men trying to walk silently and only barely not succeeding. Lia didn't hear, but she felt the change in Hunter's posture, and looked up to ask a question.

Hunter stopped her with a finger to her lips. Lia nodded, frightened now, but with enough presence of mind to follow her lead. Hunter kept them walking slowly down the middle of the way, obvious under the lightstrings, until they rounded a corner out of their pursuers' sight. Then she hurried the med into the shadow of a doorway. It brought back another night in the city, another girl she had tried to protect, annuals ago. Hunter had saved her from the mob, that girl, only to deliver her to a different kind of death. For a moment she saw that other face instead of Lia's. *I'm sorry*, she said again to the withered husk on the altar. *I should have let you run.*

"Echo, what is it?" Lia whispered.

"Shh. We're being followed." She pushed memory and the med deeper into the shadows, listening hard. Feet pounded down the street behind them, then paused. Her sensitive hearing picked up their pursuers' indecision, a few steps forward, a few to the side. A tongue of light licked this way and that, trying to pick up some taste of their prey. *Keep going*, Hunter urged them silently. *Don't turn.*

The light flickered this way. Two figures, features indistinguishable in the dark, worked their way cautiously down the alley. The one in front held something in one hand that he swung back and forth from doorway to doorway across the alley as his partner cast the light into each shadowy crevice. Some kind of weapon, from the way he moved. Hunter edged silently in front of Lia, one hand pressing the med's shoulder to keep her crouched low, putting herself between Lia and their pursuers.

They were only a few doorways down. Hunter felt the med's pulse pounding at the base of her neck. She gave a little squeeze, reassurance and warning. The med nodded silently against her hand.

Two doorways. One. The men paused again. *That's far enough. You must have missed us at the turn. Go back the way you came.*

Whispered conversation that even she could not make out.

Go.

The men turned away. One step, and another, and another. Hunter eased to standing, pulling Lia up behind her. The Warder's stronghold was only around the next corner. The med was fast, light on her feet. They only needed to outrun the men for a hundred paces. The length of the alley would be enough of a start. Hunter bounced a little on her toes, getting ready.

The chance never came. Hunter heard an unfamiliar metallic click, then the light swung back suddenly, pinning her squarely in the doorframe. Before she could move, there was a sharp *pop*, and the stone beside her exploded into splinters. Something hit her arm, hard enough to knock her sideways. Lia cried out, sounding more surprised than hurt.

The man holding the lantern must have jumped at the noise; the light lurched away, swung back to pick them out again. Hunter pushed herself out of the doorway with her good hand, running straight at the men. She was in arm's reach before the man with the weapon could bring it to bear a second time. She grabbed the front of the weapon, pushing it down instinctively. There was another loud *pop* and metal jerked hotly under her hand. Her nose twitched at a harsh acrid smell. She wrenched the thing out of the man's grip and swung it, still one-handed, in an arc that ended suddenly in a dull thud against his skull. The thing in her hand barked yet again, singeing her fingers. The man dropped without another sound. His companion cursed and swung the lantern at her, striking her injured arm. Stars exploded in her vision and she nearly fell. He snatched the weapon back, aimed it straight into her face. She heard a dull *click*. Nothing else happened. He cursed again, then unaccountably turned and ran.

She thrust herself upright, ready, but there was no further attack. Gingerly, she made her way back to the doorway. The med raised the piece of brick she had in her hand. Her face was flecked with dark spots in the starlight. Hunter caught her wrist as she began to swing the brick. "It's me."

"Echo?"

Hunter nodded, then realized the med couldn't see her in the dim light. "Yes. Are you hurt?"

"N-no. I don't think so." Lia's voice shook a little, now that the danger had passed. "No." Already settling. "What was that?"

"I don't know. Let's get out of here."

Her arm had begun to hurt in earnest by the time they made it back to the clinic. "Saints!" the med gasped, seeing Hunter's sodden sleeve in the light. It was Hunter's blood on her face. "Let me take a look at that."

Hunter flexed the arm gently, craning her neck to see the crimson streak that scored the muscle, below the shoulder. The med probed gently, flinching harder than Hunter when her fingers felt the spot. "There's something in there."

"A splinter from the rock?"

"I don't know. It feels strange." Lia hesitated. "It needs to come out."

Hunter nodded. "Go ahead."

By the time Lia was done she was pale, and Hunter was glad she herself had lain down before they started. She took a deep breath and sat back up, slowly. Just a little dizzy, not too bad. She looked into the bloody basin. "What is that?"

The med poked at it with an equally bloody finger. "I don't know." She held it to the light, a slightly misshapen, roundish blob.

Hunter felt a chill that had nothing to do with the wound. She took the evil little thing and stared at it. "It's a projectile."

"I don't understand."

"That thing the man had"—Lia hadn't seen it in the dark—"it was a projectile weapon." *Exey's proof?* Her head swam.

The Bender was right. This changed everything. *Saints.* If Loro had had this in the square . . .

The med stared at it in revulsion. "I didn't know there was such a thing."

"There isn't supposed to be," Hunter said grimly, slipping the fragment into her pocket while the med affixed a bandage to her arm.

Lia's hands shook the tiniest fraction. "Did you recognize them?"

"No. I didn't get a good look, but I don't think it was anyone I've seen before."

Lia was thinking hard, despite the shock. "We were still in the edge; they must just have been troublemakers."

"Maybe. It would be an awfully big coincidence."

"You think they might have been after you? Who would dare? Besides—" Lia hesitated, then went on with a little grimace. "If they were after you, they would have known it was me with you. I can't believe anyone would risk hurting a med, not from any clave. Not if they knew."

Hunter tested her arm carefully; it throbbed with every motion and would be worse in the morning, but she could still use it. "A weapon like that changes everything."

"It's *evil*." Lia's voice shook again. Her fingertip moved from the arm to Hunter's chest. "If that—projectile—had been this much further over, you'd be dead."

Hunter couldn't think of anything to say. That thought was nothing compared with the idea of cityens armed with such a thing. And it wouldn't take many: a few of them, in the hands of cityens who didn't scruple to use them, could do untold damage.

Maybe just against each other in alleys now, but even if the Benders were wrong about Loro, it didn't matter; it would not be long until it occurred to *someone* that the equation had changed, that the cityens were armed more powerfully than the Church. . . .

"You could be *dead*. Don't you care?" Lia's tone wavered between anger and despair. Her hand tightened on Hunter's arm, hard enough to hurt. "Don't you?"

Another wave of dizziness made it hard to put the words together. "It didn't happen, Lia. It's not worth thinking about."

The med was trembling all over now. "You never think about what might have been? What could be?"

If the stunner's wiring hadn't failed, and Tana hadn't died. If Ela hadn't gone so close to the edge. Hunter raised her good hand to her eyes, pressed until the flashing lights burned away the vision of those alternate possibilities. They had not happened. They could never have been real. Only one thing was, now, and it was almost more than she could bear. She opened her eyes again. This room, plain, clean, except where her blood had spattered it. At least that could be washed away, the room reset to its original state. Would she get another chance then, or did it always end like this?

"Echo, stay with me tonight. Please."

"It's not that bad."

Lia laughed, tears running from the corners of her eyes. "You're such a fool." She raised her hands to cradle Hunter's face. The room tilted, wavering, resettled into lines almost the same, nothing at all as they had been. "I'm asking for me, not you."

The injured arm hurt badly in the morning when she woke, and the other almost as much, where Lia's weight had trapped it through what was left of the night. Hunter rolled up, ignoring a stab of pain. With a fingertip she traced the line of the med's soft cheek, her lips, half smiling still, the strong and delicate column of her throat. Hunter did not want to move, ever again, wanted to lie there, looking at Lia's face, content in sleep, as if the small weight of metal in Hunter's arm had not tipped a balance that could never be restored.

But it had.

The Patri must be told. Such a threat to the Church could not be tolerated. What he would do to the cityens, when he found out . . . But better now, before the weapons were put to use. Most cityens were loyal; she would make him see. Perhaps, by telling him, she would be serving Church and cityens alike; that's what Exey's friends would say. She would be doing what hunters were made to do.

The Church would admit her now, she knew: she had proof of her story, in her pocket, in the torn flesh of her arm. She should be grateful for the wound: it would regain her her place in the Church, where she belonged.

Where Lia did not.

She could not go back.

She had no other choice.

She lay for a long time propped on the injured arm, watching Lia sleep until the pain became unbearable. Then she rose and slipped quietly away.

She felt hot and cold both at once. Saints knew what filth the ball had carried into her body, but the priests and their machines could probably fix whatever it was. If she were there. The Church had to know about the weapons. She had to tell the Patri. But maybe . . . Her mind turned possibilities feverishly, looking for a way, flitting through alternatives in fractured images too fast for her conscience to keep up. She knew that if she stopped to think she would be appalled at her weakness. No, worse than weakness—that could be forgiven. This was something else. Unsound. To care only about her own desires, when she had a duty to perform, to ache after one thing with all her being—no. She did not have time for judgments now.

Where was the place? Annuals ago, Tana had shown her. *A last resort*, the old hunter had said. *A way to call, for a hunter in extremis.* She cast back to that day. The alleys were different now, wider, but that didn't matter; she overlaid the map she had seen as a child on the dust she stepped through here, and it wasn't long before she found the spot. No guarantee that what she needed would be there; no way to test whether the technology still worked.

Please, by the Saint. Please be there.

She pulled aside an angled slab of rubble, not near as heavy as it looked, but the effort still made her breathless. She had lost more blood than she had realized. Her head ached, making it hard to think. It didn't matter. There, just inside the tall, narrow gap the false slab had been placed to cover . . . Squeezing into the tight space, she touched a lever that still worked smoothly, squatted by the hidden grate. She knew the words. "My service to the Church in all things," she breathed.

Into silence. Nothing lived, nothing breathed. No. *No*. She had to get word to the Church, now. This last duty, and then—she didn't know. Saint help her, she didn't know. Down the alley she heard a step, another. *Go away*, she wished, knowing they would not. "*My service to the Church in all things.*"

A tiny click. "Speak, if you would serve the Church." The voice buzzed with the faintest edge of static. Her eyes closed as relief flooded her, dizzying. There was a noise from outside. Dust drifted down on her as someone pawed around the niche. She only had seconds. *Think, Echo.* "Someone is making projectile weapons. A Wardman named Loro. He wants to stop the tithe. The Patri must know. If he sends hunters into the city unaware it will be a massacre. He has to—"

"Your words are heard." No way to know if the link was live. It could be a dead reporter, mindlessly replaying a loop.

"Tell the Patri—" She wasted a precious second to control her voice. "Tell him I still serve."

"Your words are heard."

"No—tell him—"

"Your words are heard." *Click*.

She sat in the dark with her head bowed. If only she could know the reporter was live, she could stay in the city, pretending to await the orders the Patri would find a way to send her. Precious days to stay.

She wanted them with a desperation that hurt almost as much as her arm. If she went away now, she could never return, not to things the way they were.

Not to Lia.

Then she heard the voice.

"Echo—what are *you* doing in there?" Justan, peering into the niche. Saints, Justan of all people.

"What does it look like?" She straightened, making a show of tugging at her pants.

"This's Church tech. Who were you talking to?"

"I was telling you to leave me to my business."

"That's not what it sounded like."

"That's what it was, Justan. The tech here's dead." She forced a smile. "Deserves what it got from me." *Believe me, please.* She started to walk away, but he blocked the path.

"No. I heard you talking 'bout weapons."

The words ripped away choice with a physical pain. There would be no staying now. She stopped still, not looking at him. "You must have misheard. I'm sure you did."

"No," he said stubbornly. "I don't know who you were talking t', but I know what I heard. You said something about weapons, and we found Trallen dead last night, with a big hole in his head. You know something about't. Come with me, Echo. The Warder will want to hear about this."

For the space of a breath she was tempted. But whoever had tried to kill her might try again, before she could get word to the Patri. That was her only duty now. She gave Justan one last chance. "You were right. This is a Church matter. Don't interfere with things above your place."

Hurt made his boyish face look older. "I liked you Echo, lots. But that doesn't matter now, I got my duty. And you're right, it's not for me to decide. So let's go now. The Warder'll know what to do." His hand closed over her wrist.

Poor fool. She meant only to disable him long enough for her to get away before he could raise an alarm, but he fought back with more skill than she could easily counter one-armed and wobbly from blood loss. She needed him on the ground where she could get a sleeper hold. Dropping her shoulder into his chest, she used crude strength to knock him backwards into the niche. His head struck stone with a loud crack that seemed to surprise him; he fell against the grate, eyes wide, and didn't move any more.

She wasn't sure how long she stood there, dizzy and sick.

The fierce girl appeared beside her, toeing the body dispassionately. "Dead," she said approvingly.

Hunter closed her eyes. She was hallucinating,

from the blood loss, it must be, or the wound could be poisoned. She had seen the mind wander often enough in Lia's patients, though she had never known a hunter, no matter how weak, to lose the faculty to distinguish illusion from reality. Another sign of her infirmity. She opened her eyes again, and the girl was still there.

So was Lia.

The med knelt by Justan's body, a hand at his neck. After a little while the hand moved to brush the unruly curls back from his face. Then she rose, a slow movement that seemed to take all her strength. Her face was bloodless. "He's dead."

No. Not Justan. She had only knocked him down. She only needed a few minutes' lead to get away, then he would wake, go back to his interrupted breakfast and—

"I heard you talking to him, and then I saw—Echo, you killed him."

Hunter couldn't speak.

Lia's golden eyes reflected horror. Her voice came out barely more than a whisper. "I woke up, and you were gone. I didn't know what to think, maybe that you were frightened, after we—" Lia broke off, eyes closing. Trying, Hunter knew, not to see that scene juxtaposed with this one. The monster she had given herself to. *Saints, what have I done?* The med forced herself to continue, though her voice shook so hard it was barely understandable. "I knew I had to find you, but I didn't have any idea where to look. Then the guards came in with this girl. They told me she crossed into the city a few hours ago, up North, desperate for help. She had this." Lia held up a ragged piece of Hunter's old uniform shirt. "The guards knew enough to bring her straight to me. She led me here, I don't know how."

The girl smiled proudly, scuffing away a bootprint. Then her face puckered. "Boy's sick," she said. "Bad sick."

They could not stand here in the open. "Where are the guards?" Hunter asked.

Lia's eyes darted to the niche, back. Hunter smelled the sour sharpness of her fear. "Are you going to kill me too?"

Hunter backed, hands clasped behind her, until she came up against the wall. "Please, Lia. Go back to the clinic. Forget all of this." *Say you will. I'll believe you. I won't hurt you.*

"No."

"Please, Lia. Go back."

"No!" The med's violent whisper might as well have been a shout.

Hunter's good hand lifted to touch Lia's face. "Lia, just listen to me. You have to go back. Before something happens to you too."

Lia jerked away, her face distorted with fear and fury. "Don't tell me what to do. Don't you ever tell me what to do!"

The weight of Hunter's hand dropping through the empty air was more than her legs could hold. They buckled, and only the stone digging into her back kept her from falling. Her lungs heaved for air. The sun burned through her closed eyes into her brain. Some-one, alerted by the noise or just unlucky, would find them any minute.

A shadow fell across her face.

Lia's voice still shook, but she had command of it now. "She says the child is very sick. Take me to him."

"I can't."

"I'm not abandoning a sick child somewhere in the desert without help."

Hunter scrubbed her good hand across her face. "I'll think of something."

"Listen to me." Somehow Lia found the courage to touch her arm. "You're not a med. If he dies because you couldn't—" Lia swallowed. Tears swam in her eyes. "I can't let that happen. Not to the child, not to you, even if you—" She glanced again at Justan, then resolutely back. "I don't want anyone else to die. Not if I can help it."

They made it to the forcewall unmolested.

With every step Hunter fought not to let herself fly into a thousand jagged pieces, counting single-mindedly, one, two, three, four, one, two, three, four, in the most basic ritual of self-control she knew. The girl trotted ahead, glancing back at them over her shoulder often, wordlessly urging them to hurry. Finally they rounded the last corner and came to the barrier. It hummed quietly to itself. A few scraps of fur lay outside at its feet, all that was left of some unwary animal that had come too close. The scavengers had taken care of the rest. Lia hesitated for the first time. "I've never crossed the wall." She swallowed, eyeing the remains. "All my life I've been taught that cityens who go outside die."

"You'll be safe with me."

Lia's face contracted as if she were about to laugh, or cry. The girl hopped from foot to foot, impatient to move on. Lia looked from Hunter to the child, then nodded, unable to speak.

The girl leapt through the forcewall with a little *zzzzttt*. Lia swallowed again, raising a fingertip to the invisible barrier. "It tingles."

"That's all that happens. It recognizes humans. It won't hurt you."

Lia took a breath, another, then jumped through the wall in one abrupt motion. She looked back, shaking her arms. "I thought it would be worse."

"Come on."

The girl led the way, but Hunter could have found it just as easily. By now most growing things had given way to the incessant heat; the stalks of plants that had already set their seeds in the summer rose brown and brittle like spears amidst the irregular mounded hills, but here and there the tougher specimens still showed a hint of green against the dust. Without the forcewall's haze, the patches of sky between the clouds glowed brilliant blue, and the clouds themselves showed every shade of gray and purple. A jagged streak of light split the horizon; Hunter counted fifteen heartbeats before the low rumble rolled its way to them. The faintest bitterness of ozone tickled her tongue. A few drops spattered dust by their feet, a tease; there would be no real rain until winter, and precious little then. Still, it woke smells, beyond the acrid dust.

Lia's eyes were wide, but not from fear. "It's so beautiful."

"It's the desert."

The med shook her head slowly, astonished. "I never knew."

"Come on, we have to hurry."

It wasn't far. Lia looked around, puzzled, as they stopped by a pile of rubble that looked like a dozen others they had passed, not seeing the entrance two feet from her shoulder. The girl ducked her head and was gone. "Through here," Hunter said. "Stay close to me."

They came into the chamber.

The boy lay in the back corner on a pile of rags. Even in the dim light, Hunter's sharp vision picked out the pallor around his mouth, the hollows shadowing his sunken eyes. It took Lia's slower-adjusting eyes a moment to find him. "Where—ooh." The boy stirred, hearing them, trying to push himself further into the corner, animal instinct to protect himself from predators. He was alone.

"Where's the little one?" Hunter asked.

The girl shook her head. Pain seared Hunter's nerves.

"It's me," Hunter said, dropping to her heels beside the boy. "I brought help."

"Safe?" His voice was a dry whisper.

She nodded, then, not sure he could see, said, "Yes."

Lia was already next to her, running gentle hands along his arms, legs. "What's your name?" The boy frowned, puzzled. Lia turned to Hunter, who lifted a shoulder. What did it matter? Lia's look was incredulous. "You don't know his name?"

The boy started to say something, but cut off with a wince of pain as Lia lightly touched his body. She shot a glance at Hunter, eased the rags away from the boy's swollen belly. Even in the dimness the skin showed tight and shiny red. Lia rocked back, eyes closing for a moment. Then she turned to the girl. "How long has he been like this?"

The girl stared down a minute, thinking, then held up four fingers.

"Saints." Something close to anger flashed across Lia's features as she stared at Hunter. "There's no one else to help them? This is the way they live?"

"They can fend for themselves."

Lia shook her head in disgust. "You might as well kill him too." She reached out to grab Hunter's wrist as Hunter thrust to her feet. "No, wait, I—"

Lia's voice stopped abruptly, because the girl was holding something shiny hard against her throat. Hunter's old knife, that she had left as her one gift to them.

"Don't hurt her," Hunter said to the girl as calmly as she could manage. "Lia, don't move. Don't move at all."

Lia drew the barest careful breath by way of response.

"She's my friend," Hunter said to the girl. "She wasn't going to hurt me." The girl looked doubtfully from Hunter to Lia, not removing the knife. "Let her go. She's trying to help him."

The girl was very frightened, tension limning the thin face, whitening the knuckles on the hand that held the knife. She stood frozen, like a small animal not knowing which way to run. Then she abruptly stepped away.

Lia raised a hand to rub her throat. "I'm sorry," she said shakily.

Hunter's voice came out hard, cold. "Can you help him?"

She knew, from the look in Lia's eyes. "May we speak privately?"

"There's nothing they can't—" Hunter began, but she stopped. "This way."

The daylight was bright after the dim cave. Hunter's eyes watered. She wiped an angry hand across them. Lia studied the sand. "There's something wrong inside his belly. Probably something is twisted. I've seen it often enough. Sometimes it gets better by itself. Sometimes it stays that way. Then it begins to swell, to cause pressure. When that happens, the blood doesn't flow properly. Things begin to die inside."

"Is there anything you can do?"

"I'm sorry, Echo."

The sun was squarely in Hunter's eyes, blinding her. "All right. Go home."

"What?"

"You, girl!" The child came running, but stopped dead at the sight of Hunter's face. "Take Lia back."

The girl shook her head violently. She looked back into the cave, took a step that direction. Hunter grabbed her by the arm, hard. "Do as I say."

"Echo," Lia started.

"Do you hear me? Take her back, right now."

"*Echo.*"

A hand closed on Hunter's shoulder. She dropped the girl's arm and spun, clamping her palm atop the hand. A twist, a little push, and her assailant was on her knees, wrist locked at an angle where the slightest resistance would snap tendon and bone.

"Echo, please! You're hurting me."

Rage boiled down her nerves, rendering away reason like scraps of fat off dead bones. Her arms trembled with the effort not to make the next, fatal move.

She let go all at once. Lia knelt before her, rubbing her wrist, face twisted in pain. The girl pressed up against a slab, safely out of reach, tensed to leap further if Hunter made the slightest advance.

"Saints." Hunter pressed both hands to her pounding temples. Her shoulder was on fire. Every heartbeat throbbed red against the back of her eyes. She spoke in the general direction of the girl. "Take Lia back to where she can find her way home. She'll take care of you. I promise."

Lia made her way to her feet. Her voice trembled with tears though her face was dry. "Echo—"

Hunter shook her head. "I can't go with you. I have to take care of him."

The look Lia gave her was sharp, full of frightened suspicion. Hunter closed her eyes against it. She could not stop her ears against the accusation spiraling up in Lia's voice. "What are you going to do?"

A girl, dying at the base of a cliff. Flesh soft against Hunter's breast, trusting. So easy, to make that end. Even Lia could see it in her now. Could see her do it. Finally, in the unforgiving glare of the desert, could see what had always stood before her, a thing ill made, unsound.

Unhuman.

Hunter turned and gathered up the unresisting boy with the careless strength a cityen could never match. His slight body barely made a weight against her. Lia's lips parted, but no sound came out.

No cry could have echoed louder in the stillness.

She shut her mind to everything but what needed to be done. As she turned her back she said, "I'm taking him to the Saint."

CHAPTER 20

He was brave, the little boy, enough to do a hunter
proud. Not daring to risk an encounter with cityens,
Hunter took the long way around, outside the forcewall, carrying him as gently as she could across the
broken terrain. Mindful of predators as daylight
waned, she scanned their surroundings constantly
as she walked, her head swiveling while she kept her
arms firm and still around the boy's swollen body.
Even half conscious, the child knew to keep silent; only
once, when she missed a step across a crevasse, twisting her ankle and making a back-wrenching effort to
avoid a fall that might have killed them both, did he
cry out, and even then it was bitten short. She smelled
the blood on his lips afterwards.

She had to slow after that despite the desperate instinct for haste. Her back and arms burned from the
long march bearing the boy's weight, no longer slight

in the least, and her ankle stabbed pain with every step. Something dripped down her sleeve, and she knew the wound had opened again. Her blood and the boy's, the predators would be drawn from every lair. She half saw them from the corner of her eye, padding patiently from shadow to shadow, waiting for another fall. If she did not make it to the Church before full dark, she never would.

Finally, as the light died in the west, she saw it. Above the burning spire the crossed antennas stood sentinel against her approach. She could barely remember feeling it had been her guide to home. The rose window cast a withering glare.

Another hour's stumbling march finally brought her to the forcewall. She hesitated for a half-crazed moment, imagining that it would mistake her for one of the predators that circled closer now. Then she stepped through, with a bare tingle that did not rouse the boy from what she feared was more than sleep, and onto the dusty steps. The huge doors loomed before her, blank, forbidding. A strong man with an axe had no hope against those doors; a party of strong men with a ram might move them in a day, or ten. The little knife on Hunter's belt would barely leave a scratch.

Those other defenses, though, were what she feared. Once before, Hunter had stood here with a stranger, the young woman who now lay on the altar entwined with the city's systems, but then just a frightened girl dragged back from the desert to meet her fate. That girl had found faith, but Hunter had stood beside her, hand raised to the door's implacable test, and wondered if she would be struck dead for doubting.

Her questions then were nothing to the heresies she brought with her now.

She knelt, settling the boy as softly as she could onto the top step, far enough to one side that if she fell, or if the charge passed through her, whoever came to clean up might still find him unharmed. He moaned without waking. The little breeze that had picked up with sunset brought the smell of cooking from somewhere inside the walls. Incongruously, her stomach rumbled, reminding her that she hadn't eaten since the fest. Saints. Only a day ago. A wave of nausea washed over her. She leaned over, hands on her knees, panting until it passed. She wondered if they had seen her yet. They would, once her entry attempt logged on the panels. Maybe, even if she died here, they would accept the boy.

Not even your own, the breeze whispered in the voice of a different girl, dead in the desert at the foot of a cliff. *Why him?*

Hunter straightened abruptly. She raised a fingertip. She had been taught to place a palm flat against the panel, confident and strong, but the doors didn't care; they only needed a taste. She took a deep breath and reached.

The charge flung her halfway down the steps before she even felt her finger make contact. She lay for a moment, gathering herself, then got up and did it again. This time it took longer to get up, and her hand tingled painfully. Once more, and again the door threw her back.

Three times was all the mercy it would show. Sometimes they found the body of an animal on the steps, too stupid or desperate or driven mad by the sun to stop flinging itself against the doors before the charge turned deadly. They had never, in Hunter's lifetime, found a human. *Surprise them*, she thought with a grim little laugh. She pushed herself to her feet. A broken slab alongside the path at the bottom of the steps caught her eye. Mustering her last strength, she hauled it up to the doors and laid it flat in front of them. Carefully she worked her toes under the edge until her right foot was solidly jammed, anchoring her in place. Bones would have to break before the door sent her down the steps again.

She slammed both palms against the plates.

The first instant burned all thought from her brain. Her nerve endings registered the searing agony, but she had no way to escape, no choice but to stand there, suspended by muscles locked rigid as stone in response to the charge running through her. She was dimly aware that her diaphragm had locked as well, and lungs emptied by the initial impact struggled and failed to refill. Her vision narrowed to bright exploding stars far away down a long tunnel, but the pain, the pain refused to dim, and she had a last moment of coherence to wonder if it could last forever, before one of the stars detonated in her head and she was sent hurtling into the dark with no awareness at all.

CHAPTER 21

She heard voices. That surprised her; what was there to speak in the vast emptiness of death? The constant stream of sounds would not resolve into intelligible words, no matter how hard she listened. Maybe they were some sort of hallucination, neurons firing with no external stimulus. But no, the Church taught with certainty that neurologic function ceased at the moment of death. This must be something else.

That was as far as she got for some time. No other senses returned. If there was light in this place, it did not register on her eyes, if she had eyes; she had no perception of a physical body containing whatever this was doing the thinking. Gradually she considered that perhaps she was not dead.

Despair flooded through her. What if there was no end, ever?

She tried to shut awareness down, to dive into the

impenetrable darkness enclosing her. She could not. Individual sounds began to separate from the stream, form words, string themselves into groups that she recognized as sentences, though she could not grasp their meaning.

" . . . Stable now . . . better . . . not him. No sense . . . wake . . ."

There was light.

Her eyes were open. With that realization came pain, fracturing the light into rainbows. The pain became a body, her body, battered, lying on a pallet in an enormous room with a high, vaulted ceiling laced with innumerable cables. She turned her head a fraction to the side to see the platform where the cables originated in the shrouded form at the still center.

"How . . ."

The croaking gasp was all she could manage. A pale blur blocked her view. Muscles worked hard, pulling at lenses, bringing the face into focus. "The Saint recognized you in time."

The Patri. Until this moment, she had not truly believed she would see him again. See this place, this sanctuary. The Saint in her shroud, almost close enough to touch. Something swelled painfully in Hunter's throat. The light splintered again, and she couldn't see anything at all. "Here, let me help you." A gentle arm encircled her shoulders, eased her upright.

"The boy . . ."

"The child you brought? He is safe."

"He was sick. . . ."

"He is better now." She saw him then, lying on a pallet nearby, still. Fear flashed through her; she had never seen him look so young, without the little line that creased between his eyes even when he closed them. The twisted marks of pain were smoothed away, but she could see the pulse in his neck. His face was relaxed in sleep, nothing worse. She closed her eyes, limp in every muscle. She opened them again at the Patri's words. "I have questions for you."

She struggled to compose a proper report, could only come up with, "I found the Warder."

"That isn't important now."

"But . . ." Not important? It was the reason for—everything. Tana's dead stare accused her. She must make him understand. "Patri, the cityens are angry. They have new weapons. The tithe—"

He shushed her gently. "Later, Echo, later. Try to concentrate now on what I'm asking. You passed through the forcewall yesterday, not alone."

"I'm not sure what day . . ."

"Don't worry, I know what day." Beneath the soothing tone, a hint of something else, harder. "Someone was with you. Who was it? That's what is important."

Her gaze flickered to the boy. "He was sick. I thought the Saint . . ."

"Yes, the Saint healed him. But he's not the one we're looking for. The Saint checked his denas. They aren't what we saw passing through the forcewall. Think back, carefully. It's very important. Before the boy, who else was with you?"

Memory coalesced, fragments piecing together. Not everything, but enough to give him his answer when she caught breath to speak. The girl. And Lia, of course.

Why did it matter so much?

She straightened out of the comfort of his arm, testing herself. At least she could sit unaided. Feeling was coming back to her fingers; she wriggled them, clenching and opening fists until she was sure they were under her control. Her legs were still numb, but her toes tingled painfully as whatever the doors' charge had done began to wear off. As her vision cleared, she recognized the face behind the Patri's shoulder. "Gem."

"Echo Hunter 367. It is good to see you well." The irony the girl must have intended was well hidden in her placid tone.

"You will have time to speak later," the Patri said.

Gem inclined her head in agreement. "I look forward to it." Again, perfectly placid. A challenge, perhaps, or some deeper change in the girl.

The Patri paid no attention. "Tell me what happened, Echo, when you left the city. The rest can wait."

It was so hard to compose her thoughts. "The boy was sick," she began.

"We know that, but he isn't the answer. The denas we saw were female. Who was she? Please try to remember, Echo, it's very important." It was more than impatience, it was hunger, barely restrained in his voice. This was something he wanted more than the

Warder, the tithe, even the weapons. A gift she could give him to earn her place back forever, no distance between them, no exile. All for a name she had not even been sent to find. She almost laughed, giddy, and choked on it. His hand squeezed her good shoulder gently, steadying. "Who was she?"

She looked at him, at the beginning of the approving smile in his eyes, almost enough to ease the cramp in her heart. So long, since she had seen that. Before Tana. Before Ela. All that she had done could be forgotten. So easy.

Lia. The name came to her lips, soft as a kiss.

"I can't remember," she said. A pain like the charge of the doors shot through her.

The Patri let out a long breath and leaned away. "Are you sure?"

"Yes, Patri." She did not even try to hide the tremor in her voice. "No. The past few days . . . I'm not sure. Please, if I could just have a little time. . . ." Pathetic, to beg like that, even if she weren't a hunter. What was wrong with her?

"It could be the charge," Gem said thoughtfully. "It can affect memory."

"Yes." The Patri ran a hand through his white hair. It had receded more since Hunter had seen him last. His eyes were shadowed, hiding the smile. If it had ever been there at all. What had happened to him since she was gone? "I'm sure you're right. Rest for now, Echo. I have matters to attend to here." He turned to Gem. "Take her to the domicile. Watch over her so she can sleep untroubled. After she wakes, I'm sure she'll be able to tell us more. If not," he added thoughtfully, looking at the altar, "perhaps the Saint will be able to help."

Rest evaded her. The familiar small noises of the domicile, the low whir of fans and near-silent hunter footsteps passing in the hall, were alien now after the months of city clamor. Hunter watched the moon track slowly across a window, the slanted rays only emphasizing the shadowy recesses of the cell. She should perform the relaxation techniques an old hunter had taught her when she was very small, the first time fear of the dark had to be faced instead of escaped in the comforting embrace of her bearer nun; but she could not gather herself to control her churning thoughts.

All of which centered around Lia.

What had the boards seen in her? The forcewall knew denas, nothing more; that was how it separated human from not. It could tell hunters by the tags the original priests had put in their denas, not individuals of course, but that one was a hunter. She assumed that it could tell priests as well; she had never asked. And the Saint: surely it knew the Saint, whose making was most carefully crafted of all, and who had not varied in a hundred iterations, since the first Saint ascended in that grimmest of all annuals after the Fall.

But not the cityens. They were untagged, unselected; like the animals in the desert, they mated by choice, or for lack of choice, procreating randomly. Lia was just another one of them. Why was the Patri so interested? How had the panels picked her out?

. The moon drifted past the window. Across the compound the Saint lay on the altar, her constancy a rebuke. Hunter did not deserve to be even this close. Yet she could see the sanctuary clearly in her mind: at this time of night all the light would come from the priests' panels; it would be tinting their hands and faces green as they worked, an echo of the tag the priests had placed in the first Saint's denas, that Hunter had used to track down the fugitive girl in the desert. The light would be glowing on what was left of that girl in the sanctuary, the white cloth, the wires entwined like a cage as they left her body, tethering her mind to the great circuits of the city.

What did Lia have to do with any of this?

At the edge of sleep Hunter saw the answer, but darkness overtook the thought before it was fully formed, and it fell into the abyss with the rest of consciousness.

She awoke to daylight. She started to sit up, but stopped. Gem sat at the foot of her bed, cross-legged, comfortable. Only the slightest circles beneath her eyes betrayed her.

"You watched there all night?"

Gem shrugged indifferently. She was still young; a sleepless night was nothing to her. "You heard the Patri's wishes."

Hunter gathered herself painfully to mirror Gem's position. There was little trace of girlishness in her now. Her shoulders were nearly as broad as Hunter's, the lithe musculature close to its mature development. Her face was unlined still, browned by sun, except in the tiny creases at the corner of her eyes where she had squinted often, the way the hunters did who spent long stretches in the desert. The way Hunter had, before the city.

She did not want to think of the city. That way led to Lia, and to questions she could not answer. The Patri might have ordered Gem to probe for information. To forestall her Hunter said, "Make your report, Gem Hunter 378. If you are permitted." The implication that she might not be would make Gem more likely to talk, out of sheer obstinacy.

Gem inclined her head, a brief flicker of amusement at Hunter's presumption tugging at one corner of her mouth. A few months ago she would have been angry. "I have not been told to keep information from you. I have little of substance to report on the hunters. There have been no . . . accidents . . . since you left. The younger batches are doing well in their training. The 390s are being weaned. They are making considerable fuss." Once Hunter could have smiled at that. Gem sobered. "Criya Hunter 367 did not return from the desert. We searched, but failed to recover her."

Criya. Hunter felt the shiver of something falling away forever. She remembered Tana's crooked smile. *One day I realized I was the last of my batch.* She did not want to think of Tana either, not with Gem sitting at her feet, studying her openly. The hollowness Hunter felt in her belly almost leaked into her voice. "What of the Patri? Is he well?"

"You saw him."

"He seems well, but . . ." She searched for a word that would not force Gem to deny it. "Tired. More than usual." She realized with a wrench that she did not know what was usual for him, now.

"The Materna died shortly after you were excommunicated."

"I see." Hunter had felt little attachment to that old woman, soft and vague as she always seemed, but still it was hard to imagine her gone. "The Patri must miss her."

"As he would miss any of us. There is a new one now." A pause. "Also, there have been difficulties with the Saint."

The fans in the refectory had stopped. There had been a fire. And the hunger in the Patri's eyes . . . Dread shaped itself behind her thoughts. "What kind of difficulties?"

Gem hesitated, then said again, "I have not been told to keep information from you." She glanced in the direction of the sanctuary. "The power transmission has grown erratic, and once the forcewall failed for several seconds. No harm was done, but the priests were much disturbed. The Patri has said nothing, but hunters have heard the nuns chattering about growing a new Saint."

Hunter remembered the chaos in the city when the old Saint failed, power lines burning, a child dead. Nothing close to that was happening now. Even the troubles Hunter had seen herself, beyond what Gem reported— "Surely the priests can make corrections. She still has many years to function."

Gem looked, for once, unsure. "Do you think something could have gone wrong in her making?"

"Maybe." The word was a betrayal, dishonoring that brave girl. Hunter averted her eyes from the sanctuary as she spoke. "Something can go wrong with any of our making. But there was no sign. She did what she was made to do. She was strong."

"You had to bring her back. She was afraid."

In the end she was the one who chose to return. I would have let her go. She would not blaspheme against the girl's memory by confessing that aloud. "You would be afraid too, Gem Hunter 378. Don't think otherwise."

Gem said, "I wouldn't run from my duty."

It stung, that echo of the long-ago lesson, in a room not far from here, on the day after Ela had died. The shadow of anger touched Hunter from far away. "If you had ever truly been frightened, you would not be so certain. I hope one day you will know what that fear feels like."

"Do *you,* Echo Hunter 367?"

Her dead watched from the shadows, waiting to see how Hunter would answer. She wondered if Gem ever saw Tana in her nightmares. And now the Patri asked Hunter about Lia, asked her to— She shook herself, sorry for the anger. *Even you do not deserve that lesson*, she almost told Gem, as if the girl were a child she should protect from herself. But it was not a child who regarded her now, and to that hard, unsmiling face she could not offer such a thought, only shook her head dumbly.

Gem studied her openly, curious, perhaps a bit troubled. At last she said, "It is time to go."

Limping across the compound again was like being in a dream so vivid it might be real. Hunter blinked, trying to compose herself. There were no signs of difficulty with the Saint this bright morning. Priests and nuns walked the paths, a few young hunters strode towards the training grounds with no other concern but their objective. A cohort of very small juveniles practiced stalking each other like canid pups at play, while the nuns watched from the shade of the gated yard. All of it seemed to be happening far away, as if Hunter viewed them through a priest's magnifier turned backwards.

"The 388s," Gem said, following Hunter's glance.

"Of course," Hunter snapped. But her eyes lingered on the nuns. One, brown haired, shorter than the others, laughed, a bright sound out of place against the dull buzz of Hunter's thoughts.

Gem eyed her sideways. "Do you wish to bathe?" she asked, her neutral tone rebuke enough. "There is time. The Patri is in communion with the Saint."

Hunter almost said no out of spite, but though someone had seen to her arm and it no longer bled, her sleeve was crusted with old blood, her clothing filthy. And she stank, she realized as her nose wrinkled in protest. She inclined her head as graciously as she could manage. "Yes, thank you."

She wished she could soak for hours, letting the heat work the aches from her injuries, the tension from her neck. Instead she cleaned herself efficiently, taking only the necessary time to scrub through the layers of filth, probing carefully to assess the damage. Her left ankle was swollen and blue, but she could move it well enough. She eased the bandage off her arm, finding the wound no worse than it should be, the flesh tender but the margins beginning to heal. The remainder was nothing more than scattered scrapes and bruises, not worth her attention. Why then did exhaustion still course through her, weakness dragging at her bones? As she brushed back wet hair grown far past hunter custom, her fingers missed the tiny weight of Lia's gold dangling from her ear. She must have lost it somewhere in the desert. No matter; it had no place here. She cupped water into her eyes again, washing away a sudden sting.

Gem studied her body without embarrassment as she rose reluctantly from the pool. "You have not been caring for yourself properly. You should eat."

As if the words activated a circuit, Hunter's stomach gurgled loudly. The day before yesterday, the fest. It seemed so much longer, as if time had stretched in unreliable ways as Hunter crossed the barrier between outside and inside the Church, one more formidable than the forcewall. She shook her head. "I should see the Patri first." Best to avoid even the smallest provocation.

"It is a minimal delay. Do not be stubborn, Echo Hunter 367. Your injuries require nutrition to heal. And," she added as Hunter set her feet wide to keep from reeling in the heat rising from the pool, "the Patri will not be pleased if you lose consciousness in your interview."

Sense, from the girl, if not kindness. It was an improvement to emerge from the grotto in clean hunter clothing, her ruined city garb left behind to be burned, she hoped; no one deserved those cast-offs. The refectory was quiet. One of the fans had stopped; the other turned slow circles, like Hunter's thoughts. It was past the morning meal; all the nuns and weanlings were already gone, though biscuits and water remained for the tardy. But three hunters still sat at the table to the side. Perhaps they had patrolled all night; Hunter saw fatigue in the set of their shoulders, the way they propped their elbows as they ate. She veered towards them, drawn to hear their reports. Gem shook her head. "Over here," she said, indicating an empty place. Reluctantly, Hunter sat. The bread tasted strange, so bland after the rough fare she had grown used to in the city, and the metallic tang of the filtration system seemed to taint the water.

The hunters, noticing them, conferred briefly. One rose and approached. "Respectfully," Gem said to Brit, "the Patri wants to be the first who speaks with her."

Brit ignored her. Expressionless, she said, "I brought the Patri your message, Echo Hunter 367."

Hunter inclined her head. Something swelled inside her, painful and glad at the same time. "I am grateful."

"He asked my opinion of its truthfulness."

Hunter's breath caught on a stabbing pain. "How did you answer?"

"I told him I could not know." The faintest line creased Brit's forehead. "But I hoped for your sake that it was."

They arrived to find the Patri's door slightly ajar. " . . . Every word," Hunter heard him say. "Anything about the original Saint." A harried priest, arms laden with prints, stumbled out the door. The Patri gestured impatiently. "Yes, enter. Gem, you may go." The click of the door behind her seemed to cut Hunter off from everything outside.

She could not make herself say the ritual words.

"I hope that you feel more like yourself this morning."

She remembered the last time she had sat here, the Patri troubled by some vague threat within the Ward, the hunter across from him thinking only how she could regain his favor. She barely recognized that stranger in her memory. "Yes, Patri."

"Good. I have often revisited those last days in my mind, Echo. I cannot be sorry, for I did what I must; but I can wish there might have been another way. We are both lucky to have this chance to start again."

For an instant, she yearned to confess everything

to him. What had happened that long-ago night with the Saint; the fear and doubt that had stalked her ever after. He would forgive her, as she had dreamed in those first awful days in the desert. He would give her back her place with Brit, Gem, the other hunters, and together they would do what must be done to preserve the Church. The city. All would be as it had been so long ago. She almost spoke. Then, impossibly, she felt a spark of anger. *Did you believe the things you said of me?* "I have fulfilled the mission, Patri."

He sat back, steepling his fingers in a gesture that recalled the Warder. "Who went with you through the forcewall, Echo?"

She sat completely still. "I'm sorry, Patri. I don't remember."

He pursed his lips. "Begin at the beginning then. Perhaps that will aid your memory. But make it brief."

Where to start, that didn't lead to Lia? This was the most dangerous kind of lie, one that involved details that would have to make sense. He would pick out any inconsistency. *Careful*, she told herself, *careful*. And underneath that, a voice keening in dismay, *How can you think to lie to him?* She didn't know, only that once she had imagined Lia here, happy, well cared for as a nun; but there was something about the Patri's interest, the acuity of his attention, that Hunter felt as the stare of a desert predator before it took a small, unsuspecting animal. She fought down a spasm of guilt, trying to find the faintest glimmer of a way to make this right for everyone. If she told the story properly, if he believed her . . . "When I was in the desert, after—after you sent me on this mission, I found some children. They were living there, abandoned."

He nodded, unsurprised. "Did you take them to the city?"

"I—no. Just a baby, that was too young to survive on its own." She swallowed. "I left the others. They didn't want to come," she added, then paused. That was beside the point. She refocused, trying to make a coherent report, owing him that, at least. "I used the baby as a means to approach the Warder. I hoped to gain his trust, and it worked. I gathered a great deal of information that was new, at least to me. There are factions among the cityens, including some that oppose the nun tithe. They have projectile weapons." She lifted her injured arm. "I intended to inform you after I acquired more details, but someone tried to kill me with one, and I was afraid that if I delayed, they might succeed before I could report at all. I decided it was best to return immediately, even with incomplete information."

"Then why," he asked mildly, "did you detour for the boy?"

Because it was the boy, and I couldn't leave him to die. "One of the other children came to get me, to bring me to him." The girl's face rose in her vision, scowling in outrage. *You are not betraying them,* she told herself. *The Church will care for her, just as they helped the boy. They'll be angry that she isn't who they're looking for, but it won't be directed at her.* She took a deep breath. "It was a girl who came for me. That must be who you saw cross the forcewall."

His eyebrows drew together. "Are you certain?"

Something in her story sounded wrong to him, she saw that from his frown. The girl was too young, or otherwise not what he expected from the patterns. No matter now. He would catch her flat out, or he would have to verify the details. That would take some time. Meanwhile, she would—

What? Defy the Church?

Saints, if she had faced the doors with that thought in her heart they would have struck her dead in an instant.

Find Lia. Warn her.

"There are gaps in my memory," she told the Patri. That might help cover any mistakes. But she still had a duty too. "About the weapons, Patri. You must not send hunters to collect the tithe now. The cityens are angry and frightened. The slightest misunderstanding may spark disaster. But they can be reasonable too. If we give them time, perhaps enlist the Warder's help . . ."

His frown deepened. "I am not asking your counsel about the tithe, or weapons. The important thing is what I saw in the patterns."

Her control began to fray. "Patri, I am speaking of preventing the threat you foresaw. Of protecting the Church *and* the cityens, even from themselves. How can anything be more important than that?"

He measured her with a hunter's cold eye. She could only imagine what he saw, an old tool damaged beyond usefulness, a ragged scrap like the clothes she had left to be burned. He stood abruptly. "Come with me."

He took her by the injured arm, inadvertently, perhaps, or a kind of lesson. She schooled her face not to show the pain.

Their abrupt entry into the sanctuary flushed priests from their chairs in a billowing of robes. "Sit," the Patri ordered them, and they subsided, but the disturbance remained. The Patri led Hunter close up to the altar, closer than she had ever been. She smelled decay, sickly sweet. The priests' hands flew over boards, stabbing and twisting controls. "Look at her, Echo. You know what is happening."

What she could see of the body was withered more than ever, worn to only the most superficial resemblance of a human form. A hand, gray and shrunken, had fallen to one side, wasted to a claw. It was much worse than it had been. Hunter had to force her voice past a constriction in her throat. "She's dying." The words left behind a burning pain. No wonder he didn't care about the weapons. "How long, Patri?"

"We don't know. A year, a few, if we can minimize the strain. Tell me, Echo. How many Saints do you think there have been?"

Baffled, she counted backwards. Two in her lifetime, four hundred annuals, maybe . . . "Thirty?" she guessed.

"Six, Echo."

Six Saints, ever?

His mouth quirked at her confusion. "They should

last a hundred annuals. That was how the first Patri planned it, to minimize the number of times they had to be copied. But the last one, only thirty. And this one—who knows. We only know the process of making them is not working anymore."

She stared at him. He had not aged like the Saint, but she could see the signs, nonetheless. The skin hung loose around his neck and sagged beneath his jawline, and his hands were spotted dark where the sun found them at the edges of his robes. From one day to the next, he had become an old man. Some day, she realized with a shock, some day not too far distant, there would be a new Patri. It was harder to envision than a new Saint.

He saw the dismay in her face. "Yes, Echo. That is why I must have answers now. I cannot leave the Church to fail."

She could not answer. Taking her silence for assent, he said, "I found something within the original prints. Words from an old priest, one of those who created the first Saint. Somehow he foresaw this disaster coming too. There were just a few lines in his writings. 'Scatter the seed,' he said. And I think that's what he did. Small bits of denas, perhaps introduced through an illness, something that spread rapidly among what was left of the population—there were many plagues in the early days. The pieces wouldn't be able to recombine until the cityens were finally able to start reproducing rapidly enough, if ever. But now, four hundred annuals later, his plan has come to fruition. The pieces *have* come together, finally. What he prayed would happen finally has."

His voice rose with a fervor she had never heard. "There's a Saint out there among the cityens, Echo. A Saint not made, but born."

The air in the sanctuary congealed into some foreign substance her lungs could not take in. "I don't understand, Patri." But inside herself, at a level deeper than words, she did. All manner of things began to make sense; she had seen the signs that foretold this, assembling themselves piece by inevitable piece. The truth, falling from the air in tiny motes like settling dust, building a whole edifice from nothing. She closed her mind, refusing to believe, before the belief became a certainty she could not evade.

"The child who was with you—or someone—" The Patri's gaze came back to her, and it took all her strength to meet it evenly. "Whoever crossed the forcewall with you had the denas of a Saint. Who was it?" She could only shake her head stupidly. The Patri drummed fingers on the altar, over and over, like a code. The sound drilled into her head. "Who *was* it?"

She flailed for sense. "There was no Saint with me. Patri, you must know that. The Saint is right here, in front of us. Gem told me you might be growing a new one, but that one would still be in the womb. I saw a woman give birth in the Bend but that was to a cityen child. . . ." The words piled one on top of the other, incoherent, meaningless babble. "It is impossible, Patri. There *couldn't* be another Saint."

His fingers stilled abruptly. Then he reached into a pocket, and laid a small scanner on the desk. When he spoke his voice was quiet, but as hard as it had been that night he had cast her out. "Listen to me, Echo. There is nothing more important in this world. You must remember who she is. You are the one hunter who can retrieve her. You must find the way."

She stood there, paralyzed as if a static wand had burned her nerves.

His eyes bored into hers. "This is the service I require. Go back into the city. Find the born Saint, and bring her to this altar. Obey me, Echo Hunter 367. Serve as you were made to do."

She sat all night in the sanctuary, staring at the wizened body there, ignored by the priests as they went about their worried work. The boards winked and flashed in patterns in the corner of her eye. It wasn't for a hunter to understand the Saint's thoughts, but there was very little of hunter left inside her now. Tana had learned to read the patterns, she'd said once. Hunter closed her eyes, seeing the play of lights through her lids. The rhythm wove itself into her brain. She reached past the Saint, towards the girl she had known, who had sacrificed herself to save the city. Surely that girl would not let it all go to waste.

Help me, Hunter begged her. *Help me see the way to serve.*

In the silence between breaths she imagined she

heard an answer: *Look with your heart. You will know the truth.*

Then the silence crashed down around her. The truth was that Hunter had failed them all.

The Saint lay wrapped in the silence, but Hunter felt her judgment. When she finally walked out the doors onto the dusty road, it was with a pain far greater than the shields had given her.

She would never be forgiven now.

CHAPTER 22

The sun was barely rising as she made her way back into the city. Even so, she was not alone, a few city-ens already moving about despite the early hour. She walked as fast as she could but, despite the clawing urge for haste, didn't run, not wanting to draw atten-tion that might end up delaying her further. She had no illusion that she would be the only hunter the Patri sent. No one followed her yet, but that time would come. She had to move fast. She was beginning to for-mulate a plan, one that involved the children and the desert and finally Lia, on whom everything depended.

By the time she reached the edge of the Ward the city had fully awakened. She bent over, fiddling un-necessarily with a bootlace to hide her face and clothes while three cityens brushed past, deep in argument. One poked a finger into the other's chest. "Are we going to let them take our daughters?" The other slapped the hand away, and for a moment she thought there would be a scuffle as they glared at each other, breathing fast. Then the third said, "Come on, this isn't the time for it. Let's get home. We have to get ready."

Her sense of urgency grew more acute. She had not lied to the Patri in one thing: she could hardly track the last few days. She calculated back quickly. A day in the desert, two nights and a day in the Church. That meant the tithe was only a day from now. Too many things, too much all coming to a crisis at once, all teetering on the edge of a cliff, like a girl whose desperate hand tore through the bushes. . . . She shook her head, trying to clear it, feeling the tension pulsing down the road, carried by the cityens the way particles carried the power down a lightstring.

Get to Lia, that was imperative. With any luck the girl would be with her, hidden in the safety of the clinic. Lia would have tried to persuade her to wait, to stay. Even a fierce child would respond to that patient, undemanding kindness. Hunter thrust down a spasm of guilt. To use the child as a decoy, while she escaped with Lia . . . The girl would hate her, but she would be safe enough in the Church. Perhaps one day she might even begin to see possibilities beyond the brute demands of survival. There was still a chance for her.

And it was Lia's only chance. In the scant time it took the Church to discover the girl was not who they sought, Hunter would have Lia beyond their reach. The med's face had opened in astonishment when she first stepped outside the confines of the forcewall. Despite her fear, she had seen beauty in the harsh expanse of sky, peace in the vast emptiness. She would learn to love it there, would choose, as the children had, the desert's honest hardships over the ugliness and chaos of the city.

Another crowd of cityens passed by, moving north towards the market square. Milse might be among them, going for bread, thinking, perhaps, with a twist of grief and anger, that he would need a little less, now that Justan was gone. . . . She wondered what Lia had told them. What Lia would say when she saw her again.

Choosing her moment, Hunter slipped across the street behind the cityens. From here it was only a few blocks to the clinic. If the line snaked around the front as usual, she would use the back entrance. The risk of exposure was nothing to the need to get to Lia quickly.

But there was no line at the clinic, not even a guard at the door. No one stopped her when she slipped through the empty anteroom. Her mouth went dry as the dusty air. She felt, before she even opened the inner door, the unnatural stillness inside.

Milse slumped at the desk, head pillowed on his arms. His tear-streaked face rose at the sound of her entry. Even before he spoke, she knew what he would say.

"Lia is gone."

The air inside the clinic pressed hot and still, depleted of oxygen. She drew the same deep breath over and over but it did nothing to slow the panicked hammering of her heart. "When was the last time anyone saw her?"

Milse seemed stunned. "We thought you were gone for good."

"*When?*"

His look turned sharp, suspicious. "The night of the fest. With *you*. Everyone is searching, but . . ." His stare ate into her. "We found Justan's body."

"I wouldn't hurt her." Her voice thinned, perilously close to shaking. "Saints, Milse, what do you think. . . . I wouldn't."

Milse's lips trembled. "I don't know what to think. I thought you cared for her, as much as someone like you could, I even imagined that you cared for *us*. But you killed Justan, didn't you? He was never anything but kind to you, Saints, he *liked* you, he was always standing up to Loro for you, and you murdered him. For what? What could he have done that he deserved to die? Then you and Lia disappeared . . . The Warder thought you had taken her to the Church. Maybe you thought she would be valuable to them somehow, a chit you could trade to regain their favor." Her belly clenched. He could not know what he was saying. "I couldn't see that, but—Saints, after Justan . . . What did you do to Lia, Echo?"

Dread settled heavy in the hollow of her gut. She should have seen Lia back to the forcewall herself. Saints, she should have done that at very least; what had she been thinking? Lia, in the desert, with only a child for protection, not even a hunter child, no matter what Hunter's fantasies of her had been . . . Dead lips pressed into the sand where the tiny predators would be eager to begin their work, blind eyes not even seeing the sky that had so astonished her. . . .

Hunter shoved back the fear, forced herself to focus. "She should have been back here the same day."

"The same day as what?"

"A child in the desert was sick. Lia went with me. She couldn't do anything, so I decided to take the boy to the Saint."

"And you left Lia alone out there?"

"Not alone, I—" With a child. Saints. Two days. Helpless in the desert. What had she done?

Hunter struggled to think. Why would they not have made it back? The girl was clever, skilled. Even burdened with Lia, it would take bad luck for her not to manage a few hours' walk back to the forcewall. An accident, a predator . . . Or maybe there was another reason. Only the girl's fear for the boy had driven her to enter the city in search of Hunter the first time; maybe asking her to do it again, even to bring Lia back where she belonged, had been too much. What, then, would she have done?

Hope sparked. Hunter had to get back to the camp. No one would have thought to search for Lia there, not yet.

"I'll find her."

The camp was deserted. There was no sign of disturbance, no indication that predators had made a kill. No recent footprints either, except her own coming to search, and she had made sure not to obscure any other signs as she moved. The scene nagged at her, something just slightly wrong. She quartered the camp again, not finding whatever it was. She stood back, surveying the whole area again. Then, despite everything, she almost smiled. The girl had done well. It was all so undisturbed that it could only have been made to look that way on purpose.

After that it was only a few minutes' work to find the brushed-over trail that made its way southeast, back towards the city. The girl had even thought to take them on a false foray north, in case someone had picked up the tracks despite her efforts to conceal them. Had she done all this out of caution, or *had* someone come searching after them? Hunter had been so nearly out of her mind that day that anyone could have followed them here from the city without her noticing. Another sin to lay to her account.

The non-trail became harder to follow as the ground changed from dust to rock to broken slab, but Hunter had a good idea where it was headed. She could see the jumbled pile of rock from here, the sheltered vantage point the girl would have sought before she led Lia across the last few lengths of open ground to the forcewall. That crossing was the most dangerous point. Hunter scoured the ground closely, dread thrumming in her ears, but found nothing. The predators had not gotten to them.

Not the predators of the desert, at least.

She slipped back inside the barrier, feeling the familiar tingle. Here the trail became clear again, doubling back towards the west. That made sense; the girl only knew one way to the Ward, and she would need to find it again to return Lia to the clinic. Easy enough to make their way along the inside perimeter until they intersected with a landmark the girl, or Lia, knew.

Hunter lost the trail for good as it began to mingle with normal city foot traffic coming north. She stopped in the shadow of a pile of rubble, wiping sweat on her sleeve. From here she could hear voices, the squeak of cartwheels, only a few hundred steps ahead, around the curve. What could have befallen them here? Even given some delay for the diversionary trail, they would have arrived long before nightfall. The girl's instincts would have urged caution, but Lia would be taking the lead now that they were in territory more familiar to her than to the girl. She would have been anxious to make it home, but she was too smart to be reckless. A few days ago she might have thought herself safe anywhere in the city, but since then she had been with Hunter when someone had tried to kill her, then the shock of Justan's death, the sick boy in the desert—even that steady heart would have been shaken. She would have stayed careful, avoided strangers, tried to find a familiar face to get her home safe to the Ward.

One of the guards, maybe, as he made his rounds. And the guards would have brought her to—

Loro, of course.

Of course. Loro.

An hour later Hunter was back to the edge between the Ward and the Bend. A few minutes after that she had a stranger's loose shirt mostly disguising her new tunic, and a man left thoughtfully in the shade who would wake up with an aching head and no explanation for finding himself half naked on the way home from market, his basket missing but all his goods laid out neatly beside him. By the time he told his story, Hunter wouldn't be needing the disguise anymore.

She set her pace just slower than the three women walking ahead of her, bending over a little as if the basket, empty except for a flattened metal bar she had pulled from some rubble as she passed, dragged at her arm. A handful of dust lightened her hair, and she kept her face low under hunched shoulders. No one would look twice at an old woman shuffling down the street. When she got to the right alley she hesitated as if confused, then meandered until she was sure that no one was paying any attention. Once between the buildings she straightened, tossing the basket off to the side, the bar now secure in a pocket, and headed at barely less than a trot straight to the door she remembered.

Hard not to think of that first small journey to the Bend with Lia. Hunter had been disoriented, uncertain what to believe, hardly able to hold to a path. Lia, walking quietly with her skirts trailing in the dust, had been a beacon already, a signal Hunter could follow to safety from any far distance, even though she hadn't known it then. That day, the cityen's messy childbirth had seemed no more than an example to be compared, unfavorably, to the orderly reproduction of hunters; yet the med's patient competence, the calm that radiated out from her to settle the mother, the anxious father, even Hunter herself—that had felt, Hunter realized now, like sanctuary.

Hunter would get her back, safe. All planning, all thought sharpened to that narrowest focus. Nothing else mattered. Nothing.

The shop door didn't budge when she tried the handle. A few cityens wandered by, eyes passing over her incuriously. She waited until they were a dozen paces past, then, using her body to shield the view from the street, she wedged the metal bar between the door and the jam, and made a sudden hard push. The lock broke with only a small cry of protest. She glanced quickly down the street, but the cityens paid no attention. She slipped inside, closing the door softly behind her.

There were no guards up here, but someone was moving in the shop below, normal working noises, footsteps, a plastic squeak, the clank of a tool being set down on a bench. Her eyes adjusted quickly to the dimness, lit only by a glow at the turn of the stairs. Four steps down from here, she remembered, then four more after the turn.

"That's quite an interesting device."

Exey jumped comically at the sound of her voice. "Saints! How long have you been there?" Belatedly, he made a grab for a small rectangular box with what had to be an antenna sticking out the top. Too late: her hand clamped across his wrist with bruising force. He shouldn't have left the thing quite so far out of reach.

"Please don't break my arm, I won't be able to work." She picked up the box with her free hand before releasing him. With just one button and the antenna, it must be a crude signaling device of some kind. A wire ran to the flex his lights were strung on. She snapped it with a sharp tug. Exey sighed. "I suppose you broke my lock too. Oh, well. I can fix them both when I get the time. Which I don't suppose you're going to give me?"

"I was thinking about your news," Hunter said, as if nothing had happened since they'd shared a ferm at the fest. "I decided I'd like to help your friends."

Exey stared. Then a smile spread slowly across his face. "Really? That's wonderful. My friends are going to be very happy." Rubbing his wrist, he straightened like a man who had just set down a heavy load. "And I can't even tell you how happy that makes me." He pointed, carefully, to the small device. "If I could signal them after all?"

"Not yet. I need some information first. The tithe is tomorrow?"

"Yes." He squinted at her, puzzled, surely wondering how she could not be certain of such a basic fact. Wondering, perhaps, if she might be a good deal less competent in other ways than he and his friends might have guessed. For once, though, he didn't say anything more.

"What else have you learned about Loro's plans to stop it?"

"Nothing. No," he added hastily when she reached for his bruised wrist again. "That won't make me any better informed. What I told you at the fest was true: what I don't know can't hurt others. And everyone knows I'm a talker, even when people aren't threatening to tear my hands off. No offense. My friends might have learned more since then, you can ask them— whenever you want to see them, I mean. There is one thing, though. . . ."

"Go on."

"There was a rumor. Word of trouble after the fest. Then no one saw you the last few days, and everyone thought . . . But you're here, so that part can't be true, can it?"

"You knew Loro was planning something, didn't you? That was the proof you told me to wait for. You let me walk into a trap."

"No! I didn't know anything about that. I told you, I was just a messenger. And anyway, I don't think that was what my friends meant by proof. They were very . . . agitated . . . when they heard you were missing."

He could be telling the truth. The ambush had happened so close to the Benders' offer, or warning, that it almost didn't make sense. She would worry about that later; it didn't matter now, not to what she had to do.

"All right, never mind. Projectile weapons, Exey. Someone attacked me with one. I want to know all about them now. What they are, what they can do. Who has them."

"Projectile weapons?" The horror in his voice sounded genuine. "You don't think—" He flinched as she smashed his signaler to pieces on the benchtop. "That I can't fix. I can't make weapons either."

"You're the best fabricator in the city. You've said so yourself. Often. You can't expect me to believe there's something you can't make that anyone else can."

He chewed his lip, caught between pride and a sensible regard for his life. "All right then, I won't. Here's the truth for you: I could make them, but I won't."

"But you know who can."

"I—"

"Saints, Exey. Lia was with me. They could have killed us both."

He sagged against the bench, looking suddenly much older. It was the look of a man who thought things that interfered with his sleep. She knew it from her own reflection. "Anyone can make them. Anyone. It's so simple." He wiped his face. "A metal ball, some powder, a little chamber to control combustion. The only trick is to seal the joint so it doesn't blow your hand off. A child could do it. Well, maybe not a child. A hunter child, perhaps." He straightened, eyes brightening. "Do you even come from children?"

Fear for Lia shivered through her veins, goading her towards violence. She locked her hands safely together behind her back. "Just tell me who has these weapons."

"Loro," he said promptly.

"Yes, I know." Her arm ached. If only he had told her at the fest, when it might have helped. "Who else? Your friends?"

He nodded reluctantly. "At least a few. We thought . . . If Loro had them, we'd better get them too, in case . . . well, just in case. But I didn't make them," he burst out. "I used one on a piece of bovine once, to see—I couldn't even eat it, after. I kept thinking, that's what it can do to a person. . . . I tried to talk them out of it. Let the Church protect us, I said. Go to the hunters, tell them, they'll take care of us. No, they said, what if the Church won't believe us? We have to take care of ourselves. But then, when I saw how you felt about Lia, I convinced them. You wouldn't let anything happen to her. You would help us." He stared at her, pleading. "You said you needed proof, and now you have it. You'll help now, won't you? Now that you know?"

"Lia is gone."

His face went gray as the dust in her hair. "What do you mean, gone?"

"Someone has taken her." Her fingers clamped over the edge of the bench behind her. She felt the metal give. "Someone I'm going to kill. If you know who it is, tell me now."

"I swear I don't," he whispered, shaking. "I swear."

"Good. You get to live. Now tell me Loro's hiding places."

CHAPTER 23

She should have thought of the warehouse herself. It was a warning: she was injured, had barely eaten or slept in the past two days—her next mistake might be the one that killed Lia. Perhaps in some twisted way Loro meant to protect the med, but he had no idea of the true danger. Only Hunter could save her. Pressed flat in the dust in a mere depression where the ground had subsided off to the side of the old road, Hunter studied the building for more than an hour, stifling the urgent temptation to storm the doors and find Lia *now*. That was weakness talking, weakness and fear. She was a hunter; she would control them.

She remembered the layout from the fest, of course: the blocky stone front with its double door, shut now and no doubt barred from the inside; two smallish openings on either side that had been windows, now glassless to let air inside; the back, behind the stage area, fallen in, old rubble scattered down to the river-bed's edge. Loro would certainly have posted lookouts at those windows, either one for each opening or at very least a man to move between them, constantly checking the broad, flat approach to the door so that no one could come near undetected. Better to find another way in.

She worked her way to the rubble field behind. The pungent stench of the river burned her nostrils, but it was much easier to move quickly here, darting from cover to cover with the advantage of the long shadows cast by the angle of the sun. The back end of the warehouse would have opened wide to accommodate cargo hauled up from the ships. Unfortunately, as she remembered, it was completely caved in. But there had to be another opening somewhere; the movement of people during the fest had told her so, and Loro would not be so stupid as to hide himself in a trap with no back exit.

Finally she found it: a break in the regular pattern of the wall where some of the concrete blocks had been moved and replaced. The slight protrusion of the false wall was barely noticeable. It ran parallel to the real wall for perhaps ten paces at the most, creating a baffle so that the actual back entrance to the building, at the blind end of the alley the two walls created, had to be approached from the side, between the walls. Because of that, guards inside wouldn't be able to see who was approaching until he got right to the entrance, but on the other hand, any attack would be slowed and funneled right into whatever trap the guards set up. She nodded in grudging approval. It was not so different from the strategy she had used at her camp in the desert.

A short while later she lay in a tight wedge against the wall behind the baffle. She had to assume there was a guard at the door, but the probability that he would come out and look around the corner just as she approached was low enough to discount. She rose and edged quickly forward, all her senses directed towards the opening. The dangerous part would be those first few feet into the funnel. Anyone waiting inside had all the advantage.

She listened hard but heard nothing. If there was a guard, he was very still. She was all the way to the opening now, and still no alarm had been raised. She gathered her feet under her until she was crouched into a muscular ball, and then launched herself around the wall into an all-out sprint through the funnel.

The guard who had fallen asleep at his formerly dull post wouldn't wake up for hours now. She eased him to the ground soundlessly, catching the blade that fell from his limp fingers before it could clang against the stone. Quickly she patted his pockets, finding nothing else useful. Too bad; a projectile weapon would have helped the odds immensely. Still crouched low against the wall, she risked a look through the open doorway.

The room she saw was currently unoccupied, stacked with miscellaneous-looking boxes and a few big pots. This must be the area behind the platform where the musicians had played. That meant that Lia and the girl, and their guards, had to be in the big front room, where the door in the wall opposite her must lead.

She frowned. It would have been easier to work in a more confined space. Now she would have to scan the whole area, locate both the prisoners and the guards, and calculate a path in and out that wouldn't put her or Lia and the girl into the way of projectiles, if the guards had them. She hoped fervently that they didn't, hoped that Loro had focused all his resources on the upcoming battle with the hunters and left only the minimum behind. She shook her head, dismissing hope. It wouldn't help her win.

She slipped across the floor to put an ear to the closed door. She heard voices, muted, a man's saying something she couldn't make out, and a remarkably vivid curse in a high snarl that could only be the fierce girl. Gruff laughter followed, and a sharp comment in a voice that pierced her chest.

Lia, alive. Until relief flooded her she didn't realize how very frightened she had been. She leaned her head against the wood door frame for a moment, eyes closed, simply listening to that voice.

Then she turned her attention to the latch, a simple metal lever. That was a stroke of luck. It lifted soundlessly, and she was five steps into the room and running hard before the guards even looked up.

More surveillance would have been better. More preparation would have been preferable. Any plan at all would have been helpful. But she had none of those, so she settled for speed. Two more steps and she launched herself into a rolling dive to her own right, so the nearest man would have to turn across his body to hit her with whatever he had in his right hand. She curled tight as her shoulder hit the floor, preserving momentum that popped her to her feet and put stunning force into the palm that slammed up under his jaw. He was still crumpling as she turned to his partner.

This man was quick. Glinting metal scythed towards her. Instead of backing she leapt towards him, inside the arc of his arm. His forearm hit hard as a club between her neck and shoulder, the knife snagging in cloth, barely scratching the skin beneath. Before he could curve the blade back into her neck she reached up across her body to clamp his arm tighter to her, then broke his elbow with a vicious outside-in swing of her other forearm. He shrieked and dropped the blade. She dropped him with a bone-crushing fist to the face.

She whirled, breathing hard, but no one else appeared.

Just Lia and the girl, roped back to back and sitting atop a barrel, the girl grinning fiercely, Lia's features pale but calm. "Echo," she breathed, twisting against the ropes. "You came back."

"How many more?" Hunter asked, retrieving the fallen knife.

"There was another one, but I think he left. I haven't seen him in a while." That might be the one Hunter had left by the door, or a fourth who could be anywhere. Either way, it wouldn't do to stay here. She sawed at the thick ropes.

Lia threw herself at Hunter as the ropes fell away, careless of the blade. Hunter jerked it safely aside as the med buried her face in her chest, shoulders shaking. She dropped her face against the med's hair, feeling the slight roughness against her lips, tasting the chemical scent of Lia's fear. She closed her eyes in naked relief.

The girl dropped down off the barrel and squatted by the man whose knife it had been, turning his face up to the light. After a moment's study of the congealing blood, she nodded in satisfaction.

"All right?" Hunter asked, straightening Lia gently. The med nodded, wiping tears. "Did they hurt you?"

"No." She drew a shaky breath. "Echo, it was Loro. He found us just when we came back inside the wall. He said the Ward wasn't safe, he brought us here instead. He said these men would take care of us, but after he left—they wouldn't have dared hurt me, but the way they started talking about her—" Lia swallowed, then glanced at the girl, who was peering through the window with a baleful look that boded ill for any enemy her eye fell on. "She almost got away. That's when they tied us up. Did you teach her to fight like that?"

Hunter shook her head. "We have to go now. Quickly." She helped Lia up, then caught her as she stumbled. "Are you sure you aren't hurt?"

"The ropes were tight, is all." Lia steadied herself, wincing.

"Let me see your hands."

Lia held them out, confused, as Hunter pulled out the tiny scanner the Patri had given her. She took the med's right hand in her left, turning it palm up. Her mouth was dry as the desert. Misunderstanding, Lia tightened her fingers in reassurance. "I'm okay, Echo, really."

Hunter pushed the button, then opened her eyes. The med's slim fingers still grasped hers. They were slender, fragile in a hunter's grasp. And pale, just a dim human whiteness in the probing blue light.

Hunter snapped the light off. The Saint in the desert had glowed the telltale green, the giveaway that had let Hunter track her down from the aircar. Maybe the Patri was wrong about Lia. She closed her eyes, afraid to hope. She had been wrong about so many things before.

"Echo, what's the matter? What's happening out there? I was so worried about you—the way you—you went off, and the boy—" Her eyes widened as she remembered. "Is he—"

"The Saint healed him."

The girl's head snapped around. "Where?"

"I left him in the Church. No, it's all right. He's safe there."

The girl hopped from one foot to the other in agitation. "Take me!"

"I can't take you. But you can go. You should." It was true, yet the sour taste of betrayal rose in her throat as she spoke. As if she sensed it, the girl's face darkened with suspicion. Hunter ignored it to continue, "You'll be safe too. They'll help you. They don't hurt children there." Hunter knelt in front of her, grasping the bony shoulders. "Listen to me. *Listen*. I told them something about you. It was a lie, a distraction, but it will take them a little while to figure that out. They'll be angry when they do."

"Echo," Lia began, but Hunter shook her head.

"They won't hurt you," she said to the girl. "It's me they'll be angry with. Just don't provoke them. Understand?" The girl nodded, still uncertain. "There's one more thing: they're going to ask you questions. Where to find me and Lia. Don't try to lie to them; they'll know."

"Find you then," the girl muttered, scowling.

"No, because we won't be here. No one will be able to find us." She waited another precious moment for the girl to comprehend. When she did, her face screwed up, the beginning of a howl of protest. "Shh. This is better. You'll be safer with them than with me." That Lia would be safer with her she could not force herself to say aloud, even when the girl's frown turned towards the med, asking with eloquent silence. "Just follow along the straight road to the Church. Go the sunset way from here, then you'll see the steeple. Stay off to the side; there are plenty of places to hide if you need to. Be careful. It's a long walk and there are predators." The girl knew the kind she meant. "Do you have questions?" The girl's stare was hard and angry. Then she shook her head. "Good. Then go."

One more moment Hunter endured that stare. Then the girl punched her right in the gut, hard enough to drive the breath from her in an astonished grunt. When she could focus again the child was gone, only the slightest scrape of light running feet betraying her flight. Hunter straightened painfully, rubbing her belly.

"Echo," Lia whispered.

"She'll be fine," Hunter said harshly. "We have to run."

"Run where?" Confusion in Lia's voice, as she remembered how Hunter had been the last time they were together. What she had done. "Echo, what happened at the Church?"

"They're going to be looking for us. We have to get away from here."

"Hunters? We'll go to the Ward. We'll hide you there. There are secret places, even hunters wouldn't find them, at least not right away, and meanwhile we'll think of something. . . . The Warder will help. Saints, the Warder! He must be so worried about me."

"We can't hide in the Ward, Lia. It's not just me. They're looking for you."

"For *me*?" Confusion gave way to fear. "Why?"

Hunter looked into her golden eyes. If Lia knew what the Church wanted, what the Patri, in his desperation, would do—that fear would always be there. The dread of what might wait around every corner, no matter how far they ran, no matter how safe they seemed. The heavy knot of apprehension, that any minute she would be exposed, betrayed, would sit in her gut as it had in Hunter's ever since the Saint . . . She could not lay that burden on Lia.

"They didn't tell me why," Hunter said.

Lia kept her face still, but Hunter saw her pupils dilate, her breathing quicken. Not all her fear was of the hunters. "Where are we going to go?"

Nowhere was safe. "To the desert. I know it best of all of them. We have a chance there."

"All right. But I need to go back to the clinic first, gather my things." Lia was speaking carefully, slowly, the way she did to her patients when their minds weren't functioning properly and she didn't want to frighten them. "Then I'll go with you." She reached for Hunter's hand, as she might for a child's.

Lia's things—of course. The prints. Hunter saw all at once the faintest hint of a way forward, like a scuff mark in the dust that might be the first track leading home. She could not see the way, not yet. But she saw in memory the prints in the clinic, in the Warder's office—stacks and stacks of them. The treasures of this world.

And the Patri was searching for answers.

Hunter took Lia's hand and started running.

They were on the outskirts of the Bend when they stumbled over the first body. Hunter had had to slow the pace for Lia, and it was nearly full dark by now. Despite the desperate need for haste, Hunter had kept them on the edges, avoiding the streets and alleys honest cityens would use, dodging and weaving past any place that might attract a hunter's slightest notice. She had begun to feel the sense of wrongness early on. Even these abandoned ways were more desolate than they should be; and the hot evening breeze carried snatches of sounds that didn't belong: a gathered crowd, shouting; and far in the distance, something large and heavy crashing to the ground. She glanced at Lia, who hadn't noticed anything amiss, other than being dragged through the city by a hunter whose mental state she had every reason to doubt.

Or maybe the med was just too breathless to question. Hunter slowed again, to a fast walk that felt like a crawl. Lia managed a half smile of gratitude and squeezed the hand she'd been holding all this time. Hunter forced herself to smile back. Another half hour, she estimated, should take them to the Ward. They would encounter cityens there, of course; it couldn't be avoided. There was no way to predict what would happen. Milse would long since have gone to the Warder, telling him Hunter had returned. They knew she had killed Justan. But she had Lia with her, unharmed, safe. The med would be proof of her good intentions. She only needed a few minutes in the clinic, then she and Lia could be gone again, before the others realized what had happened.

Hunter smelled the blood at the same time the grip on her hand tightened as Lia saved herself from a fall. "What—" The med, in the dark, couldn't see what she had tripped on, but Hunter could. She knelt by the still form, feeling for a pulse; her hand came away sticky. The body was cool. Now Lia saw it too. She shot a questioning look at Hunter.

"He's dead," Hunter said. "We have to keep going."

A hundred paces on, Lia said in a whisper taut with frustration, "One day we'll get this city to where people don't leave each other dead in the streets, even out here. One day."

"I hope so," Hunter said. To her surprise, she meant it.

But the second body was inside the Bend. Wiping her hand as clean as she could on the corpse's clothes, Hunter finally understood what the noises she'd been hearing meant. "Some kind of fight," she whispered to Lia.

"Hunters?" Lia's voice was barely audible.

"I don't think so." The sound of static wands carried a long way, and she hadn't heard it. "Stay close."

The Ward too was oddly quiet. Hunter saw lights on in living spaces, and people moving inside; but the street was as empty as she'd ever seen it. Whatever was happening, the innocent didn't want to be caught out. There was no sign of damage here, though, or anything else out of place. The fight was somewhere else then, and word had gotten back. Lia felt it too. She looked a question at Hunter. "I don't know," Hunter said. She smelled smoke, but it was far away.

They slipped into the clinic through the rear entrance. It was deserted. *Thank the Saint.* Even Milse was gone. "Where is everyone?" Lia wondered.

"I don't know," Hunter said again.

Lia frowned. "If there had been a fight, they'd bring the injured here."

The only ones we saw were dead, Hunter thought, but she did not say it aloud.

Lia said, "Echo, I can't go with you until we know what's happening. If people are hurt, if they need me—I have to stay."

"If hunters find us you won't be able to help anyone," Hunter said, more harshly than she intended. She burned to get Lia away. It had been a mistake to come back. But she had to get the prints; they might be the Saint's last hope. . . .

Hunter barred the door, then sent Lia to gather her supplies from the back room while Hunter stuffed prints into the largest packs she could find. She wracked her memory, trying to recall any reference to the Saint in the prints she had studied with Lia all those long evenings. . . . She took the ones that looked oldest. The priests could come back later for the others, and the ones in the Warder's office. She dared not delay for those, not with whatever was happening in the city adding to Lia's danger. Hunter would get her to safety in the desert, set up a camp as she had for the children, with shelter and enough food to last until Hunter could deliver the prints to the Church and return. . . .

A sharp *crack* split the air. Hunter only had time to slam the door to the back room, blocking the way to Lia, before the anteroom door came off its hinges. *Run*, she thought at Lia. Then she turned to face the hunters.

Only it wasn't hunters.

A half-dozen men, all with blue stripes down the front of their shirts, faced her in a loose half circle. Teller, Rander, the others she didn't know. Their cheeks were flushed, hair plastered wet with sweat, and they were breathing hard. It took Hunter a moment to place their expressions, then she did: stunned triumph, and not a little fear. She had seen that look on juveniles' faces, when a plan worked *too* well and began to get away from them.

The Warder burst through the door. Hope and anger warred in his face. "Milse said you had returned. Did you find her?"

Hunter calculated rapidly. The Warder would never let her take Lia. But Lia couldn't stay here. It would be the first place the hunters looked. If Hunter could draw the Warder and his men away . . . "No," she answered, putting all the fear and grief of the last few days into that one word. "But I'm still looking. I need your help. You men, come with me, I'll show you where—" She strode right past the Warder, headed for the outer door.

And she heard a click, the same sound she had heard in the alley the night of the fest.

Now she knew what it meant.

She turned back to face the Warder.

"I thought it was Loro," she whispered, horror sending a shudder through her bones. But Loro wasn't among the men.

Anguish creased the Warder's face as he brought

the evil little weapon to bear on her. Every man held one. "Don't make us use them, Echo, please."

"*Saints.*" It was so much worse than she had imagined. Worse even than she had tried to tell the Patri. The inevitable unfurled itself all too clearly in her mind. Wardmen, maybe Benders too with projectile weapons, hunters coming in to take the tithe . . . The hunters would ignore the skulking cityens—what threat could they be—right up until the moment when one of the fools fired and a hunter went down. Then there would be blood, and more firing, because that was what happened when a predator suddenly turned weak in the midst of a crowd of prey. Even in the frenzy the hunters would hesitate a fatal moment, as the ones in the market square nearly had, slave to that protective instinct bred into them from the very beginning. It would be a massacre. The Patri had made so little of her report, obsessed as he was with the Saint denas, he might not even think to warn the hunters before he sent them in. And after, the Church would retaliate. . . . And then it would be war, and the end of everything.

Saints.

The Patri had been right from the beginning. The Warder, the friendly, hapless Warder whose softness she had secretly despised even as he befriended her—he was the enemy. She stared at him, trying to see it, but could only see the man she knew, kind and frightened and helpless. Aiming a weapon that had the power to bring down the Church.

She could get to him across the few feet of floor between them, there was no doubt in her mind. The others would kill her then, but the Warder would be eliminated. Without their leader, the cityens might think twice before challenging the hunters. Maybe, maybe it would be enough to avert catastrophe. Hunter would have done her best.

But Lia would die on the altar.

It was a small sacrifice, one cityen for the city's future. Her dead, Ela and Tana and the others who had given their own lives without complaint, looked at her, silent. She didn't want to hear what they would say.

In the moment before Hunter could move, Lia opened the door.

The med took in the men, the weapons, Hunter frozen in place. The Warder. Her face went pale beneath the flush. "No. No, it can't be."

The Warder's rheumy eyes lit, though his voice broke. "Lia, my child. I thought you were dead. Thank the Saint." Outstretched arms reached to fold her close. She stood where she was, stunned. After an uncertain moment, the Warder dropped his arms.

"It's for the best, you'll see, child, I know you will."

"Those are *projectile weapons*."

The Warder looked at the thing in his hand as if surprised to find it there. "Just something to protect ourselves. It's not wrong to do that, is it?"

"Put them away." Fury laced Lia's voice. "Put them away now. I won't have those things in my clinic."

The men looked uncertainly at the Warder. Hunter

sensed their fighting hormones ebbing. They were starting to notice they were tired. Their breathing slowed, the tension gradually leaving their muscles as it dawned on them that they had survived and made it back to safety. She held herself very still. Let them focus on Lia, forget Hunter even stood there. They didn't want a confrontation with their own.

The Warder said, "We have to take responsibility for ourselves, child. We just need to be prepared, I've always taught you that."

Lia's face twisted in anguish. "Prepared for when the time comes, yes, the day the Church won't be able to help us anymore—but weapons? How will that help? Someone tried to kill Echo with one of those. And there were *bodies* on the edge."

Her accusation hung in the air. The men shifted uncomfortably. One or two slipped the devices into their pockets. *Keep talking, Lia. They'll listen to you. Make them see sense.* It might work. Hunter tightened her grip on the packs she still held, in case it didn't.

Sour-faced Teller spoke for the first time. He hadn't put his weapon away. "Benders don't know what's good for them. Never have."

Lia swung on him. "Are they going to learn it from you killing them?"

The Warder answered before Teller could. "No, Lia, my child, that's not what happened. That was an accident, a misunderstanding. Terrible, terrible, but we'll make it up to them. You'll see." He waved the weapon. "That's not what these are for."

"What, then?"

"Only to protect ourselves from the tithe."

Just like that, the men remembered a hunter stood in their midst. Weapons that were still out trained on her; the rest of them stood ready, in case she made the slightest move.

"I'm on your side, remember?" Hunter said. "The Church threw me out. I'm one of you."

The Warder's look was full of pain and confusion. "I wanted to believe you, Echo, all along. I thought you believed it yourself for a time. Your feelings for Lia . . . I can't blame you being what you are, can I? But you killed Justan. That poor sweet boy. If you could do that, what else? I can't have you at our backs when the hunters come."

Hunter's heart rate spiked. She gathered the energy, forced it into a stillness from which she could explode faster than these cityens could even imagine. She said, "If you kill hunters, the Church will destroy you."

The Warder's voice was heavy with sorrow. "The Church is dying from the inside. You feel it, Echo, I know you do. But we're beginning to live, finally, to grow and thrive and push back the darkness in our own way. What does your Patri expect us to do? Keep lying still while you steal our children? You know how we feel about them; even you, twisted as you are, you loved those children in the desert. I know you did. Would you give them up to the Church? Would you?"

Hunter didn't answer. She focused on Lia's face.

The med's eyes were wide with shock and sorrow. A protest was forming on her lips, too late.

The Warder raised his weapon. "I'm sorry, Echo. Truly."

Hunter flung the packs with all her strength. The first one caught the Warder square in the face. He stumbled into a clinic bed and fell. The weapon swung wide, barking harmlessly, sending up a puff of blue smoke.

The second pack tangled in the lightstring and pulled the whole thing down. The wire arced through the air in a sizzling shower of sparks. The room went dark except for the fire dancing at the broken wire's end. There was a sharp snap of power, and someone screamed, and the smell of burning filled the air.

Before the second pack even hit the floor Hunter launched herself at Lia. The momentum carried them crashing through the back door. Hunter slammed it behind them, hauled the med up with no thought for her gasp of pain, and dragged her running down the alley behind the clinic. She pushed Lia to the inside and a little ahead. No way to know the penetrating power of the projectiles, but they would have to pass through her body to hit Lia. All Hunter's senses strained back for the sound of pursuit, but it didn't come. A hundred paces further on she risked a quick glance behind.

Flames licked from a window. *Oh, Saint, the prints.* Cityens burst into the street, shouting for help, for water. Lia saw it too. A cry of pain burst from her, and she struggled to turn back, but Hunter forced her forward, away. She tried to make her run, but Lia stumbled once, and again, and they had to stop. Hunter cast about, and found them shelter behind the corpse of some dead building that had rotted to a mound of stone.

"We can't let this happen," Lia wept as she sank down. Her whole body shook with sobs. "We can't."

"Stay here." Hunter worked her way up the pile of rubble, testing every step and handhold to make sure she wouldn't send a cascade of rock down on top of the weeping med. By the time she got to the top her arm ached like fire. She raised her head just enough to see around the side of a fallen stone. The clinic came into view. They were still much too close. Close enough to see the buckets the cityens were passing down a line, almost to hear the steam hiss as water sloshed into the flames. Close enough to see the rising smoke snuffing out the stars, and smell hope burning as black flecks of ash drifted on the hot wind.

And when the hunters came running towards the fire she had started, she was close enough to hear the shots that brought them down.

CHAPTER 24

Hunter was almost down the other side of the rock pile and running towards the burning building before she realized what she was doing. She pulled herself back with an effort that made her bite her cheek to keep from shouting. The sharp pain helped clear her head. The hunters were dead, or they were not. Either way she couldn't help them by running mindlessly into a one-sided battle. Even if she could, she would not leave Lia alone in a burning city, not for anything.

She snaked her head around the stone again. She couldn't see where the hunters had fallen. They might still be lying in the street. Or maybe they weren't dead. They could have dragged themselves away, or been taken prisoner. The only thing she knew for sure was that they weren't fighting the cityens outside: the bucket line was still working; the flames were dying down.

She rested her forehead on her arms for a moment. The irony churned in her belly. The cityens had done her a favor: if the hunters had been coming for her and Lia, she would have killed them herself. How could she have become so desperate? It seemed annuals ago that she had asked the Patri whether he wanted her to kill the Warder for him. It would all have been so simple had he just said yes.

She made her way back down the rocks. "Lia," she said, lifting the med to her feet as gently as she could. "I'm sorry. We have to get away from here. I'm sorry." Lia just looked at her, face blank with shock, but she didn't argue as Hunter began to drag her along again.

Their progress was achingly slow, marked by detours and retraced steps as they crept towards the edge of the city, darting from shelter to shelter, shadow to shadow. Their erratic track might not hide them from a dogged pursuer, but it was the best they could do. And they might not be the focus of anyone's attention at this point: the violence had spread beyond the Ward, if it had even started there. In the distance, a heavy black column of smoke marked where another fire burned in the Bend. Groups of cityens roved everywhere, some apparently unarmed, most carrying sticks and knives. Some of the men laughed or shouted, and some of those sounded drunk on too much ferm; but most moved with what for cityens was silence, intense and focused on whatever it was they hunted. Hunter saw no one with projectile weapons, but she might not; they could be hidden anywhere in packs or clothing.

Armed or not, the gangs could still do damage; Hunter kept herself and Lia hidden, out of their way.

They only saw hunters once, towards morning. Yet again Hunter had shoved Lia back into a niche in the rubble, protecting the med with her body as men pelted by, but this time was different. These men weren't hunting, but fleeing, running full out across an empty square only a dozen paces from where Hunter and Lia cowered. They passed close enough for Hunter to see the terror on their faces. A few breaths later she knew why: three hunters came behind them, moving with deliberate speed, fanned out to drive the cityens ahead of them as they might drive small game in the desert. And the end result would be the same.

Hunter pushed Lia deeper into the niche. She crouched as low as she could and still keep the med's body sheltered. "Shh," she whispered. "Don't even breathe." She wrapped her arms around Lia's shoulders, burying the med's face in her chest, then turned her own face against the rock, so even the glint of eyes or teeth against the dark would not betray them to the hunters' sharp sight. Lia's body shook, but she stayed silent. It wouldn't matter, if the hunters got too close; they would smell the fear. Hunter's pulse pounded in her throat. She heard the whine of their static wands as they drew close. Rock chinked beneath their boots. Every muscle in Hunter's body tensed, waiting for the shock of a wand discharged between her shoulder blades. It was a long while before she realized they had passed.

She was shaking almost as hard as Lia.

Finally, near dawn, they made it to the fringe of the city. They were very close to the place Hunter had entered months ago, carrying the baby some cityen had left to die. Hunter realized she never asked what had become of it. She felt an absurd hope that it and the woman raising it were somewhere safe this night.

Meanwhile she and Lia were not. The forcewall was near, but Lia was at the end of her strength, weaving on her feet. Hunter sorted through options. She desperately wanted to be out of the city, but the Church would see them as soon as they crossed the barrier. Their best chance was with a long head start into the desert, but Lia wasn't good for more than another hour's walk, maybe not that. It wasn't near enough.

The better choice was to wait until night to cross the forcewall. That would mean hiding through the day here among the rubble and detritus. It seemed unlikely the conflict would reach this far; there was nothing worth fighting over, and no population here to do it. The worst danger would probably be the human scavengers, the failed cityens so desperate that the strife tearing at the city could not make their lives any more precarious. Perhaps, if anyone came looking, Hunter and Lia could disguise themselves among those broken people. Hunter stifled a laugh, then caught herself. She was exhausted too; she recognized the dangerous moment when the most immediate threat had passed and the temptation to relax seemed overwhelming.

Fighting the lassitude that crept into her limbs, Hunter turned to look back at the city. A column of smoke drifted gently east, over the river where the sun was rising. She smelled fire and something else, an acrid edge in the smoke that stung her nostrils even above the organic tang of the river. An occasional muffled *bang* echoed this way, dulled by distance. Crop powder, that was the smell; someone must be blowing it up on purpose. She had to tell—no. That was not her mission any longer. The Patri, the cityens—they would do what they would do. She was finished with them. Lia was here, safe, that was all that mattered anymore. Everything else was gone. A deep weariness rose to fill the void.

"The one thing we knew we couldn't let happen." Hunter heard the tears in Lia's voice. "Cityens against Church. Everything we worked for, everything we dreamed—I have to go back, Echo. They need me."

Another girl, facing the pain of her city, trying to heal it all. And the mob, chasing at her heels when she failed. *"No."* Too sharp, that tone; Lia made a tiny sound of confusion, hurt.

Hunter turned to her to make amends.

But the med's eyes were huge and frightened, and not at what she saw in the city. It was Loro who had all her attention, Loro and the weapon he held beside her face while his other hand twisted in her collar, dragging her tight against his body, between him and Hunter. He crouched a little behind her, making himself as small a target as possible. Only his head showed above the med's shoulder, and his right arm from elbow to wrist to the hand that held the projectile weapon.

Hunter took a step back, arms spread wide to show that she herself held nothing. "Let her go, Loro," she said, marveling even as she spoke at how calm her voice sounded, not even the faintest tremor to betray the terror shaking through her veins. *Stay quiet*, she urged Lia wordlessly. *Trust me. I'll get you out of this.* Other faces tried to superimpose themselves on the med's, others who thought they could trust her. She forced the visions away with a vicious effort. Lia gave the tiniest nod, as if she heard.

Loro's head jerked as another dull boom sounded from the city. "Listen to that. This morning— yesterday—a couple of hunters came into the Ward. That's what started it all. Some Wardmen went after them, and cornered them in a ruin." Hunter could imagine the scene, the hunters trapped, coldly running through every scenario that would have prevented the battle now taking place, willing to sacrifice themselves if that were the best option. Even Gem. The thought of that proud, hard strength wasted at a mob's hands brought an unexpected twist of pain.

"You can't blame them for fighting back," she said.

"It wasn't the hunters, it was the *Benders*," he cried. "They heard the firing, or maybe they knew all along. I don't know. I got there just in time to see—all of a sudden the Benders were just there, and I think our people thought it was to help, and there were three men down before they realized they were shooting at *them*. . . ." Tears of frustration and anger ran down his face. "I tried to tell him. I knew this would happen. Once the Benders knew we had weapons they would have to have them too. They're idiots, they were sure to start something like this. But the Warder said it would be all right, they would know that the Church was the enemy, not each other." His voice caught. "He couldn't understand. He's too good. He doesn't know the way people think. He thinks we're all like him. . . ."

Lia twisted in his grip, trying to face him. Her face was a mask of sorrow. "No one's blaming you, Loro. It's not your fault."

"It's *her* fault." His voice rose to a shout. "All of you. You ruin everything. Even the men I sent after you, after the fest—" He shifted his grip on Lia, holding her close to him, arm across her chest. "They wouldn't have hurt *you*. It was just to scare you, I was supposed to come after, to seem like I was saving you. . . ." *Saints*, Hunter thought. *A child, playing children's games.* He went on in a shaking voice, "But they knew what she was, and they were so afraid, they brought those weapons with them. I told them never to carry them. No one would have gotten hurt. I only wanted to show you that I could protect you better than she could."

"Is that why you left me with those men in the warehouse?"

"They were just supposed to keep you safe until I could take you away." He drew a ragged breath. "*You* get down on the ground. *Now.*" Hunter didn't dare disobey, not with that weapon next to Lia's face and Loro's control faltering. "All the way. Lie on your face, in the dirt. That's better. That's where you *all* belong. Taking our girls. Our grain. Pushing us until we're so desperate that we turn on each other when you're the real enemy."

Hunter turned her head to keep him in view, ignoring the stones pressing into the side of her face. He still held tight to Lia. She needed to separate them somehow.

"You win, Loro. You've got me, now let Lia go."

She rode out his kick to her ribs, ignoring Lia's cry of dismay. "I'm not stupid," he snarled, pulling back for another blow.

Lia pushed back against him, clutching at the arm that held her. "Please, Loro, stop. This doesn't help anyone."

"Don't worry, Lia, it will be okay. I'll get you away from here, someplace we'll be safe. From her, and all of them."

"No!". Lia's voice rose near a shout. "Saints, everyone is trying to get me away. I just want you to listen." She caught her breath, and her voice softened. "I'm sorry, Loro. I should have told you a long time ago. I just didn't want to hurt you any more, I didn't want you to lose another sister, or . . . I'm sorry. I can't go with you. You know I'd never leave the city."

"But you could go with *her*?" Loro's voice turned soft, dangerous. He tugged Lia around to face him. Hunter twisted her neck to keep them centered in her vision. Her palm closed over a handful of dust and grit.

Lie to him, please. For the Saint's sake, please lie just this once. Lia stared at him a minute, breathing hard. Then her face crumpled. She shook her head.

And then she hit him hard in the chest with both fists, and flung herself aside.

Loro cursed, whirling on Hunter, two shaking hands clenching the weapon aimed straight at her. The bones of his fingers showed white. Hunter jerked her torso off the ground, twisting and flinging the handful of dirt underhand across her body with a tearing effort.

The stinging grains caught Loro in the face. He jumped back with a reflex shout, pawing at his eyes for the critical seconds it took Hunter to jackknife to her feet. She closed the body-length gap between them in one long step, right hand reaching for his throat while her left clamped around his wrist, forcing it up and out before he could bring the weapon to bear on her or Lia, who still lay on the ground, seeming stunned. "Move!" Hunter shouted at her, but had no time to look for a response as Loro fought back with wiry strength. His free hand pummeled her head and shoulders, blows she had to take, nothing for it but to tuck her chin into her chest and shrug her shoulders up around her ears while she tried to get a better grip on his neck without letting the weapon come into play. She was still weak, she realized with the first real stab of fear. The struggle was more evenly matched than it should have been. One, then another sharp *pop* sounded close to her left ear, projectiles sent harmlessly astray as his hand jerked on the trigger. She had no idea how many times it could fire without having to be rearmed.

Loro rammed his weight forward unexpectedly, forcing her to back a step for balance. Her rear foot tangled with Lia, and for a precarious moment Hunter struggled to balance herself and Loro before they both fell atop the med. Then Lia rolled out of the way, scrambling off to the side on all fours. Hunter took one more step backwards, dropping almost to one knee as if she could no longer hold Loro's weight. As he fell forward into the gap the feint created, she straightened her leg with all her strength, reached her front foot behind his heel, and twisted, pushing him backwards with the hand still on his neck. He tried to jump away but his leg caught on her hooking foot. She jerked the foot up and gave one last hard shove, and Loro hit the ground flat on his back, too fast to brace for the fall. The impact drove a harsh whoop of air from his lungs. The weapon bounced away somewhere out of reach.

Hunter followed him down, knee in his chest, both hands closing around his throat. He hammered at her with his fists, panic giving him a burst of strength. He must have gotten hold of a rock; something gave with a sickening crunch in her side as he struck. She felt the blows only vaguely, a minor annoyance while she concentrated all her effort on choking the life from him. Lia was shouting something, but she couldn't make out the words over the thunder in her head. Loro's face grew mottled, struggles subsiding into irregular reflex jerks. Strangulation was not the cleanest method, but it would suffice. At least, she thought dimly, he deserved it, unlike so many of her victims.

She stared into his dusky face, gave a last squeeze, lifting his head off the dirt and slamming it down, then sat back on her heels astride his chest, disgusted and sick.

His breath rattled a few times irregularly, then caught a rhythm, rasping in and out with a dying-engine wheeze.

Hunter's own breath came in harsh sobs of exhaustion. Every gasp stabbed white with pain, and one ear burned fiercely where a fist had crushed it against her skull. Arms came around her shoulders, not an attack, but Lia, kneeling alongside her, murmuring something wordless, trying to help her up. She straightened a little, struggling to find room for air. She needed to restrain Loro before he regained consciousness, but for the moment she could only sit there, trying to rub her vision clear and wondering what she was going to do next.

Lia's face was a mask of grime, tears washing down in two clean tracks. It reminded Hunter of something she had seen once, a long time gone, she couldn't recall what. Lia pulled back with an abrupt flinch. *Remembering what she held*, Hunter thought wearily, but then she realized the med's wide eyes were focused over her shoulder.

"Finish the task, Echo Hunter 367."

Hunter rose with a dizzying effort. "Run, Lia," she

said flatly. She knew the med would not. It didn't matter anyway; there was nowhere for her to go. Hunter tasted defeat, sharp and metallic, more bitter than the blood in her mouth. She took a last look past the forcewall at the desert stretching empty out to the edge of the world, then turned to face the city again, and Gem.

They were not mirror images any longer. Gem stood easily, weight balanced on her toes, shoulders loose and arms free, the stunner in her hand held relaxed and ready, Hunter and Lia both comfortably in its range. Despite the heat her face was barely flushed, only a faint patch of sweat darkening the immaculate cloth of her shirt. By contrast Hunter felt old and shabby, hair full of dust and scratched face stinging. She took a step forward, and her bones creaked. Gem leapt lightly down from the outcropping, gesturing at Loro with the stunner. Hunter had no doubts whatever that it had been altered to kill, and not by any accident of the wiring this time. "He is dangerous, to you and to the Church. You defeated him; why would you not finish the task?"

She could barely explain it to herself, let alone Gem. Instead of trying, she just shrugged. The motion hurt the shoulder she had strained throwing the first handful of dust. Perplexingly Gem nodded, seeming unsurprised. Perhaps she expected Hunter to fail by now. Hunter felt too weary even to be insulted. The girl's sharp gaze moved on to Lia with a mixture of curiosity and respect. "You were taking her the long way around to the Church."

Lia spoke for the first time, eyes locked on Gem as if she'd never seen a hunter before. "We weren't going to the Church."

Gem cocked her head. "Ah. You haven't told her, have you?"

"Told me what?" Lia asked sharply. Hunter's stomach tightened in the certainty of a coming blow. She could not meet Lia's eyes.

"It was sensible not to," Gem said thoughtfully. It was the exact tone Hunter used to take analyzing the actions of a juvenile in a post-exercise debriefing. "Especially if you knew that boy was following you. She might have resisted, and you would have had to fight both of them at once."

Gem walked closer to the med, at an angle that kept Hunter fully in the stunner's field, and Lia between them as well. Gem studied Lia frankly, seeming satisfied overall with what she saw; but when she moved away, there was a question in her eyes. "I never saw the Saint before she ascended. Is this what she looked like, Echo Hunter 367?"

"No." That girl had been frightened, haunted by the duty she ran away from. By Hunter, who had stalked her through the desert, just as she had Ela, and dragged her back from the tiny camp she had made, so desperate to escape Sainthood that she would rather face a painful death in the desert than life on the altar. Even confused as she was now, Lia had nothing in common with that girl.

Except dawning in her eyes was the same certainty

that had been the Saint's, in the end, of a duty that could never be forsaken. "Echo, what lie did you tell them?" Lia whispered.

Hunter shook her head helplessly, mute. Lia turned to Gem, demanding, "Tell me what is going on."

"What do you know about the Saint?" Gem asked in that same dispassionate tone, as if it were no more than a classroom exercise.

"The Saint preserves the Church, and the Church preserves the city," Lia began by rote, but Gem interrupted.

"No, I don't mean that. About the Saint herself, the one on the altar now?"

Confused, Lia pursed her mouth as she cast back in memory. "I saw her once," she said slowly. "That night . . . We knew the old Saint was dying, of course. Sometimes the grid flickered, or the water pumps cut on and off. But that night . . . the lights went out, and stayed out. I was sure the forcewall was out too. I didn't know what would happen. Then something exploded, and a little boy was killed. I was in the street, by chance, and I heard the noise, and ran to help, even though I could see that it was already too late. But before I could do anything, this woman—a child, really—stepped forward and laid her hand on him. Then I knew, and the crowd knew, who she was." Lia's golden eyes grew luminous, and the hair on Hunter's neck prickled, just as it had that night. "For just a minute, I thought—everyone thought—that she was going to bring him back. I *felt* it, something in the air, like the feeling when you stand near the forcewall, something so real. . . . But then she didn't." The med paused, then went on in a more normal voice. "The crowd turned ugly then. If they had caught her they would have killed her, I'm sure of it. I don't think she would even have tried to escape. But there was a hunter there who—"

She stopped, a hand to her mouth. "Oh, Echo. It was *you*."

Hunter couldn't find words.

"You saved her." Lia's face lit in the beginnings of a smile. She cupped a hand to Hunter's aching cheek. "You saved her."

Hunter's voice finally tore free. "*I took her to the Church.* She didn't want to go, and I made her. I let them—" She broke off, choking down dust until she could speak something closer to sense. "She's dying now. On the altar."

"Already?" Lia's eyes flicked from Hunter to Gem for confirmation. That tiny betrayal stung.

"Yes," Gem said gravely. "Much sooner than expected."

"But I thought . . . Doesn't making a Saint take a long time? How can you have another one ready so soon?"

The silence hanging in the air answered her. "Saints," Lia whispered. "There isn't another one, is there?" She looked at them both, really frightened now. "What are we going to do?"

Hunter leapt at Gem. The stunwand brushed her ribs long before her hands could reach their target, and she crumpled at Gem's feet. Lia flew to her side, kneeling, skirt whitening in the dust. Darkness circled Hunter's vision, but she was still conscious, barely. "No," she wheezed, struggling to reach the stunner in Gem's hand. Her flailing arm, nerveless, only struck the med instead. She lay still then, worse than useless. "Gem, please."

Gem seemed to look at her from a long way above. "I'm sorry, Echo," she said, "but there is no point trying to escape the truth." She turned to Lia, and her voice grew soft. "I never saw the old Saint, before she ascended. I have heard the story, of course, and to be honest, I doubted her worthiness. A Saint who tried to run . . . I've begun to see, though, why Echo Hunter 367 believed in her." Gem smiled a little, oddly sad. "And why she has done as she has done. But that doesn't matter. You see—" She broke off, cocking her head again at the med. "What is your name?"

"Lia," the med replied, startled.

"Lia," Gem repeated. "I'll remember." She bent down, helping the med to her feet tenderly. "You see, Lia, the Church hasn't made a new Saint. But we've found one."

And as Hunter made one last desperate effort to rise, writhing in the dust, Gem looked down, a strange expression on her face. Respect, Hunter realized dimly. After all this time. Then Gem knelt, and pressed the trigger, and the darkness closed over everything.

CHAPTER 25

She woke abruptly, facing a wall. Every part of her body hurt, so much that she could barely draw breath. Her hands were bound with a length of old cable twisted around both wrists and wrapped around her waist so that neither hand could quite reach the other. Gem's doing, no doubt. She struggled frantically for a moment then stopped. *You're a hunter. Act like one.*

A familiar low hum, strong enough to send a tiny vibration through the stone floor, ran like a foundation under the intermittent sounds of motion, the light brush of cloth over limbs, the click of fingernails across boards and panels. She smelled warm stone cooling, priests, and the slight underlying taint of decay. And beyond that, the organic spice mix of the city, muted now by sweat and dust but unmistakable nonetheless.

Lia.

Gem had brought them both to the sanctuary.

No one seemed to have noticed Hunter's panicked thrashing. *Lucky*, she told herself bitterly. *Or maybe you're no concern to them at all.* She had to get free. She rolled slowly onto her side. Her head pounded so horribly that it was a moment before she could open her eyes.

The first thing she saw was Lia's face, whiter than the dust that streaked it. That was all she had to see. Hunter knew they had told her. The med was leaning over the altar, doing something to the Saint. Her sleeves were pushed up and her eyes half closed in concentration, exactly as Hunter had seen her a hundred times in the clinic. A trio of priests worked around her, their hands busy with tools and wire. Nearby, the Patri and another handful of priests huddled in intense consultation over the main boards.

Hunter must have made some sound. Gem padded over, boots silent against the worn stone. She hauled Hunter up without apparent effort. When she let go, Hunter nearly fell, saved only by the young hunter's quick grab. Humiliated, Hunter had to accept Gem's help to stumble the dozen painful steps across the sanctuary.

Lia flung herself against her, wrapping her arms around her in a fierce hug, dropping her face into Hunter's shoulder. Hunter's bound hands could only reach to the med's waist, resting atop her thin hips as if about to lead her in some twisted dance. For an instant the feel of Lia's body pressed against hers was the only thing that mattered in the world. "Have they hurt you?" she whispered, ignoring Gem and the priests and the Patri.

Lia shook her head against Hunter's shoulder. "No. Are you all right?" There were tears in her voice. Hunter held her as close as she could.

"I'm fine. Shh."

"I made them let me see the children. The little boy is getting better. The girl made it, she wasn't hurt. You were right, Echo, sending her here." She tried to laugh, face still pressed into Hunter's shirt. "She fits right in."

They will make her into one of us. Foolish, the little twist of pain that thought brought. The girl would be safer in the Church than anywhere else. If any place were safe now: a faint tremor registered through the soles of Hunter's boots, a distant part of the city trembling. The urgency in the priests' movements, their hesitation and sudden darting stabs at the dials, told her the danger was far from over. "What's happening?"

The Patri turned. The sight of his face shocked her. Dark circles ringed his eyes, and the skin hung loose from his face as if the flesh had withered under it in the days since she had last seen him. He gestured at the lights dancing across the boards, the Saint screaming alarm. "Show her."

Gem extricated Hunter from Lia's embrace and half led, half pulled her up the ladder-like vestibule stairs that went up to the loft. Through the gaps between treads Hunter saw nuns and weanlings huddled beneath the staircase, the weanlings silent, the nuns weeping softly. Indine stood guard in front of them, solid as the Church doors.

One look through the rose window told Hunter everything.

The battle had boiled right up to the Church. Cityens mobbed the road and the ground along both sides, groups of them surging and falling back, clots breaking off into individual battles as they fought one another, then reabsorbing into the main body, the whole mass moving inexorably forward. Some of the cityens dragged carts or carried sacks over their shoulders. Even through the window Hunter could hear the shouts, the curses, the occasional sharp *pop* of a projectile weapon. Between the cityens and the Church doors, hunters had thrown up a barricade, barrels and refectory tables and all manner of debris. They crouched behind, projtrodes ready. Occasionally one would lift a head over the barrier, sight quickly on the nearest cityen, and fire. The mob would fall back, momentarily discouraged, then push forward again.

Gem said, "Their projectile weapons are making it difficult to defend ourselves without excessive casualties. I had some trouble to get through." Her lips twitched. "I would have left you, but the woman would have none of it. She is very stubborn."

A giddy laugh rose in Hunter's throat at the image of Lia arguing with Gem over Hunter's insensible body. She choked it back. "What about Loro?"

"The boy? He was none of my concern."

"Don't let them do this to her, Gem."

The young hunter met her eyes evenly. "Systems are failing all through the Church, Echo Hunter 367. The cityens will break through the barricade soon. Then we'll have to decide whether to start killing them, or step aside and let them overrun the compound and all the buildings."

Saints. No wonder the Patri looked like that.

The floor shook at some distant explosion. "Crop powder," Gem said. That explained the sacks.

Downstairs the Church doors groaned open. "Echo?" Lia called anxiously.

Hunter flung herself down the ladder by the rails, ignoring the skin burning off her palms. She tripped at the bottom, stumbling over a weanling. "Indine," she croaked as she climbed back to her feet. "Get them below ground. They'll be safer there."

"The Patri gave no order."

"*Go!*" Hunter snapped, already turning for the sanctuary. The trampled weanling, too much asked of her, began to wail. Indine shot a look that way, lips thinning, then nodded, taking the weanling's hand. Gem, jumping lightly from the ladder, delayed to help marshal the others. Hunter left them to it, limping with what speed she could manage back to Lia.

Three hunters and a man entered the sanctuary. Brit and Delen, bearing heavy packs, and Ava beside them, hand pinioning the Warder. "The aircar failed," Brit said to Lia. "This was all we could carry." Priests snatched the packs, began rooting through prints in desperate haste. "We found this man as well. He tried to stop us."

The Warder's forehead was smeared with soot, clothing torn and singed, though he appeared otherwise unharmed. His old vest had been shredded in the tumult, the remaining rags hanging from his shoulders; nervous fingers plucked at air where the hem had disintegrated. His face seemed to have dissolved into a featureless dough of fear and dismay, but it lightened when his rheumy eyes found Lia. "Lia, my child, what are you doing here?"

She turned a closed face on him. "Trying to stop what you started."

The Patri tore himself away from the boards. "What is all this?"

"I sent them," Lia said, a hint of defiance in her voice. "The prints might help. I didn't expect them to bring the Warder."

A muscle twitched beneath the Patri's eye. He caught the Warder by the collar. "See what your disobedience has wrought."

The Warder bobbed his head, larynx working, but he found the strength somewhere to meet the Patri's eyes. "The Church started this long ago. I only wanted to protect my people. The children. I thought you would see reason." His hands clenched, and tears choked his voice. "I didn't imagine you'd rather kill us all. But it's not too late. It's not, I'm sure. Withdraw from the city. Without hunters to provoke them, tempers will cool the sooner. I beg you, please."

The Patri shoved him back to Ava in disgust. He stabbed his finger at a glowing dot on his boards. "We arranged a fire near the granary. That will draw them away from the Church."

Lia whirled on the Patri in dismay. "You're burning the grain?"

"It shouldn't get that close. Not if they use sense. If they don't . . ." The Patri shrugged, face hard. "We have enough stored here to last the winter."

"The cityens would starve!" The shocked accusation was out of Hunter's mouth before her mind even formed the words.

"Do you think I don't know that?" It was the closest to anguish she had ever seen on the Patri's face. For the first time in her life she thought, *He has no plan*. No: *there is no plan*. Even in the worst days of her exile, she had been certain that he worked according to a grand vision, whether she could ever understand it or not. There had been a kind of comfort in that knowledge, cold as it was. But now even that was ripped away. Even he did not know what to do. "What do you expect?" he went on, his voice rising. "They resisted the tithe. They killed hunters. If cityens die it will set us back a hundred annuals, but if the Church dies it will be the end of everything. *Everything*."

"Besides," Gem said in a sensible tone, "we're not the ones doing it. They're still fighting each other, mostly. At least for now. Fortunately they're not very efficient."

"How can you talk that way?" Lia cried. "Efficiency? They aren't your machines."

At that moment lights blinked once, twice, then steadied, dimmer than before. A priest at the altar made a small sound of alarm, holding up a frayed piece of wire. One of his fellows rushed forward to help him strip and reconnect it. The Warder's eyes widened, anger giving way to fear. "Your machines are dying, aren't they? The Saint? It's happening already? How can that be, I thought—"

The Patri said, "The city's struggles weaken her. But the new Saint will be strong. We'll make the Church what it was again."

Lia's eyes flicked to the altar, then closed. Her lips compressed in a thin line, hands fisting at her sides. Hunter strained against her bonds to touch the med's arm, all the comfort she could offer. Ava and Delen exchanged uneasy glances. If Hunter could have spared a thought she would have been sorry for them. No lesson had prepared them for all this.

The floor shook with another, louder rumble. Lights flickered, came on, flickered out, leaving them in near darkness, the only illumination a faint glimmer from the boards, and a brighter glow at the altar where scurrying priests buzzed and fluttered around the Saint. Yet another flash, and a priest fell with a wordless scream of pain, and the smell of something burning. It smelled like food. A coil of nausea wrapped around Hunter's belly.

Lia ran to the Saint. She laid a palm atop the withered body while the priests scrambled around them, her lips moving almost silently, her face intent. Hunter just made out the murmured words of comfort. "Shh, you'll be fine, I'm here, don't worry, you'll be fine. . . ." Hunter's vision blurred; unable to raise her hands, she could only shake her head angrily to try to clear her sight.

The Warder had begun to babble. "The prints, I understand now, yes, we'll go back to the Ward. There are more in my office, many more, and Lia is such a gifted healer. A bit of time and surely she'll find some way—"

The Patri's furious arm swept a pile of prints to the floor in a crash. "There is no more time!"

In the shocked silence every face turned to him. Even the priests froze at their boards, stunned, their hands suspended above dials and switches.

The Patri calmed himself with a hunterlike effort. "Begin preparations for the ascension." He took Lia gently by the shoulders, drawing her away from the altar. "Come, child. They have work to do, and you must make ready."

"Lia?" The Warder's face crumpled as understanding dawned. "Oh, no, my child. No, it cannot be. This must just be some terrible misunderstanding. You mustn't do this. Get away from her!"

He tried to grab for the Patri, but Ava held him back. "Get him out of here," the Patri snarled.

"No, you mustn't make her. . . ." The Warder's voice

died, his pleading gaze jumped from Lia to the Patri, and finally to Hunter. "You—you brought her here for *this*?"

A searing pain scorched Hunter's heart. As if she felt it, Lia shook free of the Patri, coming to Hunter's side. "Leave her alone," she said. "You don't know anything about it."

Only Ava's hand kept the Warder upright as his knees gave way. His face dropped into his hands; his shoulders shook. The Patri made a wordless sound of disgust, turning away. But then the Warder gathered himself to search out Lia's face again, something besides sorrow touching his filmy eyes. "I'm sorry, child. I've been beyond a fool, and I know you can never forgive me." He struggled upright; Hunter could almost hear his old bones creak. "If I could take it all back, I would. If I had known, I never would have . . . But if you are to be the Saint, there will be more good in the Church than I could ever imagine." He covered his eyes again for a moment, then found a tremulous smile for the hunter beside him. "Young Ava, again, isn't it? This time it is I who have not done so well. But if you let me go, I will try to make it up. I set those people on that road out there; I might yet be able to talk some sense into them. At least I can try."

"There's no point," Hunter said harshly. "They won't listen. It would be a waste."

The Warder plucked a thread from the shreds of his sweater, squinting at it in the dim light. "Sometimes I pull one of these and the whole thing comes unraveled." He flicked it away. "You never know." He limped towards the doors. No one moved to stop him.

"Wait." Lia ran to him, pressed her cheek to his. "Go with the Saints."

Brit looked after him. "I might increase the odds of his success. With your permission, Patri."

A faint line drew between the Patri's brows. After a moment, he nodded, thin-lipped. Brit inclined her head to him, then, after a long, measuring look, to Lia. Then she was gone.

The Patri laid a hand on Lia's shoulder. "Come. I will help you."

"No," Hunter said. She forced herself between them. Gem cuffed her away, not hard, but it was enough to send stars across her vision. She stood swaying uselessly, trying not to fall.

"We all have our duty," the Patri said heavily. "Let her do hers."

"It's not her duty to die for you!" Hunter cried. "Saints, is that all you know? There has to be another way. You don't have to do this. You didn't have to have Gem kill Tana. Saints, if you had just told me the truth—none of this had to happen!"

Gem said, "I told the truth. The weapon misfired."

"Because *he* tampered with it?"

The Patri let out an impatient breath. "This is ridiculous. I had no part in Tana's death."

"I don't believe you," Hunter said flatly. Once it would have chilled her heart, such blasphemy. Now she wished the Church would strike her dead, to prove that it was able.

Nothing happened.

The Patri loomed so close she could smell the sour sweat beneath his robes. Behind him on the altar the priests worked quickly, efficiently now, a new purpose to their motions. Hunter's heart hammered in fear. "I owe you no explanation," the Patri said, "but I will tell you anyway. Perhaps this last lesson will do you good. Yes, Tana came to see me that night. About Gem, and other things that troubled her. She asked me what I was going to do, and I told her I didn't know, beyond to trust the Saint. She began to laugh. She said the Saint had said the same thing. It made no sense to me. She was still laughing when she left."

A chill spread through Hunter's veins. *There is a plan*, Tana had told her, with that wry grin that had made it seem as if she saw everything from a very great distance. It wasn't her own imminent death that would have given her that look. And there had also been the oddly compassionate way she had spoken to Hunter, tried, in her own dry way, to comfort her. She had seen the way the future twisted around both of them, weaving threads into one knotted plan binding tight as any rope.

Only not the Patri's plan. And not Tana's either. Not Tana's alone.

I think I've learned to read the patterns. And I don't like her answers.

Hunter stared at the shrouded figure on the altar. *Not you. Not you.*

Lia laid a tender hand on the Saint's brow beneath the wire crown. "Oh, Echo . . . She knew. She knew exactly what she had to do."

The Patri stared at the Saint, eyes narrowed at first, then growing round with wonder. When he spoke, his voice was hushed with awe. "She did it because of you. The last hunter she knew, before she ascended. The one who brought her back from the desert. There was more that happened than you ever told, wasn't there? Enough for her to know—" His eyes alit on Lia. "The patterns that were out there, the wild Saint—she made sure that Echo would do it again. Would find *you*, and bring you here to save us."

Gem took an involuntary step back, eyes widening like a child's as she suddenly saw the pattern. She bowed ever so slightly towards the figure on the altar. "We are made to serve," she said, her voice oddly choked.

"No," Hunter whispered. "*No.*"

Lia took Hunter's bound hands. "It was the only way. She had to drive you away from all this." Lia's gesture took in the priests, the Patri, the Saint herself. "She knew you could only find me if your heart was free to search."

"No," Hunter said again. Heat built behind her eyes. *I don't care whose plan it was. I won't let it happen.*

All thought narrowed into one tight beam. Get Lia away, get her far from here, to freedom and a chance to live. That one last mission she could accomplish. Hunter took a deep, slow breath, drawing up the final reserves of strength. The Patri stood close to Lia. If Hunter had him, they would have to listen to her. But she only had one chance. If Gem got to her first it would be no contest.

She was starting to move when the floor bucked, throwing her off balance. Her ribs hit into the hard edge of the altar with a pain that turned her vision black, and she tasted blood. Though her ears hadn't registered the noise from the blast, all sound was muffled, coming through from a great distance. Dust choked her, and a fit of coughing almost sent her the rest of the way into unconsciousness. She fought it back with some last thread of discipline.

Think like a hunter, she ordered herself. *One last time. Think.*

The cold slab under her hands was the altar. She fumbled, fingers searching as far as her bonds permitted, then finding what they sought. Pulling with the last of her strength, she hauled herself up, refusing to consider what she was clambering over until she perched precariously at the top, then feeling her way along the ropelike cable until she felt the connector. She grasped one side in each hand and stopped. Still the blackness refused to lift. She stayed where she was, gasping for breath.

It took a moment to realize that the sparks across her vision, flashing in time to a grinding wheeze, came from a source outside her eyes. Blink, blink, blink, and then catch, the emergency lights coming on as some-one, a priest it must be, hand cranked a generator. In the dimness Hunter saw Lia, safe in the circle of Gem's arm. The med's eyes scanned the room, searching, the way she searched a body for injury. Then she found Hunter's face.

Gem followed Lia's gaze. The young hunter's raised hand suddenly held projtrodes, aimed dead at Hunter. Ava and Delen split off, flanking the altar on either side, static wands ready.

Hunter crouched over the Saint, aware now that her hands were wrapped around the snake of cable running from the Saint's crown to the priests' boards. The priests around the altar stood frozen in horror. Even through the thick walls of the sanctuary she could hear the occasional distant boom of something exploding, like a heart beating fit to burst.

"Let her go," Hunter ordered.

"Echo Hunter 367, cease," the Patri thundered. "You will destroy the Church."

"We don't deserve to survive," Hunter cried. "All of this, since the Fall—for nothing. A waste that only put off the inevitable. You think you know so much, you and your priests and your order and your Church. You think the Church has saved us, since the Fall, and it has, but for what? For what? *Not* for this. We didn't save the city, we brought all this on it. It isn't what we were taught, not what we tell ourselves, but it's what we'll always come to—protecting ourselves, not the cityens. Betraying them to keep things the way we say they have to be. Look at us. We're all unsound. The Saint, wearing out so soon. The hunters we have to cull because they don't copy true. Saints, do you think I don't know what I am?" She heard Lia's wordless gasp of protest, went on recklessly, now that all was lost— "*All* of this is only a damaged copy of what it should have been. It can't go on like this. It has to change." Her hands clenched on the conduit. "I won't let it go on. Let Lia go, or I'll kill the Saint."

They all gaped at her in disbelief, the Patri, Gem, even the priests who tore their eyes from their boards to watch the calamity unfold. Lia too, until she turned her face away. Gem's arm tightened, pulling her closer in a gesture that seemed to draw some cord tighter around Hunter's strangling heart.

Fury distorted the Patri's face. "Enough of your blasphemy! Gem." Gem raised her trodes, reluctantly it seemed, but her hand was steady. Hunter felt a coldness settle in her bones. It was the end. She could take the junction down, or evade the trodes, but not both. And she would not let them have Lia. She raised the cable as best she could, showing it clearly so they could make no mistake of her intentions. Gem hesitated, casting a glance at the Patri.

"Even she wouldn't sacrifice the whole city," he said flatly. "It's time." He motioned, and priests came forward eagerly to take Lia's arms.

Lia tore herself free. "*I'll* tell you when it's time. *If* it's time." Before the priests could stop her, she scrambled up beside Hunter on the altar. Seeing the Patri's consternation, she gave a harsh laugh. "The mind has to be willing when the crown goes on, doesn't it? Yes, I thought as much. Otherwise Gem would have tapped me over the head in the desert and I would never have awakened." Her smile fled, and she swallowed, averting her eyes from the Saint. "At least not as myself. So now you listen to me, all of you. Look, *look* at what's happening. We're tearing ourselves to pieces. Don't you see? *All* of us. Our plans, our schemes—we have to stop it. Echo's right. We can't go on like this."

"I'll get you out of here," Hunter promised. "I'll find a way."

"I'm so sorry, Echo. If it were just you and me—" Lia stopped Hunter's protest with a gentle finger on her lips. "We're like that fierce little girl of yours—almost ready to stand on our own, but not quite yet. For a while we'll still need the Church's help." She scowled down at the Patri. "But all of you need to listen. You have a choice to make: help us grow up, or bring another Fall. And, Gem, you might as well put those down. Echo goes free and unharmed, or you'll never get a thing from me. And don't think you can wait until—after— and do it then. I'll know. Believe me, I'll know."

"What can she be to you?" the Patri asked, bewilderment thinning his voice. "She's a hunter. A tool, nothing more. She's not even a true copy, just a dangerous mistake. She knows, she confessed it herself. Don't you see?"

Lia drew Hunter around to face her. Hunter felt that look to her core, shamed, at the sweat and dirt caking her face, at the way her hands shook on the conduit; most of all, at the way she would let Saint and Church and city fall to ruins in a heartbeat if it meant saving Lia. The Patri was wrong. She wasn't dangerous. She was worthless.

"It's you who doesn't see," Lia said softly. Her hand caressed Hunter's cheek, withdrew. Then the med crossed her arms, looking down at the Patri and hunters and priests. "I'm telling you: it's time for everything to change. Now you decide if you're ready." And then her breath caught, and her voice began to shake. "But hurry."

The Patri stood staring blankly for so long that Hunter wondered if the strain had broken his mind. Then something lit behind his eyes, lifting his sagging features and filling them with desperate hope. He bowed his head, then raised his face to the altar, lifting his palms wide in offering. "My service to the Saint in all things."

Lia, white face streaked silver with tears, bowed her head into her hands, then nodded.

"I won't let you do this," Hunter cried. "Look at her. *Look at her.*"

Lia did. Her wise, calm gaze took in the Saint's wizened face beneath the crown, the skin stretched tight across bone worn free of every trace of human softness, the sunken eyes that stared at visions nothing living could see. When Lia looked up, her lips were trembling but her golden eyes, melting with tears, held nothing but compassion.

"No!" Hunter's grip tightened on the junction, beginning to pull it apart. The Saint's wasted body twitched.

Lia laid her hands gently atop Hunter's. The touch shot through Hunter's nerves like the pain of the Church doors, paralyzing her. "Echo, you know I have to. I can save them—the cityens, the hunters even. The children." She was weeping in earnest now, tears running down her face, her voice trembling with them. "But I can't do it by myself." She drew a quivering breath, then steadied. "Yours will be the last face I see. Please, Echo. I love you. Give me that to take with me."

Hunter strained against the bonds until she held Lia's face between her hands. Every instinct screamed protest. Pain ripped through her chest with each beat of her heart. She touched her lips to the med's forehead, then her mouth. She tasted tears, salty as blood. They stood like that for a moment out of time. Then: "Look at me," Hunter said at last. "I love you."

Lia looked at her, and smiled.

Half blind with anguish, scarcely able to breathe, Hunter held Lia's face between her hands as the med eased the crown off the dying Saint and slipped it over her own head. Hunter kept her eyes locked on Lia's, refusing to blink, willing every breath, every last heartbeat to Lia through that gaze they shared, ignoring everything else in the world, aware of nothing but Lia, even as the lights came on full bright, the boards flashed and spun into a steady rhythm, as the others, no more than shadows in the corner of her eye, pointed and murmured in amazement at the Church coming back to life, as the sounds of battle faded away and died. She saw Lia's face transfixed with awe and wonder, her golden eyes burning brightly as a beacon, glowing from within. She heard the sharp intake of breath, felt the body sag against her as the thought, the awareness, all that was Lia spun burning through the wires, out across the city she would heal.

She saw Lia looking back at her for one last moment.

And then she saw the Saint ascend.

The engines strained at their very limits, pushed as far as Gem dared beyond the last relay's range. No one had come this far in living memory. Even out here Hunter could still smell smoke, an acrid reminder of disaster that would linger for days, though most of the fires had been put out by now. The city had new scars to bear, wounds that might take a lifetime to heal. A hunter in another hundred annuals, if there were still hunters then, might survey the dead areas, spare a moment to ponder what had happened, then turn without further thought to whatever task she had at hand.

Hunter wondered how much of what she had come to know was left, and who; she pictured Exey standing in his workshop, surveying and contemplating and already grinning his crooked grin as he imagined what he could craft out of the ruins. Brit had limped in, hurt but likely to survive. No one had seen the Warder, but then, they might not; there was much to accomplish in the city and cityens were already organizing themselves to take care of what they could without any hunter's help.

Hunter wouldn't be there to see it; she had her own task, one that no one else could do. She hopped out of the aircar as lightly as her stiff bones could manage. Her pack, bearing little more than a receiver to hunt signals crossing the empty air, a few basic supplies, and the rewired stunner Gem had handed her without comment, made an insignificant load.

Gem said, "Ava and Delen and the others are already gathering the rest of the Warder's prints. Perhaps the priests will have found answers by the time you get back."

Hunter was strangely touched by Gem's faith in her return. But she said, feeling the slightest curve come to her lips, "Are you wishing my search to be for nothing, Gem?"

"Of course not." A pause. "The Saint made a good choice, Echo Hunter 367. Both Saints."

It was a moment before Hunter could speak. "You should be getting back, Gem; the Church needs you."

"Echo." Her young self looked down at her from the open hatch. "I swear to you, I will protect her with my life."

"That is a formidable thing, Gem Hunter 378."

One last time Gem studied her, searching for mockery, finding none. Then the young hunter nodded. "Goodbye, Echo Hunter 367."

She stood there until the whine of the aircar's engines, protesting against the dust and the distance from the Saint, died into nothing. The vast emptiness of the desert spread before her. If there were other cities, other Saints, they could remain hidden there for lifetimes.

But Criya had said once that Hunter was good at finding things. She had only been half right, Hunter thought. Not just finding things, but bringing them home.

Hunter stood still, listening. As always, the answer was silence. No words sounded in her ears. No voice spoke within her mind.

But now that she knew how, she could hear. Echo hitched the pack higher on her shoulder and took the first step forward, while her Saint whispered endlessly in her heart.

ACKNOWLEDGMENTS

More people than I can thank here contributed to this book. I would like to name a few: my parents, who made reading as natural as breathing. My brother and sister, who helpfully suggested that I dedicate this book "to my siblings, without whom so much more might have been accomplished." Other than that, they're the best siblings a person could have. The kind and brilliant Kelley Eskridge at Sterling Editing, for helping my dream come true. My agent, Mary C. Moore, who pulled my story out of the slush. Rebecca Lucash at Harper Voyager Impulse, who is a pleasure to work with. And most of all my wife, Mary, for everything.

ABOUT THE AUTHOR

STACEY BERG is a medical researcher who writes speculative fiction. Her work as a physician-scientist provides the inspiration for many of her stories. She lives with her wife in Houston and is a member of the Writers' League of Texas. When she's not writing, she practices kung fu and runs half marathons.

Discover great authors, exclusive offers, and more at hc.com.